Friedrich Schiller

ESSAYS

The German Library: Volume 17

Volkmar Sander, General Editor

Friedrich Schiller

ESSAYS

Edited by Walter Hinderer
and Daniel O. Dahlstrom

CONTINUUM · NEW YORK

2005
The Continuum International Publishing Group Inc
15 East 26 Street, New York, NY 10010

The German Library
is published in cooperation with Deutsches Haus,
New York University.
This volume has been supported by a grant
from the funds of Stifterverband für die Deutsche Wissenschaft.

Printed in the United States of America

Library of Congress Cataloging-in-Publication Data

Schiller, Friedrich, 1759–1805.
[Essays. English. Selections]
Essays / Friedrich Schiller ; edited by Walter Hinderer and Daniel O. Dahlstrom.
p. cm. — (The German library ; v. 17)
Includes bibliographical references.
ISBN 0-8264-0712-9 (alk. paper) — ISBN 0-8264-0713-7 (pbk. : alk. paper)
1. Aesthetics. 2. Schiller, Friedrich, 1759–1805—Aesthetics. 3. Criticism. I. Hinderer, Walter, 1934– . II. Dahlstrom, Daniel O. III. Title. IV. Series.
B3086.S31 1993
111′.85—dc20 93-9855
CIP

Acknowledgments will be found on page 261, which constitutes an extension of the copyright page.

Contents

Introduction

If Socrates in the *Politeia* appears as a naive philosopher of poetry, the protagonist of a dramatic poem outlawing poetry for the good of the state, then Schiller in the essays assembled in the present volume is, by contrast, a self-conscious advocate of the political necessity and philosophical indispensability of poetry and art. In style and substance these essays contradict both the notion that there is a doctrinal purity to philosophy and morality, somehow removed from the emotional pull of the imagination, and the notion that the efficacy of poetry and poetic feelings is anarchal and detachable from reflection on human nature and destiny. Not surprisingly, Schiller has had his share of critics on both scores. Referring to Schiller's *Wallenstein,* Goethe objected that "those two great aids, history and philosophy, get in the way of parts of the work and prevent its purely poetic success." At the same time Fichte inveighed against the poetic quality of Schiller's philosophical writings: "You bind the powers of the imagination, which can only be free, and want to force them to think. But they cannot." Not without a measure of arrogance, Schiller countered Fichte's complaint by declaring: "I do not desire merely to make my thoughts clear to others but to give them my entire soul and to influence their sensuous and intellectual capabilities."

There were times, it bears noting, when Schiller was not always convinced that he had succeeded in merging philosophy and poetry. In a letter to Goethe he seems to accept a basic difference between philosophical and poetic domains as he confesses to vacillating "like some sort of hermaphrodite" between abstract conceptions and concrete perceptions: "Usually, the poet overcame me when I should have been doing philosophy and the philosophical spirit took command when I was supposed to be writing poetry." Nevertheless, the idea of the synthetic unity of reason and imagination is a dominant notion of Schiller's aesthetic writings. This notion is in fact an integral part of the defining theme of Schiller's aesthetics: the concrete totality of human nature as both a fusion of individual and sociopolitical development, and a synthesis of historical and artistic accomplishment.

Whereas the interpenetration of historical and philosophical, personal and social dimensions is perfectly consistent with the underlying synthetic message of Schiller's aesthetic writings, it gives his discussion of these themes a sometimes confusing complexity. He has an irritating tendency to jump from one context to another without giving sufficient warning of his intention to do so. No sooner, for example, in the *Letters on the Aesthetic Education of Man* has Schiller defined the fundamental aspects of personal development than these same aspects are identified as the foundations of history in general. Similarly, the theory of cultural-philosophical triads in "On Naive and Sentimental Poetry" is immediately transformed into three steps of an experiment that is at once political, aesthetic, and personal.

Although Schiller moves confidently and perhaps at times too casually between such diverse contexts, this synthetic penchant does not lead him, as it does the German Romantics, to poeticize all aspects of life. There is without question a *mode utopique* to Schiller's thinking, but his method is utopian precisely because it combines the analysis and criticism of social and political reality with intellectual experimentation and development of "new possibilities." The failures of society and of the contemporary context in which Schiller was writing are readily discernible from his anticipation of what the world ideally should be.

Given the complexity and myriad directions of Schiller's thinking, his aesthetic essays can be difficult to read without some sort of compass. Accordingly, in this introduction, the central features and objectives of Schiller's program of anthropological aesthetics, from its inception in his earliest writings to the *Letters on the Aesthetic Education of Man* in particular, are sketched, followed by a review of the implications of this program for criticism and its distinctively historical dimensions, as outlined in *On Naive and Sentimental Poetry* and in the other essays on sublimity, pathos, and the art of tragedy in the present volume. Schiller's program is placed, finally, within the context of classical and modern philosophical perspectives, in the light of both his appropriation of Kant's critical philosophy and his anticipation of German idealism.

Schiller's Anthropological Aesthetics

The aesthetic vision of the totality of human nature, so fundamental to Schiller's thought, is also an essential feature of the educational program of the eighteenth century from Lessing, Wieland, and Herder to Goethe and on to Jean Paul and Hölderlin. Echoing a theme from Wieland's *Contributions to the Secret History of Human Understanding and Development* (1770) and Herder's *Letters in Promotion of Humanity* (1772), Schiller identifies art as the means of human self-completion. "It is not just poetic licence but philosophical truth," Schiller observes in Letter 21 *On the Aesthetic Education of Man,* "when we call beauty our second creator." In the essay *On Grace and Dignity,* Schiller notes that nature gives man, in contrast to animals and plants, "only his destiny," leaving up to him "its fulfillment." As a person, man has accordingly "alone of all beings the privilege of breaking the chain of necessity by his will," that is to say, by free action or art (in the broadest sense of the term).

In Schiller's eyes, in other words, nature supplies the condition of the possibility of existence, but the expansion and the fulfillment of this possibility lie within the power of the individual. The artists' duty is to cultivate and ennoble human nature *(natura)* through art *(ars)*. As Schiller puts it in his philosophical poem *The Artists* (1789), "mankind's dignity" is placed in the artist's own hands. Schiller's philosophy of art thus constitutes a kind of anthropological aesthetics, involving a program of education that is both personal and sociopolitical precisely because it is aesthetic.

At the root of this anthropological perspective is Schiller's view that there is a basic dynamism to human nature, propelled by a drive towards synthesis that is experienced as an aesthetic condition. Clearly evident in his earliest works, such as the dissertation

Philosophy of Physiology (1779) and *Essay on the Connection between the Animal and Spiritual Nature of Man* (1780), Schiller's synthetic approach to anthropology can be traced in part to his early medical training and alignment with the contemporary discipline of physiology, the so-called "philosophy of physicians" who propagated the unity of psyche and soma. In Schiller's hands this unity becomes the dynamic offspring of an endless, utopian endeavor. "The destiny of man," Schiller declares in his dissertation, is "to be God's peer. . . . Man's ideal is infinite: but the spirit is eternal. Eternity is the measure of infinity. In other words, the spirit will develop infinitely but will never attain its ideal." Here Schiller articulates his fundamental anthropological perspective, namely, that there is, indeed, a unity to human nature but it is a unity that consists precisely in a creative and ongoing synthesis of an underlying duality. In the eleventh letter from *The Aesthetic Education of Man* this perspective is formulated as a dialectic between "person" and "condition."

Schiller introduces the concept of "transmutative force" in order to heal the "rift between the world and the spirit" of which he speaks in his dissertation. In a lecture entitled *What Can a Good, Permanent Stage Really Achieve* (1784) he locates this possibility in "aesthetic sense." Though he delineates this "mediating condition" in greater detail in the *Letters on the Aesthetic Education of Man*, already in this early lecture the "aesthetic sense" or the "feeling for the beautiful" has the function of recreating human potential diminished or suppressed by the demands of business and profession.

The way to a higher stage of humanity and of politics leads through art. "In order to solve that problem of politics in practice," Schiller advises, "it must be approached through the problem of aesthetics, because it is only through Beauty that man makes his way to freedom" (Letter 2). As Schiller puts it in *On Grace and Dignity*, human beings can suppress their physical nature in favor of rationality or they can fully succumb to their sensuous nature or they can find a harmony between the demands of nature and reason. In each case there is an obvious political and aesthetic parallel to the anthropological condition: a stifling monarchy and regimented tastes correspond to the first condition, whereas political anarchy and tastelessness correspond to the second. The third condition, on the other hand, unites in a "beautiful" bond grace and dignity, predilection and obligation, and—ideally—law and freedom.

In the *Letters on the Aesthetic Education of Man* this third condition is characterized as an "aesthetic condition" on an individual level and as an "aesthetic state" on a political level. The aesthetic state is the "totality of human potential," which is reduced or eliminated under other conditions. A prerequisite for this "state of freedom" is the aesthetic condition, a condition achievable only through art since art alone frees human beings from the opposing drives of nature and culture, body and soul, and leads them to experience their own freedom, thereby enabling them to realize all their possibilities. While the physical quality of a thing can directly relate to "our sensual condition," the logical quality to "our reason," and the moral quality to "our will," the aesthetic quality alone relates to all our different abilities together. In other words, only aesthetic experience is able "to cultivate the totality of our sensuous and intellectual abilities in the greatest possible harmony."

This aesthetic state is clearly an ideal, corresponding to Schiller's early notion of the human destiny of "being a peer of God." Behind this ideal there is an objective that can be traced throughout Schiller's aesthetic writings: to stimulate human beings to the optimal realization of their potential. For this reason, Schiller opposes anything that threatens this realization: repressive political institutions and one-sided cultural developments in which principles dominate feelings or emotions get the better of principles. Because human actions are often unilaterally determined by either a physical or an intellectual power, art plays a decisive role as a corrective and mediator between the two powers.

Schiller's Historiological Criticism

If in his critical essays of 1782 Schiller appears to consider painting in poetry to be dangerous and to prefer, as in drama, a manipulation of emotions, his positive assessment of the poetry of Friedrich Matthison in 1794 puts greater value on the painterly depictive form in poetry. Here he claims that we actually view "every painterly and poetic composition as a piece of music" and apply "to a certain extent the same laws to them." This reasoning places the modern propinquity of poetry and music in an anthropological context, since the poet should not just "affect the heart," but should also "*determine* the state of our sensibility."* In the assessment of Matthisson's poems as in other writings of the 1790s, Schiller speaks of the aesthetic and human necessity that the individual merge with the species. This necessity underlies the two demands he makes of a work of art: first, the "necessary relationship to its object (objective truth)," and second, the "necessary relationship of this object . . . to the human abilities of feeling (subjective generality)." Fulfilling these demands is the task of the sentimental operation elaborated in *Naive and Sentimental Poetry*, an operation that Schiller claims is the prerequisite for aesthetic and human progress. Every aesthetic progress in fact requires progress along these lines on the part of the individual human being. As Schiller puts this matter in a critical review of the poetry of Gottfried August Bürger in 1791, the poet's "first and most important duty" is the "greatest possible" ennoblement of his own "individuality" and its purification "to the purest and most glorious humanity." Thus, according to Schiller, deficits in literary works can and should be attributed to the person who created them. Values missing in the person cannot be contained in the artistic production.

At the same time, the poet is hardly free of his age and culture. Perhaps the most pregnant aspects of Schiller's post-Enlightenment reflections on aesthetics and art is his refusal to consider them apart from their historical context and, indeed, apart from a conception of the history of human development altogether. In other words, Schiller's conception of criticism, his account of artistic and aesthetic criteria, is embedded in a historiology, a logos of human history. According to that logos, the totality of human nature in the ancient world expressed itself in the reality surrounding the poet. This situation, however, no longer exists and the modern

*This insight has ramifications for philosophical prose as well as for poetry. In his essay *On the Necessary Limitations in the Use of Beauty of Form Particularly When Expounding on Philosophical Truths* (1795), Schiller declares that the scientific style of exposition with its concern for principles and the appeal to imagination typical of popular expositions are to be combined in a synthesis of "beautiful literary manner."

artist must recreate in and from himself—in other words, sentimentally—through the "depiction of the ideal" what is no longer achievable by naively "imitating reality."

In this way, Schiller captures the difference between ancient and modern poetry as a contrast between naive and sentimental art (without denying the existence of ancient sentimentality and modern naïveté). Whereas the ancient poets move us through nature, the modern poets touch us with ideas. The naive art of the ancients "depicts the *object with all its limitations, individualizing* it," while the sentimental art of the moderns consists in removing "*all limitations* from its object, *idealizing* it." The individualizing typical of naive art and the idealizing characteristic of sentimental art can lead to two different sorts of excesses. Naive poetry may produce an "object without thought or reflection," and sentimental poetry may degenerate into "a play of thought and reflection without object."

The central thesis of *Naive and Sentimental Poetry,* Schiller's final major work on aesthetics, is that "nature brings [man] to unity with himself, art separates and divides him, and through the ideal he returns to unity." Modern art, as opposed to ancient art, has the unique opportunity and obligation to lead humanity back to lost nature, though now on a higher level, or, in other words, to lead it back to a unity by means of the ideal. Thus, Schiller demands of the sentimental poet that he spiritualize "[the] raw material from the inside out through the subject," that he recover "through reflection the poetic content that the exterior sensibility had lacked," and that he supplement "nature through the idea." The poet's task is to transform a limited objective into an infinite one by means of a sentimental operation. Once again, this operation is possible only if the poet has cultivated and educated himself as an individual correspondingly.

Schiller wrote to Wilhelm von Humboldt on December 25, 1795, that the relationship between "naive and sentimental *poetry* . . . [is the same as that between] naive and sentimental *humanity.*" Accordingly, in *Naive and Sentimental Poetry* the path taken by modern poets is regarded as the same path that human beings as individuals and as a species must take. Since the ideal is infinite, however, the "cultured human being" or idealist can never achieve the corresponding perfection, though the "natural human being" or realist is quite capable of doing so. However, Schiller adds, the goals in each case, namely, the goals "reached for through culture" and those "*achieved* through nature," are quite different. From this comparison he concludes that the idealist goal of modern humanity is "immensely preferable" to the realist goal of the more natural humanity in antiquity. Although an "infinite greatness" has been attained by the realist or the naive poet of antiquity, the infinite greatness of the idealist or sentimental poet is something ever approximated. Hence, human progress is possible only if human beings "cultivate" themselves, that is to say, if they move from the naive to the sentimental stage.

The modern poet is distinguished by the fact that he gives expression to his own thoughts and feelings as such. He applies his ideas to experience and communicates directly to his readers his own reflections on the relation between ideals and reality or experience. For this reason, the modern poet is confronted with three possible states of affairs: agreement or disagreement or both agreement and disagreement between the ideal and the real. In *Naive and Sentimental Poetry* Schiller demonstrates how three basic types of poetry—satire, idyll, and elegy—correspond respectively to a contradiction between the real state and the ideal, a harmony between them, and alternating states of contradiction (movement) and harmony (stillness).

Characteristically, despite pleas for the indispensability and even inevitability of sentimental poetry in the present age (exemplified by his critique of Rousseau), Schiller does not consider sentimental poetry the end of art and human development. In a letter to Humboldt dated December 25, 1795, Schiller explains that if sentimental culture or humanity is "*complete* . . . it is no longer sentimental, but ideal . . . I present the sentimental as only *striving after* the ideal." Moreover, "every true genius," Schiller insists, "must be naive, or he is no genius."* Only the concepts of both naïveté

*Goethe, in particular, represents to Schiller the naive poet-genius who, to be sure, for want of an adequate surrounding reality, must escape into the sentimental operation. In a letter to Goethe on August 23, 1794, he explains: "Now, since you were born a German, since your Grecian spirit was contained in a Nordic creation, you had no other choice but either to become a Nordic artist or, according to your imagination and with the help of your ability to think and to reflect, to replace that which reality denied you and thus from the interior and in a rational manner, to give birth to a Greece."

and sentimentality include the necessary content and form to give "*mankind its most complete possible expression*" and unify "the idea of mankind into one." The "ideal of human nature," as Schiller notes toward the end of his essay, is divided between both types of poet, although it is not "completely achieved . . . by either."

Nevertheless, this synthetic ideal is the very entelechy of history, as Schiller conceives it. Naive poetry is followed by sentimental and finally by ideal poetry, just as naive humanity is followed by sentimental and finally by ideal humanity. The latter—ideal—phase actually leads back "to nature on the path of reason and of freedom." In a 1793 discussion of a work by Wilhem von Humboldt, in other words, two years before his last great essay on aesthetics, he observes: "During the first phase there were the Greeks. We are in the second phase. We can only hope for the third, and then one won't want to wish the Greeks back either."

Over the years, Schiller formulated various "fundamental laws" that, hand in hand with his conception of humanity's development, have pronounced aesthetic implications. The first such law, the "fundamental law of mixed nature," emerged from his second dissertation: "the activities of the body correspond to the activities of the mind, i.e., any overexertion of the mind will always result in an overexertion of certain bodily functions, just as the equilibrium of the former or the harmonious activity of our spiritual faculties is associated with the most perfect balance of the latter."

From this law of psychosomatic interdependence, as we might call it today, Schiller develops his poetological definition of pathetic depiction in the form of "the two fundamental laws of all tragic art" (which apply particularly to his youthful dramas). In two essays, which originally belonged together and are included in the present volume, *On the Sublime* (1793) and *On the Pathetic* (1793), Schiller expands on these "fundamental laws": "They are *first*: depiction of suffering nature; *second:* depiction of moral independence in suffering." Similarly in another essay included here, *On the Art of Tragedy* (1792), Schiller emphasizes the need for the protagonists of tragedy to be portrayed as both sensuous and moral, in order that their suffering may arouse our sympathy, the very purpose of tragedy. The feeling of the sublime itself, Schiller declares in the final short essay of the current volume, *Concerning the Sublime* (1793), is a mixture of anguish and joy, preferred by noble souls even over pleasure, precisely because this feeling testifies to a moral principle within us that is independent of all the stirrings of the sensuous side of our nature.

Schiller expands on a corresponding set of fundamental laws in Letter 11 of *On the Aesthetic Education of Man*. "Two fundamental laws of sensuo-rational nature" are involved, which he explains as follows: the first fundamental law "insists upon absolute *reality*": man should "turn everything that is mere form into [a part of] the world, and make all his potentialities fully manifest." The second fundamental law "insists upon absolute *formality*": man should "eradicate everything in himself which is merely [part of the] world and bring harmony into all his changes; in other words: he is to externalize all that is within him, and give form to all that is outside him." Both these tasks, conceived "in their highest fulfillment," Schiller goes on to say, "lead us back to that concept of divinity from which I started." In his last major work on aesthetics, *On Naive and Sentimental Poetry,* Schiller returns to this "concept of divinity" through elaboration of the dualistic typology of the "inner spiritual form," the "noteworthy psychological antagonism among men," and the division into the two basic types: realists and idealists. To the extent that these dualisms or antagonisms are eliminated, that "concept of divinity," the "ideal of human nature," appears.

In the end, Schiller maintains, only a synthesis of naive and sentimental poetry can "give human nature its complete expression" and thereby realize the whole range of human potential, that state of being "a peer of God" sought in the first dissertation. Thus, in Schiller's final considerations of this theme, the arts of idealizing and of naturalizing approach one another more closely, at least in theory. In a letter to Goethe September 14, 1797, Schiller neatly sums up his conception of art: "Two things have to be part of the poet and the artist: that he lifts himself above reality and that he remains within the sensuous realm. Where these two are joined, there is aesthetic art."

Schiller's Philosophical Synthesis

Two philosophical perspectives can be said to vie for Schiller's intellectual soul. The one perspective, undoubtedly reinforced by his relationship to Goethe, is classical; it looks to nature for inspiration and to humanity in its infancy, to the Greek world, for guidance; art's task is to recover and sustain a *graceful* naturalness that defines the beautiful. The other perspective is decidedly modern, receiving its definitive articulation in the transcendental philosophy of Kant, someone taken by the sublimity of a humanity that sets conditions for the very understanding of nature and possesses moral *dignity* by being able to free itself from the grip of nature and tradition. The latter perspective is more pronounced in Schiller's aesthetic essays, at least in the sense that, as might be expected in theoretical writings, he makes use of the terminology dominating the philosophical debate of his day.

Schiller's Appropriation of Kantian Themes and Terminology*

One of the central aims of Kant's *Critique of Pure Reason* is to demonstrate that Hume's scepticism is unwarranted; scientists can rightly assume that there is some specific cause or sufficient reason for every particular event that transpires within the natural order. Nature, construed as the complex of phenomena studied by science, is thoroughly determined. This theoretical and even mechanistic sense of "nature" surfaces repeatedly in Schiller's aesthetic writings, for example, in references to nature's "physical necessity" (Letter 3) and to the rational manner in which nature always acts (*Concerning the Sublime*), existing "according to its own immutable laws" (*On Naive and Sentimental Poetry*). However, nature exhibits this determinism, in Kant's view, only as the sum of appearances or phenomena. What nature or the reality of things might be beyond the realm of what can be experienced lies beyond the reach of science; such is the realm of speculative metaphysics,

*While Kant's considerable influence on Schiller is unmistakable, there is also some evidence of the possibility that Schiller influenced Kant. Kant emphasizes that, while humans share a sense of the pleasurable with all animals and an appreciation of the good with all rational entities, the experience of beauty is distinctively human. A similar theme is declared a year earlier by Schiller in *The Artists*: "Die *Kunst,* o Mensch, hast du allein." In a lengthy footnote to the second edition of his *Religion* essay, Kant responds to a criticism of him advanced by Schiller in *Grace and Dignity.*

the progeny of the ideas of pure reason (for example, the idea of God as a first cause). Throughout his aesthetic writings, Schiller also frequently uses "idea" in this technical sense, signifying something that can be entertained without being known.*

Although such ideas have only heuristic and no explanatory value for science, the idea of freedom, the idea of an unconditioned condition or spontaneous causality of human action, lies at the basis of morality. In the *Critique of Practical Reason* Kant argues that the idea of freedom and the "unconditional practical law" (ultimately, the moral law of treating persons as ends and never simply as means) reciprocally imply each other. What a person ought to do is not, indeed, finally cannot, be based upon nature and science; it can only be based upon an ideal and someone is free if and only if (or, better, to the extent that) he or she acts, not on the basis of nature's determinations or knowledge of them, but on the basis of that ideal. The same point is driven home by Schiller in what he calls "the transcendental way" in Letters 10 through 15, which he bases upon the difference between an individual's (moral) "person" and (material) "condition."

Kant's first two critiques thus establish two sets of principles, largely embraced by Schiller, that respectively underlie science and morality. As far as can be *known*, these principles are not incompatible since they govern the two distinct realms of nature and of freedom respectively, that is to say, things as they appear and things as they are supposed to be. There is, however, a "gap," as Kant himself calls it, between the two realms, raising the gnawing question of the ultimate relation between them. To be sure, the findings of natural science are no more based on morality than the morality of an action is based on some calculation of the prospects in the nature of things for the happiness of those affected by the action, including the agent (a claim emphatically echoed by Schiller in Letter 19). Yet, the very idea of morality requires that the gap between the realms of nature and morality can be bridged or, in other words, that nature can be transformed into a moral world.

*A rational idea *[Vernunftidee]* is a category no longer related by the understanding *[Verstand]* to some actual or possible experience in nature, but rather extended by reason alone *[reine Vernunft]*—through an illusory, but in itself noncontradictory, natural, and unavoidable process that Kant calls *dialectic*—to the thought of something unconditioned. In a sense the title "critique of pure reason" is short for

In the *Critique of Judgment* Kant finds a subjective basis for a "transition" from the realm of nature to that of morality and that basis is the experience of the beautiful and the sublime. While insisting that a genuine judgment that something is beautiful or sublime cannot be motivated by moral interests any more than by scientific or sensuous interests, Kant also recognizes that both the beautiful and the sublime are "purposeful in relation to moral feeling." "The beautiful," he notes, "prepares us to love something, even nature itself, disinterestedly; the sublime to prize it even against our (sensuous) interest." Beauty, for Kant, is a universally shared, yet "disinterested" delight that the sheer form of something affords a person precisely by putting the mind's ability to imagine and to reflect into a state of free play. So construed, beauty is a "symbol of morality," presenting an analogy to morality that is itself universally respected as the freedom of a will in conformity with laws dictated by reason. Given this analogy, Kant concludes, the appreciation of beauty "makes possible the transition from the allurements of the senses to a habitual moral interest without too violent a step." Not by preaching, but by bringing a certain refinement to society, fine art *(schöne Kunst)* provides a kind of training for the moral rule of reason.

Schiller's *Letters on the Aesthetic Education of Man* are in great part a response to what he saw as the tragedy of the French Revolution: a brutal attempt to turn a people's natural instincts into moral virtue overnight, the fate of a people "not yet ripe for civil liberty" because of what they lacked in "human liberty." "Any durable reform," Schiller wrote the duke of Augustenburg, "must emanate from a way of thinking, and where the principle is rotten, nothing healthy or benign can grow. The character of its citizens alone creates and upholds the state and makes political and civilian freedom possible." With the tragedy of the French Revolution in mind, Schiller bases the theme of his letters, dedicated to the duke of Augustenburg, on precisely the argument outlined by Kant for the necessity of a "transition" from a natural state to a moral one. In Schiller's work, this transition takes the form of what he revealingly labels both "the aesthetic condition" and "aesthetic freedom." Like

"critique of the ideas of pure reason." Kant also distinguishes aesthetic ideas from rational ideas, but Schiller seems to have been most taken by the latter.

Kant, Schiller emphasizes how beauty frees the mind from relating to objects solely on the basis of desire, and by the sheer play(fulness) involved in the experience of beauty it makes possible "a transition into the world of spirit."* Yet, there are several passages in Schiller's aesthetic writings where he goes beyond Kant by claiming that the aesthetic condition is a *necessary* condition for the development of morality (Letter 23) and that this condition is itself a "gift of nature" (Letter 24, "On the Naive").

As a necessary corollary to the more exalted role he assigns to the aesthetic condition and to nature, ideal beauty is for Schiller not a mere form (a spatial and/or temporal *Gestalt* or *Spiel*), as it was for Kant, but rather "the living form." Whereas Kant construed beauty as a pleasure derived merely from the free play of mental faculties, Schiller's conception of beauty as the living form satisfies the ideal "play-drive" in human beings that optimally integrates two radically opposing drives; a sensuous or material drive for change (becoming) and a formal drive for permanence (being), which results in a conception of beauty as a dynamic, exuberant unity of opposites (Letter 15: "the material constraint of natural laws and the spiritual constraint of moral laws").

So construed, the aesthetic condition is not only the means of passing from a natural condition to a moral one, but also the means for incorporating morality within nature, in other words, for the effective execution of moral ideals in nature. The play of aesthetics in effect combines and thereby realizes both natural and moral ends, allowing Schiller to conclude that beauty is the very "consummation of humanity." The full realization of moral ideals in human nature can only take place in nature, and that is as much as to say that there can be no moral dignity without grace.

Underlying this classically inspired transformation of Kant's aesthetics is Schiller's insight that one is a human being in the full sense of the word only when he or she plays (Letter 15). Schiller adds that play, understood as the complete fusion of grace and dignity, "was long ago alive and operative in the art and in the feeling of the Greeks." In this way, Schiller gives a historical name and added significance to Kant's model (described, but not identi-

*For these and other such references to the "transition" see Letters 3, 15, and 20–25.

fied at the conclusion to the critique of aesthetic judgment) of a people finding the mean between nature and a higher culture. In *Naive and Sentimental Poetry* the beautiful naïveté of the ancient Greeks is presented as an irrecoverable, sentimental ideal.

Schiller's conception of the naïveté of nature and the human race in its infancy is thus, as he himself suggests, an idea that only a modern could have. Yet, precisely by means of this conception, Schiller is able to grasp nature as both the point of departure and the aim of freedom and not merely, as it seemed to be for Kant, as freedom's foe or at least its indifferent accomplice. Nature herself, Schiller argues at one point, makes the "transition" to aesthetic play (Letter 27).

Not only Kant's concept of nature, but also his perspective on culture is transformed by being placed within the classical horizons of Schiller's thought. Culture is defined by Kant as nature's ultimate purpose, "ultimate" because culture disciplines and shapes our desires "to make us receptive to purposes higher than nature itself can provide." For Schiller "the task of culture" is indeed based upon Kant's demonstration that the realms of nature and morality are not incompatible since each is the provenance of a distinct drive (sensuousness and reason respectively) directed at a distinct object. However, culture does not exist, as Kant supposed, simply to prepare human beings to live for a purpose that transcends nature, but rather, as Schiller puts it in Letter 13 and again in Letter 24, precisely to make sure that each realm is given its due, seeing to their utmost purity "even while they are being most intimately fused." Once again, Schiller emphasizes the need to view aesthetic culture as a transition not merely from nature, but also from an unfeeling, purely rational morality to "the ideal of beautiful humanity."

In a certain sense Schiller's preoccupation with Kant's conception of the sublime in several of the aesthetic writings in his volume may be seen as the complement, if not the counterpoint, to his more classical view of culture and nature. Kant restricts the sublime to natural phenomena that appear either so immense ("the mathematical sublime") that, as the very word suggests, we cannot hope to find the proper measure for them or so ominous ("the dynamical sublime"), that if they were to threaten us, we would have no means of physically resisting them. In both cases (renamed by Schiller the "theoretical" and the "practical sublime") nature presents itself as anything but a beautiful harmony of elements in which human beings might thrive. Yet here, too, Schiller is transforming Kant's account even as he builds upon it and, in the process, preparing the way for the German idealism that followed. Whereas Kant restricts his account of the dynamical sublime largely to natural phenomena, Schiller considers the practical sublimity of specific human themes, actions, and characters both in real life and in the fine art *(schöne Kunst)* of tragedy. Kant explained how the pleasure afforded by the dynamic sort of sublimity depends upon simultaneously recognizing a natural threat to one's physical existence and a moral capacity or freedom to defy nature, come what may. Schiller enlarges on Kant's analysis, noting how much more pleasurable it is, both in and outside the theater, when what is threatened is not only one's life but also one's moral vocation and character. At the same time, since tragedy is one of the fine or beautiful arts *(schöne Künste)*, by identifying the practically sublime as the object of tragedy and the source of its pleasures, Schiller brings together what Kant kept separate: the form of beauty and the formlessness of the sublime. As was the case in his account of the beautiful in terms of the "play-drive," Schiller's reflections move to a point where the thought of a unity of opposites, the centerpiece of German idealism, seems inevitable.

Schiller and German Idealism

It is not insignificant that, despite their quarrel in the interim, Fichte is the only contemporary German philosopher, aside from Kant, explicitly mentioned by Schiller in the revised as well as the original version of the Letters. In Letter 4 he refers his readers to "his friend" Fichte's *Lectures on the Vocation of a Scholar* for the derivation of the ideal and the task of realizing it; in Letter 13 as he addresses culture's task of doing justice to both sensuous and rational drives in terms of a concept of reciprocal action ("the idea of humanity in the most proper sense of the word"), Schiller speaks of Fichte's "admirable" outline of this concept and its importance in *Fundaments of the Theory of Knowledge*. Both references are highly revealing; the stridently ethical character of Fichte's philosophy and his insistence on grasping a dynamic unity of opposites in order to get at the bottom of Kant's transcendental philosophy are unmistakable in Schiller's own critical revisions of Kant's achievement.

Not surprisingly, these references to Fichte together with Schiller's rethinking of *la querelle des anciens et des modernes* point also to the themes having the greatest impact on the three former seminarians at the Stift in Tübingen: Hölderlin, Schelling, and Hegel. Each of them saw himself not as a future pastor but as a *Volkserzieher*, an "educator of the people," and each would herald, in one way or another, the idealist notion of the absolute union of subject and object and, from another point of view, the absolute union of the individual and the species. After reading just the first two installments of Schiller's *Aesthetic Letters* in April 1795, Hegel writes Schelling that they are a "masterpiece." Hölderlin writes Schiller himself in September 1795, affirming that the absolute union of things is aesthetic and, six months later, he is planning his own "New Letters on the Aesthetic Education of Man." Schelling, after an intensive study of *Naive and Sentimental Poetry*, explicitly argues for the aesthetic character of the absolute in his *System of Transcendental Idealism* of 1800.

In his mature work Hegel also develops the theme of the aesthetic character of the absolute, conceived as spirit, encompassing the individual (subjective spirit, nature become self-conscious) and the community (objective spirit, moral and mutual self-consciousness), though he subordinates that aesthetic character to supposedly higher forms of this self-conscious unity, namely, religion and philosophy. Nevertheless, even in later years, in his lectures on aesthetics, he pays special tribute to Schiller's "great service of having broken through the Kantian subjectivity and abstraction and having dared to go beyond it, grasping unity and reconciliation as the truth intellectually and realizing it artistically." Moreover, in Schiller's writings—for example, Letter 18 ("nature (sense) everywhere unites, the intellect everywhere separates, but reason reunites"), the concluding pages of *Concerning the Sublime*, and part 3 of *Naive and Sentimental Poetry*—there is an obvious anticipation of Hegel's own dialectical use of *Aufhebung* as a term for the dynamic unifying of opposites that preserves their differences and that, consequently, cannot be the object of a mere intuition, intellectual or aesthetic (as it was for Schelling and apparently Hegel himself in 1800).

There is perhaps no clearer illustration of Schiller's influential role in the development of German idealism out of Kant's transcendental philosophy than his own use of Kant's table of categories to clarify the relation between naive and sentimental poetry and ways of feeling (as well as the corresponding historical relation between ancients and moderns, the natural and the ideal). Kant distinguishes his table of twelve categories into four classes, in each of which the second category is a negation of the first, while the third category "springs from the combination of the first with the second." The parallel that Schiller draws in this connection is illustrated in the following chart:

Kant		Schiller	
Class	E.g.,		
Categories	Quantity	Poetry	History
First	Unity	Naive	Nature
Second	Plurality	Sentimental	Art
Third	Totality	Ideal	Ideal

The ideal, in poetry as in human history, is thus not to be conceived as the mere negation or opposite of naïveté and nature, but rather as an attempt to combine naïveté and nature with their opposites (the sentimentality or art produced by reflection, *Verstand*)—or, in crypto-Hegelian terms, to recover *something like* naïveté and nature by negating the negation of them.

It is not, of course, as though people will be able to return to the same nature that pervades naive poetry. Indeed, Schiller belabors the relative strengths and weaknesses and, ultimately, the irreconcilability of naive and sentimental poetry and of the realist and the idealist—except in the case of "a few rare individuals, who hopefully there always have been and always will be." Thus, even though his own understanding of the liberating, aesthetic recovery of nature provides the cognitive model for idealistic speculations about an absolute encompassing both nature and human history, Schiller himself does not indulge in such speculations. Nature indelibly marks the realist or idealist for what he is and Schiller, like Kant and Aristotle, recognized all too well that history is a story told by men. In this respect Schiller remains faithful to both his classical and transcendental perspectives and to his vocation as a poet.

Just as speculations about art in Schiller's essays always carry over into political, cultural-historical, and anthropological questions, so too do his discourses on politics, cultural history, and anthropology always lead directly back to art—the most important aid in the consideration of human concerns. There is perhaps no more apt justification of this synthetic character of Schiller's aesthetics than Schiller's words to Charlotte von Schimmelmann in a letter of November 4, 1795: "The highest philosophy ends in a poetic idea, so do the highest morality and the highest politics. It is the poetic spirit that indicates the ideal to all three, and to approach it is their greatest perfection."

W. H.
D. O. D.

All translations are based upon volumes 20 and 21 of *Schillers Werke,* Nationalausgabe: Philosophische Schriften, Unter Mitwirkung von Helmut Koopman, herausgegeben von Benno von Wiese (Weimar: Hermann Böhlaus Nachfolger, 1962). Numbers placed between brackets—e.g., [417]—within the translation indicate the respective page of the text in the Nationalausgabe.

On the Art of Tragedy*

There is something about a state of emotion, all by itself and independent of any relation of its object to our betterment or detriment, that enchants us. We strive to put ourselves in such a state, even if it should involve some sacrifice. This urge lies at the bottom of our most ordinary pleasures; it scarcely even comes up for consideration whether in the process the emotion be directed at something desirable or abhorrent and whether by its nature it be pleasant or painful. Indeed, experience teaches that an unpleasant emotion has greater appeal for us and consequently that the pleasure of an emotion stands in directly inverse relation to its content. It is a universal phenomenon in human nature that what is sad, what is terrible, and even what we dread captivate us with an allure in itself irresistible. We find the sight of misery and horror repugnant and yet with the same force we feel ourselves drawn to it. Filled with expectation, people crowd around somebody telling the story of a murder; we hungrily devour the most fantastic ghost stories, and the more such tales make our hair stand on end, the better.

This excitement expresses itself more vividly in the case of objects actually observed. Viewed from shore, a storm at sea sinking an entire fleet would captivate our fantasy just as powerfully as it

On the Art of Tragedy (Über die tragische Kunst), originating in a lecture in the summer of 1790, was first completed in the winter of 1791 and appeared in the second part *("Zweites Stück")* of Schiller's periodical, *Neue Thalia* (Leipzig: Göschen, 1792), vol. 1, pp. 176–228.

offends our sensitive heart. It is difficult to believe with Lucretius that this unnatural sort of pleasure springs from a comparison of our own safety with the perceived danger. Think of how immense a procession of people accompanies a criminal to the scene of his torments! Neither the pleasure deriving from a satisfied love of justice nor the ignoble delight resulting from some gratified lust for revenge can explain this phenomenon. In the hearts of the spectators this unfortunate soul can even be forgiven and compassion of the most upright sort may busy itself with his preservation. Nevertheless, with more or less strength, a need is stirred in the [149] spectator to focus eye and ear, out of curiosity, on the individual's expression of suffering. If someone with breeding and more refined feelings constitutes an exception here such that this need is not stirred, it is not because the urge is not at all present in him, but because he is overwhelmed by the pain and strength of his compassion or because he is held in check by laws of propriety. Nature's child, unencumbered by any feelings of tender humanity, gives itself up to this powerful pull without shame. This need must accordingly be based on the original disposition of the human mind and must be explicable by some universal, psychological law.

Yet, even if we find these raw, natural feelings incompatible with the dignity of human nature and for that reason hesitate to establish a law for the entire species on this basis, there are still enough experiences to put beyond doubt the reality and the universality of the pleasure that people take in painful emotions. The painful struggle between opposing inclinations or duties, while a source of misery for the individual undergoing it, captivates us when we consider it. With ever-mounting pleasure we follow the progression of a passion to the abyss into which it drags its unfortunate victim. The same tender feelings that frighten us back from the sight of physical suffering or even from the physical expression of moral suffering, allow us, in sympathy with the pure moral pain, to feel a pleasure simply all the sweeter. The interest with which we dwell on the portrayals of such themes is universal.

Naturally, this holds only for the emotion *communicated or felt afterwards*. For the close relation of the *original* emotion to our instinct for happiness usually concerns and preoccupies us too much to leave room for the pleasure imparted by the emotion of itself, free from any connection with self-interest. So for someone who is actually in the grip of a painful passion, the feeling of pain is overwhelming, however much the portrayal of his mental state is able to delight the listener or onlooker. In spite of this, even for the individual undergoing it, the original emotion, although painful, [150] is not utterly devoid of pleasure. Only the degrees of this pleasure vary, depending upon the individual's frame of mind. If there were not some enjoyment in uneasiness, doubt, and fear, then games of chance would hold incomparably fewer attractions for us, people would never plunge into dangers out of sheer foolhardiness, and even the sympathy with another's suffering would never be more enchanting than precisely when the illusion is greatest and we most mistake ourselves for him. This does not mean, however, that the unpleasant emotions afford pleasure in and of themselves, a claim that surely no one would dream of making. It is sufficient if these states of mind merely provide the conditions under which certain types of pleasure are possible for us. Minds that are especially receptive to *these* types of pleasure, and long for them above all, will for that reason more easily reconcile themselves to these unpleasant conditions. And even in the most turbulent storms of passion they will not entirely lose their freedom.

The displeasure we feel in the face of adverse emotions proceeds from the relation of its object to our sensuous or moral capabilities, just as the pleasure in agreeable emotions springs from these very same sources. Then, too, the degree of freedom capable of being asserted in emotions corresponds to the relation of a human being's moral nature to his sensuous nature. In addition, since what is moral, as is well known, is not a matter of our choice, whereas sensuous urges, on the other hand, are—or at least are supposed to be—subordinated to the dictates of reason and consequently are in our power, it becomes clear that it is possible to maintain a complete freedom in regard to all emotions that have to do with the selfish instinct and to be master of the intensity those emotions are supposed to attain. This intensity will be weaker precisely to the degree that the moral sense maintains the upper hand over the human being's instinct for happiness [or urge to be happy] and to the degree that selfish adherence to his individual ego is diminished by his obedience of the universal laws of reason. In a state of emotion such an individual will thus feel the object's relation to his instinct for happiness far less and, as a consequence, [151] will also experience far less of the displeasure springing solely from this relation. On the other hand, he will notice all the more the relation of this very object to his moral life; and precisely for this reason he will also be all the more receptive to the pleasure that, by virtue of the relation to morality, often permeates the most excruciating suffering of sensuous life. Such a frame of mind is most capable of enjoying the pleasure of empathy and even preserving the original emotion within the limitations of someone empathizing. Thus the enormous value of a philosophy of life that weakens the feeling for our individuality by constantly referring to universal laws, that teaches us to lose our minuscule selves in the context of a larger whole, and that thereby puts us in the position of treating ourselves as we do others. This sublime spiritual disposition is the lot of strong and philosophical minds who, through assiduous work on themselves, have learned to control the selfish instinct. Even the most painful loss does not drive them beyond the sort of composed melancholy that is always capable of being combined with a noticeable degree of pleasure. Only such minds, who alone are capable of separating themselves from themselves, enjoy the privilege of taking part in themselves and feeling their own suffering in the gentle reflection of sympathy.

The foregoing already contains enough hints to make us attentive to the sources of the pleasure secured by emotion in itself and by a sad emotion in particular. As has been seen, this pleasure is greater in minds that are moral and it works all the more freely, the more the mind is independent of selfish urges. Moreover, this pleasure has greater vitality and strength in emotions of sadness where self-love is enfeebled, than in emotions of joy that presuppose some satisfaction on the part of self-love. Hence, it grows where the selfish urge is scorned and it diminishes where this urge is flattered. Now, we are not acquainted with more than two sorts of sources of pleasure: the satisfaction of the urge to be happy and the fulfillment of moral laws. Hence, a pleasure proven not to have sprung from the first source must have its origin necessarily in the second source. It is from our moral nature, then, [152] that the pleasure emanates by means of which painful emotions captivate us when we hear of them and in certain cases, even when they are originally felt, still touch us in a pleasurable way.

People have tried to explain the pleasure afforded by compassion in several different ways. Yet, most accounts proved unsatisfactory because people looked to the accompanying circumstances rather than to the nature of the emotion itself for the explanation for this phenomenon. For many the pleasure of empathy is nothing other than the pleasure the soul takes in its sensitivity; for others it is the pleasure of powerfully engaged forces, the robust efficacy of desires, in short, a satisfaction of the urge to act. Others have it springing from the discovery of morally beautiful features of character, made visible by the struggle with misfortune and passion. In each case, however, it remains unclear why precisely the pain itself, the actual *suffering* in the objects of the compassion, attracts us more powerfully than anything else does, since according to the above explanations a weaker degree of suffering apparently should be more conducive to the alleged causes of our pleasure in being stirred. The vividness and strength of the images awakened in our fantasy, the moral excellence of the persons suffering, the empathizing individual's glance back at himself—all these things can probably enhance the pleasure of the emotion, but they are not the cause that produces it. Of course, a feeble soul's suffering or a scoundrel's pain does not secure us this enjoyment, but the reason for this is that they do not arouse our sympathies to the degree that a suffering hero or a virtuous but struggling person does. Our original question recurs again and again: why is it precisely the very intensity of the suffering that determines the intensity of the sympathetic pleasure we have in an emotion? The question can be answered in no other way than by acknowledging that the very assault on our sensuous life is the condition for igniting that power of mind, whose activity produces the pleasure that we take in sympathetic suffering.

Now, this power is none other than reason. To the extent that its unimpeded effectiveness as an activity belonging absolutely to the self deserves above all to be called an activity, and to the extent that the mind feels itself completely independent and free only when it acts morally, to this extent, [153] the pleasure that sorrowful, tragic emotions give us originates in the satisfaction of the urge to act. But in this regard, too, it is not the number, nor the liveliness of the images, nor even the effectiveness of desires in general, but rather a specific type of image and the effectiveness of a specific desire, produced by reason, that lie at the basis of this pleasure.

Hence, it is because it satisfies the instinct to act, that we generally find the emotion communicated enchanting. The sorrowful emotion realizes that effect to a higher degree because it satisfies this instinct to a higher degree. Only when it is in the state of its complete freedom, only when it is conscious of its rational nature does the mind express its highest activity, since there alone does it wield a power superior to any resistance.

That very state of mind, therefore, that above all proclaims this power and awakens this higher activity, is the *most purposeful* to a rational being and the most satisfying for the instinct to act. Hence, it must be linked with a superior degree of pleasure.* The tragic emotion transports us into such a state and the pleasure of that emotion must surpass the pleasure of joyful emotions precisely to the degree that the moral capacity within us is elevated above the sensuous capacity.

What is merely a subordinate member in the entire system of purposes may be taken out of this context by art and pursued as the chief purpose. For nature pleasure may be only an intermediate purpose, for art it is the supreme purpose. Thus, it is a part of the purpose of art not to neglect, above all, the great pleasure contained in the sorrowful, tragic emotion. The particular art that establishes the pleasure of sympathy as its purpose is called the *art of tragedy* in the most general sense of the term.

Art realizes its purpose through an *imitation of nature,* inasmuch as it fulfills the conditions under which pleasure becomes possible in actuality. To this end, art combines the most disparate [154] arrangements of nature according to some understandable plan in order to achieve as its ultimate purpose what nature produces merely as a by-product. The art of tragedy will thus imitate nature in those actions most apt to arouse sympathizing emotion.

In order, then, to prescribe to the art of tragedy its general procedure, it is above all necessary to know the conditions under which the pleasure of the emotion would be produced with the most certainty and the greatest force, and in accordance with ordinary

*See the essay on the basis of the pleasure in tragic themes. [Schiller is refering to his essay *Über den grund des Vergnügens an tragischen gegenständen,* which appeared in *Neue Thalia,* Bd. I, Stück 1 (1792).]

experience. At the same time it is also necessary to be aware of those circumstances that inhibit or even destroy that pleasure.

Experience provides two contrasting causes of hindering the pleasure taken in emotions: either the compassion is too feeble or it is so strongly aroused that the emotion communicated acquires the potency of an original emotion. The reason for the former, in turn, can lie either in the weakness of the impression we receive from the original suffering, in which case we say that our hearts are left cold and we feel neither pain nor pleasure; or it can lie in the more powerful feelings that combat the received impression and, by their preponderance in the mind, weaken or completely stifle the pleasure of compassion.

In accord with what was maintained in the preceding essay about the basis of the pleasure taken in tragic themes, in the case of any tragic emotion some incongruity [or something at odds with a purpose: *Zweckwidrigkeit*] is represented, which, if the emotion is to be alluring, always leads to a representation of some higher purposiveness *[Zweckmäßigkeit]*. Then it is a matter of the relation of these two opposed images to one another, whether pleasure or displeasure is supposed to stand out in the emotion. If the representation of the incongruity is more potent than the representation of the opposite, or if the purpose frustrated is more important than the one realized, the displeasure will have the upper hand every time. This may be true *objectively* of the human race in general, or merely *subjectively* of particular individuals. [155]

If the displeasure with the cause of a misfortune becomes too strong, it weakens our sympathy for the individual suffering it. Two completely different sensations cannot be present in the mind to a high degree at the same time. Indignation at the instigator of the suffering becomes the dominant emotion and every other feeling has to give way to it. Thus our compassion is always diminished somewhat, if the unfortunate soul, with whom we should be empathizing, fell to his ruin because of his own unforgiveable crime, or if out of despondency and due to the infirmity of his intellect he does not know how to pull himself up from this mess, supposing that he still could do so. Despite the mistreatment by his thankless daughters, no little damage is done to our sympathy for the unfortunate Lear by the fact that this childish old man gave his crown away so frivolously and divided his love among his daughters so imprudently. In Kronegk's tragedy, *Olint and Sophronia,* even the most frightful suffering that we see these two martyrs exposed to for their beliefs can only feebly arouse our sympathy and their sublime heroism can only faintly inspire our admiration, because madness alone can commit such an act as that by which Olint led himself and his entire people to the brink of disaster.

Our compassion is no less weakened if our souls are filled with revulsion at the perpetrator of some calamity, when we should be pitying the innocent victims of it. The supreme perfection of a work always suffers when the writer of the tragedy cannot make do without a villain and is forced to derive the degree of suffering from the degree of malice. Shakespeare's Iago and Lady Macbeth, Cleopatra in the *Rodogune,* Franz Moor in the *Räuber,* testify to this claim. A writer who knows where his best interests lie will bring the misfortune about, not through a malicious will intending it and still less through a lack of understanding, but through the force of circumstances. If the misfortune springs, not from immoral sources, but rather from external things that neither have a will nor are subject to one, then our compassion is purer and, at least, is not diminished by any [156] image of moral incongruity. But, then, the participating spectator cannot be spared the unpleasant feeling of an incongruity in nature, which in this case only moral purposiveness can redeem. Our sympathy ascends to a much higher level when both the person suffering and the person causing the suffering become objects of sympathy. This can only happen when the person causing the suffering arouses neither our hate nor our contempt. Instead, against his inclination, he is brought to a point where he becomes the origin of the misfortune. Thus it is especially beautiful in the case of the German *Iphigenia* that the Taurian king, the only one standing in the way of the wishes of Orestes and his sisters, never loses our respect and in the end even elicits our love.

As moving as this genre is, even it is surpassed by that genre where the cause of the misfortune not only does not contradict morality, but is only possible because of morality, and where the mutual suffering springs merely from the image of someone causing suffering. The situation of Chimene and Roderich in Pierre Corneille's *Cid,* indisputably the masterpiece of the tragic stage as far as intrigue is concerned, is of this sort. Love of honor and a child's duty arm Roderich against the father of his beloved and his bravery renders him the victor over the father. Love of honor and a child's duty awaken in Chimene, the daughter of the one defeated, a formidable accusor and prosecutor of Roderich. Both act contrary to their inclinations, inclinations that make them tremble, with so much anguish, at the tragedy of the objective they pursue and yet, with the same zeal, make their senses of moral duty bring this tragedy about. Thus, both win our highest respect, because they fulfill a moral duty at the cost of inclination; both kindle our compassion to the utmost, because they suffer voluntarily and on the basis of a motivation that makes them worthy of the highest degree of respect. Our sympathy here is, as a result, so little disturbed by contrary feelings that it blazes with twice the intensity. The sheer impossibility of combining the idea of misfortune with someone who could not be more deserving of good fortune might still cast a gloom, like a cloud of pain, over the pleasure gained from our sympathy. A great deal is already [157] gained from the fact that our indignation over this frustration of purposes is not directed at any moral entity, but instead is *diverted* to the most innocuous of places, namely, to necessity. Being blindly subject to fate is, nonetheless, always humiliating and debilitating for entities that are free and self-determining. This is why the most splendid pieces of the Greek stage leave something to be desired, since in all these pieces appeal is ultimately made to necessity and our reason, demanding reason as it does, is always left with some untied knot.

However, even this resolves itself and, with it, every hint of displeasure disappears at the highest and final stage to which a morally formed person can ascend and to which the art that touches us can elevate itself. This happens when even that dissatisfaction with fate falls to the wayside, losing itself in the presentiment or rather in a distinct consciousness of a teleological connection among things, a sublime order, a benevolent will. Then, allied with our pleasure in moral harmony there is the invigorating image of the most perfect purposiveness in the entire expanse of nature. Its apparent violation, which in a single case caused pain, becomes simply a goad to our reason to search out general laws for a justification of this particular case and to resolve the isolated dissonance within the grand harmony. Greek art never elevated itself to this pure height of tragic emotion, because neither the folk religion nor even the philosophy of the Greeks went this far. It is reserved for modern art, which enjoys the advantage of receiving a purer material from a more refined philosophy, to fulfill this highest demand and *thus* to unfold the complete moral dignity of art. If it were actually necessary for us moderns to renounce trying again and again to revive Greek art where it cannot be surpassed, then tragedy alone might constitute an exception. Perhaps in its case alone does our scientific culture replace the theft that it has otherwise perpetrated on art in general.

Just as the tragic emotion is weakened by the intermingling of contrary images and feelings, and the pleasure of that emotion is accordingly [158] diminished, so, on the other hand, by coming too close to the original emotion, it can be excessive, to such a degree that the pain becomes overwhelming. It has been noted that the displeasure in emotions has its origin in the relation of its object to our sensuous life, just as the pleasure in emotions is based on the relation of that very emotion to our moral life. Thus a definite relation between sensuous life and moral life is presupposed, which decides the relation of displeasure to pleasure in sorrowful emotions and which cannot be altered or inverted without at the same time inverting the emotional feelings of pleasure and pain or transforming them into their opposite. The livelier the awakening of sensuous life, the weaker the effect of moral life and, vice versa, the more the former loses in power, the more the latter will gain in strength. Thus, what gives the sensuous life an upper hand in our mind inhibits moral life and hence cannot help but detract from that pleasure we take in emotions flowing from this moral life alone. In corresponding fashion everything that provides some impetus to the moral life in our minds takes the sting out of pain even in original passions. Our sensuous life, however, actually gains the upper hand when the images of suffering become so vivid that they leave us no possibility of distinguishing the communicated passion from an original one, that is, of distinguishing ourselves from the suffering subject, or truth from fiction. Likewise, it gets the upper hand when it is nourished by an accumulation of sensuous objects and by the blinding light that an overexcited imagination casts over them. Nothing, on the other hand, is more apt to show it the way back to its limitations than *moral ideas* transcending the sensuous order. An oppressed reason supports itself on these ideas like spiritual props in order to raise itself above the gloomy fog of feelings to a brighter horizon. Thus the great attraction that general truths and moral sayings, interspersed at the right place in dramatic dialogue, have had for all civilized peoples, and thus, too, the almost exaggerated use already made [159] of them by the Greeks. After a long, unrelenting state of simple suffering, caused by the bondage of the senses, nothing is more welcome to a mind that is moral than to be reawakened to the possibility of acting on its own and have its freedom reinstated.

Enough concerning the causes which restrict our sympathy and stand in the way of the pleasure afforded by the sorrowful emotion. We need now to enumerate the conditions for furthering sympathy and awakening the pleasure of the emotion in the most reliable and powerful manner.

All sympathy presupposes *images* of suffering. The degree of sympathy depends upon the vividness, veracity, completeness, and length of the suffering.

I. The *more vivid and lively* the images, the more the mind is invited to be active, the more its sensuous character is aroused, and thus the more its moral capacity is challenged to resist. Images of suffering may, however, be sustained in two different ways that are not conducive to the impression's vividness in the same manner. Suffering we are witness to affects us with incomparably greater strength than suffering we first hear about through narration or description. The former overwhelms the free play of our imagination and, since it affects the sensuous side of us directly, it penetrates our hearts in the shortest way possible. In narration, on the other hand, some particular matter is first raised to a universal level and, then, on the basis of this, the particular matter is known. Thus from the outset, owing to this necessary operation of the intellect, a considerable portion of the impression's strength is removed. A weaker impression will, however, not take complete control of the mind and will give extraneous images room to disturb its effect and attenuate the attention paid it. Quite often the narrative presentation also transports us from the state of mind of the person acting to that of the narrator, thus interrupting the illusion so necessary to the sympathy. As often as the narrator intrudes himself in the first person, a pause arises in the action and hence unavoidably also in the emotion we share. This occurs, too, when the dramatist forgets himself in the dialogue and [160] places in the mouth of the person speaking, observations that only an indifferent onlooker could have made. Hardly any of our modern tragedies may be free of this mistake, but the French alone have elevated it to a rule. An immediate, vivid presence and visualization are therefore necessary, to give our images of suffering the intensity required for a high level of emotion.

2. Yet we can receive the most vivid impressions of some suffering, without being brought to any noticeable degree of compassion, if these impressions lack *truthfulness*. We have to make ourselves a *concept* of the suffering we are supposed to be taking part in. That requires that the concept coincide with something already previously at hand in us. The possibility of compassion rests namely upon the perception or presupposition of a *similarity* between us and the subject suffering. Everywhere that this similarity can be detected, compassion is necessary; where it is lacking, compassion is impossible. The more visible and the greater the similarity, the livelier our compassion is; the slighter the similarity, the weaker the compassion. If we are supposed to enter into the emotion of another, then all the *inner* conditions for this emotion must be present within us, so that the *external* cause, which gave rise to the emotion by being joined with those conditions, can exert a similar effect on us. Without forcing ourselves to exchange places with him, we must be capable of putting ourselves all at once in his position. Yet, how is it possible to feel someone else's condition within *ourselves,* if we have not previously found ourselves in the condition that the other person is in?

This similarity is a matter of the mind's entire foundation, insofar as this is universal and necessary. But it is preeminently our *moral nature* that is universal and necessary. Sensuous capabilities can be determined in different ways through contingent causes; even our cognitive capabilities are dependent upon conditions that change. Only our moral life is founded on itself and is, precisely for this reason, most suited to provide a universal and sure standard for this similarity. Thus, if we [161] find that an image agrees with our form of thinking and feeling, if it already has a certain kinship with our own sequence of thoughts, and if it is easily grasped by our minds, we call that image "true." If the similarity concerns something peculiar to our minds, that is to say, if it is a matter of determinations of the general character of human nature that are *particular* to us, something that may be disregarded without detriment to this general character, then this image is true merely for *us*. If it concerns the universal and necessary form that we presuppose for the entire species, then the truth is immediately to be deemed objective. For the Romans the elder Brutus's judgment and the suicide of Cato have subjective truth. The actions of these two men flow from images and feelings that do not follow immediately from the universal character of human nature, but rather immediately from a human nature determined in a particular way. In order to share these feelings with them, one must possess a Roman's sensibilities or at least be capable of momentarily assuming them. On the other hand, one needs to be nothing more than simply a *human being* to be transported to a state of high emotion by the heroic sacrifice of a Leonidas, by the peaceful surrender of an Aristid, by the freely accepted death of a Socrates; or to be brought to tears by the terrible turn of fortune of a Darius at Thranes. In contrast with those images mentioned above, we grant these sorts of images an objective truth because they agree with the nature of *all* subjects and, by that fact, uphold a universality and necessity as rigorous as if they were independent of every subjective condition.

Furthermore, the portrayal that is subjectively true, just because it is a matter of contingent determinations, is not for that reason to be confused with arbitrary determinations. Even what is subjectively true flows ultimately from the universal structure of the human mind that becomes determined in a particular way solely by virtue of particular conditions, and both the universal structure and the particular determinations are equally necessary conditions of what is subjectively true. If it had contradicted the universal laws of human nature, Cato's decision could not have been even subjectively true. The sphere within which depictions of the latter sort are effective is simply narrower, because they presuppose determinations other than those [162] universal ones. The art of tragedy can make use of this subjectively true scenario with considerable, intensive effect, if it is willing to forsake the extensiveness of its effect. Still, what is unconditionally true, what is simply *human* in human relations, will always be its most fertile material, since with this material alone it is assured of the *universality* of the impression it makes, without having to relinquish the *strength* of the impression.

3. Thirdly, in addition to the vividness and truthfulness of tragic depictions, *completeness* is required. Nothing that must be conveyed from the outside in order to set the mind in motion in the way intended may be omitted in the representation. If a member of the audience—even if he is disposed to the Roman mentality—is to make Cato's state of mind his own, that is, if he is to consider the republican's decision his own decision, then he must come to see that this decision is based not merely on the Roman soul, but also on the circumstances. The entire context and scope of the situation, outside as well as inside Cato, must lie before the viewer's eyes, and not a single link may be missing from the chain of determinations, to which the Roman's final decision is connected as something necessary. Generally, even the genuineness of a depiction is not recognizable without this completeness, since only the similarity of the *circumstances,* which we have to see perfectly, can justify our judgment about the similarity of the *feelings*. For the emotion springs only from the union of external and internal conditions. If what is to be determined is whether we would have acted like Cato, then above all else we must think of ourselves as being completely in Cato's own external situation. Only then are we justified in holding our feelings up against his, in making some inference on the basis of the similarity, and in passing judgment on the truth of the similarity.

This completeness of the depiction is only possible by combining several individual images and feelings, which are related to one another as cause and effect and in their connection constitute a complete unit for us to contemplate. If they are to touch us in a lively way, all these images must make an immediate impression on our sensuous character and, since the narrative form [163] always weakens this impression, these images must be caused by some contemporaneous action. Thus, for the completeness of the depiction of something tragic, a series of individual, perceptible actions are necessary, actions that are bound up with the tragic action as to a whole.

4. Finally, the images of the suffering must work on us *incessantly,*

if they are to stir up a high level of emotion. The passion produced in us by others' sufferings is a state of coercion from which we rush to free ourselves and it is all too easy for the illusion so indispensable for compassion to disappear. For this reason, our minds must be forcibly fettered to these images and robbed of the freedom of tearing themselves away from the illusion prematurely. For this purpose the liveliness of the images and the strength of the impressions that overcome our sensuous character are not adequate, since the more vehemently the sensitive capabilities are agitated, the more vigorously the power of the soul reacts to subdue this impression. Yet the writer who wants to touch us may not weaken this spontaneous power. For the great enjoyment that tragic emotions provide us lies precisely in this power's struggle with the sensuous suffering. Thus, if the mind, in spite of the spontaneity with which it resists, should remain fixed on the feelings of suffering, then these must be skillfully and periodically interrupted, even dissolved by contrary feelings—in order then to return with increasing strength and to renew the liveliness of the first impression all that more often. *Variation* of the feelings is the mightiest means against weariness and the effects of habit. This variation revives the exhausted sensuousness and staggering the force of the impressions beckons the spontaneous faculty to the respective resistance. This faculty must be ceaselessly at work maintaining its freedom against coercion by sensuousness, but it must not triumph before the end and even less may it succumb in the struggle. Otherwise, in the first case the suffering is done away with, in the second the activity, and only the union of the two genuinely arouses the emotion. The great secret of the art of tragedy [164] consists precisely in the skillful management of this conflict; there the secret is revealed in its most brilliant light.

Also necessary is a series of alternating images, in other words, a purposive combination of several actions corresponding to these images. With these actions the central action unwinds perfectly and through it the intended tragic effect, like a spool of thread from the spindle, so that the mind finally is ensnared as by an unbreakable net. The artist, if I may be permitted this image, first economically gathers all the *individual* rays of light belonging to the object that he makes the tool of his tragic purpose and in his hands they become the lightning that ignites all hearts. While the novice hurls the entire lightning bolt of terror and fear into our heads all at once and without effect, the artist reaches his goal step-by-step through simple, little strokes and penetrates the soul in its *entirety*, precisely because he touched it only gradually and incrementally.

If we draw up now the results from the foregoing investigations, then the following conditions lie at the basis of tragedy's emotion. *First,* the object of our sympathy must belong to our nature in the complete sense of the word, and the action, in which we are supposed to participate, must be moral, that is, it must be conceived within the realm of freedom. *Second,* the suffering as well as the sources and extent of it must be communicated completely within a sequence of connected events and, of course, *third,* it must be realized in a perceptible way, not presented in mediated fashion through description, but through action directly. The art in tragedy combines and fulfills all these conditions.

Tragedy is, accordingly, a literary imitation of a coherent series of events (of a complete action) that shows us human beings in a state of suffering and has the purpose of arousing our sympathy.

It is, first, *imitation*—of an action. The concept of imitation distinguishes it from the other genres of literature, which merely narrate or describe. In tragedies the individual events are placed before the imagination [165] or the senses as present the moment they are occurring; this takes place immediately, without the interposition of some third thing. Due to their very form, the epic, the novel, and the simple narration move the action into the background because they insert the narrator between the reader and the persons acting. However, as is well known, what is placed in the background, what is over with, weakens the impression and the accompanying emotion, What is present strengthens it. All narrative forms make what is present into something past; all *dramatic* forms make the past something present.

Tragedy is secondly imitation of a series of *events,* an *action.* By imitating, tragedy depicts not only the feelings and passion of the persons in the tragedy, but also the events from which those feelings and passions originated and on the occasion of which they came to be expressed. This distinguishes it from the lyrical types of literature that, to be sure, poetically imitate specific states of mind just as much, but not actions. An elegy, a song, or an ode can through imitation place before our eyes the poet's present state of mind, conditioned by particular circumstances (be it in his own person or in some ideal person). To this extent they overlap with the concept of tragedy, but they still do not constitute a tragedy, since they limit themselves merely to depicting feelings. Even more essential differences lie in the different purpose of these types of literature.

Thirdly, tragedy is imitation of a *complete action*. A single event, as tragic as it might be, still does not yield a tragedy. Several occurrences, grounded in one another as cause and effect, must be bound together purposefully into a whole, if the truth, that is to say, the congruence of an imagined passion, character, and the like with the nature of our soul, is to be recognized. This congruence is the sole basis of our participation. If we do not feel that in the same circumstances we ourselves would have suffered in just the same way and would have acted in just the same way, then our sympathy will never be aroused. Thus, it is a matter of our pursuing the represented action in its entire context, of our seeing it flow from the soul of its originator with the cooperation of external circumstances by a natural [166] progression. Thus before our eyes the curiosity of Oedipus or the jealousy of Othello arises and grows and is consummated. Also, in this way alone is it possible to compensate for the great distance between the peace of an innocent soul and the torments of a criminal's conscience, between the proud certainty of someone blessed and his terrifying demise, in short, between the reader's calm mood at the beginning and the passionate arousal of his feelings at the end of the action.

A series of several, related incidents is required to incite an alteration in the movements of our minds, a change that intensifies attentiveness and summons up every capacity of our spirit. This change also revives an urge to act that has grown weary, incensing it all the more furiously by delaying its gratification. In moral life and nowhere else does the mind find help against the suffering of sensuous life. Thus, to provoke this with even greater pressure, the tragedian must prolong the torments on the sensuous side. But he must also show this side some satisfaction in order to make the victory for morality all the more difficult and all the more glorious. Both are possible only through a series of actions that are wisely selected and combined for this purpose.

Tragedy is, fourthly, *poetic* imitation of an action warranting our sympathy and, for that reason, it is set in contrast to *historical* imitation. It would be the latter if it pursued a historian's purpose, in other words, if it aimed at *instructing* us about things that had happened and how they happened. In such a case it would have to hold itself strictly to historical accuracy, since it would attain its aim only by faithfully presenting what actually happened. Tragedy, however, has a *poetic* purpose, that is to say, it presents an action in order to *move* us and, by moving us, to *delight* us. If then it treats some given material for this purpose, it becomes *free* in the imitation precisely for this reason. It continues to have the power, indeed, the obligation of subordinating the historical truth to the laws of the literary art and of reworking the given material as the art requires. Since, however, [167] it is in a position to achieve *its* purpose, namely, the emotion, only on the condition of utterly conforming to the laws of nature, it is subject to the rigorous law of natural truth without its historical freedom being violated in any way. In contrast to "historical truth" this natural truth is called the "poetic truth." Thus it is understandable how poetic truth often suffers when historical truth is strictly observed and, vice versa, how much more poetic truth stands to gain when historical truth is rudely violated. Since the writer of tragedy, just like any writer, is only subject to the law of poetic truth, the most conscientious observance of historical truth can never relieve him of his duty as a writer nor can it ever provide him with an excuse for overstepping the poetic truth or for being uninteresting. Thus it betrays quite limited conceptions of the art of tragedy, indeed, of literary art in general, when a writer of tragedies is dragged before the tribunal of history and *instruction* is demanded from someone who, by his very name, commits himself solely to stirring and delighting us. Even then, when the writer himself, because of a nervous submissiveness to historical truth, is supposed to have foregone his artistic license and tacitly given history jurisdiction over his work, art has every right to summon him before *its* tribunal. If a death of a Hermann, a Minona, or a Prince of Stromberg, for all the accuracy of their adherence to the costumes, people, and character of the times, did not pass the test here, they would be called mediocre tragedies.

Fifthly, tragedy is imitation of an action, which *shows* us *human beings in a state of suffering*. The expression, *human being*, is not at all idle and serves to draw quite precisely the boundaries within which tragedy is limited in the choice of its subject matter. Only the suffering of entities both sensuous and moral, such as we are, can arouse our sympathy. Thus, beings who declare themselves free from all *morality,* such as the evil demons painted by folk superstition or by a writer's imagination, and humans similar to them; also beings who are free [168] from the coercion of *sensuousness,* such as we regard pure intellects, and humans who have extricated themselves from this coercion to a greater extent than human weakness permits—all these are equally unfit for tragedy. In general, the concept of suffering and of a suffering in which we are supposed to participate already determines that only *human beings* in the full sense of the word can be the object of the suffering. A pure intellect cannot suffer and a human subject that approaches this pure intellect to an uncommon degree can never arouse a great degree of pathos, since his moral nature too readily provides protection against the suffering of a weak sensuous character. A thoroughly sensuous individual devoid of morality and those that come close to this are, of course, capable of the most frightening level of suffering because their sensuous nature acts on a level that is overwhelming. Without the support of any moral feeling, these individuals fall prey to such pain. Theirs is a thoroughly helpless kind of suffering, an absolute inertia of reason, and we turn away from such suffering with indignation and disgust. The writer of tragedy thus rightly prefers mixed characters and his ideal hero is as far removed from what is utterly contemptible as from what is perfect.

The tragedy, finally, combines all these features *in order to arouse the emotion of compassion.* Many of the scenarios constructed by the writer of a tragedy may quite legitimately be used for some other purpose, for example, a moral purpose, a historical purpose, and so on. Yet, the fact that the writer aims precisely at stirring up sympathy and nothing else frees him from all demands that are not connected with this purpose. At the same time, however, this fact also obliges him to take his bearings from this ultimate purpose every time he applies the rules previously determined.

The final ground, to which all rules for a specific literary genre refer, is called the *purpose* of this genre. The combination of means through which a literary genre achieves its purpose is called its *form.* Accordingly, purpose and form stand in the most precise sort of relationship to one another. The form is determined and necessarily prescribed by the purpose and the [169] realized purpose will be the result of the fortuitously observed form.

Since every literary genre pursues a purpose peculiar to it, it will distinguish itself precisely for this reason from the rest by virtue of a distinctive form, since the form is the means by which it achieves its purpose. Precisely what it alone accomplishes, in contrast to the rest, it must accomplish thanks to the quality that it alone possesses in contrast to the others. The purpose of tragedy is *emotion,* its form is *imitation* of an action leading to suffering. Several literary genres can share with tragedy the same sort of action as their subject matter. Several literary genres are able to pursue tragedy's purpose—the emotion—although not as their main purpose. The difference turns on the relation of the form to the purpose, that is, how the genre treats its subject matter in view of its purpose or, in other words, how it achieves its purpose by means of its subject matter.

If the purpose of tragedy is to arouse the emotion of compassion, but its form is the *means* of achieving this purpose, then imitation of a poignant action is the central concept behind all the conditions for arousing the compassionate emotion in the most powerful way. Thus, the form of tragedy is the form most conducive to arousing the compassionate emotion.

The product of a literary genre is perfect, if the peculiar form of this literary genre has been best utilized to achieve its purpose. A tragedy, therefore, is perfect when the tragedy's form, namely, the imitation of a poignant action, has been best utilized to arouse the compassionate emotion. The most perfect tragedy would thus be one in which the compassion aroused is the effect less of the material than of the form of tragedy, employed in the most effective way. This may stand for the *ideal* of tragedy.

Many tragic plays, even those full of great poetic beauty, are dramatically flawed because they do not seek to achieve the purpose of the tragedy through the best utilization of the form of tragedy. Others are flawed because they use the tragic form to achieve [170] some other purpose than that of tragedy. Not a few of our most beloved pieces move us solely because of the material and we are generous or inattentive enough to attribute to the clumsy artist as a point of merit what is simply a feature of the material. In the case of other pieces we appear to forget completely the aim for which the dramatist has gathered us together and, satisfied at being pleasantly entertained by glittering games of imagination and wit, we do not once notice that we leave the theater with cold hearts. Must an honorable art (since what speaks to the divine part of our being is honorable) make its case through such contestants before *such* referees? Only for mediocre writers is the audience's satisfaction encouraging; for the genius, it is insulting and threatening.

Translated by Daniel O. Dahlstrom

On the Sublime*

(Toward the Further Development of Some Kantian Ideas)

We call an object *sublime* if, whenever the object is presented or represented, our sensuous nature feels its limits, but our rational nature feels its superiority, its freedom from limits. Thus, we come up short against a sublime object *physically,* but we elevate ourselves above it *morally,* namely, through ideas.

Only as sensuous beings are we dependent; as rational beings we are free.

A sublime subject matter gives us *in the first place* a feeling of our dependency as natural beings, because *in the second place* it makes us aware of the independence that, as rational beings, we assert over nature, as much *inside* as *outside* ourselves.

We are dependent insofar as something *outside* us contains the reason why something is possible *inside* us.

As long as nature outside us conforms to conditions under which something becomes possible inside us, we cannot feel our dependency. If we are to become conscious of that dependency, then nature must be represented as conflicting with what for us is a *need* and yet is *possible* only through nature's compliance. Or, in other

---

**On the Sublime (Vom Erhabenen)* appeared in the third volume (which contains parts 1–3) of Schiller's periodical *Neue Thalia* (Leipzig: Göschen, 1793), pp. 320–66.

words, nature must stand in contradiction to our instincts or drives *[Triebe]*.

Now all instincts at work within us as sensuous beings may be reduced to two fundamental instincts. First, we possess an instinct to alter the condition we find ourselves in, to express our existence, to be effective, all of which amount to acquiring representations or notions for ourselves. This fundamental instinct can thus be called "the instinct to represent things to ourselves" or, in short, "the cognitive instinct" *[Vorstellungstrieb]*. Second, we possess an instinct to maintain the condition we find ourselves in, to continue our existence, an instinct called "the instinct for self-preservation" *[Trieb der Selbsterhaltung]*.

The cognitive instinct concerns knowing; the instinct for self-preservation concerns feelings, in other words, inner perceptions of existence. [172]

By virtue of these two sorts of instincts we are *dependent* upon nature in two ways. The first kind of dependence becomes evident to us if the natural conditions for arriving at various sorts of knowledge are missing. We experience the second kind of dependency when nature contradicts the conditions that make it possible for us to continue to exist. In a parallel way, with the help of reason, we maintain our *independence* from nature in two senses: *first,* because (in a theoretical sense) we pass beyond natural conditions and can *think* more than we know; *second,* because (in a practical sense) we set ourselves above natural conditions and, by means of our will, can contradict our *desires*. When perception of some subject matter allows us to experience the former, it is *theoretically magnificent*, something cognitively sublime. A subject matter providing us with the feeling of the independence of our will is *practically magnificent,* a sublimeness of character *[ein Erhabenes der Gesinnung]*.

In the case of what is theoretically-sublime, the cognitive instinct is contradicted by nature as an *object of knowledge*. In the case of what is practically-sublime, the instinct to preserve ourselves is contradicted by nature as an *object of feeling*. In the former scenario nature is considered merely as an object that should have expanded our knowledge; in the latter case it is represented as a power that can determine *our* own condition. Kant accordingly names the practically-sublime "the sublimity of power" or "the dynamically sublime" in contrast to the mathematically sublime. However, since it is in no way possible on the basis of the concepts *dynamic* and *mathematical* to make clear or not whether the sphere of the sublime is exhausted by this division, I have preferred the division into the *theoretically-sublime* and the *practically-sublime.*

In what way we are dependent upon natural conditions in our cognitions and become conscious of this dependency will be sufficiently elaborated in the development of the theoretically-sublime. That our existence as sensuous beings is dependent upon natural conditions outside us is scarcely in need of a proof of its own. As soon as nature outside us alters its specific relationship to us, on which our physical well-being is based, our [173] existence in the world afforded by the senses and connected to this physical well-being is also immediately challenged and endangered. Nature thus has in its power the conditions under which we exist and, in order that we pay attention to this relationship to nature, so indispensable to our existence, a vigilant sentry has been given to our physical life in the form of the *self-preservation instinct* and a warning has been given to this instinct in the form of *pain.* Thus, the moment our physical condition undergoes a change that threatens to transform it into its opposite, pain calls attention to the danger and summons the instinct of self-preservation to resist.

If the danger is of *the sort* that any resistance on our part would be futile, then *fear* must arise. Hence, if the existence of an object conflicts with the conditions of our own existence and if we do not feel ourselves up to its power, it is an object of fear, something *frightening.*

But it is only frightening for us as sensuous beings, because only as such are we dependent upon nature. That inside us that is not nature and not subordinated to natural law has nothing to fear from nature outside us, considered as a force. Represented as a force capable of determining our physical condition but having no power over our will, nature is *dynamically* or *practically* sublime.

The practically-sublime thus is distinct from the theoretically-sublime in that the former conflicts with the conditions of our existence, while the theoretically-sublime conflicts only with the conditions of knowledge. An object is theoretically-sublime insofar as it brings with it the notion *[Vorstellung]* of infinity, something the imagination does not feel itself capable of depicting. An object is practically-sublime insofar as it brings with it the notion of a danger that we do not feel ourselves capable of overcoming with our physical powers. We succumb in the attempt to grasp the idea *[Vorstellung]* of the theoretically-sublime or to resist the force of the practically-sublime. A peaceful ocean is an example of the former, a stormy ocean an example of the latter. An enormously high tower or mountain can provide something sublime for cognition. If it looms down over [174] us, it will turn into something sublime for our emotional state. Again, both have this much in common with one another: precisely by contradicting the conditions of our existing and acting respectively, they disclose the very power within us that does not feel itself bound to these conditions, that is to say, a power that, on the one hand, is able to think more than the senses can apprehend and, on the other hand, fears nothing as far as its independence is concerned and suffers no violence in expressing itself, even if the senses accompanying it should be overcome by the frightful power of nature.

Yet, although both sorts of sublimity have a similar relation to our power of reason, they stand in a completely different relation to the sensuous side of us, and this is the basis for an important difference between them, a difference in strength as well as interest.

The theoretically-sublime contradicts the cognitive instinct, the practically-sublime the preservation instinct. In the first case what is contested is only an individual expression of the cognitive power of the senses. In the second case, however, what is contested is the ultimate basis of any possible expression of this power, namely, its very existence.

Now, of course, there is some displeasure involved in every failed attempt to know, since by this means an active instinct is confounded. Yet this displeasure can never amount to pain as long as we know that our existence is not dependent on the success or failure of such knowing and our self-respect does not suffer in the process.

However, if an object clashes with the conditions of our existence and the immediate sensation of it would cause *pain,* the image of the object inspires *fright.* For, in order to preserve the power itself, nature would have had to make arrangements completely different from those that it found necessary to sustain the activity of that power. In the case of a *frightful* object, then, the sensuous side of our nature is engaged in a quite different way than it is in the case of something infinite, since the self-preservation instinct clamors much more loudly than the cognitive instinct does. It is altogether different whether we have to fear losing a single notion or the basis of any possible notion, namely, our existence in the world of the senses, [175] in other words, whether we have to fear for existence itself or for a single expression of it.

However, precisely for this reason, namely, because the *frightful* object assails our sensuous nature more violently than something *infinite* does, the distance between capabilities of the senses and capabilities that go beyond the senses is felt all the more keenly. Reason's superiority and the mind's inner freedom become all the more conspicuous. Since, then, the entire essence of the sublime rests upon the consciousness of this rational freedom of ours, and all pleasure afforded by the sublime is grounded precisely in this consciousness alone, it follows of itself (as experience also teaches) that the aesthetic image of what is *frightful* must stir us more powerfully and more pleasantly than the representation of the *infinite* does, and that the practically-sublime has, accordingly, a very great advantage over the theoretically-sublime, as far as the strength of the feeling is concerned.

While what is theoretically-magnificent actually expands only our *scope,* what is practically-magnificent, the dynamically-sublime, expands our *power.* Only by means of the latter do we really experience our true and complete independence from *nature.* For feeling oneself to be independent of natural conditions in the mere act of knowing and in one's entire inward existence is completely different from feeling oneself to be transported and elevated to a point beyond fate, beyond all contingencies, and beyond all natural necessity. Nothing matters more to a human being as a sensuous being than his existence, and no dependency is more oppressive to him than this, to regard nature as the very power reigning over his existence. He feels himself free of this dependency when he is witness to the practically-sublime. "The irresistible power of nature," Kant says, "of course provides us, regarded as sensuous beings, with the knowledge of our impotence; but at the same time it uncovers in us a capacity to judge ourselves independently of nature, and a superiority over nature. This superiority grounds a self-preservation of a sort completely different from the kind that can be contested by nature outside us and endangered—in this process the *humanity* in our person remains unvanquished, although *the human being* would have to succumb to that power of nature. In this way," he continues, "the frightful power of nature is judged aesthetically [176] by us to be sublime, because it calls up in us a power of ours, that is not of nature, to regard as *trivial* everything for which we are concerned as sensuous beings: goods, health, and life. Hence, too, for ourselves and for our existence as persons, we consider that might of nature—to which, of course, we are subject as far as those goods are concerned—no power to which we would have to submit ourselves when it comes to the question of our supreme principles and maintaining or forsaking them. Therefore," he concludes, "nature here is called 'sublime' because it elevates the imagination to the portrayal of those very instances, in which the mind can render itself capable of feeling the unique sublimity of its own calling."

This sublimity of our rational character—this, our practical independence from nature, must, indeed, be distinguished from the sort of superiority that we know how to assert over nature as a power in individual instances, owing to either our physical or our intellectual powers. There is, of course, also something magnificent, but not at all sublime about this latter sort of superiority in itself. For example, a human being who struggles with a wild animal and subdues it by the strength of his arm or even by cunning; a raging river like the Nile whose power is broken by dams, and which the human intellect, by gathering its overflow in canals, can even transform from a destructive object into a useful one; a ship at sea that by its ingenious design is in a position to defy all the violence of the furious elements; in short, all those cases where by means of his inventive intellect the human being has forced nature to obey him and to serve his aims, even where nature is superior to him as a power and equipped to bring about his demise. All these cases, I say, do not awaken a feeling of the sublime, although they have something analogous to it and for that reason, in the aesthetic evaluation, are also pleasing. Yet why are they not sublime, given the fact that they make evident the superiority of humans over nature?

To answer this question we must return to the concept of the sublime, where the reason may be easily uncovered. According to this concept, the only sublime object is the object that is superior to us [177] as *natural beings,* but from which we feel ourselves absolutely independent as rational beings, as beings not belonging to nature. Thus, on the basis of this conception, all *natural means* employed by human beings to withstand the power of nature are *excluded* from the category of the sublime. For this concept demands unconditionally that as natural beings we be no match for the object, and yet feel ourselves to be independent of it, owing to what in us is not of nature (and this is nothing other than pure reason). However, all those means cited, through which the human being is superior to nature (skillfulness, cunning, and physical strength), are taken from nature and hence they belong to the human being as a natural being. Accordingly, it is not as an intelligent being but as a sensuous being that a human being withstands those natural objects, that is to say, not morally through his inner freedom, but physically through application of natural forces. Also, it is not because he is an intelligent being that he is not overcome by these objects, but rather because as a sensuous being he is already superior to them. Yet where his physical powers are sufficient, there is nothing that could force him to have recourse to his intellectual self, to the inner self-sufficiency of his rational powers.

Therefore, for the feeling of the sublime it is absolutely requisite that we see ourselves with absolutely no *physical means of resistance* and look to our nonphysical self for help. The sort of object involved must therefore be *frightening* to the sensuous side of us, and that is no longer the case, the moment we feel ourselves equal to it through natural powers.

This is also confirmed by experience. The mightiest natural force is less sublime precisely to the degree to which it appears to be tamed by human beings, and it rapidly becomes sublime again as soon as it confounds human artifice. As a natural force superior to us, a horse that still gallops around wild and unbridled in the forests can be *frightening* and can even provide a subject matter for a sublime portrayal. Once tamed and harnessed to the yoke or before the wagons, the very same horse loses that frightfulness and thereby everything sublime about it. But if this horse, after it has been broken in, tears loose of its reins and, bucking in anger under its rider, violently regains [178] its freedom, it is once again frightening and becomes sublime once more.

A human being's physical superiority over natural forces is therefore so little a reason for something being sublime that almost everywhere that superiority is encountered it weakens or completely destroys the sublimity of the object. We can, of course, with considerable pleasure, dwell on the human skill that is capable of subduing the wildest forces of nature. Yet the source of this pleasure is *logical* and not *aesthetic;* it is a result of reflection and is not inspired by the immediate image of something.

Hence, nature is practically sublime only where it is *frightening.* But then the question arises: is this also the case in reverse? Is it also practically sublime wherever it is *frightening?*

Here we must return once again to the concept of the sublime. As essential as it is that we feel ourselves as sensuous beings to be dependent upon the object, it is just as essential, on the other hand, that we feel ourselves as rational beings to be independent of that very object. Where the former is missing, where there is nothing in the object that frightens our sensuous nature, no sublimity is possible. Where the latter is absent, that is to say, where the object is *merely* frightening and we do not feel ourselves as rational beings to be superior to it, then sublimity is just as remote a possibility.

In order to experience something frightening as sublime and take pleasure in it, inner freedom on the part of the mind is an absolute requisite. Indeed, something frightening can be sublime merely by the fact that it allows us to experience our independence, our mind's freedom. Actual and serious fear, however, overcomes all freedom of mind.

Therefore, the sublime object must, of course, be frightening, but it may not incite actual fear. Fear is a condition of *suffering* and *violence;* only in a detached consideration of something and through the feeling of the activity inside ourselves can we take pleasure in something sublime. Thus either the fearful object may not direct its power at us at all or, if this happens, then [179] our spirit must remain free, while our sensuous nature is being overwhelmed. This latter case is, however, extremely rare, and demands an *elevation* of human nature that can scarcely be considered possible in an individual. For where we actually find ourselves in danger, where we ourselves are the object of an inimical natural power, aesthetic judgment is finished. As sublime as a storm at sea may be when viewed from the shore, those who find themselves on the ship devastated by the storm are just as little disposed to pass this aesthetic judgment on it.

Hence, we are concerned only with the first case where we are able, of course, to witness the might of the frightful object but without it being directed at us, in other words, where we *know* that we are *safe* from that very object. It is only in the imagination, then, that we put ourselves in a position where this power could affect us and all resistance would be in vain. What is terrifying thus exists solely in the representation *[Vorstellung]* of it; yet even the mere representation of danger, if it is vivid enough, sets the preservation instinct in motion and the result is something analogous to what the actual sensation would produce. A shudder grips us, a feeling of anxiety stirs, our sensuous nature is aroused. And without this onset of actual suffering, without this serious attack on our existence, we would merely be playing with the object. And it must be *serious,* at least in the sensation, if reason is supposed to have recourse to the idea of its freedom. Consciousness of the freedom within us can be valid and worthwhile only insofar as it is serious about this; but it cannot be serious if we are merely playing with the representation of the danger.

I have said that we must be safe and secure if we are to enjoy what is *frightening*. Now there are, however, instances of misfortune and danger from which a human being can never know that he is safe and yet the representation of these misfortunes and dangers can still be and even actually is sublime. The concept of safety thus cannot be restricted to the fact that someone knows that he is physically out of danger, as, for example, when someone peers down into an enormous depression from a high and well-secured parapet or [180] looks down at a stormy lake from a height. In such cases the fearlessness is, of course, based upon the certainty that one cannot be affected. But on what would anyone be willing to base his security in the face of fate, the omnipresent power of the divinity, painful diseases, poignant losses, or death? Here there is no physical basis at hand at all for putting oneself at ease. If we reflect on fate in its frightfulness, then we must without hesitation admit to ourselves that we are anything but removed from it.

There is accordingly a twofold basis for security. In the face of such evils as it is in our physical power to elude, we can have external, physical security. However, when confronted by the sort of evils that we are in no position to resist or evade by any natural means, we can have merely inner or moral security. This distinction is important, especially in relation to the sublime.

Physical security provides an immediate reason for our sensuous nature to be at ease, completely unrelated to our inner or moral condition. Thus, too, nothing at all is required to be able to regard an object without fear if we find ourselves in this physical safety when confronted by the object. For just this reason, one finds a far greater uniformity to people's judgments about the sublimity of *such objects,* the sighting of which is bound up with this physical security, than about those objects in the face of which one has only moral security. The cause is obvious. Physical security is beneficial to everyone in the same way. Moral security, on the other hand, presupposes a state of mind not found in all individuals. Yet, because this physical security holds only for our sensuous nature, it possesses nothing of itself that could please our rational nature and its influence is merely negative, in that it simply keeps the self-preservation instinct from being frightened and the freedom of mind from being overwhelmed.

In the case of inner or *moral security* things are completely different. This security is, of course, also a basis for putting our *sensuous nature* at ease (otherwise it would itself be sublime), but it is so only [181] indirectly, through ideas of reason. We look upon the fearful without fear because we feel ourselves to be beyond the reach of its power over us as natural beings, either through the consciousness of our *innocence* or through the thoughts of the *indestructibility of our being.* This moral security and certitude thus postulate, as we see, *ideas of religion,* since only *religion,* not *morality,* sets out grounds for putting our sensuous nature at ease. Morality inexorably follows the prescription of reason, without any regard for the interest of our sensuous nature. It is religion, however, that seeks to establish a reconciliation, an agreement between the demands of reason and the inclinations of our sensuous nature. Hence, for moral security it does not at all suffice that we possess a moral disposition. Rather, it is also necessary that we think of *nature* in accord with the *moral law* or, what in this case is one and the same, that we think of nature under the sway of a pure rational being. Death, for example, is one such object in the face of which we have *only* moral security. For most people (since most people by far are more sensuous than they are rational) the vivid representation of all the terrors of death, joined with the certainty of being unable to escape it, would make it quite impossible to combine this image with as much composure as an aesthetic judgment requires—if the rational belief in an immortality, even for our sensuous nature, did not provide a tolerable way out.

Yet this must not be understood as though the image of death, if combined with sublimity, sustains this sublimity through the idea of immortality.—Nothing could be further from the truth!—The idea of immortality, as I am taking it to be here, can put our instinct to survive, that is to say, our sensuous nature, at ease and I must note, once and for all, that as far as making a sublime impression is concerned, our sensuous nature with its demands must be completely set aside and every basis for reassuring us must be sought in reason alone. Thus, the very idea of immortality, in which our sensuous side to a certain extent is still given its due (as it is put forward in all positive religions), [182] can contribute nothing at all to the representation of death as a sublime object. Rather this idea must simply stand, as it were, in the background in order to come to the aid of our sensuous nature alone, in case the latter feels desperate and defenseless, exposed to all the terror of being annihilated, and threatened by the prospect of succumbing to this violent assault. If this idea of immortality, however, becomes the prevailing idea in the mind, death loses it *fearfulness* and the *sublime* disappears.

If the divinity is represented in its omniscience, holiness, and might—an omniscience that illuminates all the crevices and corners of the human heart, a holiness that permits no impure emotion, and a might that has our physical fate in its power—it is a *fearful* image and can thus become a *sublime* one. We can have no physical security against the effects of this might, since it is as impossible to *elude* it as it is to *resist* it. We are thus left with only moral security that we base upon the justice of this being, together with our innocence. Because we are conscious of our innocence and thus secure in the face of the godhead, we look without terror upon the terrifying phenomena by means of which it makes its power known. When this unbounded, irresistible, and all-present power is represented, that moral security makes it possible for us not to lose our freedom of mind completely, for when that is gone, the mind is in no mood to make an aesthetic judgment. Yet this feeling of security, even though it has a moral basis, cannot be the cause of the sublime, for in the end it only provides a basis for reassuring our sensuous nature. This sense of security satisfies the instinct for self-preservation, but the sublime is never based upon the satisfaction of our instincts. If the image of divinity is to be practically (dynamically) sublime, then we have to tie the feeling of our security *not to our existence* but rather *to our principles.* It has to be irrelevant to us how we fare as natural beings in the process, if we feel that, simply as intellects, we are independent of the effects of its might. But we feel that as rational beings we are not dependent even on divine omnipotence [183] since even that omnipotence cannot destroy our autonomy, cannot determine our will against our principles. Only insofar, therefore, as we deny the divinity all *natural influence* on *determinations of our will,* is the representation of its power dynamically sublime.

As far as what determines the will is concerned, feeling that one is independent of the divinity means nothing else than being conscious that the divinity could never *as a force* act upon the will. Since, however, the pure will must always coincide with the divine will, there can never be a case where, on the basis of pure reason, we determine ourselves in a way that goes against the divine will. Hence we deny the divinity influence on our will merely insofar as we are conscious that *the divinity could influence the determinations of our wills only through its agreement with the pure law of reason within us,* that is to say, not through authority, not through reward or punishment, not through regard for the divinity's might. Our reason venerates in the divinity nothing but its holiness and also fears nothing but its disapproval—and even this only insofar as our reason recognizes in the divine reason its own law. It is not a matter of divine *caprice* to approve or disapprove of our sentiments; that is determined instead by our behavior. In the sole case, therefore, where the divinity could become fearful for us, namely, in its disapproval, we are not dependent upon it. Hence, represented as a power capable, of course, of destroying our *existence,* but as long as we still have this existence, unable to have any influence on the actions of our reason, the divinity is dynamically sublime—and only the religion that imparts this image of the divinity to us bears the seal of sublimity within it.* [184]

The object of the practically-sublime must be frightening to the sensuous side of human nature; an evil must threaten our physical condition and the representation of the danger must set our self-preservation instinct in motion.

As far as the emotion involved in the preservation-instinct is concerned, our *intelligible self*, namely, that within us that is not of nature, must distinguish itself from the sensuous side of our being and become aware of its self-sufficiency, of its independence from everything that can affect its physical nature. In short, it must become conscious of its freedom.

This freedom, however, is in an unqualified sense only moral, not physical. Not as sensuous beings and neither through our natural powers nor through our intellect may we feel superior to the fearful object. For then our security would always be a function merely of physical causes; in effect, it would be empirical and as a result there would always remain a dependency upon nature. Instead, it must be completely irrelevant to us how we fare as sensuous beings in the process, and our freedom must consist merely in the fact that we regard, our physical condition, determined as it can be by nature, as something external and alien, having no influence on our moral person, and as something we do not count as part of our self. [185]

---

*This analysis of the concept of the dynamically sublime, Kant says, seems to be contradicted by the fact that we are used to representing God in a violent storm, an earthquake, and so on, as an angry power and yet as sublime, in which case it would be as foolish as it is frivolous on our part to imagine a superiority of mind over the effects of such a power. Here, not a feeling of the sublimity of our own nature, but rather far more a feeling of dejection and submission seems to be the frame of mind best suited to the appearance of such an object. In religion in general, throwing oneself down and adoring with contrite gestures full of fear seem to be the only appropriate behavior in the presence of the divinity, behavior most peoples have also accordingly taken up. But, he continues, this frame of mind is not at all necessarily bound up with the idea of the *sublimity* of a religion. The human being conscious of his own guilt and thus having cause to fear is not at all in a frame of mind to wonder at the divine greatness. Only when his conscience is clean, do those effects of the divine power serve to give him a sublime idea of the divinity, inasmuch as he is then elevated above the *fear* of the effects of this power through the feeling of his own sublime disposition. He stands in awe *[Ehrfurcht]*, not in fear *[Furcht]*, of the divinity. On the other hand, superstition feels only fear and anxiety toward divinity, without esteeming it. Out of such feeling there can never arise a religion

Someone who overcomes what is fearful is ***magnificent** [groß]*. Someone who, even while succumbing to the fearful, does not fear it, is *sublime [erhaben].*

Hannibal was magnificent from a theoretical point of view, since he forged a passage over the untrodden Alps to Italy. He was magnificent in a practical sense, or sublime, only in misfortune.

Hercules was magnificent because he undertook and completed his twelve tasks.

Prometheus was sublime because, fettered to the Caucasus, he did not regret his deed and did not acknowledge having done anything wrong.

An individual can display magnificence in *good fortune*, sublimity only in *misfortune.*

Hence, any object that shows us our impotence as natural beings is practically-sublime, as long as it also discloses a capacity within us to resist that is of a completely different order. This capacity does *not,* of course, remove the danger to our physical existence, but (what is infinitely more) separates our physical existence from our personhood. Hence, when something sublime is represented or entertained, we become conscious, not of *material* security in a single instance, but rather of an *ideal* security extending over all possible instances. This is accordingly based, not on overturning or overcoming in any sense a danger threatening us, but rather on removing the sole and ultimate condition for something to be a danger to us. The experience of the sublime removes this condition by teaching us to regard the sensuous part of our being, what alone is subject to the danger, as an external, natural thing that has no effect at all on what we genuinely are as persons, our moral selves.

Having established the concept of the practically-sublime, we are in a position to classify it in terms of both the variety of objects that arouse it and the variety of our relationships to these objects.

There are three sorts of things that we distinguish in the representation of the sublime: *first,* the power of some natural object; *second,* the relation of this power to our capacity to resist it physically; *third,* the relation of this power to the [186] moral person

---

of uprightness, but only ingratiation and the solicitation of favor. Kant's *Critique of Aesthetic Judgment. Analytic of the Sublime.*

within us. The sublime is thus the effect of three images following upon one another: (1) an objective, physical power, (2) our subjective, physical impotence, and (3) our subjective, moral superiority. Although essentially all three elements must be combined in every representation of the sublime, it is nevertheless a contingent matter how we arrive at a representation of them, and this fact is the basis for a central, twofold distinction with respect to the sublimity of power.

1. Either some subject matter *[Gegenstand]* simply as a power or, in other words, the objective cause of suffering but not the suffering itself may be presented for viewing, and it is left to the individual making the judgment to produce the image of the suffering in himself and transform that subject matter into an object *[Objekt]* of fear by virtue of its relation to the preservation instinct and into something sublime by virtue of its relation to the moral person within him.

2. Or, in addition to the subject matter as a power, its fearfulness for human beings, the suffering itself, may be objectively represented as well, leaving nothing else for the individual making the judgment to do but apply it to his moral condition and produce something sublime out of something fearful.

An object *[Objekt]* of the first class is contemplatively-sublime, an object of the second class is pathetically-sublime.

I. The Contemplative Sublimity of Power

The kinds of subject matter that show us nothing mo[illegible] power of nature far superior to our own, but otherwise leave it up to us to relate that power to our physical state or to our moral character as persons, are sublime solely in a contemplative sense. I characterize them [187] in this way because they do not take hold of the mind with such ferocity that it is unable to continue calmly contemplating them. In the case of what is contemplatively sublime it is mostly a matter of the mind's own activity, because only one of the conditions of sublimity is provided externally, while the other two must be realized by the individual himself. For this reason the effect of the contemplatively sublime is neither as intense nor as widespread as the effect of the practically sublime. The effect is *not as widespread* because not everyone has sufficient imagination to produce in themselves a vivid image of the danger, nor do they all have enough moral self-sufficiency and fortitude not to try to avoid such an image. The effect is *not as powerful,* because the image of the danger in this case, even if it is quite vividly awakened, is nonetheless always *voluntary,* and it is much easier for the mind to remain in control of an image that it produced of itself. Hence, the contemplatively-sublime produces a slighter, but also less mixed sort of enjoyment.

For the contemplatively-sublime, nature provides nothing but some power-laden subject matter. It is left to the imagination to make something out of this that is frightening to humanity. How the sublime precisely turns out depends upon whether the part played by the imagination in producing what is fearful is respectively great or small, and whether the imagination does its job openly or furtively.

An abyss appearing at our feet, a thunderstorm, a flaming volcano, a mass of rock looming over us as though it were about to plunge down on us, a storm at sea, a bitter winter in the polar regions, a summer in the tropics, ferocious or poisonous animals, a flood—all these and more are the sorts of natural forces in the face of which our capacity to resist counts for nothing, natural forces that contradict our physical existence. Even certain ideal objects such as, for example, *time* considered as a power working quietly but inexorably, *necessity* with its rigorous laws from which no natural being can escape, and even the moral idea of *duty* that behaves often enough like an inimical power toward our physical existence, [188] become fearful objects as soon as the *imagination* relates them to the preservation instinct, and they become sublime as soon as *reason* applies them to its supreme laws. In all these cases, however, since the fantasy first adds the fearful character and it is completely up to us to suppress an idea that we have produced ourselves, these objects belong to the class of the contemplatively-sublime.

Yet the image of danger still has a *real* basis here, and what is required is merely the simple operation of connecting the existence of these things with our physical existence in a *single* image. If this is done, something frightful is then present. Fantasy need contribute nothing on its own; instead it simply clings to what is presented to it.

Quite often subject matters taken from nature and in themselves neutral, are subjectively transformed by the intervention of fantasy into frightful powers, and fantasy itself does not merely *discover* what is frightful through comparison, *but rather creates* it quite arbitrarily without an adequate, objective basis for it. This is the case for the *extraordinary* and the *indeterminate.*

For humanity in its infancy, where the imagination works in the most unencumbered way, everything unusual is terrifying. In each unexpected appearance of nature people believe they see an enemy, an enemy armed against their existence. At the same time the preservation instinct is at work meeting this attack. In this period the preservation instinct is their unbridled master and, since this instinct is anxious and cowardly, its domination is a realm of terror and fear. The superstition formed in this epoch is correspondingly dark and fearful, and even the morals bear this hostile, gloomy character. One finds people who arm themselves before they dress, and they grab first for the sword when meeting a stranger. The custom of the ancient Taureans, to sacrifice to Diana every newcomer who had the misfortune to land on their coast, scarcely had any other origin than *fear.* For only a human being *formed in a depraved way* and not someone merely *unformed* is so barbaric that he rages against what can do him no harm. [189]

This fear of everything extraordinary disappears, to be sure, with the rise of culture, but not so completely that no trace of it remains in the *aesthetic* contemplation of nature, where people deliberately give themselves up to the play of fantasy. Writers know this quite well and accordingly do not fail to make use of *extraordinary* things, at least as an ingredient in what is frightful. A profound quiet, an immense emptiness, a sudden light in the dark are in themselves quite neutral things, distinguished by nothing but their extraordinariness and unusualness. Nevertheless, they arouse a feeling of fright or, at least, intensify its impression, and for that reason are suited to be something sublime.

If Virgil wants to scare us about the realm of Hades, he draws our attention above all to its emptiness and stillness. He calls it *loca nocte late tacentia,* "that silent, expansive plain of night," *domos vacuas Ditis et inania regna,* "the empty dwellings and hollow realms of Pluto."

During the initiations into the mysteries of the ancients a fearful, solemn impression was especially preferred, and to this end people also made use of silence in particular. A profound quiet provides the imagination with a free space to play and intensifies the expectation of something frightful that is supposed to come. In devotional exercises the silence observed by an entire community gathered together is a very effective means of prodding their fantasies and putting their minds in a solemn mood. Even folk superstition makes use of silence in its delusions, for, as is well known, a profound quiet must be observed if someone has to dig for a treasure. In the enchanted palaces of fairy tales a deathly silence reigns, awakening horrors, and it is part of the natural history of enchanted forests that nothing living moves within them. Even *loneliness* is frightful as soon as it is neither voluntary nor passing, such as, for example, the banishment to an uninhabited island. A far-flung desert, a solitary forest several miles long, losing one's way around a seemingly boundless lake—these are the sort of simple images that can stir up fears and should be used in poetry to depict the sublime. However, here (in the case of [190] loneliness) there is already an objective basis of the fear, since the idea of a great loneliness also brings with it the idea of *helplessness*.

Fantasy proves itself to be far more skilled at making something terrifying out of something *mysterious,* indeterminate, and *impenetrable*. Here it is in its genuine element with a wide range of possibilities open to it, given the fact that the actual world sets no boundaries to it and its operations are not limited to any particular case. Yet, that it is inclined precisely to what is *terrible* and that the unknown is a source of *fear* more than hope, lies in the nature of the preservation instinct that guides it. Revulsion works with incomparably greater speed and force than desire does, and for this reason we rather suppose something bad than expect something good lying behind what is unknown.

Darkness can be terrifying and precisely for that reason is suited to the sublime. Yet it is not terrifying in itself, but rather because it conceals objects from us and thus delivers us up to the full force of the imagination. As soon as the danger becomes clear, a considerable part of the fear disappears. The sense of sight, the primary sentry of our existence, fails us in the darkness and we feel ourselves defenselessly exposed to the hidden danger. For this reason superstition puts all appearances of spirits at the midnight hour, and the realm of death is represented as a realm of endless night. In the writings of Homer, where humanity still speaks its most natural language, darkness is portrayed as one of the greatest evils.

> There lie the land and the city of the people of Chimer.
> Constantly they grope in the night and fog, and ne'er
> Does the God of the shining sun show them a beam of
> light;
>
> Instead, these wretched people lie enveloped by
> terrifying night.
>
> *Odyssey* (eleventh song)

> "Jupiter," the brave Ajax calls out in the darkness of the battle, "free the Greeks from this darkness. Let it become day, let these eyes see, and then, if it is your will, let me fall in light."
>
> *Iliad* [191]

Even the *indeterminate* is an ingredient of the terrible, and for no other reason than because it gives the imagination freedom to paint the picture as it sees fit. What is determinate, on the other hand, leads to distinct knowledge and withdraws the object from the arbitrary play of fantasy, because it subjects the object to the intellect.

Homer's portrayal of the underworld is all the more frightful, precisely because it, as it were, swims in a fog and the shapes of the spirits in Ossian are nothing but ethereal cloud formations, leaving it to fantasy to provide the contours at will.

Everything that is *hidden,* everything *full of mystery,* contributes to what is terrifying and is therefore capable of sublimity. Of this sort is the inscription on the temple of Isis at Sais, in Egypt. "I am all that is, that has been, and that will be. No mortal man has lifted my veil." It is precisely this uncertainty and mysteriousness that lend the terrifying character to people's images of the future after death. These feelings are expressed quite successfully in Hamlet's well-known soliloquy.

The description that Tacitus gives us of the solemn procession of the goddess Hertha becomes sublime in a terrifying way because of the darkness he spreads over it. The goddess's coach disappears into the deepest recesses of the forest and no one employed for this mysterious service comes back alive. With a shudder one wonders what it might be that costs the life of someone who sees it, *quod tantum morituri vident.*

All religions have their mysteries that support a holy fright and, just as the majesty of divinity dwells in the all-holy behind the curtain, so the majesty of kings surrounds itself with mystery in order, by means of this artificial invisibility, to keep the respect of their subjects in a state of constant trepidation.

These are the most distinguished subspecies of the power that is contemplatively-sublime, and since it is grounded in the moral vocation common to every human being, one is justified in presupposing a receptiveness to it on the part of all [192] human subjects. The lack of this receptiveness cannot be excused by some contingency of nature, as in the case of merely sensuous feelings; rather it may be considered an imperfection in the subject. At times one finds cognitive sublimity combined with the sublimity of power and the effect is all the greater, if not only the sensuous capacity to resist, but even the capacity to portray finds its match in an object and the sensuous side of human nature with its twofold demand [of knowing and living] is scorned.

II. The Pathetically Sublime

If something is presented to us in an objective way, not merely as a power in general, but at the same time as a power having catastrophic consequences for people—in other words, if it does not merely *show,* but also actually *expresses* its power in a hostile manner—then the imagination is no longer free to refer it to the preservation-instinct or not; instead, the imagination now *must* do so, it is objectively required to do so. Yet actual suffering does not permit an aesthetic judgment, since such suffering overcomes the mind's freedom. Thus, the fearful object may not demonstrate its destructive power on the individual judging, that is, we may not *ourselves* suffer, or rather we may suffer only *sympathetically.* However, even if the suffering we sympathize with exists *outside* us, it is too violent for our sensuous nature. The empathizing pain overwhelms all aesthetic enjoyment. Suffering can become aesthetic and arouse a feeling of sublimity only when either it is a mere illusion and fabrication or (in case it had happened in reality) it is presented, not immediately to the senses, but to the imagination. The image of another's suffering, combined with emotion and the consciousness of the moral freedom within us, is *pathetically sublime.*

The sympathy or the empathizing (shared) emotion is no free expression of our mind, that we [193] would first have to produce spontaneously in ourselves. Rather it is an involuntary affection *[Affektion]* on the part of our capacity to have feelings, determined by natural law. It does not at all depend upon our will whether we want to share in the suffering of some creature. The moment we have an image of it, we *must* feel it. *Nature,* not our *freedom* acts, and the movement of the mind hurries ahead of the decision.

Therefore, as soon as we hold on to the image of some suffering objectively, then, by virtue of the unchanging natural law of sympathy, a feeling for this suffering must follow within ourselves. By this means we make it our own, as it were. We *suffer with. Empathy* or *compassion* means not merely the shared grief, the fact of being moved by another's misfortune, but rather every sorrowful emotion, without distinction, which we feel when we enter into someone else's feelings. Hence, there are as many sorts of empathy as there are diverse sorts of suffering originally: empathizing fear, empathizing fright, empathizing anxiety, empathizing anger, empathizing despair.

Yet, if what arouses the emotion (or what is pathetic) is supposed to provide a basis for the sublime, it may not be pressed to the point where one is actually *suffering oneself.* Even in the midst of the most violent emotion we must *distinguish* ourselves from the individual who himself suffers, for the freedom of spirit is gone as soon as the illusion is transformed into the complete truth.

If empathizing is elevated to such a pitch that we seriously confuse ourselves with the person suffering, then we no longer control the emotion, but rather it controls us. On the other hand, if the sympathy remains within its aesthetic boundaries, then it combines two chief conditions of the sublime: a sensuously vital image of the suffering together with the feeling of one's own security.

But this feeling of security when faced with the image of someone else's suffering is in no sense the *basis* of what is sublime, and is not at all the *source* of the pleasure we draw from this image. The pathetic becomes sublime only through the consciousness of our moral, not our physical freedom. Not because we see ourselves [194] removed from this suffering by our good fortune (for then we would still always have a very poor guarantee of our security), but rather because we feel our moral self to be removed from the causality of this suffering, namely, from its influence upon what determines our willing, it *elevates [erhebt]* our mind and becomes *pathetically* sublime.

It is not absolutely necessary that one actually feel the strength of soul within oneself to assert one's moral freedom in the face of a seriously immanent danger. We are talking here, not about what *happens,* but rather about what *should* and *can* happen; in other words, we are talking about our *calling,* not about what we actually *do;* about our power, not about its use. Because we see a heavily loaded freighter go down in the storm, we are able to feel ourselves quite unhappily in the position of the merchant, whose entire estate is swallowed up by the water. Yet at the same time, we still feel as well that this loss only concerns contingent things and that we have a duty to rise above it. However, nothing can be a duty if it cannot be realized, and what *should* happen must *be able* to happen. That, however, we *can* regard a loss with indifference, a loss that is rightly so poignant for us as sensuous beings, proves that there is a capacity within us to act according to laws completely different from those of the sensuous faculties, a capacity having nothing in common with natural instinct. Everything that makes us conscious of this capacity within us is *sublime.*

One can quite rightly say, therefore, that one will endure the loss of goods with nothing less than composure. This does not hinder the feelings of the sublime at all—if one only feels that one *should* disregard the loss and that a duty exists to allow it no influence on the self-determining of reason. Of course, all the aesthetic power of the magnificent and the sublime is lost on someone who does not even have a sense *for that duty.*

Hence, at least a capacity of the mind to become conscious of its rational determination and a receptivity to the idea of duty are indispensable, even if at the same time one also recognizes the limits that the weakness of humanity [195] may have set to their exercise. In general, it would be dangerous for the enjoyment of the good as well as of the sublime, if one could only have a sense for what one has oneself achieved or what one trusts oneself to achieve. But it is a basic feature of humanity, and one worthy of respect, that humanity acknowledges a good thing, at least in *aesthetic* judgments, even if it would have to speak *against* itself, and that it pays homage to the pure ideas of reason, at least in feeling, even if it does not always have sufficient strength actually to *act* on those ideas.

Consequently, two main conditions must be met for the *pathetically sublime: first,* a vivid image of *suffering,* in order to awaken the emotion of compassion with the proper strength, and *second,* an image of the *resistance* to the suffering, in order to call into consciousness the mind's inner freedom. Only by virtue of the first condition does the object become *pathetic,* only by virtue of the second condition does the pathetic become at the same time something *sublime.*

From this basic principle flow the two fundamental laws of all tragic art. These are *first:* portrayal of the suffering nature; *second,* portrayal of moral independence in the suffering.

Translated by Daniel O. Dahlstrom

On the Pathetic*

Portrayal of suffering—as mere suffering—is never the end of art, but as a means to this end it is of the utmost importance to art. The ultimate purpose of art is to depict what transcends the realm of the senses and the art of tragedy in particular accomplishes this by displaying morality's independence, its freedom, in the throes of passion, from nature's laws. The principle of freedom within us makes itself known only by the resistance it exerts against the power of feelings, while the resistance can be measured only by the strength of the onslaught of feelings. Thus, in order for human *intelligence* to reveal itself as a force independent of nature, it is necessary for nature first to demonstrate all its might before our eyes. The *sensuous being* must *suffer* deeply and vehemently, the pathos must be present, so that the rational being can testify to its independence and, *by acting,* can present itself.

We can never know whether a *state of mind* is a result of its moral strength, if we have not been convinced that it is not the result of insensitivity. To master feelings that only gently stroke the surface of the soul in passing is no art. It is another thing, however, for the mind to maintain its freedom in a storm that stirs up an individual's entire sensuous nature; then a capacity to resist is required that is infinitely superior to all the power of nature. Thus,

***On the Pathetic (Über das Pathetische)* appeared in the third volume (which contains parts 1–3) of Schiller's periodical *Neue Thalia* (Leipzig: Göschen, 1793), vol. III, 366–94.

only by means of the most vivid depiction of the nature suffering do we succeed in portraying moral freedom. Before we pay homage to the tragic hero as a rational person and believe in the strength of his soul, he must have first established himself in our eyes as someone who is sensitive and feels.

Pathos is, therefore, the first and indispensable demand made of the tragic artist and the artist may press the depiction of suffering as far as is possible *without detracting from his final purpose,* in other words, without suppressing the moral freedom. He must, as it were, give his hero or [197] his reader the complete, full salvo of suffering, since otherwise it always remains problematic whether the hero's resistance to that suffering is an act of the mind, that is to say, something *positive* and not rather merely something *negative,* in short, a deficiency.

The latter is the case in earlier tragedies of the French, where we never or only quite rarely confront the *suffering nature* face-to-face; for the most part we see instead only diffident poets declaiming or bombastic comedians. The icy tone of the declamation stifles any genuine naturalness and the cherished *propriety* of the heroes of French tragedies makes it utterly impossible for them to portray humanity as it really is. Everywhere, even in the right setting, *propriety* falsifies the expression of nature and yet the latter is what art constantly demands. We can scarcely believe that a hero of a French tragedy *suffers,* since he expresses how he feels in the manner of the calmest of men and the constant concern for the impression being made on others never lets him indulge the natural freedom within him. The kings, princesses, and heroes of a Corneille and Voltaire never forget their *position* even in the most passionate suffering and would far sooner doff their *humanity* than surrender their *dignity.* They are like the kings and emperors in the old picture books, who take their crowns with them to bed.

How completely different are the *Greeks* and those moderns who write in the spirit of the Greeks! The Greek is never ashamed of nature, he grants sensuousness the full complement of its rights and is nevertheless certain that he will never be enslaved by it. His profound and correct understanding of things allows him to distinguish what is incidental (what bad taste makes the centerpiece of its works) from what is essential. Yet everything about a human being that is not a matter of his humanity is incidental to him. The

Greek artist, who has to portray a Laocoön, a Niobe, a Philoctetus, is not aware of a princess, a king, and a prince; he latches on to the human being alone. For this reason the wise sculptor discards the clothing and shows us stark-naked figures, although he knows full well that this was not the case in real life. In his eyes clothes are something incidental, something to which [198] what is essential may never be subordinated. After all, the laws of decorum or need are not the laws of art. The sculptor is supposed to, indeed, he wants to show us *human beings,* and since garments conceal, he rightly gets rid of them.

Just as the Greek sculptor tosses aside the useless and restrictive burden of clothes in order to make more room for *human nature,* so the Greek poet sets his human beings free from the coercion of convention that is just as useless and just as restrictive. He liberates people from all the diffident laws of decorum, laws that only afflict them and hide the nature within them. In the writings of Homer and in the tragedies a suffering nature speaks to our hearts genuinely, uprightly, and penetratingly; all passions have free play and no feeling is held back by some rule about what is appropriate. The heroes are as susceptible as others are to every sort of human suffering; they are heroes precisely because they feel the suffering intensely and inwardly and yet are not overcome by it. They love life as ardently as we do, but this sentiment does not so dominate them that they are unable to sacrifice life, if the duties of honor or humanity require it. Philoctetus fills the Greek stage with his lamentations; even the furious Hercules does not suppress his pain. Iphigenia, destined to be a sacrifice, confesses with moving candor the pain of taking leave forever of the light of day. Nowhere does the Greek seek his glory by dulling the suffering or by indifference to it, but rather by *enduring* the suffering with every feeling for it. Even the Greek gods must pay homage to nature, whenever the poet seeks to bring them closer to humanity. The wounded Mars cries out with pain as loudly as ten thousand men and Venus, scratched by a lance, climbs Olympus *weeping* and cursing all battles.

This gentle sensitivity to suffering, this warm and upright nature that lies there with that vulnerability and genuineness, this nature that moves us so profoundly and so vividly in Greek works of art, is a model to be imitated by all artists, and a law [199] prescribed to art by the Greek genius. *Nature* always makes the first demand on the human being, a demand that may never be disavowed. For the human being—before being anything else—is an entity who feels. *Reason* makes the second demand on the human being, since a human is an entity who feels rationally, a moral person, and it is this person's duty not to let nature prevail over him but rather to master it. Only then, if *first* justice has been done to *Nature* and if, *second, Reason* has maintained its right, is it permissible for *Propriety* to make the *third* demand on the human being and to require of him regard for society in the expression of feelings and reflections and to show himself to be a *civilized* being.

Depicting the suffering nature is the first law of the art of tragedy. Portraying moral resistance to the suffering is the second law.

The emotion, as emotion, is something neutral and the depiction of it, regarded with respect to itself alone, would be devoid of any aesthetic value. For, to repeat once again, nothing concerned exclusively with the sensuous nature is worthy of portrayal. Thus, not only all (maudlin) emotions that have a merely sedating effect, but in general all emotions, even those of the *highest intensity,* whatever sort of emotions they be, are beneath the dignity of the art of tragedy.

Maudlin emotions, those merely tender stirrings, belong to the domain of *what is agreeable,* and fine art has nothing to do with this domain. These emotions simply gratify the senses through a kind of diffusion or lulling, and they refer solely to the outer, not to the inner state of the human being. Many of our novels and tragedies, especially the so-called dramas (something between a comedy and a tragedy) and the beloved family portrait, belong to this class. Their only effect is to empty the tear ducts and pleasurably alleviate the vascular system. But the spirit goes away empty and the nobler power inside the human being is in no way fortified by all this. Thus, many an individual, Kant says, feels himself *edified [erbaut]* by a sermon, yet in the course of it nothing at all has been *erected [aufgebaut]* within him. [200] Even modern music seems to prefer to aim only at sensuousness. By doing so, it flatters the reigning taste that wants only to be pleasantly titillated, and not to be taken hold of, not to be powerfully moved, not to be ennobled. Everything *maudlin* is thus preferred. However noisy a concert hall, everyone is suddenly all ears if a maudlin passage is performed. Then on all faces there usually appears an expression of sensuality, verging on something brutish, and intoxicated eyes swim, the open mouth is all desire, a voluptuous trembling seizes the entire body, breathing is quick and faint, in short, all the symptoms of inebriation appear—clear proof that the senses are feasting, but that the spirit or the principle of human freedom is falling prey to the violence of the sensuous impression. All these emotions, I say, are excluded from art by a noble and masculine sort of taste, because such emotions simply gratify the *senses* and nothing more and art has nothing to do with this.

Also excluded, on the other hand, are all those degrees of passion that merely *afflict* the senses, without at the same time compensating the spirit for that affliction. By their *painfulness* they suppress the mind's freedom no less than *debauchery* does and, for that reason, they can produce only revulsion and no emotion worthy of art. Art must delight the spirit and oblige freedom. Anyone who falls victim to pain is simply a tormented animal and no longer a suffering human being, for a moral resistance to suffering is absolutely required of a human being and only by this means is the principle of freedom within him, intelligence, able to make itself known.

For this reason, those very artists and poets who believe that pathos is achieved merely by the *sensuous* force of passion and by the most vivid possible depiction of suffering have a rather shabby understanding of their art. They forget that suffering itself can never be the *ultimate purpose* of the depiction or the *immediate* source of the pleasure we feel in what is tragic. The pathetic is aesthetic only insofar as it is sublime. Yet, effects [201] traceable to a sensuous source and based merely on the fact that the ability to feel is affected are never sublime, however much force they may also exhibit. For everything sublime stems *only* from reason.

A display of passion alone (the most pleasurable as well as the most painful) without any portrayal of the power of resistance beyond the senses is called *common* or *vulgar,* while the opposite is called *noble*. Everywhere they are employed, *noble* and *common* are concepts that characterize a reference to participation or lack of participation in an action or a work, by the part of human nature that transcends the senses. Nothing is *noble* unless it springs from reason; everything our sensuous constitution brings forth for itself is *common* or *vulgar.* We say of a human being, "he acts *in a vulgar way*" if he merely follows the impulses of his sensuous urges. He acts *uprightly* if he follows his urges only in view of laws. He acts *nobly* if he follows reason alone without regard for his urges. We call the shape of a face *common* if it in no way acquaints us with the individual's intelligence, *telling* if the features of the face are determined by his spirit, and *noble* if the features are determined by a spirit that is pure. We call an architectural work *common* if it shows us nothing but physical purposes. We call it *noble* if, independent of all physical purposes, it at the same time portrays ideas.

Therefore, I say that good taste permits no display of passion alone, however so powerful, if it only expresses physical suffering and physical resistance without at the same time making visible the nobler side of humanity, the presence of a capacity beyond the senses. The obvious reason for this, as has already been developed, is the fact that only the resistance to suffering, never the suffering in itself, is pathetic and deserves to be portrayed. Thus, the absolutely highest peak of any passion is denied the artist as well as the writer. For all such levels of passion suppress the force resisting from within or rather already presuppose its suppression, since no passion can reach its ultimate level as long as human intelligence still manages some resistance.

Now the question arises: by what means does this power of resistance beyond the senses make itself known [202] in a passion? By no other means than by taking control of or, more generally, by doing battle with the passion. I say "the *passion*" because it can do battle with the senses, too, but that is not a fight with the passion, but rather with the cause of the passion—not a moral, but rather a physical resistance that even a worm exerts if someone steps on it or a bull if someone wounds him, without awakening pathos on that account. That someone suffering seeks to express his feelings, to get rid of his foe, or to bring an ailing limb to safety—all these he has in common with every animal and instinct already takes over here without first putting a question to his will. That work of instinct is thus as yet not an act of his humanity, it does not yet disclose that he is an intelligent being. The senses, to be sure, will always do battle with their enemy, but never with themselves.

The struggle with passion, on the other hand, is a struggle with the sensuous side of human nature and, therefore, presupposes something distinct from this sensuousness. Against the object that causes him suffering a human being can defend himself with the help of his intellect and the strength of his muscles; against the suffering itself he has no other weapons than ideas of reason.

Thus, in order for pathos to take place, these ideas must appear in the portrayal or be awakened through it. Ideas, however, in the proper and positive sense of the word, may not be portrayed, since nothing in intuition can correspond to them. But, of course, in a negative and indirect way they may be portrayed, if something is presented to intuition, the conditions for which we vainly search in *nature*. Each phenomenon whose ultimate ground cannot be derived from the world of the senses is an indirect portrayal of something beyond the senses.

How then does art succeed in representing something that lies beyond nature without making use of supernatural means? What kind of phenomenon must that be which is brought about by natural forces (since otherwise it would not appear) and nevertheless cannot be derived from physical causes without contradiction? This is the problem; how then does the artist solve it? [203]

We must remember that there are two sorts of phenomena that can be detected in someone caught up in a state of passion. The first sort are those that belong to him simply as an animal and, as such, merely follow the laws of nature without his will being able to control those phenomena or without the independent power in him generally being able to have immediate influence on them. Instinct produces them immediately and they blindly obey its laws. The organs for the circulation of blood, the respiratory organs, and the entire surface of the skin are, for example, of this sort. But even the organs that have been subordinated to the will do not always await the will's decision. Instead the instinct often sets them immediately in motion, especially where pain or danger threatens the physical condition. Thus our arm is, of course, under the will's control, but if we unknowingly grab something hot, then pulling the hand back is certainly no act of the will. Rather, the instinct alone accomplishes it. Indeed, language is, even more so, something certainly standing under the will's control and yet, as soon as some considerable pain or simply a strong emotion surprises us, instinct can also manage even this organ and work of the intellect as it sees fit, without first asking the will. Let the most composed Stoic suddenly catch sight of something altogether wondrous or something unexpectedly terrifying, let him stand near someone slipping and about to fall into an abyss, and he will, as a result, involuntarily emit a loud cry and, of course, not some barely articulate sound, but a quite distinct word. The *nature* within him will have acted sooner than the *will.* This, therefore, serves as proof that there are phenomena in a human being that cannot be attributed to his person as an intelligent being but rather merely to his instinct as a force of nature.

Now, however, *secondly,* a human being also exhibits phenomena that are subject to the will's influence and control of the will or that we at least can regard as such, that is to say, phenomena that the will *could have prevented.* Thus, the *person* and not *instinct* has to answer for these phenomena. It is for instinct, with blind zeal, to be concerned about the interests of sensuality, [204] but it is for the person to curb instinct through regard for laws. Instinct of itself respects no law, but it is up to the person to see to it that no instinctive act violates the prescriptions of reason. This much, therefore, is certain: instinct alone does not unconditionally have to determine all the phenomena or appearances of a human being in a state of passion. Instead, the human will can set a limit to instinct. If instinct alone determines all human phenomena, then nothing more is at hand that could call to mind a *person.* It is simply a natural entity, in effect, an animal, that we have before us, since *animal* is the term for every natural entity controlled by instinct. If, therefore, the person is supposed to be depicted, then some phenomena must occur in the human being that have been determined either contrary to instinct or at least not by instinct. Even the fact that they were not determined by instinct is enough to direct us to a higher source, as soon as it becomes obvious to us that instinct would have had to determine matters in a completely different way, had its power not been broken.

Now we are in a position to indicate how the independent power within a human being that transcends his sensuous nature, namely, his moral self, can be portrayed in a state of passion. This is done by having all the sides of a human being that simply obey nature—sides that the will is able to manage either never at all or at least not under certain circumstances—betray the presence of suffering, while no trace of this suffering or only a slight trace of it is evident in those sides not subject to instinct's *blind* violence and not necessarily observing nature's laws. The latter sides of a human being thus appear free to a certain extent. In the disharmony between those features of the animal nature stamped by the law of necessity and those determined by the spirit in its spontaneousness, the presence of a *principle transcending the senses* in a human being becomes recognizable, a principle that can set a limit to the workings of nature and thus, precisely for that reason, makes apparent its distinctness from nature. The merely animal side of a human being follows nature's laws and [205] hence may appear stifled by the violence of passion. Thus, the full strength of the suffering reveals itself in this side of a human being and serves, as it were, as a measure for assessing resistance to it. For the strength of the resistance or the moral power within the human being can be only evaluated in terms of the strength of the attack on it. The more decisively and the more violently the passion expresses itself in the *animal realm,* yet without being able to maintain the same force in the *human realm,* the more evident the latter realm becomes. The moral independence of the human reveals itself all the more gloriously, the portrayal becomes all the more pathetic, and the *pathos* all the more sublime.*

This aesthetic principle is made visible in the pillars of the ancients, though it is difficult to conceptualize and to put in words the impression made by seeing them with one's own eyes. The group of Laocoön and his children is to some extent a measure for

*By the *animal realm* I understand the entire system of those human phenomena that are subject to the blind force of natural instinct and are completely explicable without presupposing any freedom of will. However, by the *human realm* I understand those phenomena that receive their laws from freedom. Now during a performance, if there is a *lack* of passion in the animal realm, it leaves us cold. On the other hand, if passion *predominates* in the human realm, it disgusts and revolts us. Within the animal realm passion must always remain *unresolved;* otherwise pathos is missing. A resolution may be found solely within the human realm. Thus, a person suffering, pictured as grumbling and whining, will only touch us faintly, since within the animal realm the pain is already resolved by gripes and tears. Bitter, silent pain seizes us far more potently, where we find no help from *nature,* but rather must have recourse to something lying beyond all that is natural. The pathos and the power of tragedy lie precisely in this *reference to something transcending sensuality.*

what the pictorial arts of the ancients could achieve in terms of pathos. "Laocoön," Winckelmann tells us in his history of art (page 699 of the Vienna quartal edition),

> is a nature in excruciating pain, formed in the image of a man who tries to gather together the conscious strength of spirit against it. While his suffering swells up his muscles and strains his nerves, [206] the spirit is armed with strength and appears in the forehead that has been driven upwards and in the chest that raises itself up by the clinched breathing and by holding back any expression of feeling, in order to take hold of the pain and to confine it to itself. The anxious sighing that he draws into himself as he takes a breath exhausts his lower body, hollowing out the sides and allowing us to determine the movements of his intestines. Yet his own suffering appears to afflict him far less than does the pain of his children who turn their faces to their father and cry for help. The father's heart reveals itself in the agonizing eyes and compassion seems to swim in a cloudy vapor up to those same eyes. His face grieves but does not cry out, his eyes are turned to help of a higher kind. The mouth is full of agony and the sunken lower lip heavy with that same agony; in the upper lip, drawn upwards, this agony is mixed with pain that ascends with a rage of despair over an undeserved, unworthy suffering, making the nose swell and revealing itself in the flared and upwards-drawn nostrils. Beneath the forehead, as though united in a single point, the battle is drawn between pain and resistance and it is drawn with magnificent truthfulness. For, while the pain drives the eyebrows upwards, the struggle against that pain presses the flesh above the eyes downwards and against the upper eyelid, so that the eye is almost completely covered by the overstretched flesh. The nature that the artist could not render more beautiful he has sought to show more exposed, more intense, and more powerful. The greatest beauty reveals itself where the most excruciating pain is placed. The left side, where the viper pores out his venom with a ferocious bite, is the very spot that appears to suffer the most violently from this sensation nearest the heart. His legs attempt to lift themselves up in order to tear themselves away from his curse; no part of the body is at rest, even the traces of the chisel help signify a skin that is becoming stiff.

How genuinely and how sensitively the intellect's battle with the suffering of the sensuous nature is developed in this depiction and how accurately the phenomena are presented in which animality [207] and humanity, nature's coercion and reason's freedom, reveal themselves! As is well-known, Virgil depicted the same scene in his *Aeneid,* but it was not part of the epic poet's plan to dwell, as the sculptor must, on Laocoön's state of mind. For Virgil the entire story is merely a subplot and the purpose it is meant to serve is sufficiently achieved merely by depicting the physical state, without needing to let us look deep into the soul of the suffering figure. For he intends, not so much to move us to sympathy, as to instill us with terror. The poet's duty in this respect was thus merely negative, namely, not to overdo the portrayal of the suffering nature such that in the process every expression of humanity and moral resistance would be lost. For if he had overdone the depiction of suffering, it would have inevitably been followed by a sense of repugnance and disgust. So he stuck to portraying the *cause* of the suffering, the frightfulness of the two snakes and the fury of their assault on their victim, considering it appropriate to enlarge in more detail upon this cause than upon the victim's feelings. He only passes quickly over these feelings, because it must have been important to him to maintain undiminished the image of a divinely ordained punishment and the impression of terror. Had he, on the other hand, let us know as much about the person of Laocoön as the sculptor did, then the hero in the plot would no longer have been the wrathful divinity, but rather the suffering human being, and the episode would have lost its purposefulness for the epic as a whole.

People are already acquainted with Virgil's account of the Laocoön story from Lessing's splendid commentary. But the purpose of Lessing's use of the story was merely to make evident the boundaries between poetic and pictorial depiction by means of an example, not to develop the concept of pathos from it. To the latter end, however, it appears to me no less useful and, with your permission, I will run through it one more time in this regard.

> . . . suddenly—and I shudder to recall it—
> Two serpents were to be seen swimming across
> From Tenedos breasting the calm sea waters
> In ring upon vast ring swirling together

Towards the shore. Their blood-red heads [208]
And necks went towering up above the waves,
The rest of their length went thrashing through the water
Squirming colossal coils, churning the sea
In a breaking foaming wake—then they made the shore,
Their bloodshot eyes ablaze, the flickering forks
Of their tongues playing about their mouths.

Aeneid ii, 203–11*

The first of the three conditions of the sublimeness of power, cited above, is given here, namely, a mighty force of nature, equipped to destroy and scornful of any resistance. Yet, that this might is also *frightening* and becomes *sublime,* depends upon two distinct operations of the mind, that is to say, on two images we spontaneously produce in ourselves. *In the first place,* because we consider this irresistible power of nature together with the human being's weak capacity to withstand it physically, we know that it is frightening. *In the second place,* because we compare it to our will and call to mind our will's absolute independence from every natural influence, it becomes for us a sublime object. These two connections, however, are *our* doing. The poet gives us nothing further than an object furnished with considerable power and striving to exert it. If we *tremble* before that object, this happens merely because we *think* of ourselves or a creature similar to us struggling with it. If in the course of this trembling we feel ourselves elevated *[erhaben],* then it is because we become conscious that, even as a victim of this power, we would have nothing to fear for ourselves insofar as we are free, in other words, for the autonomy of the determinations of our wills. In short, the depiction up to this point is sublime in a purely contemplative sense.

---

* Ecce autem gemini Tenedo tranquilla per alta
(horresco referens) immensis orbibus angues
incumbunt pelago, pariterque ad littora tendunt.
Pectora quorum inter fluctus arrecta, jubaeque [208]
sanquineae exsuperant undas, pars caetera pontum
pone legit, sinuatque immensa volumine terga.
Fit sonitus spumante salo, jamque arva tenebant,
ardenteis oculos suffecti sanguine et igni,
sibila lambebant linguis vibrantibus ora.

English translations are taken from Vergil, *The Aeneid,* Translated by Patric Dickinson (New York: New American Library, 1961), pp. 34–35.

We scattered in every direction
white with fear at the sight.
But they made straight and purposefully on
towards Laocoön.

Aeneid ii, 212–13*

What is powerful is at the same time *presented* as something frightening, and what is contemplatively sublime turns into something pathetic. We see it actually enter into conflict with the impotent human being. Laocoön or us, the difference in the effect is only a matter of degree. The instinct to sympathize arouses the instinct for preservation, the monster lets loose on—us, and all escaping is in vain. [209]

Now it is no longer up to us to measure this might against our own and try to relate it to our existence. This is happening in the object itself without any help from us. Our fear accordingly does not have, as in the preceding case, a merely subjective basis in our mind, but rather an objective basis in the object. For, even if we recognize the whole of this as a mere fiction of the imagination, still we distinguish in this fiction an image, communicated to us from outside ourselves, from another image that we spontaneously produce in ourselves.

The mind thus loses a portion of its freedom, since it receives from outside it, what it previously produced through its spontaneity. The image of danger gains an appearance of objective reality and the passion becomes something serious.

Now, were we nothing but sensuous beings that only obey the self-preservation instinct, we would stand still here and remain in a condition of mere suffering. But there is something within us that takes no part in the stimulations of our sensuous nature, something whose activity is not oriented toward any physical conditions. Depending on how this spontaneous principle (the moral disposition) has developed itself in a mind, more or less room will be left to the suffering nature and more or less spontaneity will remain in the passion.

In moral minds what is frightening (in the imagination) passes

---

* Diffugimus visu exsangues, illi agmine certo
Laocoonta petunt.

quickly and easily over into the sublime. Just as the imagination loses its freedom, so reason makes its freedom obtain; the mind *extends itself all the more inwardly simply because it finds limits outwardly.* Driven from all the fortifications that might afford a sensuous being some physical protection, we dive into the invincible fortress that our moral freedom constitutes and, precisely by this means, we attain an absolute and infinite security, while we give up for lost what is a merely relative and precarious bulwark in the field of appearance. But for this very reason, because it must have come to these physical straits before we look to our moral nature for help, we are able to purchase this lofty feeling of freedom only with our suffering. The common soul simply remains caught up [210] in this suffering and never feels more than fear in the sublimity of pathos. An independent mind, on the other hand, makes the transition from just this suffering to the sense of his loftiest power of acting; he knows how to produce something sublime from each fearful thing.

> They made for Laocoön; and first each serpent
> Seized one of his little boys and wrapping itself
> In squeezing coils around him snapped and swallowed
> The wretched limbs
>
> *Aeneid* ii, 213–15*

It makes for a great effect, the fact that the moral human (the father) is attacked before the physical human is. All emotions are more aesthetic secondhand, and no sympathy is stronger than the sympathy we feel with sympathy.

> Then, as Laocoon rushed to their rescue
> Waving a weapon, the serpents seized on him and
> Enwound him in their huge spirals
>
> *Aeneid* ii, 215–16†

The time was right to make us respect the hero as a moral person

---

* Laocconta petunt, ac primum parva deorum
corpora gnatorum serpens amplexus uterque
implicat, ac miseros morsu depascitur artus.

† Post ipsum, auxilio subeuntem ac tela ferentem
corripiunt.

and the poet seized this moment. From his description we are aware of the full might and fury of the inimical monsters and we know how futile all resistance is. Were Laocoön merely an ordinary human being, he would perceive where his interest lies and, like the rest of the Trojans, would seek safety in a speedy flight from the scene. But he has a heart in him and the danger to his children holds him back—to his own demise. This feature alone already makes him worthy of all our sympathy. Whenever the vipers would have taken hold of him, it would have moved and shaken us. The fact, however, that it occurs precisely at *that* moment when he deserves our respect as a father, the fact that his demise is represented as the immediate result of fulfilling his paternal duty, as the consequence of the tender concern for his children—this ignites our participation to the utmost. It is now as though he freely chooses to surrender himself to the disaster and his death becomes an action of his will.

In all pathos, therefore, the senses as well as the spirit must take an interest, the former on account of the suffering, the spirit on account of the freedom involved. If a portrayal of pathos lacks [211] an expression of nature suffering, it has no *aesthetic* force and our hearts are left cold. If it lacks an expression of an ethical propensity, then, for all its sensuous force, it will never be *pathetic* and it will inevitably enrage our sensibilities. In the midst of all the mind's freedom it must always be apparent that a human being is suffering just as in the midst of all the suffering of humanity there must always be a glimmer of an independent spirit or a spirit capable of being independent.

Independence of spirit in a state of suffering can reveal itself in two sorts of ways. Either *negatively,* if the physical side of the human being does not legislate to the ethical side and his *condition* is not allowed to be cause of his *sentiments;* or *positively,* if the ethical side of the human being *legislates* to the physical side and his sentiments have some causal influence on his condition. A sublime *composure* springs from the former scenario, sublime *action* from the latter.

Every character not dependent upon fate provides an instance of sublime composure. "A brave soul, doing battle with disaster," Seneca says, "is an alluring spectacle, even for the gods." The Roman Senate after the debacle at Cannae provides us such a sight. Even Milton's Lucifer, when he looks around him for the first time in hell, his future home, fills us with a feeling of amazement, because of this strength of soul. ". . . hail horrors," he calls out, "hail

> Infernal world and thou profoundest hell
> Receive thy new possessor; one who brings
> A mind not to be changed by place or time.
> The mind is its own place, and in itself
> Can make a heav'n of hell, a hell of heav'n.
> What matter here, if I be still the same, . . .
> And what should I be, all but less than he
> Whom thunder hath made greater? here at least
> We shall be free. . . ."

Medea's reply in the tragedy belongs to the same class.

A sublime composure may be *observed,* since it depends upon a coexistence of things. Sublime action, on the other hand, may only be *thought,* since it depends upon a succession, and understanding is required in order for the suffering to be inferred from a free decision. Thus, sublime composures alone are suited to the work of pictorial and plastic artists, since these sorts of artists can successfully depict only things that are coexistent, [212] while the poet can enlarge upon both coexistent and successive things. Even if the plastic or pictorial artist has to portray a sublime *action,* he must transform it into a sublime *composure.*

Sublimity of action requires not only that a human being's suffering have no influence on his moral disposition, but rather vice versa, that the suffering be far more the work of his moral character. This can take place in two sorts of ways. Either mediately and according to the law of freedom, if he *chooses* the suffering out of respect for some sort of duty. In this case the representation of duty as a *motive* determines him and his suffering is an *act of will.* Or immediately and according to the law of necessity, if he morally *atones* for not doing his duty. In this case the representation of duty as a *power* determines him and his suffering is merely an *effect.* An example of the former is provided us by Regulus, when he surrendered to the Carthaginians' thirst for revenge, in order not to break his word. He would have served as an example of the latter case, if he had broken his word and the consciousness of this guilt had made him miserable. In both cases the suffering has a moral basis, only with the difference that in the first case he shows us his moral character, in the second merely that he is subject to moral concerns, that he has a moral vocation. In the first case he appears as a morally significant person, in the second case merely as an aesthetically significant object.

This latter difference is important for the art of tragedy and for that reason deserves a more detailed discussion.

Simply from the standpoint of an aesthetic evaluation, a human being is already a sublime object if he demonstrates the dignity of the human vocation by virtue of his *condition,* even supposing that we are not to find this vocation realized in his *person.* Only if he conducts himself at the same time as a person in a manner consistent with that vocation does he become sublime from a moral point of view. That is to say, he becomes sublime in the moral sense only when it is not merely his capability, but rather the use of this capability that warrants our respect or, in other words, only when his actual conduct is as dignified as his innate potential. It is one thing for us in the course of our judgment to direct our attention at the moral capability in general and the possibility of a will that is absolutely free, and quite another thing for us to direct our attention at the [213] use of this capability and the actualization of this absolute freedom.

These are two different focuses, I say, and this divergence lies not somehow merely in the objects judged, but rather in the diverse ways of judging. The same object can be disagreeable to us from a moral point of view and yet be quite attractive to us from an aesthetic point of view. But even if the same object satisfies us in both instances, it has this effect in each case in a completely different way. That it is aesthetically useful does not make it morally satisfying and it does not become aesthetically useful by the fact that it is morally satisfying.

I think, for example, of the self-sacrifice of Leonidas at Thermopylae. Judged from a moral perspective, this action portrays for me the moral law being carried out in complete contradiction of instinct. Judged aesthetically, it portrays to me the moral capability of a human being, independent of all coercion by instinct. This action *satisfies* my moral sense (reason) while it *delights* my aesthetic sense (imagination).

For this diversity in my feelings in regard to the same object I offer the following explanation.

Just as what we are is divided into two principles or natures, so, too, corresponding to this division, are our feelings divided into two completely different genera. As rational beings we feel approval or disapproval, as sensuous beings we feel pleasure or displeasure. Both sorts of feelings, those of approval and those of pleasure, are based on a satisfaction. The former is based on satisfaction of a *claim,* since reason merely *demands,* but does not crave anything. The feeling of pleasure is based on satisfaction of a *desire,* since the senses only have *cravings* and cannot make demands. The demands of reason and the cravings of the senses are related to one another as necessity is to want. Both, therefore, are subsumed under the concept of exigency, simply with the distinction, that the exigency of reason is unconditioned while the exigency of the senses only takes place under conditions. In both cases, however, the satisfaction is contingent. Hence, every feeling of pleasure as well as of approval is based in the end on the agreement [214] of something contingent with something necessary. If what is necessary is an imperative, there will be approval; if it is a want, then pleasure will be the sensation. In both cases, the more contingent the satisfaction is, the more intense it is.

Now, at the bottom of every moral evaluation there lies a demand by reason that things be done morally, and there is an unconditioned exigency at hand that we intend what is right. But because the will is free, it is (physically) a contingent matter whether we actually do it. If we, then, actually do so, this agreement of contingency with the rational imperative in the exercise of freedom is approved or applauded and, of course, all the more so if the conflict of inclinations makes *this* exercise of freedom more contingent and more doubtful.

In the case, on the other hand, of an aesthetic evaluation, the object is related to *the needs of the imagination,* and the imagination cannot *command,* but can merely *desire* that what is contingent be in agreement with its interest. The interest of the imagination, however, consists in this: to keep itself in play *free from laws.* There is nothing more at odds with this inclination to "not be tied down" than the will's moral obligation that determines the object of the will in the most rigorous fashion. Moreover, since the moral obligation of the will is the object of moral judgment, one readily sees that the imagination could not profit from this sort of judging. Still, a moral obligation of the will is thinkable only on the supposition that the will is in absolutely no way dependent on the compulsion of natural urges. The *possibility* of freedom thus postulates freedom and hence in this respect perfectly agrees with the interests of fantasy. Yet, since fantasy cannot, through its need, prescribe to the will of individuals as reason can through its imperative, any linking of the capacity for freedom with fantasy is something that happens by chance and thus, as a concurrence of the contingent and the (conditionally) necessary, it must arouse pleasure. Hence, if we judge Leonidas's deed *from a moral point of view,* we then regard it from a standpoint where its necessity strikes us more than its contingency does. [215] If, on the other hand, we judge it *from an aesthetic point of view,* then we consider it from a standpoint where its contingency is on display far more than its necessity is. It is a *duty* for every will, to act in a certain way, as soon as it is a free will. However, that there is a freedom of will at all that makes it possible so to act, this is a *favor* bestowed by nature on that very capability in need of freedom. Hence, if the moral sense—reason—judges a virtuous action, then the approval is the highest sort possible, because reason can never find *more* than it demands and only seldom finds *as much* as it demands. On the other hand, if the aesthetic sense—the imagination—judges the same action, then a positive kind of pleasure ensues, since the imagination can never demand that nature be in agreement with its needs and has to be surprised by their actual satisfaction as by some stroke of luck. We applaud the fact that Leonidas *actually made* the heroic decision that he did, but we shout for joy, we are thrilled that he *could* make it.

The difference between the two sorts of judgment strikes us even more clearly, if someone begins with an action, regarding which the moral and the aesthetic judgments turn out differently. Take the self-immolation of Peregrinus Protheus at Olympia. Judging from a moral point of view, I cannot approve of this action since I find mixed motives at work there and the *duty* to preserve oneself is set aside for the sake of such motives. Yet, judged from an aesthetic point of view, the action pleases me and, of course, it does so because it testifies to a capacity of the will to withstand even the mightiest of all instincts, the *instinct* for self-preservation. In evaluating the action aesthetically, I forget about the individual, that is to say, I abstract from the relation of *his* will to the law of the will and regard the human will generally, namely, as a capacity of the species in relation to the power of nature as a whole. When I do this, I do not pay attention to whether it was a purely moral disposition or whether it was simply a more powerful sensuous appeal that suppressed the self-preservation instinct in the fanatic Peregrin. In the moral evaluation of the action, [216] it has been seen, self-preservation was represented as a *duty* and the violation of this duty was accordingly offensive. In the aesthetic evaluation, on the other hand, self-preservation was regarded as an *interest* and setting this interest aside was rather enjoyable. In the latter sort of judging, then, the operation is precisely the reverse of that in the former. When we make aesthetic judgments, we put a sensuously limited individual and a pathologically vulnerable will up against the absolute law of the will and the infinite duty of spirits, whereas when we make moral judgments, we contrast the absolute capacity of the will and the infinite *power* of spirits with the compulsions of nature and the limitations inherent in sensuousness. Thus the aesthetic judgment leaves us free, it elevates and inspires us, because we find ourselves with an apparent advantage over our sensuousness, already by virtue of the mere capacity to will in an absolute way, in other words, by virtue of the mere propensity for morality, since the sheer possibility of refusing to be coerced by nature flatters our need to be free. Thus the moral judgment limits and humbles us, since we find ourselves, in every particular act of the will, more or less at a disadvantage in the face of what is an absolute law for the will. The fact that the will is limited to being determined in one way alone, a limitation demanded by duty, is at odds with the instinct for freedom on the part of fantasy. In making aesthetic judgments we veer from actual things to possibilities and rise up from the individual to the species, while in making moral judgments we descend from the possible to the actual and enclose the species within the limitations of the individual. No wonder, then, that we feel ourselves broadened in aesthetic judgments, but confined and restricted in moral judgments.* [217]

*This analysis, I might recall in passing, also explains the diverse aesthetic impressions that the Kantian representation of duty usually makes on its various critics.

From all this it follows, then, that moral and aesthetic judgments, far from supporting one another, stand rather in each other's way, since they point the mind in two diametrically opposed directions. For the law abidingness demanded by reason as a moral judge is inconsistent with the lack of restraint required by imagination as an aesthetic judge. Thus an object will be all the less suitable to some aesthetic use the more it qualifies for some moral use. If a writer, nevertheless, has to select this sort of object for his theme, then he will do well to treat it in such a way that our reason is not so much focused on the *rule* governing the will as our fantasy is focused on the *capacity* of the will. For his own sake the writer must take this route, since our freedom marks the end of his realm. Only as long as we look outside ourselves are we *his;* as soon as we reach inside our own bosoms, he has lost us. This, however, is inevitably the outcome from the moment a theme no longer *is regarded by us as a phenomenon,* but rather *stands in judgment over us* as a *law.*

For a *writer's* purposes the only thing useful about even expressions of the most sublime virtue is the *power* they possess. He does not bother in the slightest about the orientation of the power. Even if he places the [218] most perfect paradigm of morality before our eyes, the writer has no other purpose *and may have no other purpose* than to fascinate us by the consideration of it. Now, however, only what benefits us as individuals can fascinate us and only

---

One part of the public that should not be dismissed finds this representation of duty rather humiliating; another finds it infinitely uplifting for the heart. Both are right and the reason for this contradiction lies simply in the diverse standpoints from which each regards this matter. Merely doing our duty is, to be sure, nothing great; insofar as the best we can manage to do is simply to fulfill our obligations and yet doing this even shabbily is our duty, there is nothing inspiring in the highest virtue. However, to fulfill one's obligations faithfully and perseveringly in the face of all the limitations of a sensuous nature, to follow the holy law of spirits steadfastly despite the shackles of matter, is certainly elevating and admirable. As far as the world of spirits is concerned, in other words, our virtue is nothing meritorious and however much it may cost us, we will always *be useless knaves.* On the other hand, as far as the world of the senses is concerned, our virtue is an object all that much more sublime. Insofar, then, as we judge our actions morally and refer them to the moral law, we will have little cause to be proud of our moral life. However, insofar as we look to the possibility of these actions and relate the capacity of our mind lying at the bottom of these actions to the phenomenal world, that is to say, insofar as we judge aesthetically, we may be allowed a certain feeling for ourselves, indeed, this is even necessary, since we uncover a principle within us that is incomparably great and infinite.

what elevates our spiritual capacity can fascinate us in a spiritual sense. But how can another's dutifulness benefit *us* as individuals and enhance our spiritual power? That someone *actually* does his duty depends upon a contingent use *he* makes of his freedom and, precisely for that reason, it can prove nothing as far as we are concerned. It is merely the *capacity* for a similar dutifulness that we share with him and the fact that we see our own capacity in his that explain why we feel our spiritual power elevated. It is, therefore, merely via the representation of its possibility that the actual exercise of an absolutely free willing pleases our aesthetic sense.

One becomes even more convinced of this, if one contemplates how little the poetic power of the impression made on us by moral characters or plots depends on their *historical reality*. Because all aesthetic effect is based on the *poetic,* not the historic truth, none of our satisfaction with ideal characters is lost by recalling that they are poetic fictions. The poetic truth consists, not in the fact that something actually happened, but rather in the fact that it could happen, thus, in the internal possibility of the matter. The aesthetic force must, accordingly, already lie in the possibility depicted.

Even in regard to actual events of historical persons what is poetic is not their existence, but rather the capability that their existence makes known. The fact that these persons actually lived and that these events actually ensued can, to be sure, very often enhance our pleasure, but this adds something alien that is far more detrimental than conducive to the poetic impression. People have long believed that they do a service to the literature of our fatherland by recommending national themes to writers for their work. By this means, it was claimed, Greek poetry gained such mastery over hearts and minds, because it painted native scenes and immortalized native deeds. It is not to be denied that [219] the poetry of antiquity, owing to this feature, accomplished things that modern poetry cannot pride itself in having done. But are these the accomplishments of the art and the poet? Woe to the Greek genius for art, if it had nothing but this circumstantial advantage over the genius of the moderns, and woe to the artistic taste of the Greeks if it had first to be acquired by means of such historical relevancies in its poets' works! Only a barbarian sort of taste needs the prod of private interest in order to be taken by beauty and only a bungler elicits from some material a power that he despairs being able to give a form to. Poetry should not pass through the cold regions of memory, it should never make eruditeness its expounder nor self-interest its advocate. It should affect the heart because it flowed from the heart and it should aim, not at the citizen in the human being, but rather at the human being in the citizen.

It is fortunate that the true genius does not pay much heed to the pointers people take pains to impart to him, more on the basis of opinion than of competence. Otherwise Sulzer and his followers would have given German poetry a quite ambivalent form. To shape humans morally and to ignite nationalistic feelings in the citizen is, to be sure, a very honorable mandate for the poet and the muses know best how closely the arts of the sublime and the beautiful are connected with this. Yet what the poetic art indirectly does quite splendidly, it would only succeed at very badly, were it to attempt that directly. The art of poetry never carries on any particular business among men and one could not choose a more inappropriate tool to see to it that a particular charge, a job, is well managed. Its sphere of effect is the totality of human nature and only insofar as it has an influence on the character, is it able to have influence on the particular actions of that character. Poetry can come to be for the human being, what love is for the hero. It can neither counsel him nor join him in battle nor otherwise do any work for him, but it can develop him into a hero, call him to action, and equip him with the strength to be everything he ought to be. [220]

Hence, the aesthetic power with which the sublimeness of character and action take hold of us rests in no way upon reason's interest in things *being* done rightly, but rather upon imagination's interest in it *being possible* that things are done rightly. That is to say, it is in the interest of the imagination that no feeling, however powerful, be capable of subduing the freedom of the mind. This possibility lies, however, in every hardy expression of freedom and the power of the will, and only where the poet hits upon this, has he found a fitting subject matter to portray. As far as *his* interest is concerned, it makes no difference if he intends to take his heroes from the class of pernicious or of good characters, since the very measure of power required for good can quite often, for that reason, be demanded in something evil. When we make aesthetic judgments, we focus far more on power than on its orientation and far more on freedom than on lawfulness. This becomes obvious enough from the very fact that we would rather watch power and freedom expressed at the cost of lawfulness than watch lawfulness expressed at the cost of power and freedom. That is to say, as soon as scenarios arise where the moral law is coupled with impulses whose force threatens to carry away the will, the character rises in aesthetic quality if he is able to withstand those impulses. A man of vice begins to interest us as soon as he is forced to risk happiness and life in order to carry out his pernicious will. Someone virtuous, on the other hand, loses our interest in the same proportion as his happiness necessitates his good conduct. Revenge, for example, is indisputably an ignoble and even base emotion. Nevertheless, revenge becomes aesthetic as soon as it exacts a painful sacrifice from those who carry it out. Through the act of murdering her children, Medea aims at Jason's heart, but at the same time she breaks her own and her revenge becomes aesthetically sublime as soon as we see the tender mother.

The aesthetic judgment contains in these cases more truth than one usually believes. Vices that testify to strength of will clearly proclaim a greater potential for truly moral freedom than do virtues that draw on inclinations for support. [221] For it costs the inveterate villain only a single victory over himself, a single reversal of maxims, to turn all that constancy and firmness of will he expends on evil into something good. Why else is it that we contemptuously dismiss the mediocre character and with spine-tingling amazement often follow every step of the utterly pernicious character? Without question, the reason is that in the former case we give up on even the possibility of the sort of willing that is absolutely free, while in every utterance of the villain, on the other hand, we observe that he can rise up to the full dignity of humanity through a single act of will.

Consequently, in aesthetic judgments we are interested, not in morality of itself, but simply in freedom, and morality can please our imagination only insofar as it makes that freedom visible. It is thus an obvious confounding of boundaries, for people to demand moral purposefulness in aesthetic things and to want to drive imagination from its rightful domain as a means to expanding reason's realm. Either the imagination will have to be completely subjugated and then all aesthetic effect is lost, or it will share its dominance with reason and then, indeed, not much will have been gained for morality. By pursuing two divergent aims, people will run the risk of failing both. Moral legitimacy will fetter the freedom inherent in fantasy and the imagination's capriciousness will destroy the necessity dictated by reason.

Translated by Daniel O. Dahlstrom

Concerning the Sublime*

"No human being is obliged to be obliged!" Nathan the Jew says to the Dervish, words true to a far greater extent than people would perhaps like to admit. The will is what distinguishes the human race, and reason itself is nothing but the will's everlasting rule. All of nature acts in a rational manner; the human prerogative is simply to act in a rational manner consciously and deliberately. All other things must; the human being is the entity that wills.

Precisely for this reason, nothing is so beneath the dignity of a human being as to suffer violence, for it destroys the individual's humanity. Whoever inflicts it on us, is at odds with nothing less than our humanity; whoever cowardly suffers it, tosses his humanity aside. Yet this claim to absolute freedom from all brute force seems to presuppose an entity in possession of a power sufficient to repel every other power from it. If a claim of this sort is found in an entity that does not occupy the highest echelon in the realm of forces, then the result is an ill-fated contradiction between desire and capability.

Every human being finds himself in this position. He is surrounded by countless forces, all superior to him and all playing the

---

**Concerning the Sublime (Über das Erhabene)* first appeared in the third part of *Kleinere prosaische Schriften* (Leipzig: Crusius, 1801), pp. 3–43. The editors of the National Edition think it improbable, given its Kantian terms and agreement with *On the Sublime* and *On the Pathetic,* that the essay was drafted much later than these pieces. Its approximate date is accordingly set between 1794 and 1796.

master over him. Yet because of his nature he claims not to have to endure violence. His intellect, to be sure, artfully enhances his natural powers, and up to a certain point he actually succeeds in physically mastering everything else physical. There is a remedy for everything, so goes the proverb, everything, that is, but death. Yet if this, in the strictest sense, actually is the sole exception, it would still subvert the entire concept of a human being. He can no longer be the sort of entity that wills, if there is even a single case where he absolutely must do what he does not want to do. This singular, terrifying case of *simply being necessitated to do what he does not want to do,* will haunt him like a ghost and hand him over to the blind terrors of [39] the imagination, something that is actually the case for the majority of people. His exalted freedom is absolutely nothing, if he is even bound in a single, solitary instance. Culture is supposed to put humans in a state of freedom and to assist in realizing the concept of a human person as a whole. Thus it is supposed to make him capable of asserting his will, for the human being is the entity that wills.

This is possible in two sorts of ways. Either *realistically,* when the human being opposes brute force with brute force, when as a part of nature he masters nature; or *idealistically,* when he takes a step beyond nature and thereby negates the concept of brute force in regard to himself. What helps him accomplish the former is called "physical culture." The human being shapes his intellect and his sensuous powers either in order to make the forces of nature, in accordance with their own laws, into tools of his will, or in order to put himself in a position of safety when confronted with those effects of natural forces that he cannot steer. Yet the forces of nature may be mastered or thwarted only up to a certain point. Beyond this point they elude the power of a human being and subjugate the human being to themselves.

Hence, human freedom would quickly be at an end, if a human being were capable only of physical culture. However, he is supposed to be a human being without exception; thus, in no case is he supposed to suffer or undergo something *against* his will. If he can no longer oppose physical forces with a corresponding physical force, then nothing else remains for him to do to avoid suffering violence than *to do completely away with a relation* so deleterious to him and to *destroy conceptually* a brute force that he in fact must endure. However, to destroy a force conceptually means nothing other than to submit to it voluntarily. The culture that renders him adept at this is called "the moral culture."

A human being who is morally cultivated, and only this sort of human being, is completely free. He is either superior to nature as a power or he is in harmony with it. Nothing that nature does to him is violence, since it has already become *his own action* before it gets to him, and the dynamism of nature never reaches him, since he deliberately cuts himself off from everything that nature can reach. Morality teaches this kind of sensibility [40] under the concept of resignation to necessity, and religion teaches it under the concept of commitment to divine counsel. Yet this sensibility, if it is to be a work of free choice and deliberation, requires from the outset a greater clarity of thinking and a higher energy of will than people are accustomed to having in practical life. Fortunately, however, in the rational nature of a human being there is not only a moral predisposition that can be developed by the intellect, but also an *aesthetic* tendency toward this moral development within his sensuously rational nature, that is to say, his human nature, a tendency that can be awakened by certain sensuous themes and cultivated by purifying his feelings in line with this idealistic impetus of the mind. I turn now to the treatment of this predisposition that is, to be sure, conceptually and essentially idealistic, but also quite clearly apparent in the life of the realist, even though he does not allow for it in his system.*

Developed feelings for beauty are, of course, already sufficient to render us independent of the power of nature up to a certain point. A mind so ennobled that it is touched more by the forms than by the material of things and derives unbounded joy from reflection merely on the manner of something's appearance, without any view toward possessing it, such a mind bears within itself an inner, ineradicable fullness of life. And because it has no need to acquire the objects among which it dwells, it is also in no danger of being robbed of them. However, in the end, even an appearance requires a body for it to reveal itself to, and, hence, as long as there

---

*Just as nothing, in general, can be called "truly idealistic" but what the consummate realist actually and unconsciously practices and only denies due to an inconsistency on his part.

is even a need for a beautiful appearance alone, a need for the *existence* of objects remains and, as a consequence, our satisfaction is still dependent upon nature's power over all that exists. It is, of course, one thing to feel a desire for beautiful and good objects and quite another thing altogether to desire simply that the objects present be beautiful and good. The latter, but not the former, can exist together with the greatest freedom [41] of mind. We can demand that what is present at hand be beautiful and good, but we can only wish for the beautiful and the good to be present. That very mental attitude that is indifferent to the existence of the beautiful and good and perfect, yet with the most uncompromising rigor demands that what exists be good and beautiful and perfect, is appropriately called "magnificent" and "sublime," since it contains all the real features of a beautiful character without sharing its limitations.

It is a sign of good and beautiful, but in each case feeble souls, always to be pressing impatiently for the existence of their moral ideals, and to be painfully struck by the obstacles to this. Such people put themselves in a position of being tragically dependent upon chance, and it can always be safely said in advance that they leave too much to the material component in moral and aesthetic matters and that they will fail the supreme test of character and taste. Those who are morally defective should not cause us *suffering* and pain, which always testifies more to an unsatisfied need than to an unfulfilled demand. The demand that goes unfulfilled should be accompanied by a more robust sort of emotion, strengthening the mind and fortifying it in its power rather than making it meek and forlorn.

Nature gives us two genii to accompany us through life. The one, sociable and comely, shortens our trouble-filled journey with its cheerful games; it eases the bonds of necessity for us, and in the midst of joy and levity it guides us to those dangerous places where we must act as pure spirits and lay aside everything corporeal, in other words, it leads us to the knowledge of truth and to the exercise of duty. Here it abandons us, since its realm is only the world of the senses and its earthly wings cannot carry it beyond this world. But then another genius steps forward, a strong-armed genius, serious and silent, that carries us across the dizzying depth.

In the first of these genii one recognizes the feeling of the beautiful, in the second the feeling of the sublime. The beautiful is already an expression of freedom, of course, but not of the sort that lifts us above the power of nature and extricates us from every corporeal influence. Rather it is of the sort that [42] we appreciate as human beings within nature. When it comes to beauty we feel that we are free because sensuous urges harmonize with the law of reason. In the case of the sublime we feel free because those sensuous urges have no influence on the legislation of reason, since the spirit acts here as if it stood under no laws other than its own.

The feeling of the sublime is a mixed feeling. It is a combination of *being in anguish* (at its peak this expresses itself as a shudder) and *being happy* (something that can escalate to a kind of ecstasy). This combination, although it is not actually pleasure, is still preferred by noble souls over all pleasure. This synthesis of two contradictory sensations in a single feeling establishes our moral self-sufficiency in an irrefutable manner. For, since it is absolutely impossible for the same object to be related to us in two contradictory ways, it follows from the fact that *we ourselves* are related to the object in two contrasting ways, that two opposite natures must be united within us. Moreover, when the object is presented or represented, the ways these two opposite natures respectively take an interest in it are completely contrary to one another. Thus, by means of the feeling of the sublime, we experience that the state of our mind is not necessarily oriented to the state of our senses, that the laws of nature are not necessarily our laws as well, and that we have within us a self-sufficient principle that is independent of all sensuous stirrings.

There are two sorts of sublime object. Either we relate the object to our *powers of comprehension* and succumb in the attempt to form a picture or a concept of it, or we relate it to our *powers of living* and regard it as a might against which our own might amounts to nothing. Yet, although the sublimity of the object brings on the painful feeling of our limitations in the one case as in the other, still we do not flee it; instead we are irresistibly drawn to it. Would this be possible at all, if the limits of our imagination were also the limits of our powers of comprehension? Would we really want to be reminded of the omnipotence of the forces of nature, if we had nothing else in reserve but what can [43] become a prey to nature? We delight in what is sensuously infinite, because we are able to think what the senses no longer grasp and what the intellect no longer understands. We are enchanted by what is fearful, because we are able to want what our instincts abhor and to spurn what they desire. We readily let the imagination meet its match in the realm of appearances, since the latter remains, in the end, only a sensuous force triumphing over another sensuous force. Yet nature in its utter unboundedness cannot attain the absolute grandeur within us. We gladly subject our well-being and our existence to physical necessity, because this is precisely what reminds us that it has no control over principles basic to us. The human being is in the hands of nature, but the will of man is in his own hands.

In this way nature has wielded a sensuous means to teach us that we are more than simply sensuous. It has known how to employ even sensations to lead us to the realization that we have been subjected to their brute force in nothing less than the manner of a slave. This is a completely different effect than can be accomplished by beauty, namely, by the beauty of the actual world, since even the sublime must lose itself in something ideally beautiful. Reason and sensuality harmonize in the case of what is beautiful, and only on account of this harmony does it hold any charms for us. Thus, through beauty alone we would never learn that we are called to prove ourselves to be pure intellects and are capable of doing so. In what is sublime, on the other hand, there is *no* harmony of reason and sensuousness and the spell that captivates our minds lies precisely in this contradiction. Here the physical and the moral sides of the human being are severed from one another in the sharpest possible way, for it is precisely when confronted by such objects that the physical side feels only its limitations, while the moral side experiences its *power*. The moral side of human nature is infinitely elevated by the very thing that forces the physical side of human nature into the ground.

A human being, I want to assume, ought to possess all the virtues that together constitute a *beautiful character*. He ought to find pleasure in the exercise of justice, charity, temperance, fortitude, and fidelity. [44] All the duties that circumstances require of him should become child's play, and fortune should make no action difficult that his outgoing heart might demand of him. Is there anyone who is not elated by such a beautiful harmony of natural urges with reason's precepts and who can refrain from loving such a person? Yet can we really be certain, with all our fondness for him, that he actually is someone virtuous and that virtue exists at all? Unless he was a fool, this individual could not have acted otherwise if he were aiming at the same time for nothing more than pleasant sensations and he would have had to disdain what was to his own advantage if he had any desire to be wicked. It is possible that the source of his actions is pure, but he must work that out in his own heart and *we* see nothing of this. We see him do no more than even a merely prudent man would have to do, who makes pleasure his god. The world of the senses thus explains the entire phenomenon of his virtue, and we have no need at all to look beyond this world for an explanation of it.

However, suppose this very same man suddenly suffers a great misfortune. Suppose that he is robbed of his possessions and that his good name is dragged through the mud. Suppose that illnesses confine him to an excruciating sickbed, that death takes from him all who love him, and that everyone he trusted abandons him in his time of need. Let people look for him in this situation and demand of the unfortunate soul that he practice the very same virtues that he had been so ready to practice when luck smiled on him. If in these circumstances they find that he is the exact same man, if poverty has not lessened his charity, nor ingratitude his readiness to serve, nor pain his equanimity, nor his own misfortune his ability to share in another's happiness, if one notices the changed situation in his stature but not in his behavior, in the content but not the form of his action—then, of course, no explanation on the basis of the *concept of nature* is any longer sufficient. (According to this concept it is absolutely necessary that something in the present, as an effect, be grounded in something in the past as its cause.) For nothing [45] can be more contradictory than that the effect remains the same while the cause has turned into its opposite. Accordingly, every natural sort of explanation must be rejected and we must completely give up attempting to derive the behavior from the circumstance. The explanation of the behavior must be removed from the physical order of the world and transferred to a completely different order. While reason *[Vernunft]* with its ideas can ascend to this level, the understanding *[Verstand]* with its concepts cannot grasp it. This discovery of an absolute, moral capability, bound to no natural condition, gives the melancholy feeling (taking hold of us when we look at such an individual) that completely distinctive, unspeakable charm, that sublimity that no pleasure of the sense, however noble it be, can ever compete with.

The sublime thus fashions for us a point of departure from the sensuous world in which the beautiful would gladly detain us forever. Not gradually (since there is no transition from dependency to freedom), but only suddenly and through a kind of shock, does something sublime tear the independent spirit loose from the net a sophisticated sensuousness uses to ensnare it. The more transparently this net is woven, the tighter its hold on the spirit. To a great extent that sophisticated sensuousness has won the day in people's minds due to the imperceptible influence of an effete taste, and in the seductive dress of spiritual beauty it has succeeded in forcing itself into the innermost seat of moral legislation and poisoning the sacredness of maxims there at their source. Yet, in spite of all this, often a single sublime emotion is enough to rip the web of deception apart, suddenly giving back to the tethered spirit all its mobility, revealing its true vocation and necessitating a feeling of its dignity, at least for the moment. Beauty in the shape of the goddess Calypso had enchanted the courageous son of Ulysses, and by the power of her charms she long held him captive on her island. Although he was simply lying in the arms of lust, he long believed that he was paying homage to an immortal divinity. But suddenly, in the shape of Mentor, a sublime impression took hold of him; he recalled his higher calling, dove into the waves, and was free. [46]

The sublime, like the beautiful, is lavishly diffused throughout the whole of nature, and the capacity to feel both the beautiful and the sublime is placed in all human beings. But the seedlings of these feelings develop unevenly and must be helped along by art. It is already part of nature's purpose that we first rush toward beauty while still fleeing the sublime. For beauty is our nursemaid in childhood and, indeed, is supposed to guide us from the raw state of nature to a state of refinement. Yet, although it is our first love and our sensitivity to it unfolds earliest, nature has nonetheless taken care that it mature slowly and that, in order to develop fully, it await the formation of the understanding and the heart. If taste were to attain to full maturity before truth and morality were implanted in our hearts and in a manner superior to the way that can happen by means of taste, then the world presented by the senses would remain forever the limit of our aspirations. Neither in our conceptions nor in our sensibilities would we go beyond it, and what cannot be imagined would also have no reality for us. But fortunately it is part of nature's arrangement that, of all the capabilities of the mind, taste, although blossoming first, reaches maturity last. In the intervening period enough time is won to implant a wealth of conceptions in the head and a treasure chest of principles in the heart, and then in particular to develop out of reason a sensitivity to the grandeur and the sublimity in things.

As long as the human being was merely slave of physical necessity, as long as he found no way out of the narrow circle of needs and did not have a clue to the lofty *demonic* freedom lurking in his heart, the *inscrutability* of nature could only remind him of the limitations of his mind and the *destructiveness* of nature could only remind him of his physical impotence. Thus, he was forced to pass meekly over the former and to turn in fright away from the latter. Yet no sooner does the detached consideration of things make a place for him over against the blind onslaught of natural forces, and no sooner does he discover amidst this torrent of appearances something enduring in his own being, [47] than the wild masses of nature around him begin to speak to his heart in a completely different language and the relative majesty outside him becomes the mirror for him of the absolute grandeur within him. Then, without fear and quivering with pleasure, he draws nearer to these images of horror produced by his imagination and he deliberately summons up all the power of this faculty to portray the sensuously infinite so that, when this effort nevertheless fails, he might feel that much more keenly the superiority of his ideas over the best that the sensuous side of his nature is capable of accomplishing. The sight of unlimited distances and of heights disappearing from view, the expansive ocean at his feet, and the even vaster ocean above him, snatch his spirit away from the narrow sphere of actual things and the oppressive confinement of physical life. The simple majesty of nature holds out to him a far grander standard for appreciating things and, surrounded by nature's magnificent formations, he no longer puts up with the trivial in the way he thinks. Who knows how many luminous thoughts and heroic decisions, that no study cell or social salon could have been brought into the world, were given birth on a walk as the mind courageously wrestled with the great spirit of nature. The character of city people, crippled and frayed as it is, readily turns to trifles, while the nomad's sensibilities remain as open and free as the firmament under which he camps. Who knows whether this considerable difference is not to be ascribed in part to the fact that the urban dweller is so less frequently in intercourse with the great genius of nature!

However, it is not merely what lies beyond the imagination's reach, namely, the quantitatively sublime, it is also what lies beyond the intellect's comprehension, namely, *confusion,* that can help portray what transcends the senses and can give an impetus to the mind, provided that the confusion advances to a certain level and announces itself as nature's doing (since otherwise it is contemptible). Is there anyone who would not rather linger amidst the inspiring disorder of a natural landscape than pass time in the insipid regularity of a French garden? Who would not rather marvel at the miraculous struggle beween fertility and devastation on the plains of Sicily or feast his eyes on Scotland's wild cataracts and misty mountain ranges, on Ossian's magnificent nature, than admire the straight lines of Holland's bitter, patient victory over the most stubborn of the elements? [48] No one will deny that people are physically better cared for in Batavia's pastures than under Vesuvius's treacherous crater or that the intellect that wants to comprehend things and put them in order is far better served by an inn's orderly garden than by a natural landscape in the wild. People have, however, need of something more than merely to live and enjoy themselves; they are called to more than simply grasping the phenomena surrounding them.

What makes the untamed and bizarre character of physical creation so appealing to the sensitive traveler is the very thing that opens up the source of a completely unique pleasure to minds capable of being inspired even within the murky anarchy of the moral world. Of course, there are people who employ the *intellect's* faint torch to cast light on the immense household of nature and are only concerned with reducing its audacious disorder to some sort of harmony; such people can find no satisfaction in a world where erratic contingency seems to rule more than some wise plan does, and where, in most cases by far, merit and fortune contradict one other. They want to have everything as organized in the grand course of the world as it is in a well-run inn, and if they fail to find this orderliness (and it has to be assumed that they will not), then there is nothing left for them to do but expect from a future existence and from another nature the satisfaction present and past existence have not given them. If, on the other hand, they deliberately give up trying to bring this lawless chaos of phenomena under some cognitive unity, then what they give up for lost on one side they gain in abundance from another side. Owing to the complete lack of some connection in the form of a purpose among this throng of phenomena, the latter become overwhelming and useless to the understanding that must depend upon that form of connection. Yet it is precisely this utter lack of some purposeful connection among the phenomena that makes them an all the more accurate sensuous image for pure reason. In this wild prodigiousness of nature reason finds portrayed its own independence from natural conditions. For if one removes from a series of things every manner of connection among them, then one has a concept of independence that is in surprising agreement with pure reason's concept of freedom. Under this idea of freedom that it derives from itself, [49] reason thus encompasses in a unity that is thought, what the understanding cannot combine into a unity that is known. Through this idea reason subjects the endless play of phenomena to itself and thus at the same time asserts its power over the understanding as a faculty conditioned by the senses. Now, if one recalls how valuable it must be for a rational being to become conscious of its independence from nature's laws, then one grasps how it happens that people with a sublime temperament can consider themselves compensated by this idea of freedom for every mistake in knowing. For a noble mind, freedom with all its moral contradictions and physical evils is an infinitely more interesting spectacle than prosperity and order without freedom, where the sheep patiently follow the shepherd and the self-controlled will demeans itself to being a useful part of some clockwork. While in the latter case the human being merely becomes an ingenious product of nature, one of the more fortunate citizens of its realm, freedom makes him a citizen and co-regent of a higher system. Having the lowliest place in this system, moreover, is infinitely more honorable than occupying the highest echelon in the physical order.

Considered from this perspective and *only* from this perspective, world history is for me a sublime object. The world as a historical object is at bottom nothing but the conflict of natural forces among themselves and with human freedom. History reports to us the success of this engagement. As far as history has evolved until now, it has far greater acts of nature (among which all human emotions must be numbered) to relate than of self-sufficient reason. The latter sort of rationality has been able to assert its might only through individuals who are exceptions to natural law, such as a Cato, Aristides, Phocion, and similar men. If one approaches history only with great expectations of being illuminated and of learning, how very disappointed one is! The claims of experience refute all the well-meant attempts of philosophy to bring what the moral world *demands* into harmony with what the real world *does*. As obliging as nature [50] is in its *organic realm* where it orients or appears to orient itself to the regulative principles of judgment, it is just as intransigent in the realm of freedom, tearing loose from the reins with which the speculative spirit would so much like to hold it captive and direct it.

How completely different it is if one gives up trying to *explain* nature and makes this inscrutability itself the standpoint of the evaluation. Viewed as a whole, nature flaunts all the rules prescribed to it by our understanding; going its own willful, uninhibited way, it tramples into the dust the creations of both wisdom and chance with the same indifference; it sweeps away the important as well as the trivial, bringing the noble as well as the ordinary down with it in the same demise; at one point it preserves a world of ants while at another point it seizes and crushes human beings, its most splendid creation, in its gargantuan arms; frequently, in a careless moment, it squanders accomplishments that had cost it the most effort, while it just as often takes centuries to construct some work of folly. Precisely these facts, in a word, this defection of nature as a whole from the scientific rules to which it is subject in its individual appearances, makes apparent the absolute impossibility of explaining *nature itself* by means of *natural laws* and of having obtain for the realm of nature as a whole what obtains *within* it. As a result, the mind cannot resist being driven from the world of appearances to the world of ideas, from the conditioned to the unconditioned.

The frightfulness and destructiveness of nature take us even further than its sensuous infinity does, as long, namely, as we merely remain detached observers of nature. Of course, a sensuous individual as well as the sensuous side of a rational individual fear nothing so much as to be at odds with this power that has well-being and existence at its command.

The supreme ideal we strive after is to remain on friendly terms with the physical world as the guardian of our happiness without on that account being required to break with the moral world that determines our dignity. Now, as is well known, it is not always a matter of serving two masters, and even if (an almost impossible case) duty should never come into conflict with need, natural necessity still enters into no agreement with the human being [51] and neither his power nor his skill can secure him against the treachery of fate. Thus, it is good for him if he has learned to endure what he cannot change and to surrender with dignity what he cannot save! Instances can occur where fate scales all the ramparts on which he has based his security and there is nothing left for him to do but take flight in the sacred freedom of spirits—where there is no other means of pacifying life's urges than willing them—and no other means of withstanding nature's might than accommodating it and, through a deliberate transformation [*Aufhebung*] of all sensuous interest, doing oneself in morally before some power does so physically.

Sublime emotions strengthen him toward this end as does a more frequent intercourse with the devastating character of nature, both where it displays its destructive might to him merely from afar and where it actually exerts this might against his fellow human beings. The pathetic is an artificial misfortune and, like the true misfortune, it puts us in *immediate contact* with the spiritual law that reigns in our bosoms. Yet genuine misfortune does not always choose its man and its time well. Often it surprises us when we are defenseless and, what is worse, it frequently *renders* us *defenseless*. The artificial misfortune of the pathetic, on the other hand, finds us fully equipped and, since it is merely imagined, the self-sufficient principle in our minds gets room to assert its absolute independence. Thus, the more often it renews this act of independence, the more accomplished the human spirit becomes and it acquires an ever greater advantage over sensuous urges, such that when a serious misfortune finally does arise in the midst of these imagined and artificial ones, that person is in a position to treat it as an artificial one and transform actual suffering into a sublime emotion—a human being can soar no higher! The pathetic, one can thus say, is an inoculation against unavoidable fate, robbing fate of its perniciousness and diverting its attack to a human being's strength.

Away, then, with the coddling that is based upon a false understanding and with the frail, pampered taste that throws a veil over the stern face of necessity and, in order to put itself [52] in a sensuously advantageous position, *lies* about some sort of harmony between well-being and good behavior, a harmony of which there are no traces in the real world. On brow after brow cruel fate shows itself to us. There is salvation for us, not in ignorance of the dangers camped around us—for ultimately this ignorance must come to an end—but only in the *acquaintance* with those dangers. To make this acquaintance we are helped along by the terrifying and magnificent spectacle [*Schauspiel*] of change destroying everything and re-creating it and then destroying it once again, a spectacle of ruin at times eating slowly away at things, other times suddenly assaulting them. History provides ample examples of the pathetic picture of humanity *wrestling* with fate, a picture of the incessant flight of fortune, of confidence betrayed, injustice triumphant, and innocence violated. Imitating these images, the art of tragedy places them before our eyes. For does there exist anyone anywhere in the world with a moral disposition that is not completely degenerate who can *read* about the stubborn yet futile struggle of Mithridates, about the demise of the cities of Syracuse and Carthage, *and* can dwell on such scenes without shivering in wonder at necessity's stern law, without momentarily reining in his desires, and without clutching for what is constant in his bosom, after being seized by this eternal infidelity of everything sensuous? The capacity to feel the sublime is thus one of the most glorious dispositions in human nature, deserving our *respect* due to its origin in a self-sufficient capacity to think and will; because of its influence on moral human beings, it deserves as well to be developed in the most complete possible manner. The beautiful renders itself deserving on account of the *humanness* in a human being, the sublime on account of the *purely demonic* in him. Because it is our calling to orient ourselves, in the face of all sensuous limitations, according to the lawbook of pure spirits, the sublime must come to the assistance of the beautiful in order to make the *aesthetic education* a complete whole and expand the human heart's sensitivity to the entire scope of our calling, extending even beyond the world of the senses. [53]

Without beautiful things there would be a constant battle between our natural calling and our rational calling. In the effort to do justice to our *spiritual vocation,* we would neglect our *humanity* and, prepared at any moment for the departure from the world of the senses, we would constantly remain strangers in this sphere of acting assigned to us. Without sublime things, beauty would make us forget our dignity. Through the inertia of an uninterrupted pleasure we would lose the strength of *character* and, tied to this *contingent form of existence* by bonds that cannot be dissolved, we would lose sight of our permanent vocation and our true fatherland. Only if the sublime is married to the beautiful and our sensitivity to both has been shaped in equal measure, are we complete citizens of nature, without on that account being its slaves, and without squandering our citizenship in the intelligible world.

Now, of course, nature on its own presents objects in abundance on which the ability to feel the beautiful and the sublime could be exercised. Yet here, as elsewhere, people are better served by something secondhand than by something firsthand. People prefer to receive from art a material that has been prepared and selected than to have to draw it themselves painstakingly and indigently from the murky wells of nature. The mimetic drive to picture things [*der nachahmende Bildungstrieb*] cannot receive an *impression* without immediately striving for a lively *expression;* in every beautiful or magnificent form of nature it sees a challenge to wrestle with that form. This drive has a tremendous advantage over that natural form, namely, the advantage of being permitted to treat as the main purpose and as a unique whole the very thing that nature, in the course of pursuing a purpose more pertinent to the natural order, merely takes up in passing—if nature does not, indeed, unintentionally toss it completely aside. Either nature *suffers violence* in its beautiful organic formations (through some deficiency in the individual material or through intrusion of heterogeneous forces) or nature *does violence* in its magnificent, pathetic scenarios, acting as a force on human beings. Since nature can still become aesthetic simply as an object of unforced observation if either of the above takes place, then [54] its imitator, in the form of the pictorial and plastic arts [*bildende Kunst*], is completely free. For art of this sort detaches all the contingent limitations from its object and also leaves the mind of the observer free because it imitates only the *appearance* and not the *actuality*. Yet, since all the magic of the sublime and the beautiful lies only in the appearance and not in the content, art possesses all the advantages of nature without sharing its chains.

Translated by Daniel O. Dahlstrom

Letters on the Aesthetic Education of Man*

Si c'est la raison, qui fait l'homme,
c'est le sentiment, qui le conduit.
—Rousseau

First Letter

I have, then, your gracious permission to submit the results of my inquiry *concerning art and beauty* in the form of a series of letters. Sensible as I am of the gravity of such an undertaking, I am also alive to its attraction and its worth. I shall be treating of a subject that has a direct connection with all that is best in human happiness, and no very distant connection with what is noblest in our moral nature. I shall be pleading the cause of beauty before a heart that is as fully sensible of her power as it is prompt to act upon it, a heart that, in an inquiry where one is bound to invoke feelings

* *On the Aesthetic Education of Man* first appeared as a complete and revised text in volume 3 of *Kleinere prosaische Schriften* (Leipzig: Crusius, 1801) pp. 44–309. The text was originally published in 1795 in three installments of *Die Horen,* volume 2, with Letters 1–9 (pp. 7–48) appearing in January, Letters 10–16 (pp. 51–94) in February, and Letters 17–27 (pp. 45–124) in June.

no less often than principles, will relieve me of the heaviest part of my labors.

What I would have asked of you as a favor, you in your largesse impose upon me as a duty, thus leaving me the appearance of merit where I am in fact only yielding to inclination. The free mode of procedure you prescribe implies for me no constraint; on the contrary, it answers to a need of my own. Little practiced in the use of scholastic modes, I am scarcely in danger of offending against good taste by their abuse. My ideas, derived from constant communing with myself rather than from any rich experience of the world or from reading, will be unable to deny their origin: the last reproach they are likely to incur is that of sectarianism, and they are more liable to collapse out of inherent weakness than to maintain themselves with the support of authority and borrowed strength.

True, I shall not attempt to hide from you that it is for the most part Kantian principles on which the following theses will be based. But you must ascribe it to my ineptitude rather than to those principles if in the course of this inquiry you should be reminded of any particular philosophical school. No, the freedom of your mind shall, I can promise you, remain inviolable. Your own feeling will provide me with the material on which to build, your own free powers of thought dictate the laws according to which we are to proceed.

Concerning those ideas that prevail in the practical part of the Kantian system only the philosophers are at variance; the rest of mankind, I believe I can show, have always been agreed. Once divested of their technical form, they stand revealed as the immemorial pronouncements of common reason, and as data of that moral instinct that nature in her wisdom appointed man's guardian until, through the enlightenment of his understanding, he should have arrived at years of discretion. But it is precisely this technical form, whereby truth is made manifest to the intellect, which veils it again from our feeling. For alas! intellect must first destroy the object of inner sense if it would make it *its own*. Like the analytical chemist, the philosopher can only discover how things are combined by analyzing them, only lay bare the workings of spontaneous nature by subjecting them to the torment of his own techniques. In order to lay hold of the fleeting phenomenon, he must first bind it in the fetters of rule, tear its fair body to pieces by reducing it to concepts, and preserve its living spirit in a sorry skeleton of words. Is it any wonder that natural feeling cannot find itself again in such an image, or that in the account of the analytical thinker truth should appear as paradox?

I too, therefore, would crave some measure of forbearance if the following investigations, in trying to bring the subject of inquiry closer to the understanding, were to transport it beyond reach of the senses. What was asserted above of moral experience, must hold even more of the phenomenon we call beauty. For its whole magic resides in its mystery, and in dissolving the essential amalgam of its elements we find we have dissolved its very being.

Second Letter

But should it not be possible to make better use of the freedom you accord me than by keeping your attention fixed upon the domain of the fine arts? Is it not, to say the least, untimely to be casting around for a code of laws for the aesthetic world at a moment when the affairs of the moral offer interest of so much more urgent concern, and when the spirit of philosophical inquiry is being expressly challenged by present circumstances to concern itself with that most perfect of all the works to be achieved by the art of man: the construction of true political freedom?

I would not wish to live in a century other than my own, or to have worked for any other. We are citizens of our own age no less than of our own state. And if it is deemed unseemly, or even inadmissible, to exempt ourselves from the morals and customs of the circle in which we live, why should it be less of a duty to allow the needs and taste of our own epoch some voice in our choice of activity?

But the verdict of this epoch does not, by any means, seem to be going in favor of art, not at least of the kind of art to which alone my inquiry will be directed. The course of events has given the spirit of the age a direction that threatens to remove it even further from the art of the ideal. This kind of art must abandon actuality, and soar with becoming boldness above our wants and needs; for art is a daughter of freedom, and takes her orders from the necessity inherent in minds, not from the exigencies of matter.

But at the present time material needs reign supreme and bend a degraded humanity beneath their tyrannical yoke. *Utility* is the great idol of our age, to which all powers are in thrall and to which all talent must pay homage. Weighed in this crude balance, the insubstantial merits of art scarce tip the scale, and, bereft of all encouragement, she shuns the noisy marketplace of our century. The spirit of philosophical inquiry itself is wresting from the imagination one province after another, and the frontiers of art contract the more the boundaries of science expand.

Expectantly the gaze of philosopher and man of the world alike is fixed on the political scene, where now, so it is believed, the very fate of mankind is being debated. Does it not betray a culpable indifference to the common weal not to take part in this general debate? If this great action is, by reason of its cause and its consequences, of urgent concern to everyone who calls himself man, it must, by virtue of its method of procedure, be of quite special interest to everyone who has learned to think for himself. For a question that has hitherto always been decided by the blind right of might, is now, so it seems, being brought before the tribunal of pure reason itself, and anyone who is at all capable of putting himself at the center of things, and of raising himself from an individual into a representative of the species, may consider himself at once a member of this tribunal, and at the same time, in his capacity of human being and citizen of the world, an interested party who finds himself more or less closely involved in the outcome of the case. It is, therefore, not merely his own cause that is being decided in this great action; judgment is to be passed according to laws that he, as a reasonable being, is himself competent and entitled to dictate.

How tempting it would be for me to investigate such a subject in company with one who is as acute a thinker as he is a liberal citizen of the world! And to leave the decision to a heart that has dedicated itself with such noble enthusiasm to the weal of humanity. What an agreeable surprise if, despite all difference in station, and the vast distance that the circumstances of the actual world make inevitable, I were, in the realm of ideas, to find my conclusions identical with those of a mind as unprejudiced as your own! That I resist this seductive temptation, and put beauty before freedom, can, I believe, not only be excused on the score of personal inclination, but also justified on principle. I hope to convince you that the theme I have chosen is far less alien to the needs of our age than to its taste. More than this: if man is ever to solve that problem of politics in practice he will have to approach it through the problem of the aesthetic, because it is only through beauty that man makes his way to freedom. But this cannot be demonstrated without my first reminding you of the principles by which reason is in any case guided in matters of political legislation.

Third Letter

Nature deals no better with man than with the rest of her works: she acts for him as long as he is as yet incapable of acting for himself as a free intelligence. But what makes him man is precisely this: that he does not stop short at what nature herself made of him, but has the power of retracing by means of reason the steps she took on his behalf, of transforming the work of blind compulsion into a work of free choice, and of elevating physical necessity into moral necessity.

Out of the long slumber of the senses he awakens to consciousness and knows himself for a human being; he looks about him, and finds himself—in the state. The force of his needs threw him into this situation before he was as yet capable of exercising his freedom to choose it; compulsion organized it according to purely natural laws before *he* could do so according to the laws of reason. But with this state of compulsion, born of what nature destined him to be, and designed to this end alone, he neither could nor can rest content as a moral being. And woe to him if he could! With that same right, therefore, by virtue of which he is man, he withdraws from the dominion of blind necessity, even as in so many other respects he parts company from it by means of his freedom; even as, to take but *one* example, he obliterates by means of morality, and ennobles by means of beauty, the crude character imposed by physical need upon sexual love. And even thus does he, in his maturity, retrieve by means of a fiction the childhood of the race: he conceives, as idea, a *state of nature,* a state not indeed given him by any experience, but a necessary result of what reason destined him to be; attributes to himself in this idealized natural state a purpose of which in his actual natural state he was entirely ignorant, and a power of free choice of which he was at that time wholly incapable; and now proceeds exactly as if he were starting from scratch, and were, from sheer insight and free resolve, exchanging a state of complete independence for a state of social contracts. However skillfully, and however firmly, blind caprice may have laid the foundations of her work, however arrogantly she may maintain it, and with whatever appearance of venerability she may surround it—man is fully entitled in the course of these operations to treat it all as though it had never happened. For the work of blind forces possesses no authority before which freedom need bow, and everything must accommodate itself to the highest end that reason now decrees in him as person. This is the origin and justification of any attempt on the part of a people grown to maturity to transform its natural state into a moral one.

This natural state (as we may term any political body whose organization derives originally from forces and not from laws) is, it is true, at variance with man as moral being, for whom the only law should be to act in conformity with law. But it will just suffice for man as physical being; for he only gives himself laws in order to come to terms with forces. But physical man does *in fact* exist, whereas the existence of moral man is as yet *problematic*. If, then, reason does away with the natural state (as she of necessity must if she would put her own in its place), she jeopardizes the physical man who actually exists for the sake of a moral man who is as yet problematic, risks the very existence of society for a merely hypothetical (even though morally necessary) ideal of society. She takes from man something he actually possesses, and without which he possesses nothing, and refers him instead to something that he could and should possess. And if in so doing she should have counted on him for more than he can perform, then she would, for the sake of a humanity that he still lacks—and can without prejudice to his mere existence go on lacking—have deprived him of the means of that animal existence that is the very condition of his being human at all. Before he has had time to cleave unto the law with the full force of his moral will, she would have drawn from under his feet the ladder of nature.

What we must chiefly bear in mind, then, is that physical society *in time* must never for a moment cease to exist while moral society *as idea* is in the process of being formed; that for the sake of man's moral dignity his actual existence must never be jeopardized. When the craftsman has a timepiece to repair, he can let its wheels run down; but the living clockwork of the state must be repaired while it is still striking, and it is a question of changing the revolving wheel while it still revolves. For this reason a support must be looked for that will ensure the continuance of society, and make it independent of the natural state that is to be abolished.

This support is not to be found in the natural character of man that, selfish and violent as it is, aims at the destruction of society rather than at its preservation. Neither is it to be found in his moral character that has, *ex hypothesi,* first to be fashioned, and upon which, just because it is free, and *because it never becomes manifest,* the lawgiver could never exert influence, nor with any certainty depend. It would, therefore, be a question of abstracting from man's physical character its arbitrariness, and from his moral character its freedom; of making the first conformable to laws, and the second dependent upon sense impressions; of removing the former somewhat further from matter, and bringing the latter somewhat closer to it; and all this with the aim of bringing into being a third character that, kin to both the others, might prepare the way for a transition from the rule of mere force to the rule of law, and that, without in any way impeding the development of moral character, might on the contrary serve as a pledge in the sensible world of a morality as yet unseen.

Fourth Letter

This much is certain: only the predominance of such a character among a people makes it safe to undertake the transformation of a state in accordance with moral principles. And only such a character can guarantee that this transformation will endure. The setting up of a moral state involves being able to count on the moral law as an effective force, and free will is thereby drawn into the realm of cause and effect, where everything follows from everything else in a chain of strict necessity. But we know that the modes of determination of the human will must always remain contingent, and that it is only in absolute being that physical necessity coincides with moral necessity. If, therefore, we are to be able to count on man's moral behavior with as much certainty as we do on *natural* effects, it will itself have to *be* nature, and he will have to be led by his very impulses to the kind of conduct that is bound to proceed from a moral character. But the will of man stands completely free between duty and inclination, and no physical compulsion can, or should, encroach upon this sovereign right of his personality. If, then, man is to retain his power of choice and yet, at the same time, be a reliable link in the chain of causality, this can only be brought about through both these motive forces, inclination and duty, producing completely identical results in the world of phenomena; through the content of his volition remaining the same whatever the difference in form; that is to say, through impulse being sufficiently in harmony with reason to qualify as universal legislator.

Every individual human being, one may say, carries within him, potentially and prescriptively, an ideal man, the archetype of a human being, and it is his life's task to be, through all his changing manifestations, in harmony with the unchanging unity of this ideal.* This archetype, which is to be discerned more or less clearly in every individual, is represented by the *state,* the objective and, as it were, canonical form in which all the diversity of individual subjects strive to unite. One can, however, imagine two different ways in which man existing in time can coincide with man as idea, and, in consequence, just as many ways in which the state can assert itself in individuals; either by the ideal man suppressing empirical man, and the state annulling individuals; or else by the individual himself *becoming* the state, and man in time being *ennobled to the stature* of man as idea.

It is true that from a one-sided moral point of view this difference disappears. For reason is satisfied as long as her law obtains unconditionally. But in the complete anthropological view, where content counts no less than form, and living feeling too has a voice, the difference becomes all the more relevant. Reason does indeed demand unity; but nature demands multiplicity; and both these kinds of law make their claim upon man. The law of reason is imprinted upon him by an incorruptible consciousness; the law of nature by

*I refer to a recent publication by my friend Fichte, *Lectures on the Vocation of a Scholar,* in which illuminating deductions are drawn from this proposition in a way not hitherto attempted.

an ineradicable feeling. Hence it will always argue a still defective education if the moral character is able to assert itself only by sacrificing the natural. And a political constitution will still be very imperfect if it is able to achieve unity only by suppressing variety. The state should not only respect the objective and generic character in its individual subjects; it should also honor their subjective and specific character, and in extending the invisible realm of morals take care not to depopulate the sensible realm of appearance.

When the artisan lays hands upon the formless mass in order to shape it to his ends, he has no scruple in doing it violence; for the natural material he is working merits no respect for itself, and his concern is not with the whole for the sake of the parts, but with the parts for the sake of the whole. When the artist lays hands upon the same mass, he has just as little scruple in doing it violence; but he avoids showing it. For the material he is handling he has not a whit more respect than has the artisan; but the eye that would seek to protect the freedom of the material he will endeavor to deceive by a show of yielding to this latter. With the pedagogic or the political artist things are very different indeed. For him man is at once the material on which he works and the goal toward which he strives. In this case the end turns back upon itself and becomes identical with the medium; and it is only inasmuch as the whole serves the parts that the parts are in any way bound to submit to the whole. The statesman-artist must approach his material with a quite different kind of respect from that which the maker of beauty feigns toward his. The consideration he must accord to its uniqueness and individuality is not merely subjective, and aimed at creating an illusion for the senses, but objective and directed to its innermost being.

But just because the state is to be an organization formed by itself and for itself, it can only become a reality inasmuch as its parts have been tuned up to the idea of the whole. Because the state serves to represent that ideal and objective humanity that exists in the heart of each of its citizens, it will have to observe toward those citizens the same relationship as each has to himself, and will be able to honor their subjective humanity only *to the extent* that this has been ennobled in the direction of objective humanity. Once man is inwardly at one with himself, he will be able to preserve his individuality however much he may universalize his conduct, and the state will be merely the interpreter of his own finest instinct, a clearer formulation of his own sense of what is right. If, on the other hand, in the character of a whole people, subjective man sets his face against objective man with such vehemence of contradiction that the victory of the latter can only be ensured by the suppression of the former, then the state too will have to adopt toward its citizens the solemn rigor of the law, and ruthlessly trample underfoot such powerfully seditious individualism in order not to fall a victim to it.

But man can be at odds with himself in two ways: either as savage, when feeling predominates over principle; or as barbarian, when principle destroys feeling. The savage despises civilization, and acknowledges nature as his sovereign mistress. The barbarian derides and dishonors nature, but, more contemptible than the savage, as often as not continues to be the slave of his slave. The man of culture makes a friend of nature, and honors her freedom while curbing only her caprice.

Consequently, whenever reason starts to introduce the unity of the moral law into any actually existing society, she must beware of damaging the variety of nature. And whenever nature endeavors to maintain her variety within the moral framework of society, moral unity must not suffer any infringement thereby. Removed alike from uniformity and from confusion, there abides the triumph of form. *Wholeness* of character must therefore be present in any people capable, and worthy, of exchanging a state of compulsion for a state of freedom.

Fifth Letter

Is this the character that the present age, that contemporary events, present to us? Let me turn my attention at once to the object most in evidence on this enormous canvas.

True, the authority of received opinion has declined, arbitrary rule is unmasked and, though still armed with power, can no longer, even by devious means, maintain the appearance of dignity. Man has roused himself from his long indolence and self-deception and, by an impressive majority, is demanding restitution of his inalienable rights. But he is not just demanding this; over there, and over here, he is rising up to seize by force what, in his opinion, has been wrongfully denied him. The fabric of the natural state is tottering, its rotting foundations giving way, and there seems to be a *physical* possibility of setting law upon the throne, of honoring man at last as an end in himself, and making true freedom the basis of political associations. Vain hope! The *moral* possibility is lacking, and a moment so prodigal of opportunity finds a generation unprepared to receive it.

Man portrays himself in his actions. And what a figure he cuts in the drama of the present time! On the one hand, a return to the savage state; on the other, to complete lethargy: in other words, to the two extremes of human depravity, and both united in a single epoch!

Among the lower and more numerous classes we are confronted with crude, lawless instincts, unleashed with the loosening of the bonds of civil order, and hastening with ungovernable fury to their animal satisfactions. It may well be that objective humanity had cause for complaint against the state; subjective humanity must respect its institutions. Can the state be blamed for having disregarded the dignity of human beings as long as it was still a question of ensuring their very existence? Or for having hastened to divide and unite by the [mechanical] forces of gravity and cohesion, while there could as yet be no thought of any [organic] formative principle from within? Its very dissolution provides the justification of its existence. For society, released from its controls, is falling back into the kingdom of the elements, instead of hastening upwards into the realm of organic life.

The cultivated classes, on the other hand, offer the even more repugnant spectacle of lethargy, and of a depravation of character that offends the more because culture itself is its source. I no longer recall which of the ancient or modern philosophers it was who remarked that the nobler a thing is, the more repulsive it is when it decays; but we shall find that this is no less true in the moral sphere. The child of nature, when he breaks loose, turns into a madman; the creature of civilization into a knave. That enlightenment of the mind, which is the not altogether groundless boast of our refined classes, has had on the whole so little of an ennobling influence on feeling and character that it has tended rather to bolster up depravity by providing it with the support of precepts. We disown nature in her rightful sphere only to submit to her tyranny in the moral, and while resisting the impact she makes upon our senses are content to take over her principles. The sham propriety of our manners refuses her the *first* say—which would be pardonable—only to concede to her in our materialistic ethics the *final* and decisive one. In the very bosom of the most exquisitely developed social life egotism has founded its system, and without ever acquiring therefrom a heart that is truly sociable, we suffer all the contagions and afflictions of society. We subject our free judgment to its despotic opinion, our feeling to its fantastic customs, our will to its seductions; only our caprice we do uphold against its sacred rights. Proud self-sufficiency contracts the heart of the man of the world, a heart that in natural man still often beats in sympathy; and as from a city in flames each man seeks only to save from the general destruction his own wretched belongings. Only by completely abjuring sensibility can we, so it is thought, be safe from its aberrations; and the ridicule that often acts as a salutary chastener of the enthusiast is equally unsparing in its desecration of the noblest feeling. Civilization, far from setting us free, in fact creates some new need with every new power it develops in us. The fetters of the physical tighten ever more alarmingly, so that fear of losing what we have stifles even the most burning impulse toward improvement, and the maxim of passive obedience passes for the supreme wisdom of life. Thus do we see the spirit of the age wavering between perversity and brutality, between unnaturalness and mere nature, between superstition and moral unbelief; and it is only through an equilibrium of evils that it is still sometimes kept within bounds.

Sixth Letter

Have I not perhaps been too hard on our age in the picture I have just drawn? That is scarcely the reproach I anticipate. Rather a different one: that I have tried to make it prove too much. Such a portrait, you will tell me, does indeed resemble mankind as it is today; but does it not also resemble any people caught up in the process of civilization, since all of them, without exception, must fall away from nature by the abuse of reason before they can return to her by the use of reason?

Closer attention to the character of our age will, however, reveal an astonishing contrast between contemporary forms of humanity and earlier ones, especially the Greek. The reputation for culture and refinement, on which we otherwise rightly pride ourselves vis-à-vis humanity in its *merely* natural state, can avail us nothing against the natural humanity of the Greeks. For they were wedded to all the delights of art and all the dignity of wisdom, without however, like us, falling a prey to their seduction. The Greeks put us to shame not only by a simplicity to which our age is a stranger; they are at the same time our rivals, indeed often our models, in those very excellences with which we are wont to console ourselves for the unnaturalness of our manners. In fullness of form no less than of content, at once philosophic and creative, sensitive and energetic, the Greeks combined the first youth of imagination with the manhood of reason in a glorious manifestation of humanity.

At that first fair awakening of the powers of the mind, sense and intellect did not as yet rule over strictly separate domains; for no dissension had as yet provoked them into hostile partition and mutual demarcation of their frontiers. Poetry had not as yet coquetted with wit, nor speculation prostituted itself to sophistry. Both of them could, when need arose, exchange functions, since each in its own fashion paid honor to truth. However high the mind might soar, it always drew matter lovingly along with it; and however fine and sharp the distinctions it might make, it never proceeded to mutilate. It did indeed divide human nature into its several aspects, and project these in magnified form into the divinities of its glorious pantheon; but not by tearing it to pieces; rather by combining its aspects in different proportions, for in no single one of their deities was humanity in its entirety ever lacking. How different with us moderns! With us too the image of the human species is projected in magnified form into separate individuals—but as fragments, not in different combinations, with the result that one has to go the rounds from one individual to another in order to be able to piece together a complete image of the species. With us, one might almost be tempted to assert, the various faculties appear as separate in practice as they are distinguished by the psychologist in theory, and we see not merely individuals, but whole classes of men, developing but one part of their potentialities, while of the rest, as in stunted growths, only vestigial traces remain.

I do not underrate the advantages that the human race today, considered as a whole and weighed in the balance of intellect, can boast in the face of what is best in the ancient world. But it has to take up the challenge in serried ranks, and let whole measure itself against whole. What individual modern could sally forth and engage, man against man, with an individual Athenian for the prize of humanity?

Whence this disadvantage among individuals when the species as a whole is at such an advantage? Why was the individual Greek qualified to be the representative of his age, and why can no single modern venture as much? Because it was from all-unifying nature that the former, and from the all-dividing intellect that the latter, received their respective forms.

It was civilization itself that inflicted this wound upon modern man. Once the increase of empirical knowledge, and more exact modes of thought, made sharper divisions between the sciences inevitable, and once the increasingly complex machinery of state necessitated a more rigorous separation of ranks and occupations, then the inner unity of human nature was severed too, and a disastrous conflict set its harmonious powers at variance. The intuitive and the speculative understanding now withdrew in hostility to take up positions in their respective fields, whose frontiers they now began to guard with jealous mistrust; and with this confining of our activity to a particular sphere we have given ourselves a master within, who not infrequently ends by suppressing the rest of our potentialities. While in the one a riotous imagination ravages the hard-won fruits of the intellect, in another the spirit of abstraction stifles the fire at which the heart should have warmed itself and the imagination been kindled.

This disorganization, which was first started within man by civilization and learning, was made complete and universal by the new spirit of government. It was scarcely to be expected that the simple organization of the early republics should have survived the simplicity of early manners and conditions; but instead of rising to a higher form of organic existence it degenerated into a crude and clumsy mechanism. That polypoid character of the Greek states, in which every individual enjoyed an independent existence but could, when need arose, grow into the whole organism, now made way for an ingenious clockwork, in which, out of the piecing together of innumerable but lifeless parts, a mechanical kind of collective life ensued. State and church, laws and customs, were now torn asunder; enjoyment was divorced from labor, the means from the end, the effort from the reward. Everlastingly chained to a single little fragment of the whole, man himself develops into nothing but a fragment; everlastingly in his ear the monotonous sound of the wheel that he turns, he never develops the harmony of his being, and instead of putting the stamp of humanity upon his own nature, he becomes nothing more than the imprint of his occupation or of his specialized knowledge. But even that meager, fragmentary participation, by which individual members of the state are still linked to the whole, does not depend upon forms that they spontaneously prescribe for themselves (for how could one entrust to their freedom of action a mechanism so intricate and so fearful of light and enlightenment?); it is dictated to them with meticulous exactitude by means of a formulary that inhibits all freedom of thought. The dead letter takes the place of living understanding, and a good memory is a safer guide than imagination and feeling.

When the community makes his office the measure of the man; when in one of its citizens it prizes nothing but memory, in another a mere tabularizing intelligence, in a third only mechanical skill; when, in the one case, indifferent to character, it insists exclusively on knowledge, yet is, in another, ready to condone any amount of obscurantist thinking as long as it is accompanied by a spirit of order and law-abiding behavior; when, moreover, it insists on special skills being developed with a degree of intensity that is only commensurate with its readiness to absolve the individual citizen from developing himself in extensity—can we wonder that the remaining aptitudes of the psyche are neglected in order to give undivided attention to the one that will bring honor and profit? True, we know that the outstanding individual will never let the limits of his occupation dictate the limits of his activity. But a mediocre talent will consume in the office assigned him the whole meager sum of his powers, and a man has to have a mind above the ordinary if, without detriment to his calling, he is still to have time for the chosen pursuits of his leisure. Moreover, it is rarely a recommendation in the eyes of the state if a man's powers exceed the tasks he is set, or if the higher needs of the man of parts constitute a rival to the duties of his office. So jealously does the state insist on being the sole proprietor of its servants that it will more easily bring itself (and who can blame it?) to share its man with the Cytherean, than with the Uranian, Venus.

Thus little by little the concrete life of the individual is destroyed in order that the abstract idea of the whole may drag out its sorry existence, and the state remains forever a stranger to its citizens since at no point does it ever make contact with their feeling. Forced to resort to classification in order to cope with the variety of its citizens, and never to get an impression of humanity except through representation at second hand, the governing section ends up by losing sight of them altogether, confusing their concrete reality with a mere construct of the intellect; while the governed cannot but receive with indifference laws that are scarcely, if at all, directed to them as persons. Weary at last of sustaining bonds that the state does so little to facilitate, positive society begins (this has long been the fate of most European states) to disintegrate into a state of primitive morality, in which public authority has become but one party *more,* to be hated and circumvented by those who make authority necessary, and only obeyed by such as are capable of doing without it.

With this twofold pressure upon it, from within and from without, could humanity well have taken any other course than the one it actually took? In its striving after inalienable possessions in the realm of ideas, the spirit of speculation could do no other than become a stranger to the world of sense, and lose sight of matter for the sake of form. The practical spirit, by contrast, enclosed within a monotonous sphere of material objects, and within this uniformity still further confined by formulas, was bound to find the idea of an unconditioned whole receding from sight, and to become just as impoverished as its own poor sphere of activity. If the former was tempted to model the actual world on a world conceivable by the mind, and to exalt the subjective conditions of its own perceptual and conceptual faculty into laws constitutive of the existence of things, the latter plunged into the opposite extreme of judging all experience whatsoever by one particular fragment of experience, and of wanting to make the rules of its *own* occupation apply indiscriminately to all others. The one was bound to become the victim of empty subtleties, the other of narrow pedantry; for the former stood too high to discern the particular, the latter too low to survey the whole. But the damaging effects of the turn that mind thus took were not confined to knowledge and production; it affected feeling and action no less. We know that the sensibility of the psyche depends for its intensity upon the liveliness, for its scope upon the richness, of the imagination. The preponderance of the analytical faculty must, however, of necessity, deprive the imagination of its energy and warmth, while a more restricted sphere of objects must reduce its wealth. Hence the abstract thinker very often has a *cold* heart, since he dissects his impressions, and impressions can move the soul only as long as they remain whole; while the man of practical affairs often has a *narrow* heart, since his imagination, imprisoned within the unvarying confines of his own calling, is incapable of extending itself to appreciate other ways of seeing and knowing.

It was part of my procedure to uncover the disadvantageous trends in the character of our age and the reasons for them, not to point out the advantages that nature offers by way of compensation. I readily concede that, little as individuals might benefit from this fragmentation of their being, there was no other way in which the species as a whole could have progressed. With the Greeks, humanity undoubtedly reached a maximum of excellence, which could neither be maintained at that level nor rise any higher. Not maintained, because the intellect was unavoidably compelled by the store of knowledge it already possessed to dissociate itself from feeling and intuition in an attempt to arrive at exact discursive understanding; not rise any higher, because only a specific degree of clarity is compatible with a specific fullness and warmth. This degree the Greeks had attained; and had they wished to proceed to a higher stage of development, they would, like us, have had to surrender their wholeness of being and pursue truth along separate paths.

If the manifold potentialities in man were ever to be developed, there was no other way but to pit them one against the other. This antagonism of faculties and functions is the great instrument of civilization—but it is only the instrument; for as long as it persists, we are only on the way to becoming civilized. Only through individual powers in man becoming isolated, and arrogating to themselves exclusive authority, do they come into conflict with the truth of things, and force the common sense, which is otherwise content to linger with indolent complacency on outward appearance, to penentrate phenomena in depth. By pure thought usurping authority in the world of sense, while empirical thought is concerned to subject the usurper to the conditions of experience, both these powers develop to their fullest potential, and exhaust the whole range of their proper sphere. And by the very boldness with which, in the one case, imagination allows her caprice to dissolve the existing world order, she does in the other, compel reason to rise to the ultimate sources of knowing, and invoke the law of necessity against her.

One-sidedness in the exercise of his powers must, it is true, inevitably lead the individual into error; but the species as a whole to truth. Only by concentrating the whole energy of our mind into a single focal point, contracting our whole being into a single power, do we, as it were, lend wings to this individual power and lead it, by artificial means, far beyond the limits that nature seems to have assigned to it. Even as it is certain that all individuals taken together would never, with the powers of vision granted them by nature alone, have managed to detect a satellite of Jupiter that the telescope reveals to the astronomer, so it is beyond question that human powers of reflection would never have produced an analysis of the infinite or a critique of pure reason, unless, in the individuals called to perform such feats, reason had separated itself off, disentangled itself, as it were, from all matter, and by the most intense effort of abstraction armed their eyes with a glass for peering into the absolute. But will such a mind, dissolved as it were into pure intellect and pure contemplation, ever be capable of exchanging the rigorous bonds of logic for the free movement of the poetic faculty, or of grasping the concrete individuality of things with a sense innocent of preconceptions and faithful to the object? At this point nature sets limits even to the most universal genius, limits he cannot transcend; and as long as philosophy has to make its prime business the provision of safeguards against error, truth will be bound to have its martyrs.

Thus, however much the world as a whole may benefit through this fragmentary specialization of human powers, it cannot be denied that the individuals affected by it suffer under the curse of this cosmic purpose. Athletic bodies can, it is true, be developed by gymnastic exercises; beauty only through the free and harmonious play of the limbs. In the same way the keying up of individual functions of the mind can indeed produce extraordinary human beings; but only the equal tempering of them all, happy and complete human beings. And in what kind of relation would we stand to either past or future ages, if the development of human nature were to make such sacrifice necessary? We would have been the serfs of mankind; for several millenia we would have done slaves' work for them, and our mutilated nature would bear impressed upon it the shameful marks of this servitude. And all this in order that a future generation might in blissful indolence attend to the care of its moral health, and foster the free growth of its humanity!

But can man really be destined to miss himself for the sake of any purpose whatsoever? Should nature, for the sake of her own purposes, be able to rob us of a completeness that reason, for the sake of hers, enjoins upon us? It must, therefore, be wrong if the cultivation of individual powers involves the sacrifice of wholeness. Or rather, however much the law of nature tends in that direction, it must be open to us to restore by means of a higher art the totality of our nature that the arts themselves have destroyed.

Seventh Letter

Can we perhaps look for such action from the state? That is out of the question. For the state as at present constituted has been the cause of the evil, while the state as reason conceives it, far from being able to lay the foundations of this better humanity, would itself have to be founded upon it. Thus the course of my inquiry would seem to have brought me back to the point from which for a time it had deflected me. The present age, far from exhibiting that form of humanity we have recognized as the necessary condition of any moral reform of the state, shows us rather the exact opposite. If, therefore, the principles I have laid down are correct, and if experience confirms my portrayal of the present age, we must continue to regard every attempt at political reform as untimely, and every hope based upon it as chimerical, as long as the split within man is not healed, and his nature so restored to wholeness that it can itself become the artificer of the state, and guarantee the reality of this political creation of reason.

Nature in her physical creation points the way we have to take in the moral. Not until the strife of elemental forces in the lower organisms has been assuaged does she turn to the nobler creation of physical man. In the same way, the strife of elements in moral man, the conflict of blind impulse, has first to be appeased, and crude antagonisms first have ceased within him, before we can take the risk of promoting diversity. On the other hand, the independence of his character must first have become secure, and submission to external forms of authority have given way to a becoming liberty, before the diversity within him can be subjected to any ideal unity. As long as natural man still makes a lawless misuse of his license, one can scarcely run the risk of letting him glimpse his liberty; and as long as civilized man as yet makes so little use of his liberty, one can hardly deprive him of his license. The gift of liberal principles becomes a betrayal of society as a whole when it allies itself with forces still in ferment, and reinforces an already too powerful nature. The law of conformity turns into tyranny vis-à-vis the individual when it is allied with an already prevailing weakness and physical limitation, and so extinguishes the last glimmering spark of independence and individuality.

The character of the age must therefore first lift itself out of its deep degradation: on the one hand, emancipate itself from the blind forces of nature; on the other, return to her simplicity, truth, and fullness—a task for more than one century. Meanwhile I readily admit that isolated attempts may succeed. But no improvement in the body politic as a whole will thereby ensue, and discrepancies in practice will continue to belie unanimity of precepts. In other continents we shall honor humanity in the Negro; in Europe profane it in the thinker. The old principles will remain; but they will wear the dress of the century, and philosophy now lend her name to a repression formerly authorized by the Church. Fearful of freedom, which in its first tentative ventures always comes in the guise of an enemy, we shall either cast ourselves into the arms of an easy servitude or, driven to despair by a pedantic tutelage, escape into the wild libertinism of the natural state. Usurpation will invoke the weakness of human nature, insurrection its dignity; until finally blind force, that great imperatrix of human affairs, steps in and decides this pretended conflict of principles as though it were a common brawl.

Eighth Letter

Is philosophy then to retire, dejected and despairing, from this field? While the dominion of forms is being extended in every other direction, is this, the most important good of all, to remain the prey of formless chance? Is the conflict of blind forces to endure forever in the political world, and the law of sociality never to triumph over hostile self-interest?

By no means! Reason herself, it is true, will not join battle directly with this savage force that resists her weapons. No more than the son of Saturn in the *Iliad* will she descend to personal combat in this gloomy arena. But from the midst of the warriors she chooses the most worthy, equips him, as Zeus did his grandson, with divine weapons, and through his victorious strength decides the great issue.

Reason has accomplished all that she can accomplish by discovering the law and establishing it. Its execution demands a resolute will and ardor of feeling. If truth is to be victorious in her conflict with forces, she must herself first become a *force* and appoint some *drive* to be her champion in the realm of phenomena; for drives are the only motive forces in the sensible world. If she has hitherto displayed so little of her conquering power, this was due, not to the intellect that was powerless to unveil her, but to the heart that closed itself against her, and to the drive that refused to act on her behalf.

For whence comes this still so prevalent rule of prejudice, and this obscuring of minds in the face of all the light that philosophy and empirical science have kindled? Our age is enlightened; that is to say, such knowledge has been discovered and publicly disseminated as would suffice to correct at least our practical principles. The spirit of free inquiry has dissipated those false conceptions that for so long barred the approach to truth, and undermined the foundations upon which fanaticism and deception had raised their throne. Reason has purged herself of both the illusions of the senses and the delusions of sophistry, and philosophy itself, which first seduced us from our allegiance to nature, is now in loud and urgent tones calling us back to her bosom. How is it, then, that we still remain barbarians?

There must, therefore, since the cause does not lie in things themselves, be something in the disposition of men that stands in the way of the acceptance of truth, however brightly it may shine, and of the adoption of truth, however forcibly it may convince. A Sage of old felt what it was, and it lies concealed in that pregnant utterance: *sapere aude.*

Dare to be wise! It is energy and courage that are required to combat the obstacles that both indolence of nature and cowardice of heart put in the way of our true enlightenment. Not for nothing does the ancient myth make the goddess of wisdom emerge fully armed from the head of Jupiter. For her very first action is a warlike one. Even at birth she has to fight a hard battle with the senses, which are loath to be snatched from their sweet repose. The majority of men are far too wearied and exhausted by the struggle for existence to gird themselves for a new and harder struggle against error. Happy to escape the hard labor of thinking for themselves, they are only too glad to resign to others the guardianship of their thoughts. And if it should happen that higher promptings stir within them, they embrace with avid faith the formulas that state and priesthood hold in readiness for such an event. If these unhappy men deserve our compassion, we are rightly contemptuous of those others whom a kindlier fate has freed from the yoke of physical needs, but who by their own choice continue to bow beneath it. Such people prefer the twilight of obscure ideas, where feeling is given full rein, and fancy can fashion at will convenient images, to the rays of truth that put to flight the fond delusions of their dreams. It is on precisely these illusions, which the unwelcome light of knowledge is meant to dissipate, that they have founded the whole edifice of their happiness—how can they be expected to pay so dearly for a truth that begins by depriving them of all they hold dear? They would first have to be wise in order to love wisdom: a truth already felt by him who gave philosophy her name.

It is not, then, enough to say that all enlightenment of the understanding is worthy of respect only inasmuch as it reacts upon character. To a certain extent it also proceeds from character, since the way to the head must be opened through the heart. The development of man's capacity for feeling is, therefore, the more urgent need of our age, not merely because it can be a means of making better insights effective for living, but precisely because it provides the impulse for bettering our insights.

Ninth Letter

But is this not, perhaps, to argue in a circle? Intellectual education is to bring about moral education, and yet moral education is to be the condition of intellectual education? All improvement in the political sphere is to proceed from the ennobling of character—but how under the influence of a barbarous constitution is character ever to become ennobled? To this end we should, presumably, have to seek out some instrument not provided by the state, and to open up living springs that, whatever the political corruption, would remain clear and pure.

I have now reached the point to which all my preceding reflections have been tending. This instrument is fine art; such living springs are opened up in its immortal exemplars.

Art, like science, is absolved from all positive constraint and from all conventions introduced by man; both rejoice in absolute *immunity* from human arbitrariness. The political legislator may put their territory out of bounds; he cannot rule within it. He can proscribe the lover of truth; truth itself will prevail. He can humiliate the artist; but art he cannot falsify. True, nothing is more common than for both, science as well as art, to pay homage to the spirit of the age, or for creative minds to accept the critical standards of prevailing taste. In epochs where character becomes rigid and obdurate, we find science keeping a strict watch over its frontiers, and art moving in the heavy shackles of rules; in those where it becomes enervated and flabby, science will strive to please, and art to gratify. For whole centuries thinkers and artists will do their best to submerge truth and beauty in the depths of a degraded humanity; it is they themselves who are drowned there, while truth and beauty, with their own indestructible vitality, struggle triumphantly to the surface.

The artist is indeed the child of his age; but woe to him if he is at the same time its ward or, worse still, its minion! Let some beneficent deity snatch the suckling betimes from his mother's breast, nourish him with the milk of a better age, and suffer him to come to maturity under a distant Grecian sky. Then, when he has become a man, let him return, a stranger, to his own century; not, however, to gladden it by his appearance, but rather, terrible like Agamemnon's son, to cleanse and to purify it. His theme he will, indeed, take from the present; but his form he will borrow from a nobler time, nay, from beyond time altogether, from the absolute, unchanging, unity of his being. Here, from the pure ether of his genius, the living source of beauty flows down, untainted by the corruption of the generations and ages wallowing in the dark eddies below. The theme of his work may be degraded by vagaries of the public mood, even as this has been known to ennoble it; but its form, inviolate, will remain immune from such vicissitudes. The Roman of the first century had long been bowing the knee before his emperors when statues still portrayed him erect; temples continued to be sacred to the eye long after the gods had become objects of derision; and the infamous crimes of a Nero or a Commodus were put to shame by the noble style of the building whose frame lent them cover. Humanity has lost its dignity; but art has rescued it and preserved it in significant stone. Truth lives on in the illusion of art, and it is from this copy, or afterimage, that the original image will once again be restored. Just as the nobility of art *survived* the nobility of nature, so now art goes before her, a voice rousing from slumber and preparing the shape of things to come. Even before truth's triumphant light can penetrate the recesses of the human heart, the poet's imagination will intercept its rays, and the peaks of humanity will be radiant while the dews of night still linger in the valley.

But how is the artist to protect himself against the corruption of the age that besets him on all sides? By disdaining its opinion. Let him direct his gaze upwards, to the dignity of his calling and the universal law, not downwards toward fortune and the needs of daily life. Free alike from the futile busyness that would fain set its mark upon the fleeting moment, and from the impatient spirit of enthusiasm that applies the measure of the absolute to the sorry products of time, let him leave the sphere of the actual to the intellect, which is at home there, while he strives to produce the ideal out of the union of what is possible with what is necessary. Let him express this ideal both in semblance and in truth, set the stamp of it upon the play of his imagination as upon the seriousness of his conduct, let him express it in all sensuous and spiritual forms, and silently project it into the infinity of time.

But not everyone whose soul glows with this ideal was granted either the creative tranquillity or the spirit of long patience required to imprint it upon the silent stone, or pour it into the sober mould of words, and so entrust it to the executory hands of time. Far too impetuous to proceed by such unobtrusive means, the divine impulse to form often hurls itself directly upon present-day reality and upon the life of action, and undertakes to fashion anew the formless material presented by the moral world. The misfortunes of the human race speak urgently to the man of feeling; its degradation more urgently still; enthusiasm is kindled, and in vigorous souls ardent longing drives impatiently on toward action. But did he ever ask himself whether those disorders in the moral world offend his reason, or whether they do not rather wound his self-love? If he does not yet know the answer, he will detect it by the zeal with which he insists upon specific and prompt results. The pure moral impulse is directed towards the absolute. For such an impulse time does not exist, and the future turns into the present from the moment that it is seen to develop with inevitable necessity out of the present. In the eyes of a reason that knows no limits, the direction is at once the destination, and the way is completed from the moment it is trodden.

To the young friend of truth and beauty who would inquire of me how, despite all the opposition of his century, he is to satisfy the noble impulses of his heart, I would make answer: impart to the world you would influence a *direction* toward the good, and the quiet rhythm of time will bring it to fullfillment. You will have given it this direction if, by your teaching, you have elevated its thoughts to the necessary and the eternal, if, by your actions and your creations, you have transformed the necessary and the eternal into an object of the heart's desire. The edifice of error and caprice will fall—it must fall, indeed it has already fallen—from the moment you are certain that it is on the point of giving way. But it is in man's inner being that it must give way, not just in the externals he presents to the world. It is in the modest sanctuary of your heart that you must rear victorious truth, and project it out of yourself in the form of beauty, so that not only thought can pay it homage, but sense, too, lay loving hold on its appearance. And lest you should find yourself receiving from the world as it is the model you yourself should be providing, do not venture into its equivocal company without first being sure that you bear within your own heart an escort from the world of the ideal. Live with your century; but do not be its creature. Work for your contemporaries; but create what they need, not what they praise. Without sharing their guilt, yet share with noble resignation in their punishment, and bow your head freely beneath the yoke that they find as difficult to dispense with as to bear. By the steadfast courage with which you disdain their good fortune, you will show them that it is not through cowardice that you consent to share their sufferings. Think of them as they ought to be, when called upon to influence them; think of them as they are, when tempted to act on their behalf. In seeking their approval appeal to what is best in them, but in devising their happiness recall them as they are at their worst; then your own nobility will awaken theirs, and their unworthiness not defeat your purpose. The seriousness of your principles will frighten them away, but in the play of your semblance they will be prepared to tolerate them; for their taste is purer than their heart, and it is here that you must lay hold of the timorous fugitive. In vain will you assail their precepts, in vain condemn their practice; but on their leisure hours you can try your shaping hand. Banish from their pleasures caprice, frivolity, and coarseness, and imperceptibly you will banish these from their actions and, eventually, from their inclinations too. Surround them, wherever you meet them, with the great and noble forms of genius, and encompass them about with the symbols of perfection, until semblance conquer reality, and art triumph over nature.

Tenth Letter

You are, then, in agreement with me, and persuaded by the content of my previous letters, that man can deviate from his destiny in two quite different ways; that our own age is, in fact, moving along both these false roads, and has fallen a prey, on the one hand, to coarseness, on the other, to enervation and perversity. From this twofold straying it is to be brought back by means of beauty. But how can education through beauty counter both these opposite failings at one and the same time, and unite within itself two quite incompatible qualities? Can it enchain nature in the savage, and set it free in the barbarian? Can it at the same time tense and release? And if it does not really manage to do both, how can we reasonably expect it to effect anything so important as the education of mankind?

True, we are always being told, ad nauseam, that a developed feeling for beauty refines morals, so that this would not seem to stand in need of any further proof. People base this assumption on everyday experience, which almost always shows that clarity of mind, liveliness of feeling, graciousness, yes even dignity, of conduct, are linked with a cultivated taste, and their opposite for the most part with an uncultivated one. People invoke confidently enough the example of the most civilized of all the nations of antiquity, in whom the feeling for beauty at the same time reached its highest development, and the opposite example of those partly savage, partly barbaric, peoples, who paid for their insensitivity to beauty by a coarse, or at least austere, character. Nevertheless, it sometimes occurs to thinking minds either to deny this fact or at least to doubt the legitimacy of the conclusions drawn from it. They do not think quite so ill of that savagery with which primitive peoples are usually reproached, nor quite so well of that refinement for which the cultivated are commended. Even in antiquity there were men who were by no means so convinced that aesthetic culture is a boon and a blessing, and were hence more than inclined to refuse the arts of the imagination admission to their republic.

I do not refer to those who despise the Graces because they have never experienced their favor. Those who know no other criterion of value than the effort of earning or the tangible profit, how should they be capable of appreciating the unobtrusive effect of taste on the outward appearance and on the mind and character of men? How can they help shutting their eyes to the essential advantages of an aesthetic education in view of its incidental disadvantages? A man who has himself no form will despise any grace of speech as bribery and corruption, any elegance in social intercourse as hypocrisy, any delicacy or distinction of bearing as exaggeration and affectation. He cannot forgive the darling of the Graces for brightening every circle by his company, for swaying all minds to his purpose in the world of affairs, for perhaps, through his writings, leaving the impress of his mind upon the whole century—while he, poor victim of sheer application, can with all his knowledge command no interest, nor move so much as a stone from its place. Since he cannot learn from his fortunate rival the blessed secret of pleasing, he has no choice but to bewail the perversity of human nature that honors the appearance rather than the substance.

But there are voices worthy of respect raised against the effects of beauty, and armed against it with formidable arguments drawn from experience. "It cannot be denied," they say, "that the delights of the beautiful can, in the right hands, be made to serve laudable ends. But it is by no means contrary to its nature for it to have, in the wrong hands, quite the opposite effect, and to put its soul-seducing power at the service of error and injustice. Just because taste is always concerned with form, and never with content, it finally induces in the mind a dangerous tendency to neglect reality altogether, and to sacrifice truth and morality to the alluring dress in which they appear. All substantial difference between things is lost, and appearance alone determines their worth. How many men of talent," they continue, "are not deflected by the seductive power of beauty from serious and strenuous effort, or at least misled into treating it lightly? How many of feeble intelligence are not in conflict with the social order just because the fancy of poets was pleased to present a world in which everything proceeds quite differently, in which no conventions fetter opinion, and no artifice suppresses nature? What dangerous dialectics have the passions not learned since, in the portrayals of the poets, they have been made to flaunt themselves in brilliant colors and, when in conflict with laws and duties, usually been left masters of the field? What has society profited from letting beauty prescribe the laws of social intercourse, which formerly were regulated by truth, or outward impression determine the respect that should attach to merit alone? It is true we now see all those virtues flourishing whose appearance creates a pleasing impression and confers social prestige; but, as against this, every kind of excess, too, is rampant, and every vice in vogue that is compatible with a fair exterior." And indeed it must give pause for reflection that in almost every historical epoch in which the arts flourish, and taste prevails, we find humanity at a low ebb, and cannot point to a single instance of a high degree and wide diffusion of aesthetic culture going hand in hand with political freedom and civic virtue, fine manners with good morals, refinement of conduct with truth of conduct.

As long as Athens and Sparta maintained their independence, and respect for laws served as the basis of their constitution, taste was as yet immature, art still in its infancy, and beauty far from ruling over the hearts of men. It is true that the art of poetry had already soared to sublime heights; but only on the wings of that kind of genius that we know to be closely akin to the primitive, a light wont to shine in the darkness, and evidence, therefore, against the taste of the time rather than for it. When, under Pericles and Alexander, the golden age of the arts arrived, and the rule of taste extended its sway, the strength and freedom of Greece are no longer to be found. Rhetoric falsified truth, wisdom gave offense in the mouth of a Socrates, and virtue in the life of a Phocion. The Romans, as we know, had first to exhaust their strength in the civil wars and, enervated by oriental luxury, to bow beneath the yoke of a successful ruler, before Greek art can be seen triumphing over the rigidity of their character. Nor did the light of culture dawn among the Arabs until the vigor of their warlike spirit had languished under the scepter of the Abbassids. In modern Italy the fine arts did not appear until after the glorious Lombard League was destroyed, Florence subjected to the Medicis, and in all the vigorous city-states the spirit of independence had made way for an inglorious submission. It is almost superfluous to recall the example of modern nations whose refinement increased as their independence declined. Wherever we turn our eyes in past history we find taste and freedom shunning each other, and beauty founding her sway solely upon the decline and fall of heroic virtues.

And yet it is precisely this energy of character, at whose expense aesthetic culture is commonly purchased, which is the mainspring of all that is great and excellent in man, and the lack of which no other advantage, however great, can repair. If, then, we only heed what past experience has to teach us about the influence of beauty, there is certainly no encouragement to develop feelings that are so much of a threat to the true civilization of man; and even at the risk of coarseness and harshness we shall prefer to dispense with the melting power of beauty, rather than see ourselves, with all the advantages of refinement, delivered up to her enervating influence. But perhaps *experience* is not the judgement seat before which such an issue as this can be decided. And before any weight can be attached to her evidence, it would first have to be established beyond all doubt that the beauty of which we are speaking, and the beauty against which those examples from history testify, are one and the same. But this seems to presuppose a concept of beauty derived from a source other than experience, since by means of it we are to decide whether that which in experience we call beautiful is justly entitled to the name.

This pure *rational concept* of beauty, if such could be found, would therefore—since it cannot be derived from any actual case, but rather itself corrects and regulates our judgment of every actual case—have to be discovered by a process of abstraction, and deduced from the sheer potentialities of our sensuo-rational nature. In a single word, beauty would have to be shown to be a necessary condition of human being. From now on, then, we must lift our thoughts to the pure concept of human nature; and since experience never shows us human nature as such, but only individual human beings in individual situations, we must endeavor to discover from all these individual and changing manifestations that which is absolute and unchanging, and, by the rejection of all contingent limitations, apprehend the necessary conditions of their existence. True, this transcendental way will lead us out of the familiar circle of phenomenal existence, away from the living presence of things, and cause us to tarry for a while upon the barren and naked land of abstractions. But we are, after all, struggling for a firm basis of knowledge that nothing shall shake. And he who never ventures beyond actuality will never win the prize of truth.

Eleventh Letter

When abstraction rises to the highest level it can possibly attain, it arrives at two ultimate concepts before which it must halt and recognize that here it has reached its limits. It distinguishes in man something that endures and something that constantly changes. That which endures it calls his *person,* that which changes, his *condition.*

Person and condition—the self and its determining attributes—which in the absolute being we think of as one and the same, are in the finite being eternally two. Amid all persistence of the person, the condition changes; amid all the changes of condition, the person persists. We pass from rest to activity, from passion to indifference, from agreement to contradiction; but *we* remain, and what proceeds directly from *us* remains too. In the absolute subject alone do all its determining attributes persist *with* the personality, since all of them proceed *from* the personality. *What* the Godhead is, and all that it is, it is just *because* it is. It is consequently everything for all eternity, because it is eternal.

Since in man, as finite being, person and condition are distinct, the condition can neither be grounded upon the person, nor the person upon the condition. Were the latter the case, the person would have to change; were the former the case, the condition would have to persist; hence, in each case, either the personality or the finiteness cease to be. Not because we think, will, or feel, do we exist; and not because we exist, do we think, will, or feel. We are because we are; we feel, think, and will, because outside of ourselves something other than ourselves exists too.

The person therefore must be its own ground; for what persists cannot proceed from what changes. And so we would, in the first place, have the idea of absolute being grounded upon itself, that is to say, *freedom*. The condition, on the other hand, must have a ground other than itself; it must, since it does not owe its existence to the person, i.e., is not absolute, *proceed from* something. And so we would, in the second place, have the condition of all contingent being or becoming, that is to say, *time*. "Time is the condition of all becoming" is an identical proposition, for it does nothing but assert that "succession is the condition of things succeeding one upon another."

The person, which manifests itself in the eternally persisting "I," and only in this, cannot become, cannot have a beginning in time. The reverse is rather the case; time must have its beginning in the person, since something constant must form the basis of change. For change to take place, there must be something that changes; this something cannot therefore itself be change. If we say "the flower blooms and fades," we make the flower the constant in this transformation, and endow it, as it were, with a person, in which these two conditions become manifest. To say that man has first to become, is no objection; for man is not just person pure and simple, but person situated in a particular condition. Every condition, however, every determinate existence, has its origins in time; and so man, as a phenomenal being, must also have a beginning, although the pure intelligence within him is eternal. Without time, that is to say, without becoming, he would never be a determinate being; his personality would indeed exist potentially, but not in fact. It is only through the succession of its perceptions that the enduring "I" ever becomes aware of itself as a phenomenon.

The material of activity, therefore, or the reality which the supreme intelligence creates out of itself, man has first to *receive;*

and he does in fact receive it, by way of perception, as something existing outside of him in space, and as something changing within him in time. This changing material within him is accompanied by his never-changing "I"—and to remain perpetually himself throughout all change, to convert all that he apprehends into experience, i.e., to organize it into a unity that has significance, and to transform all his modes of existence in time into a law for all times: this is the injunction laid upon him by his rational nature. Only inasmuch as he changes does he *exist;* only inasmuch as he remains unchangeable does *he* exist. Man, imagined in his perfection, would therefore be the constant unity that remains eternally itself amidst the floods of change.

Now although an infinite being, a Godhead, cannot *become,* we must surely call divine any tendency that has as its unending task the realization of that most characteristic attribute of Godhead, viz., absolute manifestation of potential (the actualization of all that is possible), and absolute unity of manifestation (the necessity of all that is made actual). A disposition to the divine man does indubitably carry within him, in his personality; the way to the divine (if we can call a way that which never leads to the goal) is opened up to him through the *senses.*

His personality, considered for itself alone, and independently of all sense material, is merely the predisposition to a possible expression of his infinite nature; and as long as he has neither perceptions nor sensations, he is nothing but form and empty potential. His sensuous nature, considered for itself alone, and apart from any spontaneous activity of the mind, can do no more than reduce him, who without it is nothing but form, into matter, but can in no wise bring it about that he becomes conjoined with matter. As long as he merely feels, merely desires and acts upon mere desire, he is as yet nothing but *world,* if by this term we understand nothing but the formless content of time. True, it is his sensuous nature alone that can turn this potential into actual power; but it is only his personality that makes all his actual activity into something that is inalienably his own. In order, therefore, not to be mere world, he must impart form to matter; in order not to be mere form, he must give reality to the predisposition he carries within him. He gives reality to form when he brings time into being, when he confronts changelessness with change, the eternal unity of his own self with the manifold variety of the world. He gives form to matter when he annuls time again, when he affirms persistence within change, and subjugates the manifold variety of the world to the unity of his own self.

From this there proceed two contrary challenges to man, the two fundamental laws of his sensuo-rational nature. The first insists upon absolute *reality:* he is to turn everything that is mere form into world, and make all his potentialities fully manifest. The second insists upon absolute *formality:* he is to destroy everything in himself that is mere world, and bring harmony into all his changes. In other words, he is to externalize all that is within him, and give form to all that is outside him. Both these tasks, conceived in their highest fulfillment, lead us back to that concept of Godhead from which I started.

Twelfth Letter

Toward the accomplishment of this twofold task—of giving reality to the necessity *within,* and subjecting to the law of necessity the reality *without*—we are impelled by two opposing forces which, since they drive us to the realization of their object, may aptly be termed drives. The first of these, which I will call the *sensuous* drive, proceeds from the physical existence of man, or his sensuous nature. Its business is to set him within the limits of time, and to turn him into matter—not to provide him with matter, since that, of course, would presuppose a free activity of the person capable of receiving such matter, and distinguishing it from the self as from that which persists. By matter in this context we understand nothing more than change, or reality that occupies time. Consequently this drive demands that there shall be change, that time shall have a content. This state, which is nothing but time occupied by content, is called sensation, and it is through this alone that physical existence makes itself known.

Since everything that exists in time exists as a *succession,* the very fact of something existing at all means that everything else is excluded. When we strike a note on an instrument, only this single note, of all those it is capable of emitting, is actually realized; when man is sensible of the present, the whole infinitude of his possible determinations is confined to this single mode of his being. Wherever, therefore, this drive functions exclusively, we inevitably find the highest degree of limitation. Man in this state is nothing but a unit of quantity, an occupied moment of time—or rather, *he* is not at all, for his personality is suspended as long as he is ruled by sensation, and swept along by the flux of time.*

The domain of this drive embraces the whole extent of man's finite being. And since form is never made manifest except in some material, nor the absolute except through the medium of limitation, it is indeed to this sensuous drive that the whole of man's phenomenal existence is ultimately tied. But although it is this drive alone that awakens and develops the potentialities of man, it is also this drive alone that makes their complete fulfillment impossible. With indestructible chains it binds the ever-soaring spirit to the world of sense, and summons abstraction from its most unfettered excursions into the infinite back to the limitations of the present. Thought may indeed escape it for the moment, and a firm will triumphantly resist its demands; but suppressed nature soon resumes her rights, and presses for reality of existence, for some content to our knowing and some purpose for our doing.

The second of the two drives, which we may call the *formal drive,* proceeds from the absolute existence of man, or from his rational nature, and is intent on giving him the freedom to bring harmony into the diversity of his manifestations, and to affirm his person among all his changes of condition. Since this person, being an absolute and indivisible unity, can never be at variance with

* For this condition of self-loss under the dominion of feeling linguistic usage has the very appropriate expression: *to be beside oneself,* i.e., to be outside of one's own self. Although this turn of phrase is only used when sensation is intensified into passion, and the condition becomes more marked by being prolonged, it can nevertheless be said that everyone is beside himself as long as he does nothing but feel. To return from this condition to self-possession is termed, equally aptly: *to be oneself again,* i.e., to return into one's own self, to restore one's person. Of someone who has fainted, by contrast, we do not say that he is beside himself, but that he is *away from himself,* i.e., he has been rapt away from his self, whereas in the former case he is merely not in his self. Consequently, someone who has come out of a faint has merely *come to himself,* which state is perfectly compatible with being beside oneself.

itself, *since we are to all eternity we ourselves,* that drive that insists on affirming the personality can never demand anything but that which is binding upon it to all eternity; hence it decides forever as it decides for this moment, and commands for this moment what it commands for ever. Consequently it embraces the whole sequence of time, which is as much as to say: it annuls time and annuls change. It wants the real to be necessary and eternal, and the eternal and the necessary to be real. In other words, it insists on truth and on the right.

If the first drive only furnishes *cases,* this second one gives *laws*—laws for every judgment, where it is a question of knowledge, laws for every will, where it is a question of action. Whether it is a case of knowing an object, i.e., of attributing objective validity to a condition of our subject, or of acting upon knowledge, i.e., of making an objective principle the determining motive of our condition—in both cases we wrest this our condition from the jurisdiction of time, and endow it with reality for all men and all times, that is with universality and necessity. Feeling can only say: this is true *for this individual* and *at this moment,* and another moment, another individual, can come along and revoke assertions made thus under the impact of momentary sensation. But once thought pronounces; *that is,* it decides for ever and aye, and the validity of its verdict is guaranteed by the personality itself, which defies all change. Inclination can only say: this is good for *you as an individual* and for *your present need;* but your individuality and your present need will be swept away by change, and what you now so ardently desire will one day become the object of your aversion. But once the moral feeling says: *this shall be,* it decides forever and aye—once you confess truth because it is truth, and practice justice because it is justice, then you have made an individual case into a law for all cases, and treated one moment of your life as if it were eternity.

Where, then, the formal drive holds sway, and the pure object acts within us, we experience the greatest enlargement of being: all limitations disappear, and from the mere unit of quantity to which the poverty of his senses reduced him, man has raised himself to *a unity of ideas* embracing the whole realm of phenomena. During this operation we are no longer in time; time, with its whole never-ending succession, is in us. We are no longer individuals; we are species. The judgment of all minds is expressed through our own, the choice of all hearts is represented by our action.

Thirteenth Letter

At first sight nothing could seem more diametrically opposed than the tendencies of these two drives, the one pressing for change, the other for changelessness. And yet it is these two drives that between them, exhaust our concept of humanity, and make a third *fundamental drive* that might possibly reconcile the two a completely unthinkable concept. How, then, are we to restore the unity of human nature that seems to be utterly destroyed by this primary and radical opposition?

It is true that their *tendencies* do indeed conflict with each other, but—and this is the point to note—not in *the same objectives,* and things that never make contact cannot collide. The sensuous drive does indeed demand change; but it does not demand the extension of this to the person and its domain, does not demand a change of principles. The formal drive insists on unity and persistence—but it does not require the condition to be stabilized as well as the person, does not require identity of sensation. The two are, therefore, not by nature opposed; and if they nevertheless seem to be so, it is because they have become opposed through a wanton transgression of nature, through mistaking their nature and function, and confusing their spheres of operation.* To watch over these,

*1. Once you postulate a primary, and therefore necessary, antagonism between these two drives, there is, of course, no other means of maintaining unity in man than by unconditionally *subordinating* the sensuous drive to the rational. From this, however, only uniformity can result, never harmony, and man goes on forever being divided. Subordination there must, of course, be; but it must be reciprocal. For even though it is true that limitation can never be the source of the absolute, and hence freedom never be dependent upon time, it is no less certain that the absolute can of itself never be the source of limitation, or a condition in time be dependent upon freedom. Both principles are, therefore, at once subordinated to each other and coordinated with each other, that is to say, they stand in reciprocal relation to one another: without form no matter, and without matter no form. (This concept of reciprocal action, and its fundamental importance, is admirably set forth in Fichte's *Fundaments of the Theory of Knowledge*, Leipzig, 1794). How things stand with the person in the realm of ideas we frankly do not know; but that it can never become manifest in the realm of time without taking on matter, of that we are certain. In this realm, therefore, matter will have some say, and not merely in a role *subordinate* to form, but also *coordinate* with it and independently of it. Neces-

and secure for each of these two drives its proper frontiers, is the task of *culture,* which is, therefore, in duty bound to do justice to both drives equally: not simply to maintain the rational against the sensuous, but the sensuous against the rational too. Hence its business is twofold: *first,* to preserve the life of sense against the encroachments of freedom; and *second,* to secure the personality against the forces of sensation. The former it achieves by developing our capacity for feeling, the latter by developing our capacity for reason.

Since the world is extension in time, i.e., change, the perfection of that faculty that connects man with the world will have to consist in maximum changeability and maximum extensity. Since the person is persistence within change, the perfection of that faculty that is to oppose change will have to be maximum autonomy and maximum intensity. The more facets his receptivity develops, the more labile it is, and the more surface it presents to phenomena, so much more world does man *apprehend,* and all the more potentialities does he develop in himself. The more power and depth the personality achieves, and the more freedom reason attains, so much more world does man *comprehend,* and all the more form does he create outside of himself. His education will therefore consist, *firstly,* in procuring for the receptive faculty the most manifold contacts with the world, and, within the purview of feeling, intensifying passivity to the utmost; *secondly,* in securing for the determining faculty the highest degree of independence from the receptive, and, within the purview of reason, intensifying activity to the utmost. Where both these aptitudes are conjoined, man will combine the greatest fullness of existence with the highest auton-

---

sary as it may be, therefore, that feeling should have no say in the realm of reason, it is no less necessary that reason should not presume to have a say in the realm of feeling. Just by assigning to each of them its own sphere, we are by that very fact excluding the other from it, and setting bounds to each, bounds that can only be transgressed *at the risk of detriment to both.*

2. In the transcendental method of philosophizing, where everything depends on clearing form of content, and obtaining necessity in its pure state, free of all admixture with the contingent, one easily falls into thinking of material things as nothing but an obstacle, and of imagining that our sensuous nature, just because it happens to be a hindrance in *this* operation, must of necessity be in conflict with reason. Such a way of thinking is, it is true, wholly alien to the *spirit of* the Kantian system, but it may very well be found in the *letter* of it.

omy and freedom, and instead of losing himself to the world, will rather draw the latter into himself in all its infinitude of phenomena, and subject it to the unity of his reason.

But man can turn these relations *upside down,* and thus miss his destiny in two different ways. He can transfer the intensity required by the active function to the passive, let his sensuous drive encroach upon the formal, and make the receptive faculty do the work of the determining one. Or he can assign to the active function that extensity that is proper to the passive, let the formal drive encroach upon the sensuous, and substitute the determining faculty for the receptive one. In the first case he will never be *himself;* in the second he will never be *anything else*; and for that very reason, therefore, he will in both cases be *neither the one nor the other,* consequently—a nonentity.*

---

*1. The pernicious effect, upon both thought and action, of an undue surrender to our sensual nature will be evident to all. Not quite so evident, although just as common, and no less important, is the nefarious influence exerted upon our knowledge and upon our conduct by a preponderance of rationality. Permit me therefore to recall, from the great number of relevant instances, just two that may serve to throw light upon the damage caused when the functions of thought and will encroach upon those of intuition and feeling.

2. One of the chief reasons why our natural sciences make such slow progress is obviously the universal, and almost uncontrollable, propensity to teleological judgments, in which, once they are used constitutively, the determining faculty is substituted for the receptive. However strong and however varied the impact made upon our organs by nature, all her manifold variety is then entirely lost upon us, because we are seeking nothing in her but what we have put into her; because, instead of letting her come *in upon us,* we are thrusting ourselves *out upon her* with all the impatient anticipations of our reason. If, then, in the course of centuries, it should happen that a man tries to approach her with his sense organs untroubled, innocent and wide open, and, thanks to this, should chance upon a multitude of phenomena that we, with our tendency to prejudge the issue, have overlooked, then we are mightily astonished that so many eyes in such broad daylight should have noticed nothing. This premature hankering after harmony before we have even got together the individual sounds that are to go to its making, this violent usurping of authority by ratiocination in a field where its right to give orders is by no means unconditional, is the reason why so many thinking minds fail to have any fruitful effect upon the advancement of science; and it would be difficult to say which has done more harm to the progress of knowledge: a sense faculty unamenable to form, or a reasoning faculty that will not stay for a content.

3. It would be no less difficult to determine which does more to impede the practice of brotherly love: the violence of our passions, which disturbs it, or the rigidity of our principles, which chills it—the egotism of our senses or the egotism of our reason. If we are to become compassionate, helpful, effective human beings, feeling and character must unite, even as wide-open senses must combine with vigor

For if the sensuous drive becomes the determining one, that is to say, if the senses assume the role of legislator and the world suppresses the person, then the world ceases to be an object precisely to the extent that it becomes a force. From the moment that man is merely a content of time, he ceases to exist, and *has* in consequence no content either. With his personality his condition, too, is annulled, because these two concepts are reciprocally related—because change demands a principle of permanence, and finite reality an infinite reality. If, on the other hand, the formal drive becomes receptive, that is to say, if thought forestalls feeling and the person supplants the world, then the person ceases to be autonomous force and subject precisely to the extent that it forces its way into the place of the object—because, in order to become manifest, the principle of permanence requires change, and absolute reality has need of limitation. From the moment that man *is* only form, he ceases to *have* a form; the annulling of his condition, consequently, involves that of his person too. In a single word, only

---

of intellect if we are to acquire experience. How can we, however laudable our precepts, how can we be just, kindly, and human toward others, if we lack the power of receiving into ourselves, faithfully and truly, natures unlike ours, of feeling our way into the situation of others, of making other people's feelings our own? But in the education we receive, no less than in that we give ourselves, this power gets repressed in exactly the measure that we seek to break the force of passions, and strengthen character by means of principles. Since it costs effort to remain true to one's principles when feeling is easily stirred, we take the easier way out and try to make character secure by blunting feeling; for it is, of course, infinitely easier to have peace and quiet from an adversary you have disarmed than to master a spirited and active foe. And this, for the most part, is the operation that is meant when people speak of *forming character;* and that, even in the best sense of the word, where it implies the cultivation of the inner, and not merely of the outer man. A man so formed will, without doubt, be immune from the danger of being crude nature or of appearing as such; but he will at the same time be armored by principle against all natural feeling, and be equally inaccessible to the claims of humanity *from without* as he is to those of humanity *from within.*

4. It is a most pernicious abuse of the ideal of perfection, to apply it in all its rigor, either in our judgments of other people, or in those cases where we have to act on their behalf. The former leads to sentimental idealism; the latter to hardness and coldness of heart. We certainly make our duty to society uncommonly easy for ourselves by mentally substituting for the *actual* man who claims our help the *ideal* man who could in all probability help himself. Severity with one's self combined with leniency toward others is a sign of the truly excellent character. But mostly the man who is lenient to others will also be lenient to himself; and he who is severe with himself will be the same with others. To be lenient to oneself and severe toward others is the most contemptible character of all.

inasmuch as he is autonomous, is there reality outside him and is he receptive to it; and only inasmuch as he is receptive, is there reality within him and is he a thinking force.

Both drives, therefore, need to have limits set to them and, inasmuch as they can be thought of as energies, need to be relaxed; the sense drive so that it does not encroach upon the domain of law, the formal drive so that it does not encroach on that of feeling. But the relaxing of the sense drive must in no wise be the result of physical impotence or blunted feeling, which never merits anything but contempt. It must be an act of free choice, an activity of the person that, by its moral intensity, moderates that of the senses and, by mastering impressions, robs them of their depth only in order to give them increased surface. It is character that must set bounds to temperament, for it is *only to profit the mind* that sense may go short. In the same way the relaxing of the formal drive must not be the result of spiritual impotence or flabbiness of thought or will; for this would only degrade man. It must, if it is to be at all praiseworthy, spring from abundance of feeling and sensation. Sense herself must, with triumphant power, remain mistress of her own domain, and resist the violence that the mind, by its usurping tactics, would fain inflict upon her. In a single word: personality must keep the sensuous drive within its proper bounds, and receptivity, or nature, must do the same with the formal drive.

Fourteenth Letter

We have now been led to the notion of a reciprocal action between the two drives, reciprocal action of such a kind that the activity of the one both gives rise to, and sets limits to, the activity of the other, and in which each in itself achieves its highest manifestation precisely by reason of the other being active.

Such reciprocal relation between the two drives is, admittedly, but a task enjoined upon us by reason, a problem that man is only capable of solving completely in the perfect consummation of his existence. It is, in the most precise sense of the word, *the idea of his human nature,* hence something infinite, to which in the course of time he can approximate ever more closely, but without ever being able to reach it. "He is not to strive for form at the cost of reality, nor for reality at the cost of form; rather is he to seek absolute being by means of a determinate being, and a determinate being by means of infinite being. He is to set up a world over against himself because he is person, and he is to be person because a world stands over against him. He is to feel because he is conscious of himself, and be conscious of himself because he feels."— That he does actually conform to this idea, that he is consequently, in the fullest sense of the word, a human being, is never brought home to him as long as he satisfies only one of these two drives to the exclusion of the other, or only satisfies them one after the other. For as long as he only feels, his person, or his absolute existence, remains a mystery to him; and as long as he only thinks, his existence in time, or his condition, does likewise. Should there, however, be cases in which he were to have this twofold experience *simultaneously,* in which he were to be at once conscious of his freedom and sensible of his existence, were, at one and the same time, to feel himself matter and come to know himself as mind, then he would in such cases, and in such cases only, have a complete intuition of his human nature, and the object that afforded him this vision would become for him a symbol of his *accomplished destiny* and, in consequence (since that is only to be attained in the totality of time), serve him as a manifestation of the infinite.

Assuming that cases of this sort could actually occur in experience, they would awaken in him a new drive that, precisely because the other two drives cooperate within it, would be opposed to each of them considered separately and could justifiably count as a new drive. The sense drive demands that there shall be change and that time shall have a content; the form drive demands that time shall be annulled and that there shall be no change. That drive, therefore, in which both the others work in concert (permit me for the time being, until I have justified the term, to call it the *play drive*), the play drive, therefore, would be directed toward annulling time *within time,* reconciling becoming with absolute being and change with identity.

The sense drive wants to *be* determined, wants to receive its object; the form drive wants *itself* to determine, wants to bring forth its object. The play drive, therefore, will endeavor so to receive as if it had itself brought forth, and so to bring forth as the intuitive sense aspires to receive.

The sense drive excludes from its subject all autonomy and freedom; the form drive excludes from its subject all dependence, all passivity. Exclusion of freedom, however, implies physical necessity, exclusion of passivity moral necessity. Both drives, therefore, exert constraint upon the psyche; the former through the laws of nature, the latter through the laws of reason. The play drive, in consequence, as the one in which both the others act in concert, will exert upon the psyche at once a moral and a physical constraint; it will, therefore, since it annuls all contingency, annul all constraint too, and set man free both physically and morally. When we embrace with passion someone who deserves our contempt, we are painfully aware of the *compulsion of nature*. When we feel hostile toward another who compels our esteem, we are painfully aware of the *compulsion of reason*. But once he has at the same time engaged our affection and won our esteem, then both the compulsion of feeling and the compulsion of reason disappear and we begin to love him, i.e., we begin to play with both our affection and our esteem.

Since, moreover, the sense drive exerts a physical, the form drive a moral constraint, the first will leave our formal, the second our material disposition at the mercy of the contingent; that is to say, it is a matter of chance whether our happiness will coincide with our perfection or our perfection with our happiness. The play drive, in consequence, in which both work in concert, will make our formal as well as our material disposition, our perfection as well as our happiness, contingent. It will therefore, just because it makes *both* contingent and because with all constraint all contingency too disappears, abolish contingency in both, and, as a result, introduce form into matter and reality into form. To the extent that it deprives feelings and passions of their dynamic power, it will bring them into harmony with the ideas of reason; and to the extent that it deprives the laws of reason of their moral compulsion, it will reconcile them with the interests of the senses.

Fifteenth Letter

I am drawing ever nearer the goal toward which I have been leading you by a not exactly encouraging path. If you will consent to follow me a few steps further along it, horizons all the wider will unfold and a pleasing prospect perhaps requite you for the labor of the journey.

The object of the sense drive, expressed in a general concept, we call *life,* in the widest sense of the term: a concept designating all material being and all that is immediately present to the senses. The object of the form drive, expressed in a general concept, we call *form,* both in the figurative and in the literal sense of this word: a concept that includes all the formal qualities of things and all the relations of these to our thinking faculties. The object of the play drive, represented in a general schema, may therefore be called *living form:* a concept serving to designate all the aesthetic qualities of phenomena and, in a word, what in the widest sense of the term we call *beauty.*

According to this explanation, if such it be, the term *beauty* is neither extended to cover the whole realm of living things nor is it merely confined to this realm. A block of marble, though it is and remains lifeless, can nevertheless, thanks to the architect or the sculptor, become living form; and a human being, though he may live and have form, is far from being on that account a living form. In order to be so, his form would have to be life, and his life form. As long as we merely think about his form, it is lifeless, a mere abstraction; as long as we merely feel his life, it is formless, a mere impression. Only when his form lives in our feeling and his life takes on form in our understanding, does he become living form; and this will always be the case whenever we adjudge him beautiful.

But because we know how to specify the elements that when combined produce beauty, this does not mean that its genesis has as yet in any way been explained; for that would require us to understand *the actual manner of their combining,* and this, like all reciprocal action between finite and infinite, remains for ever inaccessible to our probing. Reason, on transcendental grounds, makes the following demand: let there be a bond of union between the form drive and the material drive; that is to say, let there be a play drive, since only the union of reality with form, contingency with necessity, passivity with freedom, makes the concept of human nature complete. Reason must make this demand because it is reason—because it is its nature to insist on perfection and on the abolition of all limitation, and because any exclusive activity on the part of either the one drive or the other leaves human nature incomplete and gives rise to some limitation within it. Consequently, as soon as reason utters the pronouncement: let humanity exist, it has by that very pronouncement also promulgated the law: let there be beauty. Experience can provide an answer to the question *whether* there is such a thing as beauty, and we shall know the answer once experience has taught us whether there is such a thing as humanity. But *how* there can be beauty, and how humanity is possible, neither reason nor experience can tell us.

Man, as we know, is neither exclusively matter nor exclusively mind. Beauty, as the consummation of his humanity, can therefore be neither exclusively life nor exclusively form. Not mere life, as acute observers, adhering too closely to the testimony of experience, have maintained, and to which the taste of our age would fain degrade it; not mere form, as it has been adjudged by philosophers whose speculations led them too far away from experience, or by artists who, philosophizing on beauty, let themselves be too exclusively guided by the needs of their craft.* It is the object common to both drives, that is to say, the object of the play-drive. This term is fully justified by linguistic usage, which is wont to designate as "play" everything that is neither subjectively nor objectively contingent, and yet imposes no kind of constraint either from within or from without. Since, in contemplation of the beautiful, the psyche finds itself in a happy medium between the realm of law and the sphere of physical exigency, it is, precisely because it is divided between the two, removed from the constraint of the one as of the other. The material drive, like the formal drive, is wholly *earnest* in its demands; for, in the sphere of knowledge, the former is concerned with the reality, the latter with the necessity of things; while in the sphere of action, the first is directed toward the preservation of life, the second toward the maintenance of dignity: both, therefore, toward truth and toward perfection. But

* Burke, in his *Philosophical Enquiry into the Origin of Our Ideas of the Sublime and the Beautiful,* makes beauty into mere life. As far as I know, every adherent of *dogmatic* philosophy, who has ever confessed his belief on this subject, makes it into mere form: among artists, Raphael Mengs, in his *Reflections on Taste in Painting,* not to speak of others. In this, as in everything else, *critical* philosophy has opened up the way whereby empiricism can be led back to principles, and speculation back to experience.

life becomes of less consequence once human dignity enters in, and duty ceases to be a constraint once inclination exerts its pull; similarly our psyche accepts the reality of things, or material truth, with greater freedom and serenity once this latter encounters formal truth, or the law of necessity, and no longer feels constrained by abstraction once this can be accompanied by the immediacy of intuition. In a word: by entering into association with ideas all reality loses its earnestness because it then becomes *of small account;* and by coinciding with feeling necessity divests itself of its earnestness because it then becomes *of light weight.*

But, you may long have been tempted to object, is beauty not degraded by being made to consist of mere play and reduced to the level of those frivolous things that have always borne this name? Does it not belie the rational concept as well as the dignity of beauty—which is, after all, here being considered as an instrument of culture—if we limit it to *mere play?* And does it not belie the empirical concept of play—a concept that is, after all, entirely compatible with the exclusion of all taste—if we limit it merely to beauty?

But how can we speak of *mere* play, when we know that it is precisely play and play *alone,* which of all man's states and conditions is the one that makes him whole and unfolds both sides of his nature at once? What you, according to your idea of the matter, call *limitation,* I, according to mine—which I have justified by proof—call *expansion.* I, therefore, would prefer to put it exactly the opposite way round and say: the agreeable, the good, the perfect, with these man is *merely* in earnest; but with beauty he plays. True, we must not think here of the various forms of play that are in vogue in actual life, and are usually directed to very material objects. But then in actual life we should also seek in vain for the kind of beauty with which we are here concerned. The beauty we find in actual existence is precisely what the play drive we find in actual existence deserves; but with the ideal of beauty that is set up by reason, an ideal of the play drive, too, is enjoined upon man, which he must keep before his eyes in all his forms of play.

We shall not go far wrong when trying to discover a man's ideal of beauty if we inquire how he satisfies his play drive. If at the Olympic Games the peoples of Greece delighted in the bloodless combats of strength, speed, and agility, and in the nobler rivalry of talents, and if the Roman people regaled themselves with the death throes of a vanquished gladiator or of his Libyan opponent, we can, from this single trait, understand why we seek the ideal forms of a Venus, a Juno, an Apollo, not in Rome, but in Greece.* Reason, however, declares: the beautiful is to be neither mere life, nor mere form, but living form, i.e., beauty; for it imposes upon man the double law of absolute formality and absolute reality. Consequently, reason also makes the pronouncement: with beauty man shall *only play,* and it is *with beauty only* that he shall play.

For, to mince matters no longer, man only plays when he is in the fullest sense of the word a human being, and *he is only fully a human being when he plays*. This proposition, which at the moment may sound like a paradox, will take on both weight and depth of meaning once we have got as far as applying it to the twofold earnestness of duty and of destiny. It will, I promise you, prove capable of bearing the whole edifice of the art of the beautiful, and of the still more difficult art of living. But it is, after all, only in philosophy that the proposition is unexpected; it was long ago alive and operative in the art and in the feeling of the Greeks, the most distinguished exponents of both; only they transferred to Olympus what was meant to be realized on earth. Guided by the truth of that same proposition, they banished from the brow of the blessed gods all the earnestness and efforts that furrow the cheeks of mortals, no less than the empty pleasures that preserve the smoothness of a vacuous face; freed those ever-contented beings from the bonds inseparable from every purpose, every duty, every care, and made *idleness* and *indifference* the enviable portion of divinity—merely a more human name for the freest, most sublime state of being. Both the material constraint of natural laws and the spiritual constraint of moral laws were resolved in their higher concept of necessity, which embraced both worlds at once; and it was only out of the perfect union of those two necessities

* If (to confine ourselves to the modern world) we compare horse racing in London, bullfights in Madrid, *spectacles* in the Paris of former days, the gondola races in Venice, animal baiting in Vienna, and the gay attractive life of the Corso in Rome, it will not be difficult to determine the different nuances of taste among these different peoples. However, there is far less uniformity among the amusements of the common people in these different countries than there is among those of the refined classes in those same countries, a fact that it is easy to account for.

that for them true freedom could proceed. Inspired by this spirit, the Greeks effaced from the features of their ideal physiognomy, together with *inclination,* every trace of *volition* too; or rather they made both indiscernible, for they knew how to fuse them in the most intimate union. It is not grace, nor is it yet dignity, which speaks to us from the superb countenance of a *Juno Ludovisi;* it is neither the one nor the other because it is both at once. While the woman-god demands our veneration, the godlike woman kindles our love; but even as we abandon ourselves in ecstasy to her heavenly grace, her celestial self-sufficiency makes us recoil in terror. The whole figure reposes and dwells in itself, a creation completely self-contained, and, as if existing beyond space, neither yielding nor resisting; here is no force to contend with force, no frailty where temporality might break in. Irresistibly moved and drawn by those former qualities, kept at a distance by these latter, we find ourselves at one and the same time in a state of utter repose and supreme agitation, and there results that wondrous stirring of the heart for which mind has no concept nor speech any name.

Sixteenth Letter

We have seen how beauty results from the reciprocal action of two opposed drives and from the uniting of two opposed principles. The highest ideal of beauty is, therefore, to be sought in the most perfect possible union and *equilibrium* of reality and form. This equilibrium, however, remains no more than an idea, which can never be fully realized in actuality. For in actuality we shall always be left with a preponderance of the one element over the other, and the utmost that experience can achieve will consist of an *oscillation* between the two principles, in which now reality, now form, will predominate. Beauty as idea, therefore, can never be other than one and indivisible, since there can never be more than one point of equilibrium; whereas beauty in experience will be eternally twofold, because oscillation can disturb the equilibrium in twofold fashion, inclining it now to the one side, now to the other.

I observed in one of the preceding letters—and it follows with strict necessity from the foregoing argument—that we must expect from beauty at once a releasing and a tensing effect: a *releasing* effect in order to keep both the sense drive and the form drive within proper bounds; a *tensing* effect, in order to keep both at full strength. Ideally speaking, however, these two effects must be reducible to a single effect. Beauty is to release by tensing both natures uniformly, and to tense by releasing both natures uniformly. This already follows from the concept of a reciprocal action, by virtue of which both factors necessarily condition each other and are at the same time conditioned by each other, and the purest product of which is beauty. But experience offers us no single example of such perfect reciprocal action; for here it will always happen that, to a greater or lesser degree, a preponderance entails a deficiency, and a deficiency a preponderance. What, then, in the case of ideal beauty is but a distinction that is *made* in the mind, is in the case of actual beauty a difference that *exists* in fact. Ideal beauty, though one and indivisible, exhibits under different aspects a melting as well as an energizing attribute; but in experience there actually *is* a melting and an energizing type of beauty. So it is, and so it always will be, in all those cases where the absolute is set within the limitations of time, and the ideas of reason have to be realized in and through human action. Thus man, when he reflects, can conceive of virtue, truth, happiness; but man, when he acts, can only practice *virtues*, comprehend *truths*, and enjoy *happy hours*. To refer these experiences back to those abstractions—to replace morals by morality, happy events by happiness, the facts of knowledge by knowledge itself—that is the business of physical and moral education. To make beauty out of a multiplicity of beautiful objects is the task of aesthetic education.

Energizing beauty can no more preserve man from a certain residue of savagery and hardness than melting beauty can protect him from a certain degree of effeminacy and enervation. For since the effect of the former is to brace his nature, both physical and moral, and to increase its elasticity and power of prompt reaction, it can happen all too easily that the increased resistance of temperament and character will bring about a decrease in receptivity to impressions; that our gentler humanity, too, will suffer the kind of repression that ought only to be directed at our brute nature, and our brute nature profit from an increase of strength that should only be available to our free person. That is why in periods of vigor and exuberance we find true grandeur of conception coupled with the gigantic and the extravagant, sublimity of thought with the most frightening explosions of passion; that is why in epochs of discipline and form we find nature as often suppressed as mastered, as often outraged as transcended. And because the effect of melting beauty is to relax our nature, physical and moral, it happens no less easily that energy of feeling is stifled along with violence of appetite, and that character too shares the loss of power that should only overtake passion. That is why in so-called refined epochs, we see gentleness not infrequently degenerating into softness, plainness into platitude, correctness into emptiness, liberality into arbitrariness, lightness of touch into frivolity, calmness into apathy, and the most despicable caricatures in closest proximity to the most splendid specimens of humanity. The man who lives under the constraint of either matter or forms is, therefore, in need of melting beauty; for he is moved by greatness and power long before he begins to be susceptible to harmony and grace. The man who lives under the indulgent sway of taste is in need of energizing beauty; for he is only too ready, once he has reached a state of sophisticated refinement, to trifle away the strength he brought with him from the state of savagery.

And now, I think, we have explained and resolved the discrepancy commonly met with in the judgments people make about the influence of beauty, and in the value they attach to aesthetic culture. The discrepancy is explained once we remember that, in experience, there are two types of beauty, and that both parties to the argument tend to make assertions about the whole genus that each of them is only in a position to prove about one particular species of it. And the discrepancy is resolved once we distinguish a twofold need in man to which that twofold beauty corresponds. Both parties will probably turn out to be right if they can only first agree among themselves which kind of beauty and which type of humanity each has in mind.

In the rest of my inquiry I shall, therefore, pursue the path that nature herself takes with man in matters aesthetic, and setting out from the two species of beauty move upwards to the generic concept of it. I shall examine the effects of melting beauty on those who are tensed, and the effects of energizing beauty on those who are relaxed, in order finally to dissolve both these contrary modes of beauty in the unity of ideal beauty, even as those two opposing types of human being are merged in the unity of ideal man.

Seventeenth Letter

As long as it was simply a question of deriving the generic idea of beauty from the concept of human nature as such, there was no need to recall any limitations of this latter other than those that derive directly from the essence of it, and are inseparable from the concept of finiteness. Unconcerned with any of the contingent limitations to which human nature may in actual experience be subject, we derived our notion of it directly from reason as the source of all necessity, and with the ideal of human nature the ideal of beauty was automatically given too.

Now, by contrast, we descend from this region of ideas on to the stage of reality, in order to encounter man in a definite and *determinate* state, that is to say, among limitations that are not inherent in the very notion of man but derive from outward circumstance and from the contingent use of his freedom. Yet whatever diversity of limitation the idea of human nature may undergo when made manifest in any particular human being, its components alone are enough to tell us that there are, broadly speaking, only *two,* contrasting, deviations from it that can possibly occur. For if man's perfection resides in the harmonious energy of his sensuous and spiritual powers, he can, in fact, only fall short of this perfection, either through lack of harmony or through lack of energy. So that even before we have heard the testimony of experience on this matter, we are already assured in advance by pure reason that we shall find actual, consequently limited, man either in a state of tension or in a state of relaxation, according as the one-sided activity of certain of his powers is disturbing the harmony of his being, or the unity of his nature is founded upon the uniform enfeeblement of his sensuous and spiritual powers. Both these contrasting types of limitation are, as I now propose to show, removed by beauty, which restores harmony to him who is overtensed, and energy to him who is relaxed, and thus, in accordance with its nature, brings the limited condition back to an absolute condition, and makes of man a whole perfect in itself.

Beauty in the world of reality thus in no way belies the idea we formed of it by way of speculation; only it has here far less of a free hand than it had there, where we were free to apply it to the pure concept of human nature. In man, as presented by experience, beauty encounters a material already vitiated and recalcitrant, which robs her of her *ideal* perfection precisely to the extent that it interposes its own *individual* characteristics. Beauty will, therefore, in actuality never show herself except as a particular and limited species, never as pure genus; she will in tense natures lay aside something of her freedom and variety, in relaxed natures something of her vivifying power. But we, who have by now become more familiar with her true nature, should not let ourselves be confused by such discrepancies in her appearance. Far from following the ordinary run of critics, who define the concept of beauty from their individual experience of it, and make *her* responsible for the imperfections displayed by man under her influence, we know that it is, on the contrary, man himself who transfers to her the imperfections of his own individuality, who by his subjective limitation perpetually stands in the way of her perfection, and reduces the absolute ideal to two limited types of manifestation.

Melting beauty, so it was maintained, is for natures that are tense; energizing beauty for those that are relaxed. I call a man tense when he is under the compulsion of thought, no less than when he is under the compulsion of feeling. *Exclusive* domination by either of his two basic drives is for him a state of constraint and violence, and freedom lies only in the cooperation of both his natures. The man one-sidedly dominated by feeling, or the sensuously tensed man, will be released and set free by means of form; the man one-sidedly dominated by law, or the spiritually tensed man, will be released and set free by means of matter. In order to be adequate to this twofold task, melting beauty will therefore reveal herself under two different guises. *First,* as tranquil form, she will assuage the violence of life, and pave the way that leads from sensation to thought. *Secondly,* as living image, she will arm abstract form with sensuous power, lead concept back to intuition, and law back to feeling. The first of these services she renders to natural man, the second to civilized man. But since in neither case does she have completely unconditional control over her human material, but is dependent on that offered her by either the formlessness of nature or the unnaturalness of civilization, she will in both cases still bear traces of her origins, and tend to lose herself, in the one case, more in material life, in the other, more in pure and abstract form.

In order to get some idea of how beauty can become a means of putting an end to that twofold tension, we must endeavor to seek its origins in the human psyche. Resign yourself therefore to one more brief sojourn in the sphere of speculation, in order thereafter to leave it for good, and proceed, with steps made all the more sure, over the terrain of experience.

Eighteenth Letter

By means of beauty sensuous man is led to form and thought; by means of beauty spiritual man is brought back to matter and restored to the world of sense.

From this it seems to follow that there must be a state midway between matter and form, passivity and activity, and that it is into this *middle* state that beauty transports us. This is, indeed, the idea of beauty that most people form for themselves once they have begun to reflect upon her operations, and all experience points to the same conclusion. But, on the other hand, nothing is more absurd and contradictory than such an idea, since the distance between matter and form, passivity and activity, feeling and thought, is *infinite,* and there exists nothing that can conceivably mediate between them. How, then, are we to resolve this contradiction? Beauty links the two opposite conditions of feeling and thinking; yet between these two there is absolutely no middle term. The former truth we know from experience; the latter is given to us directly by reason.

This precisely is the point on which the whole question of beauty must eventually turn. And if we succeed in solving this problem satisfactorily, we shall at the same time have found the thread that will guide us through the whole labyrinth of aesthetics.

But everything here depends on two completely distinct operations that, in the investigation we are about to undertake, must of necessity support one another. Beauty, it was said, unites two conditions that *are diametrically opposed* and can never become one. It is from this opposition that we have to start; and we must first grasp it, and acknowledge it, in all its unmitigated rigor, so that these two conditions are distinguished with the utmost precision; otherwise we shall only succeed in confusing but never in uniting them. In the second place, it was said, beauty *unites* these two opposed conditions and thus destroys the opposition. Since, however, both conditions remain everlastingly opposed to each other, there is no other way of uniting them except by destroying them. Our second task, therefore, is to make this union complete; and to do it with such unmitigated thoroughness that both these conditions totally disappear in a third without leaving any trace of division behind in the new whole that has been made; otherwise we shall only succeed in distinguishing but never in uniting them. All the disputes about the concept of beauty that have ever prevailed in the world of philosophy, and to some extent still prevail today, have no other source than this: either the investigation did not start with a sufficiently strict distinction, or it was not carried through to a pure and complete synthesis. Those among the philosophers who, in reflecting on this matter, entrust themselves blindly to the guidance of their *feeling,* can arrive at no *concept* of beauty, because in the totality of their sensuous impression of it they can distinguish no separate elements. Those others, who take intellect as their exclusive guide, can never arrive at any concept of *beauty,* because in the totality that constitutes it they can discern nothing else but the parts, so that spirit and matter, even when most perfectly fused, remain for them eternally distinct. The former are afraid that by separating what in their feeling is, after all, one and indivisible, they will destroy the *dynamic* of beauty, i.e., beauty as effective force. The latter are afraid that by subsuming under a single category what in their intellect is, after all, distinct, they will destroy the *logic* of beauty, i.e., beauty as concept. The former would like to think of beauty as it actually behaves; the latter would have it behave as it is actually thought. Both, therefore, are bound to miss the truth: the former because they would make the limitations of discursive understanding vie with the infinity of nature; the latter because they would limit the infinity of nature according to the laws of discursive understanding. The first are afraid that by a too rigorous dissection they will rob beauty of some measure of her freedom; the latter are afraid that by too audacious a synthesis they will destroy the precision of their concept. The former do not, however, reflect that the freedom, in which they rightly locate the essence of beauty, is not just lawlessness but rather harmony of laws, not arbitrariness but supreme inner necessity; the latter do not reflect that the exactitude which they, no less rightly, require of beauty, does not reside in the *exclusion of certain realities,* but in the *absolute inclusion of all realities;* that it is, therefore, not limitation but infinity. We shall avoid the rocks on which both have foundered if we start from the two elements into which beauty can be divided when considered by the intellect, but subsequently ascend to the pure aesthetic unity through which it works upon our feeling, and in which the two conditions previously described completely disappear.*

Nineteenth Letter

We can distinguish in man as such two different states of determinability, the one passive, the other active, and—corresponding to these—two states of passive and active determination. The explanation of this proposition will offer the shortest way of reaching our goal.

The condition of the human mind *before* it is determined by sense impressions at all, is one of unlimited determinability. The infinity of space and time is at the disposal of the imagination to do as it likes with. And since *ex hypothesi* nothing in this whole vast realm of the possible has yet been posited, and consequently nothing as yet excluded either, we may call this condition of complete absence of determination one of *empty infinity*—which is by no means to be confused with infinite emptiness.

Now comes the moment when sense is to be stirred, and out of the endless multiplicity of possible determinations one single one

* It will have occurred to any attentive reader of the comparison I have just made that the *sensationalist* aestheticians, who attach more weight to the testimony of feeling than to that of reasoning, are by no means so far removed from the truth *in practice* as their opponents, although they are no match for them *in perspicacity.* And this is the relation we always find between nature and systematic thought. Nature (sense and intuition) always unites, intellect always divides; but reason unites once more. Before he begins to philosophize, therefore, man is nearer to truth than the philosopher who has not yet completed his investigation. Hence we can, without further examination, declare a philosophical argument to be false if, *in its results,* it has the general feeling against it; but with equal justice we may consider it suspect if, in its form and method, it has this general feeling on its side. This latter consideration may serve to console any writer who finds himself unable to set forth a process of philosophical deduction, as many readers seem to expect, just as if it were a fireside chat; while with the former we may reduce to silence anyone who would fain found new systems at the expense of ordinary common sense.

is to achieve actuality. A perception is to be born in him. What in the preceding state of mere determinability was nothing but empty potential, now becomes an effective force and acquires a content. At the same time, however, as effective force, it has limits set to it, whereas, as mere potential, it was entirely without limits. Thus reality has come into being; but infinity has been lost. In order to describe a figure in space we have to *set limits* to infinite space; in order to imagine a change in time, we have to *divide up* the totality of time. Thus it is only through limits that we attain to reality, only through *negation* or exclusion that we arrive at *position* or real affirmation, only through the surrender of our unconditional determinability that we achieve determination.

But mere exclusion would never in all eternity produce reality, nor mere sensation ever give birth to perception, unless something existed *from which* to exclude, unless through some autonomous act of the mind the negating were referred to something positive, and from no-position op-position were to ensue. This activity of the psyche we call judging or thinking; and the result of it we call *thought*.

Before we determine a point in space, space does not exist for us; but without absolute space we should never be able to determine a point at all. It is the same with time. Before we become aware of the moment, time does not exist for us; but without infinite time we should never have any awareness of the moment. We do then, admittedly, only reach the whole through the part, the limitless only through limitation; but it is no less true that we only reach the part through the whole, and limitation only through the limitless.

When, therefore, it is asserted of the beautiful that it provides man with a transition from feeling to thinking, this must in no sense be taken to mean that beauty could ever bridge the gulf separating feeling from thinking, passivity from activity. This gulf is infinite, and without the intervention of some new and independent faculty we shall never in all eternity find a particular becoming a universal, or the merely contingent turning into the necessary. Thought is the spotaneous act of this absolute faculty. The senses, it is true, have to provide the occasion for it to manifest itself; but in its actual manifestation it is so little dependent upon the senses that, on the contrary, it makes itself felt only when it is at odds with them. The autonomy with which it operates excludes all outside influence; and it is not by *providing an aid* to thought (which would imply a manifest contradiction), but merely by furnishing the thinking faculty with the freedom to express itself according to its own laws, that beauty can become a means of leading man from matter to form, from feeling to law, from a limited to an absolute existence.

But this presupposes that the freedom of the thinking powers should be inhibited, which seems to contradict the notion of an autonomous faculty. For a faculty receiving from without nothing but the material on which to work can only be impeded in its activity by the withdrawal of that material, i.e., only negatively; and we misconstrue the very nature of mind if we attribute to sensuous passions the power of being able to suppress the freedom of the spirit positively. True, experience offers us examples in plenty of the forces of reason appearing to be suppressed in proportion as the forces of sense wax more ardent. But instead of attributing that weakness of the spirit to the strength of the passions, we ought rather to put this overwhelming strength of the passions down to the weakness of the spirit; for the senses can never set themselves up against a man as a power, unless the spirit has of its own free will renounced all desire to prove itself such.

But in trying by this explanation to counter one objection, I seem to have involved myself in another, and rescued the autonomy of the psyche only at the cost of its unity. For how can the psyche produce *out of itself* at one and the same time the motive for inactivity as well as activity, unless it is itself divided, unless it is at odds with itself?

At this point we must remind ourselves that we are dealing with a finite, not with an infinite, mind. The finite mind is that which cannot become active except through being passive, which only attains to the absolute by means of limitation, and only acts and fashions inasmuch as it receives material to fashion. Such a mind will accordingly combine with the drive toward form, or toward the absolute, a drive toward matter, or toward limitation, these latter being the conditions without which it could neither possess nor satisfy the first of these drives. How far two such opposed tendencies can coexist in the same being is a problem that may well embarrass the metaphysician, but not the transcendental philosopher. The latter does not pretend to explain how things are possible, but contents himself with determining the kind of knowledge that enables us to understand how experience is possible. And since experience would be just as impossible without that opposition in the psyche as without the absolute unity of the psyche, he is perfectly justified in postulating both these concepts as equally necessary conditions of experience, without troubling himself further as to how they are to be reconciled. More over, the immanence in the mind of two fundamental drives in no way contradicts its absolute unity, as long as we make a distinction between these two drives and the *mind itself.* Both drives exist and operate *within it;* but the mind itself is neither matter nor form, neither sense nor reason—which fact does not always seem to have been taken into account by those who will only allow the human mind to be active when its operations are in accordance with reason, and declare it to be merely passive when they are at odds with reason.

Each of these two primary drives, from the time it is developed, strives inevitably, and according to its nature, toward satisfaction; but just because both are necessary, and yet strive toward opposite ends, these two compulsions cancel each other out, and the will maintains perfect freedom between them. It is, then, the will that acts as a *power* (power being the ground of all reality) vis-à-vis both drives; but neither of these can of itself act as a power against the other. Thus, not even the most positive impulse toward justice, in which he may well not be lacking, will turn the man of violence from doing an injustice; and not even the liveliest temptation to pleasure persuade the man of character to violate his principles. There is in man no other power than his will; and his inner freedom can only be destroyed by that which destroys man himself, namely, death or anything that robs him of consciousness.

It is a necessity *outside of us* that, through the medium of sensation, determines our condition, our existence in time. This life of sensation is quite involuntary, and we have no option but to submit to any impact that is made upon us. And it is no less a necessity *within us* that, at the instance of sensation and in opposition to it, awakens our personality; for self-awareness cannot be dependent upon the will that presupposes it. This original manifestation of personality is not our merit; nor is the lack of it our fault. Only of him who is conscious of himself can we demand reason, that is, absolute consistency and universality of consciousness; prior to that he is not a human being at all, and no act of humanity can be expected of him. Even as the *metaphysicist* is unable to account for the limitations imposed upon the freedom and autonomy of the mind by sensation, so the *physicist* is unable to comprehend the infinity that, at the instigation of those limitations, manifests itself within the personality. Neither philosophical abstraction nor empirical method can ever take us back to the source from which our concepts of universality and necessity derive: their early manifestation in time veils it from the scrutiny of the empirical observer, their supersensuous origin from that of the metaphysical inquirer. But enough, self-consciousness is there; and once its immutable unity is established, there is also established a law of unity for everything that is there *for* man, and for everything that is to come about *through him,* i.e., for all his knowing and for all his doing. Ineluctable, incorruptible, incomprehensible, the concepts of truth and right make their appearance at an age when we are still little more than a bundle of sensations; and without being able to say whence or how it arose, we acquire an awareness of the eternal in time, and of necessity in the sequence of chance. Thus sensation and self-consciousness both arise entirely without any effort on our part, and the origin of both lies as much beyond the reach of our will as it is beyond the orbit of our understanding.

But once they have come into being, once man has, through the medium of sensation, acquired awareness of a determinate existence, once he has, through self-consciousness, acquired awareness of his absolute existence, then these two basic drives are quickened, together with their objects. The sensuous drive awakens with our experience of life (with the beginning of our individuality); the rational drive, with our experience of law (with the beginning of our personality); and only at this point, when both have come into existence, is the basis of man's humanity established. Until this has happened, everything in him takes place according to the law of necessity. But now the hand of *nature* is withdrawn from him, and it is up to *him* to vindicate the humanity that she implanted and opened up within him. That is to say, as soon as two opposing fundamental drives are active within him, both lose their compulsion, and the opposition of two necessities gives rise to *freedom.**

*To obviate any possible misunderstanding, I would observe that, whenever there is any mention of freedom here, I do not mean that freedom that necessarily apper-

Twentieth Letter

That freedom cannot be affected by anything whatsoever follows from our very notion of freedom. But that *freedom is itself* an effect of *nature* (this word taken in its widest sense) and not the work of man, that it can, therefore, also be furthered or thwarted by natural means, follows no less inevitably from what has just been said. It arises only when man is a *complete* being, when *both* his fundamental drives are fully developed; it will, therefore, be lacking as long as he is incomplete, as long as one of the two drives is excluded, and it should be capable of being restored by anything that gives him back his completeness.

Now we can, in fact, in the species as a whole as well as in the individual human being, point to a moment in which man is not yet complete, and in which one of his two drives is exclusively active within him. We know that he begins by being nothing but life, in order to end by becoming form; that he is an individual before he is a person, and that he proceeds from limitation to infinity. The sensuous drive, therefore, comes into operation earlier than the rational, because sensation precedes consciousness, and it is this *priority* of the sensuous drive that provides the clue to the whole history of human freedom.

For there is, after all, a moment in which the life impulse, just because the form impulse is not yet running counter to it, operates as nature and as necessity; a moment in which the life of sense is a power because man has not yet begun to be a human being; for in the human being proper there cannot exist any power other than the will. But in the state of reflection into which he is now to pass, it will be precisely the opposite: reason is to be a power, and a logical or moral necessity to take the place of that physical necessity. Hence sensation as a power must first be destroyed before law can be enthroned as such. It is, therefore, not simply a matter of something beginning that was not there before; something that was

---

tains to man considered as intelligent being, and that can neither be given unto him nor taken from him, but only that freedom that is founded upon his mixed nature. By acting rationally at all man displays freedom of the first order; by acting rationally within the limits of matter, and materially under the laws of reason, he displays freedom of the second order. We might explain the latter quite simply as a natural possibility of the former.

there must first cease to be. Man cannot pass directly from feeling to thought; he must first *take one step backwards,* since only through one determination being annulled again can a contrary determination take its place. In order to exchange passivity for autonomy, a passive determination for an active one, man must therefore be momentarily *free of all determination whatsoever,* and pass through a state of pure determinability. He must consequently, in a certain sense, return to that negative state of complete absence of determination in which he found himself before anything at all had made an impression upon his senses. But that former condition was completely devoid of content; and now it is a question of combining such sheer absence of determination, and an equally unlimited determinability, with the greatest possible content, since directly from this condition something positive is to result. The determination he has received through sensation must therefore be preserved, because there must be no loss of reality; but at the same time it must, inasmuch as it is limitation, be annulled, since an unlimited determinability is to come into existence. The problem is, therefore, at one and the same time to destroy and to maintain the determination of the condition—and this is possible in one way only: *by confronting it with another determination.* The scales of the balance stand level when they are empty; but they also stand level when they contain equal weights.

Our psyche passes, then, from sensation to thought *via* a middle disposition in which sense and reason are both active *at the same time.* Precisely for this reason, however, they cancel each other out as determining forces, and bring about a negation by means of an opposition. This middle disposition, in which the psyche is subject neither to physical nor to moral constraint, and yet is active in both these ways, preeminently deserves to be called a free disposition; and if we are to call the condition of sensuous determination the physical, and the condition of rational determination the logical or moral, then we must call this condition of real and active determinability the *aesthetic.**

*For readers not altogether familiar with the precise meaning of this word, which is so much abused through ignorance, the following may serve as an explanation. Every thing which is capable of phenomenal manifestation may be thought of under four different aspects. A thing can relate directly to our sensual condition (to our being and well-being): that is its *physical* character. Or it can relate to our intellect,

Twenty-First Letter

There is, as I observed at the beginning of the last letter, a twofold condition of determinability and a twofold condition of determination. I can now clarify this statement.

The psyche may be said to be determinable simply because it is not determined at all; but it is also determinable inasmuch as it is determined in a way that does not exclude anything, i.e., when the determination it undergoes is of a kind that does not involve limitation. The former is mere indetermination (it is without limits, because it is without reality); the latter is aesthetic determinability (it has no limits, because it embraces all reality).

And the psyche may be said to be determined inasmuch as it is limited at all; but it is also determined inasmuch as it limits itself, by virtue of its own absolute power. It finds itself in the first of these two states whenever it feels; in the second, whenever it thinks. What thought is in respect of determination, therefore, the aesthetic disposition is in respect of determinability; the former is limitation by virtue of the infinite force within it, the latter is negation by virtue of the infinite abundance within it. Even as sensation and thought have one single point of contact—viz., that in both states

---

and afford us knowledge: that is its *logical* character. Or it can relate to our will, and be considered as an object of choice for a rational being: that is its *moral* character. Or, finally, it can relate to the totality of our various functions without being a definite object for any single one of them: that is its *aesthetic* character. A man can please us through his readiness to oblige; he can, through his discourse, give us food for thought; he can, through his character, fill us with respect; but finally he can also, independently of all this, and without our taking into consideration in judging him any law or any purpose, please us simply as we contemplate him and by the sheer manner of his being. Under this last named quality of being we are judging him aesthetically. Thus there is an education to health, an education to understanding, an education to morality, an education to taste and beauty. This last has as its aim the development of the whole complex of our sensual and spiritual powers in the greatest possible harmony. Because, however, misled by false notions of taste and confirmed still further in this error by false reasoning, people are inclined to include in the notion of the aesthetic the notion of the arbitrary too, I add here the superfluous comment (despite the fact that these *Letters on Aesthetic Education* are concerned with virtually nothing else but the refutation of that very error) that our psyche in the aesthetic state does indeed act freely, is in the highest degree free from all compulsion, but is in no wise free from laws; and that this aesthetic freedom is distinguishable from logical necessity in thinking, or moral necessity in willing, only by the fact that the laws according to which the psyche then behaves *do not become apparent as such,* and since they encounter no resistance, never appear as a constraint.

the psyche is determined, and man is something, either individual or person, to the exclusion of all else—but in all other respects are poles apart: so, in like manner, aesthetic determinability has one single point of contact with mere indetermination—viz., that both exclude any determinate mode of existence—while in all other respects they are to each other as nothing is to everything, hence, utterly and entirely different. If, therefore, the latter—indetermination through sheer absence of determination—was thought of as an *empty infinity,* then aesthetic freedom of determination, which is its counterpart in reality, must be regarded as an *infinity filled with content:* an idea that accords completely with the results of the foregoing inquiry.

In the aesthetic state, then, man is *naught,* if we are thinking of any particular result rather than of the totality of his powers, and considering the absence in him of any specific determination. Hence we must allow that those people are entirely right who declare beauty, and the mood it induces in us, to be completely indifferent and unfruitful as regards either *knowledge* or *character.* They are entirely right; for beauty produces no particular result whatsoever, neither for the understanding nor for the will. It accomplishes no particular purpose, neither intellectual nor moral; it discovers no individual truth, helps us to perform no individual duty and is, in short, as unfitted to provide a firm basis for character as to enlighten the understanding. By means of aesthetic culture, therefore, the personal worth of a man, or his dignity, inasmuch as this can depend solely upon himself, remains completely indeterminate; and nothing more is achieved by it than that he is henceforth enabled *by the grace of nature* to make of himself what he will—that the freedom to be what he ought to be is completely restored to him.

But precisely thereby something infinite is achieved. For as soon as we recall that it was precisely of this freedom that he was deprived by the one-sided constraint of nature in the field of sensation and by the exclusive authority of reason in the realm of thought, then we are bound to consider the power that is restored to him in the aesthetic mode as the highest of all bounties, as the gift of humanity itself. True, he possesses this humanity *in potentia* before every determinate condition into which he can conceivably enter. But he loses it in practice with every determinate condition into which he does enter. And if he is to pass into a condition of an opposite nature, this humanity must be restored to him each time anew through the life of the aesthetic.*

It is, then, not just poetic license but philosophical truth when we call beauty our second creatress. For although it only offers us the possibility of becoming human beings, and for the rest leaves it to our own free will to decide how far we wish to make this a reality, it does in this resemble our first creatress, nature, which likewise conferred upon us nothing more than the power of becoming human, leaving the use and practice of that power to our own free will and decision.

Twenty-Second Letter

If, then, in one respect the aesthetic mode of the psyche is to be regarded as *naught*—once, that is, we have an eye to particular and definite effects—it is in another respect to be looked upon as a state of *supreme reality,* once we have due regard to the absence of all limitation and to the sum total of the powers that are conjointly active within it. One cannot, then, say that those people are wrong either who declare the aesthetic state to be the most fruitful of all in respect of knowledge and morality. They are entirely right; for a disposition of the psyche that contains within it the whole of human nature, must necessarily contain within it *in potentia* every individual manifestation of it too; and a disposition of the psyche that removes all limitations from the totality of human nature must necessarily remove them from every individual manifestation of it as well. Precisely on this account, because it takes under its protection no single one of man's faculties to the exclusion of the others, it favors each and all of them without distinction; and it favors no

---

*Admittedly the rapidity with which certain types pass from sensation to thought or decision scarcely—if indeed at all—allows them to become aware of the aesthetic mode through which they must in that time necessarily pass. Such natures cannot for any length of time tolerate the state of indetermination, but press impatiently for some result that in the state of aesthetic limitlessness they cannot find. In others, by contrast, who find enjoyment more in the feeling of *total capacity* than in any *single* action, the aesthetic state tends to spread itself over a much wider area. Much as the former dread emptiness, just as little are the latter capable of tolerating limitation. I need scarcely say that the former are born for detail and subordinate occupations, the latter, provided they combine this capacity with a sense of reality, destined for wholeness and for great roles.

single one more than another for the simple reason that it is the ground of possibility of them all. Every other way of exercising its functions endows the psyche with some special aptitude—but only at the cost of some special limitation; the aesthetic alone leads to the absence of all limitation. Every other state into which we can enter refers us back to a preceding one, and requires for its termination a subsequent one; the aesthetic alone is a whole in itself, since it comprises within itself all the conditions of both its origin and its continuance. Here alone do we feel reft out of time, and our human nature expresses itself with a purity and *integrity*, as though it had as yet suffered no impairment through the intervention of external forces.

That which flatters our senses in immediate sensation exposes our susceptible and labile psyche to every impression—but only by rendering us proportionately less fitted for exertion. That which tenses our intellectual powers and invites them to form abstract concepts, strengthens our mind for every sort of resistance—but only by hardening it and depriving us of sensibility in proportion as it fosters greater independence of action. Precisely because of this, the one no less than the other must lead to exhaustion, since material cannot for long dispense with shaping power, nor power with material to be shaped. If, by contrast, we have surrendered to the enjoyment of genuine beauty, we are at such a moment master in equal degree of our passive and of our active powers, and we shall with equal ease turn to seriousness or to play, to repose or to movement, to compliance or to resistance, to the discursions of abstract thought or to the direct contemplation of phenomena.

This lofty equanimity and freedom of the spirit, combined with power and vigor, is the mood in which a genuine work of art should release us, and there is no more certain touchstone of true aesthetic excellence. If, after enjoyment of this kind, we find ourselves disposed to prefer some one particular mode of feeling or action, but unfitted or disinclined for another, this may serve as infallible proof that we have not had a *purely aesthetic* experience—whether the cause lies in the object or in our own response or, as is almost always the case, in both at once.

Since in actuality no purely aesthetic effect is ever to be met with (for man can never escape his dependence upon conditioning forces), the excellence of a work of art can never consist in anything more than a high approximation to that ideal of aesthetic purity; and whatever the degree of freedom to which it may have been sublimated, we shall still leave it in a particular mood and with some definite bias. The more general the mood and the less limited the bias produced in us by any particular art, or by any particular product of the same, then the nobler that art and the more excellent that product will be. One can test this by considering works from different arts and different works from the same art. We leave a beautiful piece of music with our feeling excited, a beautiful poem with our imagination quickened, a beautiful sculpture or building with our understanding awakened. But should anyone invite us, immediately after a sublime musical experience, to abstract thought; or employ us, immediately after a sublime poetic experience, in some routine business of everyday life; or try, immediately after the contemplation of beautiful paintings or sculptures, to inflame our imagination or surprise our feeling—he would certainly be choosing the wrong moment. The reason for this is that even the most ethereal music has, *by virtue of its material,* an even greater affinity with the senses than true aesthetic freedom really allows; that even the most successful poem partakes more of the arbitrary and casual play of the imagination, *as the medium through which it works,* than the inner lawfulness of the truly beautiful really permits; that even the most excellent sculpture—the most excellent, perhaps, most of all—does, *by virtue of its conceptual precision,* border upon the austerity of science. Nevertheless, the greater the degree of excellence attained by a work in any of these three arts, the more these particular affinities will disappear; and it is an inevitable and natural consequence of their approach to perfection that the various arts, without any displacement of their objective frontiers, tend to become ever more like each other *in their effect upon the psyche.* Music, at its most sublime, must become sheer form and affect us with the serene power of antiquity. The plastic arts, at their most perfect, must become music and move us by the immediacy of their sensuous presence. Poetry, when most fully developed, must grip us powerfully as music does, but at the same time, like the plastic arts, surround us with serene clarity. This, precisely, is the mark of perfect style in each and every art: that it is able to remove the specific limitations of the art in question without thereby destroying its specific qualities, and through a wise use of its individual peculiarities, is able to confer upon it a more general character.

And it is not just the limitations inherent in the specific character of a particular art that the artist must seek to overcome through his handling of it; it is also the limitations inherent in the particular subject matter he is treating. In a truly successful work of art the contents should effect nothing, the form everything; for only through the form is the whole man affected, through the subject matter, by contrast, only one or other of his functions. Subject matter, then, however sublime and all-embracing it may be, always has a limiting effect upon the spirit, and it is only from form that true aesthetic freedom can be looked for. Herein, then, resides the real secret of the master in any art: *that he can make his form consume his material;* and the more pretentious, the more seductive this material is in itself, the more it seeks to impose itself upon us, the more high-handedly it thrusts itself forward with effects *of its own,* or the more the beholder is inclined to get directly involved with it, then the more triumphant the art that forces it back and asserts its own kind of dominion over him. The psyche of the listener or spectator must remain completely free and inviolate; it must go forth from the magic circle of the artist pure and perfect as it came from the hands of the Creator. The most frivolous theme must be so treated that it leaves us ready to proceed directly from it to some matter of the utmost import; the most serious material must be so treated that we remain capable of exchanging it forthwith for the lightest play. Arts that affect the passions, such as tragedy, do not invalidate this: *in the first place,* they are not entirely free arts since they are enlisted in the service of a particular aim (that of pathos); and *in the second,* no true connoisseur of art will deny that works even of this class are the more perfect, the more they respect the freedom of the spirit even amid the most violent storms of passion. There does indeed exist a fine art of passion; but a fine passionate art is a contradiction in terms; for the unfailing effect of beauty is freedom from passion. No less self-contradictory is the notion of a fine art that teaches (didactic) or improves (moral); for nothing is more at variance with the concept of beauty than the notion of giving the psyche any definite bias.

But it is by no means always a proof of formlessness in the work of art itself if it makes its effect solely through its contents; this may just as often be evidence of a lack of form in him who judges it. If he is either too tensed or too relaxed, if he is used to apprehending either exclusively with the intellect or exclusively with the senses, he will, even in the case of the most successfully realized whole, attend only to the parts, and in the presence of the most beauteous form respond only to the matter. Receptive only to the *raw material*, he has first to destroy the aesthetic organization of a work before he can take pleasure in it, and laboriously scratch away until he has uncovered all those individual details that the master, with infinite skill, had caused to disappear in the harmony of the whole. The interest he takes in it is quite simply either a moral or a material interest; but what precisely it ought to be, namely, aesthetic, that it certainly is not. Such readers will enjoy a serious and moving poem as though it were a sermon, a naïve or humorous one as though it were an intoxicating drink. And if they were sufficiently lacking in taste to demand *edification* of a tragedy or an epic—and were it about the Messiah himself—they will certainly not fail to take exception to a poem in the manner of Anacreon or Catullus.

Twenty-Third Letter

I take up once more the thread of my inquiry, which I broke off only in order to apply to the practice of art, and the judgment of its works, the propositions previously established.

The transition from a passive state of feeling to an active state of thinking and willing cannot, then, take place except via a middle state of aesthetic freedom. And although this state can of itself decide nothing as regards either our insights or our convictions, thus leaving both our intellectual and our moral worth as yet entirely problematic, it is nevertheless the necessary precondition of our attaining to any insight or conviction at all. In a word, there is no other way of making sensuous man rational except by first making him aesthetic.

But, you will be tempted to object, can such mediation really be indispensable? Should truth and duty not be able, of and by themselves alone, to gain access to sensuous man? To which I must answer: they not only can, they positively must, owe their determining power to themselves alone; and nothing would be more at variance with my previous assertions than if they should seem to support the opposite view. It has been expressly proved that beauty can produce no result, neither for the understanding nor for the will; that it does not meddle in the business of either thinking or deciding; that it merely imparts the power to do both, but has no say whatsoever in the actual use of that power. In the actual use of it all other aid whatsoever is dispensed with; and the pure logical form, namely, the concept, must speak directly to the understanding, the pure moral form, namely, the law, directly to the will.

But for them to be able to do this at all, for such a thing as a pure form to exist for sensuous man at all, this, I insist, has first to be made possible by the aesthetic modulation of the psyche. Truth is not something that, like actuality or the physical existence of things, can simply be received from without. It is something produced by our thinking faculty, autonomously and by virtue of its freedom. And it is precisely this autonomy, this freedom, that is lacking in sensuous man. Sensuous man is already (physically speaking) determined, and in consequence no longer possesses free determinability. This lost determinability he will first have to recover before he can exchange his passive determination for an active one. But he cannot recover it except by either losing the passive determination that he had or *by already possessing within himself the active determination* toward which he is to proceed. Were he merely to lose the passive determination, he would at the same time lose the possibility of an active one, since thought needs a body, and form can only be realized in some material. He will, therefore, need to have the active determination already within him, need to be at one and the same time passively, and actively, determined; that is to say, he will have to become aesthetic.

Through the aesthetic modulation of the psyche, then, the autonomy of reason is already opened up within the domain of sense itself, the dominion of sensation already broken within its own frontiers, and physical man refined to the point where spiritual man only needs to start developing out of the physical according to the laws of freedom. The step from the aesthetic to the logical and moral state (i.e., from beauty to truth and duty) is hence infinitely easier than was the step from the physical state to the aesthetic (i.e., from merely blind living to form). The former step man can accomplish simply of his own free will, since it merely involves taking from himself, not giving to himself, fragmenting his nature, not enlarging it; the aesthetically tempered man will achieve universally valid judgments and universally valid actions, as soon as he has the will to do so. But the step from brute matter to beauty, in which a completely new kind of activity has to be opened up within him, must first be facilitated by the grace of nature, for his will can exert no sort of compulsion upon a temper of mind that is, after all, the very means of bringing his will into existence. In order to lead aesthetic man to understanding and lofty sentiments, one need do no more than provide him with motives of sufficient weight. To obtain the same results from sensuous man we must first alter his very nature. Aesthetic man often needs no more than the challenge of a sublime situation (which is what acts most directly upon our willpower) to make of him a hero or a sage. Sensuous man must first be transported beneath another clime.

It is, therefore, one of the most important tasks of education to subject man to form even in his purely physical life, and to make him aesthetic in every domain over which beauty is capable of extending her sway; since it is only out of the aesthetic, not out of the physical, state that the moral can develop. If man is, in every single case, to possess the power of enlarging his judgment and his will into the judgment of the species as a whole; if out of his limited existence he is to be able to find the path that will lead him through to an infinite existence, out of every dependent condition be able to wing his way toward autonomy and freedom: then we must see to it that he is in no single moment of his life a mere individual, and merely subservient to the law of nature. If he is to be fit and ready to raise himself out of the restricted cycle of natural ends toward rational purposes, then he must already have prepared himself for the latter *within the limits of the former,* and have realized his physical destiny with a certain freedom of the spirit, that is, in accordance with the laws of beauty.

And this he can indeed accomplish without in the least acting counter to his physical ends. The claims that nature makes upon him are directed merely *to what he does, to the content* of his actions; in the matter of *how* he does it, the form of his actions, the purposes of nature offer no directives whatsoever. The claims of reason, by contrast, are directed strictly toward the form of his activity. Necessary as it is, then, for his moral destiny that he should be purely moral, and display absolute autonomy, for his physical destiny it is a matter of complete indifference whether he is purely physical, and behaves with absolute passivity. In respect of the latter, it is left entirely to his own discretion whether he realizes it merely as sensuous being and natural force (i.e., as a force that only reacts as it is acted upon), or whether he will at the same time realize it as absolute force and rational being; and there should be no question as to which of these two ways is more in keeping with his human dignity. On the contrary, just as it debases and degrades him to do from physical impulse what he should have decided to do from pure motives of duty, so it dignifies and exalts him to strive for order, harmony, and infinite freedom in those matters where the common man is content merely to satisfy his legitimate desires.* In a word: in the realm of truth and morality,

---

*1. This genial and aesthetically free handling of common reality is, wherever it may be found, the mark of a *noble* soul. In general we call noble any nature that possesses the gift of transforming, purely by its manner of handling it, even the most trifling occupation, or the most petty of objects, into something infinite. We call that form noble that impresses the stamp of autonomy upon anything that by its nature merely *serves some purpose* (is a mere means). A noble nature is not content to be itself free; it must also set free everything around it, even the lifeless. Beauty, however, is the only way that freedom has of making itself manifest in appearance. That is why a face, a work of art, or the like, which expresses *intelligence* more than anything else, can never strike us as noble, any more than it is beautiful, since it emphasizes a relation of dependence (which is inseparable from purposefulness) instead of concealing it.

2. The moral philosopher does, it is true, teach us that man can never do *more* than his duty; and he is perfectly right if he merely has in mind the relation between actions and the moral law. But in the case of actions that are merely end serving, *to exceed the end, and pass beyond it* into the suprasensible (which in the present context can mean nothing more than carrying out the physical in an aesthetic manner), is in fact *to exceed duty,* since duty can only prescribe that the *will* be sacred, but not that *nature itself* shall have taken on sacral character. There is thus no possibility of a moral transcendence of duty; but there is such a thing as an aesthetic transcendence; and such conduct we call noble. But just because an element of supererogation can always be discerned in noble conduct—inasmuch as what was only required to have material value has acquired a free formal value, or, in other words, has combined with the inner value, which it ought to have, an outer value, which it could legitimately do without—for this reason many have confused aesthetic supererogation with moral, and, misled by the appearance of what is noble, have imported into morality an element of arbitrariness and contingency that would end in its entire destruction.

3. Noble conduct is to be distinguished from sublime conduct. The first transcends moral obligation; not so the latter, although we rate it incomparably higher.

feeling may have no say whatsoever; but in the sphere of being and well-being, form has every right to exist, and the play drive every right to command.

It is here, then, in the indifferent sphere of physical life, that man must make a start upon his moral life; here, while he is still passive, already start to manifest his autonomy, and while still within the limitations of sense begin to make some show of rational freedom. The law of his will he must apply even to his inclinations; he must, if you will permit me the expression, *play* the war against matter into the very territory of matter itself, so that he may be spared having to fight this dread foe on the sacred soil of freedom. He must learn to desire *more nobly,* so that he may not need *to will sublimely.* This is brought about by means of aesthetic education, which subjects to laws of beauty all those spheres of human behavior in which neither natural laws, nor yet rational laws, are binding upon human caprice, and which, in the form it gives to outer life, already opens up the inner.

Twenty-Fourth Letter

We can, then, distinguish three different moments or stages of development through which both the individual and the species as a whole must pass, inevitably and in a definite order, if they are to complete the full cycle of their destiny. Through contingent causes, deriving either from the influence of external circumstances or from the arbitrary caprice of man himself, these several periods may indeed be either lengthened or shortened, but no one of them can be left out altogether; nor can the order in which they follow each other be reversed, neither by the power of nature nor by that of the will. Man in his *physical* state merely suffers the dominion of nature; he emancipates himself from this dominion in the *aesthetic* state, and he acquires mastery over it in the *moral.*

But we do not thus esteem it because it exceeds the rational concept of its object (i.e., the moral law), but because it exceeds the empirical concept of its subject (i.e., our experience of the goodness and strength of the human will). Conversely, we do not prize noble conduct because it surpasses the nature of its subject—on the contrary, it must flow freely and without constraint out of this—but because it surpasses the nature of its object (i.e., its physical end) and passes beyond this into the realm of spirit. In the first case, one might say, we marvel at the victory that the object achieves over man; in the latter we admire the élan that man imparts to the object.

What is man before beauty cajoles from him a delight in things for their own sake, or the serenity of form tempers the savagery of life? A monotonous round of ends, a constant vacillation of judgments; self-seeking, and yet without a self; lawless, yet without freedom; a slave, yet to no rule. At this stage the world is for him merely fate, not yet object; nothing exists for him except what furthers his own existence; that which neither gives to him, nor takes from him, is not there for him at all. Each phenomenon stands before him, isolated and cut off from all other things, even as he himself is isolated and unrelated in the great chain of being. All that exists, exists for him only at the behest of the moment; every change seems to him an entirely new creation, since with the lack of necessity *within him* there is none *outside of him* either, to connect the changing forms into a universe and, though individual phenomena pass away, to hold fast upon the stage of the world the unvarying law that informs them. In vain does nature let her rich variety pass before his senses; he sees in her splendid profusion nothing but his prey, in all her might and grandeur nothing but his foe. Either he hurls himself upon objects to devour them in an access of desire; or the objects press in upon him to destroy him, and he thrusts them away in horror. In either case his relation to the world of sense is that of immediate *contact;* and eternally anguished by its pressures, ceaselessly tortured by imperious needs, he finds rest nowhere but in exhaustion, and limits nowhere but in spent desire.

> His violent passions and the Titans'
> Vigorous marrow are his . . .
> Certain heritage; yet round his brow
> Zeus forged a brazen band.
> Counsel and Patience, Wisdom, Moderation
> He shrouded from his fearful sullen glance.
> In him each passion grows to savage fury,
> And all uncheck'd his fury rages round.
>
> *Iphigenia in Tauris*

Unacquainted as yet with *his own* human dignity, he is far from respecting it in others; and, conscious of his own savage greed, he fears it in every creature that resembles him. He never sees others in himself, but only himself in others; and communal life, far from enlarging him into a representative of the species, only confines him ever more narrowly within his own individuality. In this state of sullen limitation he gropes his way through the darkness of his life until a kindly nature shifts the burden of matter from his beclouded senses, and he learns through reflection to distinguish *himself* from things, so that objects reveal themselves at last in the reflected light of consciousness.

This state of brute nature is not, I admit, to be found exactly as I have presented it here among any particular people or in any particular age. It is purely an idea; but an idea with which experience is, in certain particulars, in complete accord. Man, one may say, was never in such a completely animal condition; but he has on the other hand, never entirely escaped from it. Even among the rudest of human creatures one finds unmistakable traces of rational freedom, just as among the most cultivated peoples there are moments in plenty that recall that dismal state of nature. It is, after all, peculiar to man that he unites in his nature the highest and the lowest; and if his *moral dignity* depends on his distinguishing strictly between the one and the other, *his hope of joy and blessedness* depends on a due and proper reconciliation of the opposites he has distinguished. An education that is to bring his dignity into harmony with his happiness will, therefore, have to see to it that those two principles are maintained in their utmost purity even while they are being most intimately fused.

The first appearance of reason in man does not necessarily imply that he has started to become truly human. This has to wait upon his freedom; and the first thing reason does is to make him utterly dependent upon his senses—a phenomenon which, for all its universality and importance, has still, so it seems to me, never been properly explored. It is, as we know, through the demand for the absolute (as that which is grounded upon itself and necessary) that reason makes itself known in man. This demand, since it can never be wholly satisfied in any single condition of his physical life, forces him to leave the physical altogether, and ascend out of a limited reality into the realm of ideas. But although the true purport of such a demand is to wrest him from the bondage of time, and lead him upwards from the sensuous world towards an ideal world, it can, through a misunderstanding (almost unavoidable in this early epoch of prevailing materiality), be directed toward physical life, and instead of making man independent plunge him into the most terrifying servitude.

And this is what does in fact happen. On the wings of fancy, man leaves the narrow confines of the present in which mere animality stays bound, in order to strive toward an unlimited future. But while the infinite opens up before his reeling *imagination,* his heart has not yet ceased to live in the particular or to wait upon the moment. In the very midst of his animality the drive toward the absolute catches him unawares—and since in this state of apathy all his endeavour is directed merely toward the material and the temporal, and limited exclusively to himself as individual, he will merely be incuced by that demand to give his own individuality unlimited extension rather than to abstract from it altogether: will be led to strive, not after form, but after an unfailing supply of matter; not after changelessness, but after perpetually enduring change; and after the absolute assurance of his temporal existence. That very drive which, applied to his thinking and activity, was meant to lead him to truth and morality, brought now to bear upon his passivity and feeling, produces nothing but unlimited longing and absolute instinctual need. The first fruits which he reaps in the realm of spirit are, therefore, *care* and *fear;* both of them products of reason, not of sense; but of a reason which mistakes its object and applies its imperative directly to matter. Fruits of this same tree are all your systems of unqualified eudaemonism, whether they have as their object the present day, or the whole of our life, or—and this by no means makes them any more worthy of respect—the whole of eternity. An unlimited perpetuation of being and well-being, merely for the sake of being and well-being, is an ideal that belongs to appetite alone, hence a demand that can only be made by an animality striving toward the absolute. Thus, without gaining anything for his humanity through such manifestations of reason, man merely loses thereby the happy limitation of the animal, over which he now possesses none but the—far from enviable—advantage of having forfeited possession of the here and now in favor of longings for what is not, yet without seeking in all those limitless vistas anything but the here and now he already knows.

But even if reason does not mistake its objective and confuse the question, sense will for a long time falsify the answer. As soon as man has begun to use his intellect, and to connect the phenomena around him in the relation of cause and effect, reason, in accordance with its very definition, presses for an absolute connection and an unconditioned cause. In order to be able to postulate such a demand at all, man must already have taken a step beyond mere sense; but it is this very demand that sense now makes use of to recall her truant child. This, strictly speaking, would be the point at which he ought to leave the world of sense altogether, and soar upwards to the realm of pure ideas; for the intellect remains eternally confined within the realm of the conditioned, and goes on eternally asking questions without ever lighting upon any ultimate answer. But since the man with whom we are here concerned is not yet capable of such abstraction, that which he cannot find in his *sphere of empirical knowledge*, and does not yet seek beyond it in the sphere of pure reason, he will seek beneath it in his *sphere of feeling* and, to all appearances, find it. True, this world of sense shows him nothing that might be its own cause and subject to none but its own law; but it does show him something that knows of no cause and obeys no law. Since, then, he cannot appease his inquiring intellect by evoking any ultimate and inward cause, he manages at least to silence it with the notion of *no-cause*, and remains within the blind compulsion of matter since he is not yet capable of grasping the sublime necessity of reason. Because the life of sense knows no *purpose* other than its own advantage, and feels driven by *no cause* other than blind chance, he makes the former into the arbiter of his actions and the latter into the sovereign ruler of the world.

Even what is most sacred in man, the moral law, when it first makes its appearance in the life of sense, cannot escape such perversion. Since its voice is merely inhibitory, and against the interest of his animal self-love, it is bound to seem like something external to himself as long as he has not yet reached the point of regarding his self-love as the thing that is really external to him, and the voice of reason as his true self. Hence he merely feels the fetters that reason lays upon him, not the infinite liberation that she is capable of affording him. Without suspecting the dignity of the lawgiver within, he merely experiences its coercive force and feels the impotent resistance of a powerless subject. Because in his experience the sense drive *precedes* the moral, he assigns to the law of necessity a beginning in time too, a *positive origin*, and through this most unfortunate of all errors makes the unchangeable and eternal in himself into an accidental product of the transient. He persuades himself into regarding the concepts of right and wrong as statutes introduced by some will, not as something valid in themselves for all eternity. Just as in the explanation of particular natural phenomena he goes beyond *nature* and seeks outside of it what can only be found in the laws inherent within it, so too, in the explanation of the moral world, he goes beyond *reason* and forfeits his humanity by seeking a Godhead along these same lines. No wonder that a religion bought by the debasement of his humanity proves itself worthy of such an origin, or that man considers laws that were not binding *from* all eternity as not unconditional and not binding *to* all eternity either. His concern is not with a holy, but merely with a powerful, being. The spirit in which he worships God is therefore fear, which degrades him, not reverence, which exalts him in his own estimation.

Although these manifold aberrations from the ideal that man is meant to achieve cannot all take place in the same epoch—since in order to move from absence of thought to error of thought, from lack of will to perversion of will, he must pass through several stages—these deviations are nevertheless all attendant upon his physical condition, since in all of them the life impulse plays the master over the form impulse. Whether it, then, be that reason has not yet made its voice heard in man, and the physical still rules him with blind necessity; or that reason has not yet sufficiently purified itself of sense, and the moral is still at the service of the physical: in either case the sole principle prevailing within him is a material one, and man is, at least in his ultimate tendency, a creature of sense—with this sole difference, that in the first case he is an animal void of reason, in the second an animal endowed with reason. What he is meant to be, however, is neither of these; he is meant to be a human being. Nature is not meant to rule him exclusively, nor reason to rule him conditionally. Both these systems of rule are meant to coexist, in perfect independence of each other, and yet in perfect concord.

Twenty-Fifth Letter

As long as man, in that first physical state, is merely a passive recipient of the world of sense, i.e., does no more than feel, he is still completely one with that world; and just because he is himself nothing but world, there exists for him as yet no world. Only when, at the aesthetic stage, he puts it outside himself, or *contemplates* it, does his personality differentiate itself from it, and a world becomes manifest to him because he has ceased to be one with it.*

Contemplation (or reflection) is the first liberal relation that man establishes with the universe around him. If desire seizes directly upon its object, contemplation removes *its* object to a distance, and makes it into a true and inalienable possession by putting it beyond the reach of passion. The necessity of nature, which in the stage of mere sensation ruled him with undivided authority, begins at the stage of reflection to relax its hold upon him. In his senses there results a momentary peace; time itself, the eternally moving, stands still; and, as the divergent rays of consciousness converge, there is reflected against a background of transience an image of the infinite, namely, *form*. As soon as light dawns within man, there is no longer any night without; as soon as it grows still within him, the storm in the universe abates and the contending forces of nature come to rest between stable confines. Small wonder, then, that the most primitive poetry speaks of this great happening in the inner world of man as though it were a revolution in the outer, and symbolizes thought triumphing over the laws of time by the image of *Zeus* putting an end to the reign of Saturn.

From being a slave of nature, which he remains as long as he merely feels it, man becomes its lawgiver from the moment he begins to think it. That which hitherto merely dominated him as *force*, now stands before his eyes as *object*. Whatsoever is object for him has no power over him; for in order to be object at all, it

*I remind my readers once again that, necessary as it is to distinguish these two periods in theory, in practice they more or less merge one into the other. Nor must we imagine that there ever was a time when man found himself purely at the physical stage, or another when he had entirely freed himself from it. From the moment man *sees an object*, he is no longer in a merely physical state; and as long as he continues to see objects, he will not entirely have escaped from that physical stage; for only inasmuch as he has physical sensations is he able to see at all. In a general way, then, those three moments that I mentioned at the beginning of the twenty-fourth letter may well be considered as three different epochs, if we are thinking either of the development of mankind as a whole, or of the whole development of a single individual; but they are also to be distinguished in each single act of perception, and are, in a word, the necessary conditions of all knowledge that comes to us through the senses.

must be subjected to the power that is his. To the extent that he imparts form to matter, and for precisely as long as he imparts it, he is immune to its effects; for spirit cannot be injured by anything except that which robs it of its freedom, and man gives evidence of his freedom precisely by giving form to that which is formless. Only where sheer mass, ponderous and inchoate, holds sway, its murky contours shifting within uncertain boundaries, can fear find its seat; man is more than a match for any of nature's terrors once he knows how to give it form and convert it into an object of his contemplation. Once he begins to assert his independence in the face of nature as phenomenon, then he also asserts his dignity vis-à-vis nature as force, and with noble freedom rises in revolt against his ancient gods. Now they cast off those ghastly masks that were the anguish of his childhood and surprise him with his own image by revealing themselves as projections of his own mind. The monstrous divinity of the Oriental, which rules the world with the blind strength of a beast of prey, shrinks in the imagination of the Greeks into the friendly contours of a human being. The empire of the Titans falls, and infinite force is tamed by infinite form.

But while I was merely seeking a way out from the material world and a transition to the world of spirit, my imagination has run away with me and carried me into the very heart of this latter. Beauty, which is what we were out to seek, already lies behind us; we have o'erleapt it completely in passing from mere life directly to pure form and the pure object. But a sudden leap of this kind is contrary to human nature, and in order to keep step with this latter we shall have to turn back once more to the world of sense.

Beauty is, admittedly, the work of free contemplation, and with it we do indeed enter upon the world of ideas—but, it should be emphasized, without therefore leaving behind the world of sense, as is the case when we proceed to knowledge of truth. Truth is the pure product of abstracting from everything that is material and contingent; it is object, pure and unadulterated, in which none of the limitations of the subject may persist, pure autonomous activity without any admixture of passivity. True, even from the highest abstractions, there is a way back to sense; for thought affects our inner life of feeling, and the perception of logical and moral unity passes over into a feeling of sensuous congruence. But when we take such delight in intellectual knowledge, we distinguish very exactly between our perception and our feeling, and look upon the latter as something incidental, which could well be absent without the knowledge therefore ceasing to be knowledge or truth being any the less true. But it would be a vain undertaking to try to clear our perception of *beauty* of these connections with feeling—which is why it will not do to think of the one as the effect of the other, but is imperative to consider each as being, at the same time and reciprocally, both effect and cause. In the pleasure we take in knowledge we distinguish without difficulty the *transition* from activity to passivity, and are clearly aware that the first is over when the latter begins. In the delight we take in beauty, by contrast, no such succession of activity and passivity can be discerned; reflection is here so completely interfused with feeling that we imagine that the form is directly apprehended by sense. Beauty, then, is indeed an *object* for us, because reflection is the condition of our having any sensation of it; but it is at the same time a *state of the perceiving subject,* because feeling is a condition of our having any perception of it. Thus beauty is indeed form, because we contemplate it; but it is at the same time life, because we feel it. In a word: it is at once a state of our being and an activity we perform.

And just because it is both these things at once, beauty provides us with triumphant proof that passivity by no means excludes activity, nor matter form, nor limitation infinity—that, in consequence, the moral freedom of man is by no means abrogated through his inevitable dependence upon physical things. Beauty is proof of this and, I must add, she *alone* can furnish such proof. For since in the enjoyment of truth, or logical unity, feeling is not inevitably and of necessity one with thought, but merely follows incidentally upon it, truth can only offer us proof that sensuousness can follow upon rationality, or vice versa; but not that both exist together, nor that they reciprocally work upon each other, nor that they are absolutely and of necessity to be united. On the contrary, from the fact that feeling is excluded as long as we are thinking, and thinking excluded as long as we are feeling, the *incompatibility* of our two natures would have to be inferred; and, indeed, analytical philosophers are unable to adduce any better proof that pure reason can in practice be realized in human kind than that this is in fact enjoined upon them. But since in the enjoyment of beauty, or *aesthetic unity,* an actual *union* and interchange between matter and form, passivity and activity, momentarily takes place, the *compatibility* of our two natures, the practicability of the infinite being realized in the finite, hence the possibility of sublimest humanity, is thereby actually proven.

We need, then, no longer feel at a loss for a way that might lead us from our dependence upon sense toward moral freedom, since beauty offers us an instance of the latter being perfectly compatible with the former, an instance of man not needing to flee matter in order to manifest himself as spirit. But if he is already free while still in association with sense, as the fact of beauty teaches, and if freedom is something absolute and suprasensual, as the very notion of freedom necessarily implies, then there can no longer be any question of how he is to succeed in raising himself from the limited to the absolute, or of how, in his thinking and willing, he is to offer resistance to the life of sense, since this has already happened in beauty. There can, in a single word, no longer be any question of how he is to pass from beauty to truth, since this latter is potentially contained in the former, but only a question of how he is to clear a way for himself from common reality to aesthetic reality, from mere life-serving feelings to feelings of beauty.

Twenty-Sixth Letter

Since, as I have argued in the preceding letters, it is the aesthetic mode of the psyche that first gives rise to freedom, it is obvious that it cannot itself derive from freedom and cannot, in consequence, be of moral origin. It must be a gift of nature; the favor of fortune alone can unloose the fetters of that first physical stage and lead the savage toward beauty.

The germ of beauty is as little likely to develop where nature in her niggardliness deprives man of quickening refreshment, as where in her bounty she relieves him of any exertion—alike where sense is too blunted to feel any need, as where violence of appetite is denied satisfaction. Not where man hides himself, a *troglodyte,* in caves, eternally an isolated unit, never finding humanity *outside himself;* nor yet there were, a *nomad,* he roams in vast hordes over the face of the earth, eternally but one of a number, never finding humanity *within himself*—but only there, where, in his own hut, he discourses silently with himself and, from the moment he steps out of it, with all the rest of his kind, only there will the tender blossom of beauty unfold. There, where a limpid atmosphere opens his senses to every delicate contact, and an energizing warmth animates the exuberance of matter—there where, even in inanimate nature, the sway of blind mass has been overthrown, and form triumphant ennobles even the lowest orders of creation—there, amid the most joyous surroundings, and in that favored zone where activity alone leads to enjoyment and enjoyment alone to activity, where out of life itself the sanctity of order springs, and out of the law of order nothing but life can develop—where imagination ever flees actuality yet never strays from the simplicity of nature—here alone will sense and spirit, the receptive and the formative power, develop in that happy equilibrium that is the soul of beauty and the condition of all humanity.

And what are the outward and visible signs of the savage's entry upon humanity? If we inquire of history, however far back, we find that they are the same in all races that have emerged from the slavery of the animal condition: delight in *semblance*, and a propensity to *ornamentation* and *play*.

Supreme stupidity and supreme intelligence have a certain affinity with each other in that both of them seek only the *real* and are completely insensitive to mere semblance. Only by objects that are actually present to the senses is stupidity jerked out of its quiescence; only when its concepts can be referred back to the facts of experience is intelligence to be pacified. In a word, stupidity cannot rise above actuality, and intelligence cannot stop short of truth. Inasmuch as need of reality and attachment to the actual are merely consequences of some deficiency, then indifference to reality and interest in semblance may be regarded as a genuine enlargement of humanity and a decisive step toward culture. In the first place, this affords evidence of outward freedom: for as long as necessity dictates, and need drives, imagination remains tied to reality with powerful bonds; only when wants are stilled does it develop its unlimited potential. But it affords evidence, too, of inner freedom, since it makes us aware of a power that is able to move of its own accord, independently of any material stimulus from without, and that is sufficiently in control of energy to hold at arm's length the importunate pressure of matter. The reality of things is the work of things themselves; the semblance of things is the work of man;

and a nature that delights in semblance is no longer taking pleasure in what it receives, but in what it does.

It goes without saying that the only kind of semblance I am here concerned with is aesthetic semblance (which we distinguish from actuality and truth) and not logical semblance (which we confuse with these): semblance, therefore, which we love just because it is semblance, and not because we take it to be something better. Only the first is play, whereas the latter is mere deception. To attach value to semblance of the first kind can never be prejudicial to truth, because one is never in danger of substituting it for truth, which is after all the only way in which truth can ever be impaired. To despise it, is to despise the fine arts altogether, the very essence of which is semblance. All the same, it sometimes happens that intelligence will carry its zeal for reality to such a pitch of intolerance, that it pronounces a disparaging judgment upon the whole art of aesthetic semblance just because it is semblance. But this only happens to intelligence when it recalls the above-mentioned affinity. Of the necessary limits of aesthetic semblance I shall treat separately on some other occasion.

It is nature herself that raises man from reality to semblance, by furnishing him with two senses that lead him to knowledge of the real world through semblance alone. In the case of the eye and the ear, she herself has driven importunate matter back from the organs of sense, and the object, with which in the case of our more animal senses we have direct contact, is set at a distance from us. What we actually *see* with the eye is something different from the *sensation we receive;* for the mind leaps out across light to objects. The object of touch is a force to which we are subjected; the object of eye and ear a form that we engender. As long as man is still a savage he enjoys by means of these tactile senses alone, and at this stage the senses of semblance are merely the servants of these. Either he does not rise to the level of seeing at all, or he is at all events not satisfied with it. Once he does begin to enjoy through the eye, and seeing acquires for him a value of its own, he is already aesthetically free and the play drive has started to develop.

And as soon as the play drive begins to stir, with its pleasure in semblance, it will be followed by the shaping spirit of imitation, which treats semblance as something autonomous. Once man has got to the point of distinguishing semblance from reality, form from body, he is also in a position to abstract the one from the other, and has indeed already done so by the very fact of distinguishing between them. The capacity for imitative art is thus given with the capacity for form in general; the urge toward it rests upon a quite different endowment that I need not discuss here. Whether the artistic impulse is to develop early or late, will depend solely upon the degree of loving attachment with which man is capable of abiding with sheer semblance.

Since all actual existence derives from nature considered as alien force, whereas all semblance originates in man considered as perceiving subject, he is only availing himself of the undisputed rights of ownership when he reclaims semblance from substance, and deals with it according to laws of his own. With unrestricted freedom he is able, can he but imagine them together, actually to join together things that nature put asunder; and, conversely, to separate, can he but abstract them in his mind, things that nature has joined together. Nothing need here be sacred to him except his own law, if he but observes the demarcation separating *his* territory from the actual existence of things, that is to say from the realm of nature.

This sovereign human right he exercises in the *art of semblance;* and the more strictly he here distinguishes between mine and thine, the more scrupulously he separates form from substance, and the more complete the autonomy he is able to give to the former, then the more he will not only extend the realm of beauty, but actually preserve intact the frontiers of truth. For he cannot keep semblance clear of actuality without at the same time setting actuality free from semblance.

But it is in the *world of semblance* alone that he possesses this sovereign right, in the insubstantial realm of the imagination; and he possesses it there only as long as he scrupulously refrains from predicating real existence of it in theory, and as long as he renounces all idea of imparting real existence through it in practice. From this you see that the poet transgresses his proper limits, alike when he attributes existence to his ideal world, as when he aims at bringing about some determinate existence by means of it. For he can bring neither of these things to pass without either exceeding his rights as a poet (encroaching with his ideal upon the territory of experience, and presuming to determine actual existence by

of ideas. To such voices, therefore, the taste of our century need pay no undue heed, so long as it can stand its ground before a higher tribunal. What a more rigoristic judge of beauty could well reproach us with, is not that we attach value to aesthetic semblance (we do not attach nearly enough), but that we have not yet attained to the level of pure semblance at all, that we have not sufficiently distinguished existence from appearance, and thereby made the frontiers of each secure forever. We shall deserve this reproach as long as we cannot enjoy the beauty of living nature without coveting it, or admire the beauty of imitative art without inquiring after its purpose—as long as we still refuse imagination any absolute legislative rights of her own, and, by the kind of respect we accord to her works, go on referring her instead to the dignity of her office.

Twenty-Seventh Letter

You need have no fear for either reality or truth if the lofty conception of aesthetic semblance that I put forward in the last letter were to become universal. It will not become universal as long as man is still uncultivated enough to be in a position to misuse it; and should it become universal, this could only be brought about by the kind of culture that would automatically make any misuse of it impossible. To strive after autonomous semblance demands higher powers of abstraction, greater freedom of heart, more energy of will, than man ever needs when he confines himself to reality; and he must already have left this reality behind if he would arrive at that kind of semblance. How ill-advised he would be, then, to take the path toward the ideal in order to save himself the way to the real! From semblance as here understood we should thus have little cause to fear for reality; all the more to be feared, I would suggest, is the threat from reality to semblance. Chained as he is to the material world, man subordinates semblance to ends of his own long before he allows it autonomous existence in the ideal realm of art. For this latter to happen a complete revolution in his whole way of feeling is required, without which he would not even find himself *on the way* to the ideal. Wherever, then, we find traces of a disinterested and unconditional appreciation of pure semblance, we may infer that a revolution of this order has taken place in his nature, and that he has started to become truly human. Traces of this kind are, however, actually to be found even in his first crude attempts at *embellishing* his existence, attempts made even at the risk of possibly worsening it from the material point of view. As soon as ever he starts preferring form to substance, and jeopardizing reality for the sake of semblance (which he must, however, recognize as such), a breach has been effected in the cycle of his animal behavior, and he finds himself set upon a path to which there is no end.

Not just content with what satisfies nature, and meets his instinctual needs, he demands something over and above this: to begin with, admittedly, only a superfluity *of material things,* in order to conceal from appetite the fact that it has limits, and ensure enjoyment beyond the satisfaction of immediate needs; soon, however, a superfluity *in material things,* an aesthetic surplus, in order to satisfy the formal impulse too, and extend enjoyment beyond the satisfaction of every need. By merely gathering supplies around him for future use, and enjoying them in anticipation, he does, it is true, transcend the present moment—but without transcending time altogether. He enjoys *more,* but he does not enjoy *differently.* But when he also lets form enter into his enjoyment, and begins to notice the outward appearance of the things that satisfy his desires, then he has not merely enhanced his enjoyment in scope and degree, but also ennobled it in kind.

It is true that nature has given even to creatures without reason more than the bare necessities of existence, and shed a glimmer of freedom even into the darkness of animal life. When the lion is not gnawed by hunger, nor provoked to battle by any beast of prey, his idle strength creates an object for itself: he fills the echoing desert with a roaring that speaks defiance, and his exuberant energy enjoys its *self* in purposeless display. With what enjoyment of life do insects swarm in the sunbeam; and it is certainly not the cry of desire that we hear in the melodious warbling of the songbird. Without doubt there is freedom in these activities; but not freedom from compulsion altogether, merely from a certain kind of compulsion, compulsion from without. An animal may be said *to be at work* when the stimulus to activity is some lack; it may be said *to be at play* when the stimulus is sheer plenitude of vitality, when superabundance of life is its own incentive to action. Even inanimate nature exhibits a similar luxuriance of forces, coupled with a laxity of determination that, in that material sense, might well be called play. The tree puts forth innumerable buds that perish without ever unfolding, and sends out far more roots, branches, and leaves in search of nourishment than are ever used for the sustaining of itself or its species. Such portion of its prodigal profusion as it returns, unused and unenjoyed, to the elements, is the overplus that living things are entitled to squander in a movement of carefree joy. Thus does nature, even in her material kingdom, offer us a prelude of the illimitable, and even here remove *in part* the chains that, in the realm of form, she casts away entirely. From the compulsion of want, or *physical earnestness,* she makes the transition via the compulsion of superfluity, or *physical play,* to aesthetic play; and before she soars, in the sublime freedom of beauty, beyond the fetters of ends and purposes altogether, she makes some approach to this independence, at least from afar, in that kind of *free activity* that is at once its own end and its own means.

Like the bodily organs in man, his imagination, too, has its free movement and its material play, an activity in which, without any reference to form, it simply delights in its own absolute and unfettered power. Inasmuch as form does not yet enter this fantasy play at all, its whole charm residing in a free association of images, such play—although the prerogative of man alone—belongs merely to his animal life, and simply affords evidence of his liberation from all external physical compulsion, without as yet warranting the inference that there is any autonomous shaping power within him.*

* Most of the imaginative play that goes on in everyday life is either entirely based on this feeling for free association of ideas, or at any rate derives therefrom its greatest charm. This may not in itself be proof of a higher nature, and it may well be that it is just the most flaccid natures who tend to surrender to such unimpeded flow of images; it is nevertheless this very independence of the fantasy from external stimuli, which constitutes at least the negative condition of its creative power. Only by tearing itself free from reality does the formative power raise itself up to the ideal; and before the imagination, in its productive capacity, can act according to its own laws, it must first, in its reproductive procedures, have freed itself from alien laws. From mere lawlessness to autonomous law giving from within, there is, admittedly, still a big step to be taken; and a completely new power, the faculty for ideas, must first be brought into play. But this power, too, can now develop with greater ease, since the senses are not working against it, and the indefinite does, at least negatively, border upon the infinite.

From this play *of freely associated ideas,* which is still of a wholly material kind, and to be explained by purely natural laws, the imagination, in its attempt at a *free form,* finally makes the leap to aesthetic play. A leap it must be called, since a completely new power now goes into action; for here, for the first time, mind takes a hand as lawgiver in the operations of blind instinct, subjects the arbitrary activity of the imagination to its own immutable and eternal unity, introduces its own autonomy into the transient, and its own infinity into the life of sense. But as long as brute nature still has too much power, knowing no other law but restless hastening from change to change, it will oppose to that necessity of the spirit its own unstable caprice, to that stability its own unrest, to that autonomy its own subservience, to that sublime self-sufficiency its own insatiable discontent. The aesthetic play drive, therefore, will in its first attempts be scarcely recognizable, since the physical play drive, with its willful moods and its unruly appetites, constantly gets in the way. Hence we see uncultivated taste first seizing upon what is new and startling—on the colorful, fantastic, and bizarre, the violent and the savage—and shunning nothing so much as tranquil simplicity. It fashions grotesque shapes, loves swift transitions, exuberant forms, glaring contrasts, garish lights, and a song full of feeling. At this stage what man calls beautiful is only what excites him, what offers him material—but excites him to a resistance involving autonomous activity, but offers him material *for possible shaping.* Otherwise it would not be beauty—even for him. The form of his judgments has thus undergone an astonishing change: he seeks these objects, not because they give him something to enjoy passively, but because they provide an incentive to respond actively. They please him, not because they meet a need, but because they satisfy a law that speaks, though softly as yet, within his breast.

Soon he is no longer content that things should please him; he himself wants to please. At first, indeed, only through that which is *his;* finally through that which *he* is. The things he possesses, the things he produces, may no longer bear upon them the marks of their use, their form no longer be merely a timid expression of their function; in addition to the service they exist to render, they must at the same time reflect the genial mind that conceived them, the loving hand that wrought them, the serene and liberal spirit that chose and displayed them. Now the ancient German goes in search of glossier skins, statelier antlers, more elaborate drinking horns; and the Caledonian selects for his feasts the prettiest shells. Even weapons may no longer be mere objects of terror; they must be objects of delight as well, and the cunningly ornamented swordbelt claims no less attention than the deadly blade of the sword. Not content with introducing aesthetic superfluity into objects of necessity, the play drive as it becomes ever freer finally tears itself away from the fetters of utility altogether, and beauty in and for itself alone begins to be an object of his striving. Man *adorns* himself. Disinterested and undirected pleasure is now numbered among the necessities of existence, and what is in fact unnecessary soon becomes the best part of his delight.

And as form gradually comes upon him from without—in his dwelling, his household goods, and his apparel—so finally it begins to take possession of him himself, transforming at first only the outer, but ultimately the inner man too. Uncoordinated leaps of joy turn into dance, the unformed movements of the body into the graceful and harmonious language of gesture; the confused and indistinct cries of feeling become articulate, begin to obey the laws of rhythm, and to take on the contours of song. If the Trojan host storms on to the battlefield with piercing shrieks like a flock of cranes, the Greek army approaches it in silence, with noble and measured tread. In the former case we see only the exuberance of blind forces; in the latter, the triumph of form and the simple majesty of law.

Now compulsion of a lovelier kind binds the sexes together, and a communion of hearts helps sustain a connection but intermittently established by the fickle caprice of desire. Released from its dark bondage, the eye, less troubled now by passion, can apprehend the form of the beloved; soul looks deep into soul, and out of a selfish exchange of lust there grows a generous interchange of affection. Desire widens, and is exalted into love, once humanity has dawned in its object; and a base advantage over sense is now disdained for the sake of a nobler victory over will. The need to please subjects the all-conquering male to the gentle tribunal of taste; lust he can steal, but love must come as a gift. For this loftier prize he can only contend by virtue of form, never by virtue of matter. From being a force impinging upon feeling, he must become a form confronting the mind; he must be willing to concede freedom, because it is freedom he wishes to please. And even as beauty resolves the conflict between opposing natures in this simplest and clearest paradigm, the eternal antagonism of the sexes, so too does it resolve it—or at least aims at resolving it—in the complex whole of society, endeavoring to reconcile the gentle with the violent in the moral world after the pattern of the free union it there contrives between the strength of man and the gentleness of woman. Now weakness becomes sacred, and unbridled strength dishonorable; the injustice of nature is rectified by the magnanimity of the chivalric code. He whom no violence may alarm is disarmed by the tender blush of modesty, and tears stifle a revenge that no blood was able to assuage. Even hatred pays heed to the gentle voice of honor; the sword of the victor spares the disarmed foe, and a friendly hearth sends forth welcoming smoke to greet the stranger on that dread shore where of old only murder lay in wait for him.

In the midst of the fearful kingdom of forces, and in the midst of the sacred kingdom of laws, the aesthetic impulse to form is at work, unnoticed, on the building of a third joyous kingdom of play and of semblance, in which man is relieved of the shackles of circumstance, and released from all that might be called constraint, alike in the physical and in the moral sphere.

If in the *dynamic* state of rights it is as force that one man encounters another, and imposes limits upon his activities; if in the *ethical* state of duties man sets himself over against man with all the majesty of the law, and puts a curb upon his desires: in those circles where conduct is governed by beauty, in the *aesthetic* state, none may appear to the other except as form, or confront him except as an object of free play. *To bestow freedom by means of freedom* is the fundamental law of this kingdom.

The dynamic state can merely make society possible, by letting one nature be curbed by another; the ethical state can merely make it (morally) necessary, by subjecting the individual will to the general; the aesthetic state alone can make it real, because it consummates the will of the whole through the nature of the individual. Though it may be his needs that drive man into society, and reason that implants within him the principles of social behavior, beauty alone can confer upon him a *social character.* Taste alone brings harmony into society, because it fosters harmony in the individual. All other forms of perception divide man, because they are founded exclusively either upon the sensuous or upon the spiritual part of his being; only the aesthetic mode of perception makes of him a whole, because both his natures must be in harmony if he is to achieve it. All other forms of communication divide society, because they relate exclusively either to the private receptivity or to the private proficiency of its individual members, hence to that which distinguishes man from man; only the aesthetic mode of communication unites society, because it relates to that which is common to all. The pleasures of the senses we enjoy merely as individuals, without the genus that is immanent within us having any share in them at all; hence we cannot make the pleasures of sense universal, because we are unable to universalize our own individuality. The pleasures of knowledge we enjoy merely as genus, and by carefully removing from our judgment all trace of individuality; hence we cannot make the pleasures of reason universal, because we cannot eliminate traces of individuality from the judgments of others as we can from our own. Beauty alone do we enjoy at once as individual and as genus, i.e., as *representatives* of the human genus. The good of the senses can only make one man happy, since it is founded on appropriation, and this always involves exclusion; and it can only make this one man onesidedly happy, since his personality has no part in it. Absolute good can only bring happiness under conditions that we cannot presume to be universal; for truth is the prize of abnegation alone, and only the pure in heart believe in the pure will. Beauty alone makes the whole world happy, and each and every being forgets its limitations while under its spell.

No privilege, no autocracy of any kind, is tolerated where taste rules, and the realm of aesthetic semblance extends its sway. This realm stretches upwards to the point where reason governs with unconditioned necessity, and all that is mere matter ceases to be. It stretches downwards to the point where natural impulse reigns with blind compulsion, and form has not yet begun to appear. And even at these furthermost confines, where taste is deprived of all legislative power, it still does not allow the executive power to be wrested from it. A social appetite must renounce its self-seeking, and the agreeable, whose normal function is to seduce the senses, must cast toils of grace over the mind as well. Duty, stern voice of necessity, most moderate the censorious tone of its precepts—a tone only justified by the resistance they encounter—and show greater respect for nature through a nobler confidence in her willingness to obey them. From within the mysteries of science, taste leads knowledge out into the broad daylight of common sense, and transforms a monopoly of the schools into the common possession of human society as a whole. In the kingdom of taste even the mightiest genius must divest itself of its majesty, and stoop in all humility to the mind of a little child. Strength must allow itself to be bound by the Graces, and the lion have its defiance curbed by the bridle of a Cupid. In return, taste throws a veil of decorum over those physical desires that, in their naked form, affront the dignity of free beings; and, by a delightful illusion of freedom, conceals from us our degrading kinship with matter. On the wings of taste even that art that must cringe for payment can lift itself out of the dust; and, at the touch of her wand, the fetters of serfdom fall away from the lifeless and the living alike. In the aesthetic state everything—even the tool that serves—is a free citizen, having equal rights with the noblest; and the mind, which would force the patient mass beneath the yoke of its purposes, must here first obtain its assent. Here, therefore, in the realm of aesthetic semblance, we find that ideal of equality fulfilled that the enthusiast would fain see realized in substance. And if it is true that it is in the proximity of thrones that fine breeding comes most quickly and most perfectly to maturity, would one not have to recognize in this, as in much else, a kindly dispensation that often seems to be imposing limits upon man in the real world, only in order to spur him on to realization in an ideal world?

But does such a state of aesthetic semblance really exist? And if so, where is it to be found? As a need, it exists in every finely attuned soul; as a realized fact, we are likely to find it, like the pure church and the pure republic, only in some few chosen circles, where conduct is governed, not by some soulless imitation of the manners and morals of others, but by the aesthetic nature we have made our own; where men make their way, with undismayed simplicity and tranquil innocence, through even the most involved and complex situations, free alike of the compulsion to infringe the freedom of others in order to assert their own, as of the necessity to shed their dignity in order to manifest grace.

Translated by Elizabeth M. Wilkinson
and L. A. Willoughby

On Naive and Sentimental Poetry*

There are moments in our lives when we extend a kind of love and tender respect toward nature in plants, minerals, animals, and landscapes, as well as to human nature in children, in the customs of country folk and the primitive world. We do this, not because it makes us feel good and not even because it satisfies our intellect or taste (in both cases the reverse can often occur), but merely *because it is nature.* Every more refined human being not utterly devoid of feeling experiences this when he wanders about in the open, when he resides in the country or lingers at the monuments of ancient times, in short, whenever in the midst of man-made contexts and situations he is taken aback by the sight of nature in its simplicity. It is this interest, often elevated to a need, that lies at the bottom of our many fondnesses for flowers and animals, for simple gardens, for walks, for the land and its inhabitants, for many an artifact of remote antiquity, and the like (pro-

---

**On Naive and Sentimental Poetry* first appeared as a complete text in the second part of *Kleinere prosaische Schriften* (Leipzig: Crusius, 1800, pp. 43–76). The text was originally published in three successive issues of *Die Horen.* The first part *Über das Naive* appeared on November 24, 1795 (*Die Horen,* 4, nr. 11, pp. 3–216); the second part *Die sentimentalischen Dichter* toward the end of December (*Die Horen,* 4, nr. 12); and the final part *Beschluß der Abhandlung über naive und sentimentalische Dichter nebst einigen Bemerkungen einer charakteristischen Unterschied unter den Menschen betreffend* on January 22, 1796 (*Die Horen,* 5, nr. 1).

vided that no predilection or any other serendipitous interest comes into play here). This sort of interest in nature takes place, however, only under two conditions. It is absolutely necessary, first, that the object instilling this interest in us be *natural* or at least be considered by us to be natural, and, second, that it be *naive* (in the widest sense of the term), that is to say, nature must contrast with art and put it to shame. The moment the latter condition is joined to the former, and not before, nature becomes something naive.

Regarded in this way, nature is for us nothing but the uncoerced existence, the subsistence of things on their own, being there according to their own immutable laws.

This image is absolutely necessary if we are to take an interest in the sorts of phenomena mentioned above. If somehow by means of the most perfect sort of deception one could give an artificial flower the look of being natural, [414] if one could press the imitation of the naive in culture to a point where the illusion was complete, then the discovery that it is an imitation would utterly destroy the feeling I have been talking about.* On the basis of these considerations it becomes clear that this manner of enjoying nature is not aesthetic, but moral, for it is communicated by an idea and not immediately produced by observation. It is also in no way directed at the beauty of the forms of things. What else is it about a humble flower, a brook, a mossy rock, the chirping of birds, the humming of bees, and the like, that by itself pleases us so much? What else could even give them a claim to our love? It is not these objects, it is an idea portrayed by them that we cherish in them. We treasure the silent creativity of life in them, the fact that they act serenely on their own, being there according to their own laws; we cherish that inner necessity, that eternal oneness with themselves.

They *are* what we *were;* they are what we *should become* once

---

*Kant, to my knowledge the first person to begin reflecting on this phenomenon, recalls that if we were to find the song of the nightingale perfectly imitated by a human and if, completely moved by it, we were to give ourselves up to this impression, all our pleasure would disappear with the destruction of this illusion. See the chapter "On The Intellectual Interest in the Beautiful" in the *Critique of Aesthetic Judgment*. Anyone who has learned to wonder at the author only as a great thinker will be delighted to find here a trace of his heart and on the basis of this discovery to convince himself of the high philosophical calling of this man (a calling absolutely requiring the combination of both properties).

more. We were nature like them, and our culture should lead us along the path of reason and freedom back to nature. Thus they depict at once our lost childhood, something that remains ever dearest to us, and for this reason they fill us with a certain melancholy. Because at the same time they portray our supreme perfection in an ideal sense, they transport us into a state of sublime emotion.

Yet their perfection is not something they have deserved, since it is not the result of a decision on their part. Hence they afford us the utterly [415] distinctive pleasure of being models for us without putting us to shame. They surround us with a constant theophany, though one that is more exhilarating than blinding. What constitutes their character is exactly what ours lacks to be perfect. What distinguishes us from them is exactly what they lack to be divinelike. We are free and what they are is necessary; we alter, they remain one. Yet only if both are combined with one another—only if the will freely adheres to the law of necessity and reason maintains its rule in the face of every change in the imagination, only then does the divine or the ideal emerge. Hence in *them* we forever see what eludes us, something we must struggle for and can hope to approach in an endless progress, even though we never attain it. *In ourselves* we see an advantage that they lack, something that they either could never participate in at all, as in the case of beings devoid of reason, or can participate in only inasmuch as they proceed down the same path that *we* did, as in the case of children. Accordingly they afford us the sweetest sort of delight in the idea of our humanity, although they necessarily humble us as far as any *specific state* of our humanity is concerned.

Since this interest in nature is founded upon an idea, it is able to reveal itself only to minds receptive to ideas, that is to say, moral minds. Most people by far only affect that interest, and the universality of this sentimental taste in our times, expressing itself (especially since the appearance of certain writings) in maudlin journeys, gardens, strolls, and other penchants of this sort, is in no way a proof of the universality of this way of feeling. Still, nature will always have something of this effect even on the most callous individual. For the *potential* for morality, common to all people, is all that is needed to produce this effect and we all, without distinction, are driven to the comtemplation of *this idea,* despite the tremendous distance between our *deeds* and nature's simplicity and truth. This sensitivity to nature expresses itself in the most universal manner and in a particularly powerful fashion when it is occasioned by those objects, for example, children and primitive peoples, that are more closely connected to us, [416] placing in sharper relief for us a retrospective of ourselves and what is *unnatural* in us. People err if they believe that it is merely the image of helplessness that at certain moments makes us dwell on children with so much tenderness. That may perhaps be the case for those who would never feel anything but their own superiority in the face of weakness. However, the feeling I am talking about (that takes place only in quite distinctive moral moods and is not to be confused with the feeling stirred in us by the joyful activity of children) humbles more than it promotes self-love. Indeed, if along the way any advantage comes up for consideration, it is at least not on our side. We are moved with such emotion, not because we look down on the child from the heights of our power and perfection, but rather because we *look up* from our own *limitedness,* inseparable as it is from the *determination* we acquired at some point in time, to the boundless *determinability* in the child and to its pure innocence, and our feelings at such a moment are too visibly mixed with a certain melancholy for this source to be mistaken. In the child are exhibited the *potential* and the *calling,* in us their *fulfillment,* and the latter always remains infinitely behind that potential and that calling. The child is thus for us a realization of the ideal, not, of course, the fulfilled ideal, but the projected one. So it is in no way the representation of its neediness and limitations that moves us; completely to the contrary, it is the representation of its pure and free power, its integrity, its infiniteness, that does so. Consequently, for a person of moral substance and sensitivity a child will be a *holy* object, an object, namely, that by virtue of the magnificence of an idea overwhelms anything magnificent in experience. Whatever this object may lose in the judgment of the understanding [*Verstand*], it gains in rich measure in the judgment of reason [*Vernunft*].

Out of precisely this contradiction between the judgment of reason and that of the understanding there emerges the quite unique phenomenon of those mixed feelings awakened in us by the *naive* manner of thinking. [417] It combines *childlike* with *childish* simpleness [*Einfalt*]. Through childish simpleness a weakness is exposed to the understanding, producing that smile by which we let our *(theoretical)* superiority be known. However, as soon as we have reason to believe that this childish simpleness is at the same time childlike, and that as a consequence it is not a lack of understanding or ability but rather a loftier *(practical)* strength, a heart full of innocence and truth that leads it, on the basis of an inner grandeur, to forsake the assistance art can provide, then that triumph of the understanding is superseded, and that belittling of the child's simplemindedness turns into wonder at its simplicity [*Einfachheit*]. We feel ourselves compelled to respect the object that we smiled about earlier and, since we cast a glance back at ourselves at the same time, we also cannot avoid feeling the need to complain that we are not like that. In this way there emerges the quite unique phenomenon of a feeling in which cheerful patronizing, respect, and melancholy flow together.* For naïveté it is neces-

*In his "Remarks on the Analytic of the Sublime" (*Critique of Judgment*, page 228 [of the second, 1793 edition]) Kant also distinguishes these three sorts of ingredients in the feeling of the naive, but he gives a different explanation of them. "Something from both (the animal feeling of pleasure and the spiritual feeling of respect) are found together in naïveté that is the outbreak of the uprightness originally natural to humanity over against the art of dissembling that has become second nature. People laugh at the simplicity that does not yet understand how to pretend and still they also delight in the simplicity of nature that thwarts art in this respect. People would expect the commonplace custom of the artificial expression, carefully composed *for* show, and lo and behold it is the uncorrupted, innocent nature that they did not at all expect to find and that is revealed by someone who did not have the slightest intention of doing so. This sudden transformation of that beautiful, but false show (that usually means so very much in our judgment) into nothing, the exposure, as it were, of the rogue in us for what it is—this puts the mind in motion in two opposite directions that give a therapeutic jolt to the body. The fact, however, that something infinitely better than all the customs that people have taken on, that is to say, the fact that the purity of the manner of thinking (or at least the potential for that purity) has not been utterly extinguished in human nature, mixes seriousness and esteem into this play of the power of judgment. Yet, because the phenomenon lasts only a short time and the veil of the art of dissembling is quickly drawn again, there is also in it a mixture of pity, a tender emotion, that can be playfully combined quite well with such a good-hearted laughter and in fact usually is. At the same time this pity usually compensates for the embarrassment on the part of the individual who provides the material for the embarrassment by not yet being wise in the ways of men." I confess that this manner of explanation does not completely satisfy me and especially for this reason, that it maintains something about the naive in general that is at most true of one species of it, namely, the naïveté of surprise, of which I will speak later. Of course, it makes us *laugh* if someone in his naïveté *exposes himself*, and in many cases this laughter flows from

sary that nature be victorious over [418] art,* whether this happens against the person's knowledge and will or with full consciousness of it. In the former case it is the amusing naïveté of *surprise,* in the latter case the moving naïveté of *character.*

In the case of the naïveté of surprise, the person must be *morally* capable of denying nature. In the case of the naïveté of character, the person is not permitted to be morally capable of doing so, though we may not think the person *physically* incapable, if he is to strike us as naive. Thus the actions and prattle of children provide us with an unadulterated impression of naïveté, only as long [419] as we are not reminded of their incapacity for art and in general only take notice of the contrast between their naturalness and the artificiality in us. Naïveté is a *childlikeness, where it is no longer expected,* and precisely for that reason it cannot be attributed to actual childhood in the strictest sense.

However, in both cases, that of the naïveté of surprise as well as that of the naïveté of character, nature must be right and art wrong.

Only by virtue of this latter feature is the concept of the naive rendered complete. Passion is also natural, and the rule of propriety is something artificial, yet the victory of passion over propriety is anything but naive. On the other hand, if the same passion wins the day over affectation, over a false sort of propriety, over deception, then we have no misgivings about calling it naive.† Thus it

---

a foregoing expectation that fails to materialize. But even the naïveté of the noblest sort, naïveté of character, always arouses a *smile* that is hardly based on some expectation that has come to nothing. Instead it is only to be explained generally by the contrast between some specific behavior and the forms of conduct that are assumed and expected. I also doubt whether the pity intermingling in our feelings when confronted with naïveté of the latter sort is meant for the naive person and not rather for ourselves or rather for humanity at large, on whose demise we are reminded on such an occasion. It is all too obvious that, in the ordinary course of the world, uprightness is threatened less by physical evil than by a moral grief that necessarily has some more noble object. This object can be indeed none other than the loss of truth and simplicity in humanity.

*Perhaps I should have said with utter brevity "*the truth over deception.*" However, the concept of the naive seems to me still to include something more, since a similar feeling is stirred in us by the simplicity in general that wins out over affectation, and the natural freedom that wins out over stiffness and constraint.

†A child is naughty if, due to craving, thoughtlessness, impetuosity, it violates the dictates of a good upbringing. But it is naive if, due to a free and healthy nature,

is necessary that nature triumph over art, not through the blind force of its *dynamic magnitude*, but rather through the form of its *moral magnitude*. In short, it is necessary that it carry the day not as a matter of *neediness*, but as a matter of *inner necessity*. Not the insufficiency but rather the *illegitimacy* of art must have given nature its victory. For the insufficiency is a lack, and nothing that springs from a lack can engender respect. To be sure, in the case of the naïveté of surprise nature is always made known by the superior force of the passion and a *lack* of reflection. [420] But this lack and that superior force are by no means what constitutes the naïveté. Instead, they merely provide the occasion for nature *to follow unencumbered its own moral constitution*, namely, the law of *harmony*.

The naïveté of surprise can only occur in a human being and only insofar as the human being at that moment no longer is part of nature in its purity and innocence. It presupposes a will that is not in accord with what nature does on its own. Such an [unknowingly naive] person will be alarmed at himself if this is brought to his attention, while the naive *character*, by contrast, will wonder at people and their astonishment. In the case of the naïveté of surprise, therefore, since it is not the personal and moral character, but simply the natural character, set free by passion, that acknowledges the truth, we do not reckon this uprightness to the person's credit and our laughter is warranted mockery, uninhibited by any personal esteem for him or her. However, since here it is still a matter of the uprightness of nature breaking through the veil of falsehood, a loftier sort of satisfaction is combined with the malicious delight at having caught someone by surprise. For nature, in contrast to affectation, and truth, in contrast to deceit, must always stir respect. Thus, too, we feel an actually moral pleasure in regard

---

it dispenses with the overly affected manners characteristic of a fatuous upbringing, the stiff posturing of the dance-master, and so on. The very same thing takes place in the case of the naive when things human are transposed onto things devoid of reason (though this is in no way the proper use of the term). No one will find the sight naive, if weeds get the upper hand in a poorly attended garden. But there is certainly something naive at hand if the painstaking work of the shears in a French garden is destroyed by the wild growth of outstretching branches. Thus it is not at all naive if a trained horse, because of a natural clumsiness, performs its lesson badly; yet there is something naive about its forgetting the lesson because of a natural freedom.

to the naïveté of surprise, although it is not about a moral character.* [421]

In the case of naïveté of surprise we, of course, always have respect for ***nature,*** because we must respect the truth. In the case of naïveté of character, on the other hand, we respect the *person* and for that reason we do not merely enjoy a moral pleasure, but also experience this pleasure in regard to a moral object. In the former as in the latter case nature is *right* in that it speaks the truth. However, in the latter case it is not merely that nature is right, but also that the person is *honorable.* In the first case the uprightness of nature always embarrasses the person because the person acts involuntarily; in the second case it always brings credit to the person, provided that what the person expresses would have disgraced him or her.

We consider someone to have a naive character if in making judgments about things he overlooks their artificial and affected relations and fixes only on the simple nature of them. We expect of him everything that a wholesome nature can ascertain about things, and we completely excuse him only from what presupposes a departure from nature, whether in thinking or in feeling, or at least what presupposes an acquaintance with such a departure.

If a father tells his child that some man is languishing in poverty and the child goes over to the poor man and hands his father's wallet over to him, the action is naive: for the wholesomeness of nature acted from out of the child. In a world where the wholesomeness of nature reigned, the child would have been absolutely right to act in that way. The child looks simply at the need and at the means closest at hand for satisfying it. An extension of the right to property, such that a part of humanity perishes, is not grounded in mere nature. The action of the child thus puts the

*Since the naive rests solely on the form in which something is done or said, this property disappears from view as soon as the matter itself, either through its causes or through its effects, makes an overwhelming or even contradictory impression. Through a naïveté of this sort a crime can also be detected, but then we have neither the detachment nor the time to direct our attention to the form of the discovery; the sense of repugnance for the personal character swallows up any enjoyment of the natural character. Just as enraged feelings rob us of the moral delight with nature's uprightness as soon as we experience a crime, due to naïveté [on the part of the criminal], so our malicious joy is strangled by the compassion aroused as soon as we see someone put in danger by his naïveté.

actual world to shame, and we also acknowledge as much in our hearts by the delight we feel about that action.

If someone acquainted with the world but otherwise possessing a fair understanding of things [*gutem Verstand*] confesses his secrets to someone else who deceives him but knows how to conceal this deception cleverly, if his very forthrightness lends that person the means to do him harm, we find it naive. We laugh at him, but by the same token we still cannot [422] help admiring him. For his trust in that other person springs from the honesty of his own sensibilities. At any rate, he is naive only to the extent that this is the case.

The naive manner of thinking can thus never be a property of a degenerate human being; it can only be an attribute of children and people with a childlike disposition. The latter act and think naively, often right in the middle of sophisticated contexts of the larger world. Because of their own beautiful humanness they forget that they have to deal with a depraved world and they behave in the courts of kings with an ingenuousness and innocence such as one finds only in a pastoral world.

It is, moreover, not at all easy, always correctly to distinguish childish from childlike innocence. There are actions that hover at the outermost extreme between the two forms of innocence, and in those instances we are left completely in doubt as to whether we should laugh at the simplemindedness or revere the nobleness of that simplicity. One finds a quite remarkable instance of this in the history of the reign of *Pope Adrian the Sixth,* described for us by Mr. Schröckh with his typical thoroughness and pragmatic sort of truthfulness. This pope, a Dutchman by birth, administered the papacy at one of the most critical moments for the hierarchy, when an embittered faction unsparingly exposed the weaknesses of the Roman Church while an opposing faction had every interest in covering them up. There is no question what a genuinely naive character would have done in this case, if ever one had mistakenly ascended a chair of St. Peter. But there is indeed a question as to what extent such naïveté of character might be compatible with the role of a pope. Moreover, it was this that caused Adrian's predecessors and successors the greatest embarrassment. They uniformly adhered to the then accepted Roman system of putting nothing in order anywhere. But Adrian actually possessed the honest character of his nation and the innocence of his earlier standing. He had ascended to his lofty post from the narrow confines of a scholar, and even at the pinnacle of his new [423] dignity he did not become unfaithful to that simple character. The abuses in the Church moved him, and he was much too honest to dissimulate in public what he admitted to himself in private. In conformity with this way of thinking, he allowed himself, in the *Instruction* he dispatched with his legation to Germany, to be misled into making admissions previously unheard-of from any pope and running directly counter to the principles of this court. Among other things it says: "It is well known to us that for several years now much has transpired on this holy chair that is abhorrent. It is no wonder if this sick condition has passed from the head to the limbs, from the pope to the prelates. All of us have strayed, and for some time now there has been no one among us, not a single one, who has done something worthwhile." Again, in another place he commands his legation to declare in his name, "that he, Adrian, may not be censured for what was done by the popes prior to him and that such excesses would always have met with his disapproval, since at the time they happened he still occupied a minor position, and so on." One can easily think how such naïveté coming from the pope may have been received by the Roman clergy. The very least that people reproached him for was that he betrayed the Church to heretics. This supremely obtuse step taken by the pope would be worthy meanwhile of all our respect and admiration, if we could only convince ourselves that he had actually been naive, that is, that he had been forced simply by the natural genuineness of his character without any regard for the possible consequences, and that he would not have hesitated any less to take that step were he to have seen the full extent of the indiscretion committed. However, we have some reason to believe that he considered this step not at all so impolitic, and in his innocence went so far as to hope to have gained some very important advantage for the Church by obliging its opponents. He imagined not only that he had to take this step as an honest man, but also that he had to be able to answer for it as pope. Because he forgot that the most spurious of all structures could only be preserved by continually denying the truth, he made [424] the unforgivable mistake of following rules of conduct, that might well have obtained in the context of natural relationships, in a setting diametrically opposed to a natural one. This, of course, changes our judgment considerably. Although we cannot deny our respect for the honesty of heart from which that action flowed, this respect is not a little diminished by consideration of the fact that art here was no more a match for nature than his head was for his heart.

Every true genius must be naive or he is no genius. Naïveté alone makes someone a genius, and what someone is in the intellectual and aesthetic realm can hardly be disavowed in the moral realm. Unacquainted with the rules, those crutches of feebleness and disciplinarians of perversion, and guided solely by nature or instinct, his guardian angel, genius passes calmly and securely through all the snares of bad taste that inevitably entangle someone not a genius, if he is not clever enough to avoid them from afar. It is a gift of genius alone, always to be at home even beyond the confines of what is familiar, and to *expand* nature without *going outside* it. Occasionally, of course, even among the greatest geniuses, one comes across a case of going beyond nature, but only because even they have their moments of fantasy when they take leave of the safety of nature, either because they are carried away by the power of an example or because the degenerate taste of their age misleads them.

A genius must resolve the most complicated tasks with unassuming simplicity and ease. The egg of Columbus is the emblem for every decision of genius. Someone establishes himself as genius solely by the fact that he prevails over the entangled enterprise with simplicity. Genius proceeds not according to recognized principles but rather according to insights and feelings. But its ideas are inspirations of a god (everything wholesome nature does is divine); its feelings are laws for all times and for all races of men.

The childlike character imprinted by genius upon its works also shows up in its private life and morals. It is *chaste* because nature always is, but it is not *proper* since only what is profane is proper. It is *judicious* because nature can never be anything else, [425] but it is not *cunning*, since only art can be that. It is *faithful* to its character and inclinations, but not so much because it has principles as because nature, for all its wavering, again and again returns to its original state, always reviving the old need. It is *humble*, even shy, because genius always remains a mystery to itself, but it is not fearful since it knows nothing of the dangers on the path it treads. We know little of the private lives of the greatest geniuses, but this contention is confirmed even by the little that has been preserved for us, for example, about Sophocles, Archimedes, Hippocrates and in more recent times about Ariosto, Dante, and Tasso, about Raphael, about Albrecht Dürer, Cervantes, Shakespeare, about Fielding, Sterne, and others.

Indeed, what appears far more difficult, even a great statesman and general will exhibit a naive character if his greatness is due to his genius. Among the ancients I would call to mind here only Epaminondas and Julius Caesar, among the moderns only France's Henry the Fourth, Sweden's Gustavus Adolphus, and the czar Peter the Great. The dukes of Marlborough, Türenne, and Vendome all show us this character. Nature has assigned to the opposite sex its highest perfection as far as the naive character is concerned. The feminine addiction to being pleasing strives after nothing so much as the *illusion of being naive;* proof enough, if one had no other evidence, that the greatest power of the sex rests upon this characteristic. However, because the reigning principles of women's education are in constant conflict with this character, it is as difficult for the woman in the moral sphere as it is for the man in the intellectual sphere with the advantages of a good education to keep that splendid gift of nature from being lost. The *woman,* who for the larger world joins this moral naïveté with adroitness in her behavior, is as worthy of esteem as the scholar who combines an ingenious freedom of thought with the complete rigor of the schools.

From the naive way of thinking there flows of necessity a naive expression, as much in words as in movements, and it is the most important element of grace. With this naive [426] grace genius expresses its sublimest and profoundest thoughts, divine decrees from the mouth of a child. If the scholastic understanding, always in fear of error, hammers its words like its concepts on to the cross of grammar and logic, if it is rigid and intractable in order not to be indefinite, if it is verbose in order not to say too much, and takes the force and edge out of its thoughts so that they do not sound imprudent, then by contrast, with a single propitious stroke of the pen, genius gives its own thoughts an eternally definite, fixed, and yet completely free form [*Umriß*]. While the sign always remains different from and alien to what is signified in the case of scholastic understanding, the language of genius springs from thought as by an inner necessity and is so one with it that even concealed by the body the spirit appears as though exposed. This manner of expression, where the sign completely disappears in what is signified, and where the language, as it were, leaves naked the thought it expresses while someone else can never present that thought without at the same time concealing it, this above all is what people call ingeniousness and esprit in the style of writing.

Like the genius's self-expression in its works of spirit, innocence of heart expresses itself freely and naturally in the life of society. It is well known that people in social life deviate from the simplicity and strict genuineness of expression to the same degree that their attitudes become affected. The easily injured sense of guilt, just like the easily seduced imagination, necessarily produces a nervous condition. Without being false people often say something other than what they are thinking; people feel that it is necessary to beat about the bush in order to say things that could prove to be painful only to a sick sort of self-love, or that could prove to be dangerous only to a perverted fantasy. An ignorance of these conventional laws, together with a natural uprightness that considers every sort of crookedness and appearance of mendacity repulsive (not crudity, which it sets aside as an annoyance), produces a naïveté of expression in society, consisting in naming things by their right name and in the most straightforward manner, things that people are permitted to identify either not at all or only in some artificial way. [427] The ordinary expressions of children are of this sort. They produce laughter because of their contrast with accepted manners, yet people will always in their hearts admit to themselves that the child is right.

Taken in the proper sense, naïveté of character [*Gesinnung*] can, of course, only be ascribed to the human being as an entity not utterly subordinated to nature, although only insofar as pure nature still really acts out of him. Yet, through an effect of the poeticizing imagination, it is often transferred from rational things to things devoid of reason. Thus we often say that an animal, a landscape, a building—indeed, nature generally—possesses a naive character *[Charakter*] in contrast to human beings' arbitrariness and fantastic conceptions. In each case, however, this also demands that in our thoughts we lend a will to what lacks a will, while noting how rigorously it adheres to the law of necessity in its orientation. Dissatisfaction with our own poor use of our moral freedom and with the lack of ethical harmony in our actions easily induces the sort of mood in which we address what is devoid of reason as a person, applauding its endless uniformity and envying its calm composure as though it had actually had to struggle with a temptation to be otherwise. At such a moment we are ready to consider the prerogatives of our reason a curse and an evil and, with a vivid feeling of the imperfection of what we actually are accomplishing, we lose sight of the merits of our own potential and calling.

We then see in nonrational nature only a more fortunate sister who remained at home with her mother, while we stormed out into an alien world, arrogantly confident of our freedom. With painful urgency we long to be back where we began as soon as we experience the misery of culture and hear our mother's tender voice in the distant, foreign country of art. As long as we were mere children of nature we were happy and complete; we became free and lost both happiness and completeness. Out of this situation there spring two quite different kinds of longing for nature, a longing for its *happiness* and a longing [428] for its *completeness*. Only a sensual individual complains about the loss of the happiness that nature alone can provide; only a moral individual can mourn the loss of nature's completeness.

Ask yourself well, my sensitive friend of nature, whether your sensitivity toward nature is a matter of your torpidity yearning for rest or your offended moral sensibility yearning for harmony. If you find art repulsive and if the abuses in society drive you to the solitude of lifeless nature, ask yourself whether what disgusts you are society's exploitations, burdens, and troubles or its moral anarchy, its arbitrariness, its disorders. Your courage should [*muß*] joyfully throw itself into the former ills and replace them with the freedom that is the source of that joy. You may indeed set up nature's serene happiness as a distant goal, but only as the reward of your worthiness. Let us, therefore, hear no complaints about life's aggravations, about the inequality of conditions, about the pressure of relations, about the insecurity of possessions, about ingratitude, oppression, persecution. Freely resigned to all culture's *ills* [*Übeln*], you must submit to them and respect them as the natural condition of what alone is good. You must complain only about the evil [*Böse*] of those conditions, but not merely with feeble tears. Rather you must take care to act purely amidst those adulterations, freely amidst that bondage, steadfastly amidst the caprice of mood, lawfully amidst that anarchy. Do not be afraid of the confusion outside you, but rather of the confusion within you. Strive for unity, but do not look for it in uniformity; strive for composure, but through equanimity, not through suspension of your activity. That nature you envy in things devoid of reason is not worthy of your respect or your longing. That nature lies behind you, it must forever lie behind you. Abandoned by the guide that deceived you, you have no other choice remaining than to take hold of the law with a free consciousness and will, or fall irretrievably into a bottomless abyss.

But if you can take consolation in the loss of natural *happiness,* then let its *completeness* serve as the model for your heart. If you step out of your artificial circle toward the completeness of nature, then it stands before you in its magnificent stillness, in its naive beauty, [429] in its childlike innocence and simplicity. Dwell at that moment on this image, cultivate this feeling; it is worthy of what is most splendid in your human nature. Do not let it occur to you any longer to want to *change places* with nature. Instead, take nature up into yourself and strive to wed its unlimited advantages to your own endless prerogatives, and from the marriage of both strive to give birth to something divine. Let nature surround you like a lovely *idyll,* in which again and again you find the way back to yourself from the aberrations of art and gather the courage and new confidence about the course of life, so that the flame of the *ideal,* so easily extinguished in life's storms, is rekindled in your heart.

Recall the beauty of nature surrounding the ancient *Greeks.* Consider how confidently this people was able, under its serendipitous sky, to live with nature in the wild; consider how very much nearer to the simplicity of nature lay its manner of thinking, its way of feeling, its mores, and what a faithful copy of this is provided by the works of its poets. If one reflects upon these things, then the observation must appear strange that one encounters there so few traces of the *sentimental* interest we moderns attach to nature's settings and characteristics. There is, of course, no depiction of those scenes more exact, faithful, and detailed than that of the Greek. However, the depiction is not more exact, faithful, and detailed, and contains no more special involvement of the heart, than the depiction of a dress, a shield, a weapon, a household tool or some sort of mechanical product. He seems, in his love for the object, to make no distinction between what it is of itself and what it is through art and human will. Nature seems of more interest to his intellect and thirst for knowledge than to his moral feeling. He does not cling to nature with the fervor, sensitivity, and sweet melancholy that we moderns do. Indeed, by personifying and deifying it in its individual appearances, and by presenting its effects as actions of beings endowed with freedom, the Greek overcomes the serene necessity in it, precisely what makes it so attractive to us. His impatient fantasy leads him past it to the drama of human life. Only what is alive and free, only characters, [430] actions, and mores satisfy him. If in certain moral frames of mind *we* might wish to exchange our freedom of will (that exposes us to so much struggling with ourselves and to so many aggravations and aberrations) for the predestined but serene necessity of things devoid of reason, the fantasy of the Greeks is always busy working in precisely the opposite direction, setting up human nature already within the inanimate world and ascribing to the will influence where a blind necessity reigns.

Whence, indeed, comes this different spirit? How is it that we are so infinitely surpassed by the ancients in everything that is natural, and yet at precisely this point we are able to revere nature to a higher degree, to cling to it more intimately, and to embrace even the inanimate world with the tenderest of feelings? This is *so* because nature has disappeared from our humanity, and we reencounter it in its genuineness only outside of humanity in the inanimate world. Not our greater *naturalness* [*Naturmäßigkeit*], but the very opposite, the *unnaturalness [Naturwidrigkeit*] of our relationships, conditions, and mores forces us to fashion a satisfaction in the physical world that is not to be hoped for in the moral world. This is the satisfaction of that awakening urge for truth and simplicity that lies, like the moral predisposition from which it flows, in all human hearts as something indestructible and ineradicable. It is for this reason that the feeling with which we cling to nature is so intimately related to the feeling we have when we protest the passing of childhood and childish innocence. Our childhood is the only unmutilated nature that we still encounter in the cultivated part of humanity. Thus it is no wonder, if each footstep of nature outside us leads us back to our childhood.

In the case of the ancient Greeks it was very much different.* For them the culture had not degenerated to such a degree that nature was left behind [431] in the process. The entire edifice of their social life was erected on feelings, not on some clumsy work of art. Their theology itself was the inspiration of a naive feeling, born of a joyful imagination and not of brooding reason as is the belief of the churches of modern nations. Hence, since the Greek had not lost the nature in humanity, he also could not be surprised by nature outside humanity, and for that reason could have no pressing need for objects in which he rediscovered nature. One with himself and content in the feeling of his humanity, the Greek had to stand quietly by this humanity as his ultimate and to concern himself with bringing everything else closer to it. *We,* on the other hand, neither one with ourselves nor happy in our experiences of humanity, have no more pressing interest than to take flight from it and to remove from sight so miscarried a form.

The feeling spoken of here is thus not something that the ancients had. It is rather the same as the sort of feeling we *have for the ancients.* They felt naturally, while we feel the natural. Undoubtedly, what filled Homer's soul, as he had his divine swineherd entertain Ulysses, was a completely different feeling from what moved the soul of the young Werther when he read this song following an evening in some irritating company. Our feeling for nature is like the sick person's feeling for health.

---

*But also only in the case of the Greeks. For in order to extend life to the inanimate and to pursue the image of humanity with this zeal it is necessary to have precisely the sort of animated movement and rich fullness of human life that surrounded the Greeks. The human world of *Ossian,* for example, was shabby and uniform, while the inanimate world around him was magnificent, colossal, mighty, and thus forced itself on him, asserting its rights over human beings. Accordingly, in the songs of this poet the inanimate nature far more (than the human beings) emerges as an object of feeling. Meanwhile, even Ossian himself complains about a decline of humanity. As inconsiderable as culture's scope and depravities were among his people, the experience of it was still sufficiently vivid and intrusive to make the singer, full of high-minded feelings as he was, turn back in fear to the inanimate and pour out over his songs that elegiac sound that makes them so touching and endearing to us.

Just as nature eventually begins to disappear from human life as an *experience* and as the (acting and feeling) *subject,* we see it ascend in the world of poets as an *idea* and *object.* The very [432] nation that had gone to the greatest extremes in regard to what is unnatural and in reflection upon it must have been first affected by the phenomenon of the *naive* in the strongest way and given a name to it. This nation was, as far as I know, the *French.* Yet the naive feeling and the interest in it are naturally much older, dating from the very outset of the moral and aesthetic degeneracy. This change in the manner of feeling is, for example, already extremely evident in the case of Euripides, if he is compared with his predecessors, especially Aeschylus, even though Euripides was the favorite of his time. The same revolution can also be demonstrated among the ancient *historians.* Horace, the poet of a cultured and degenerate era, praises the serenity and joy of his Tibur and he could be named the genuine founder of this sentimental kind of poetry, since he provides a model of it that is still unsurpassed. One finds traces of this manner of feeling in Propertius and Virgil as well, among others, but less so in the case of Ovid who lacked the fullness of heart for it and who, in his exile to Tomi, painfully misses the urban delights that Horace so gladly dispensed with in his Tibur.

By virtue of the very notion of a poet, poets are everywhere the *guardians* of nature. Where they can no longer completely be this, and where they have already experienced within themselves the destructive influence of arbitrary and artificial forms or have had to contend with them, they will appear as nature's *witnesses* and *avengers.* They will either *be* nature or *seek* the lost nature. Two completely different manners of poetry spring from this fact, exhausting and demarcating the entire realm of poesy [*Poesie*]. Depending on the character of the age in which they flourish or on the impact that contingent circumstances have on their general formation and their passing states of mind, all poets who really are such will be either *naive* or *sentimental.*

The poet of the world in its youth, naive and inspired, just like the sort of person who comes closest to him in ages of artificial culture, is austere and shy. Distrustful, like the virgin [433] Diana in her forest, he flees the heart that seeks him, the need that would embrace him. The arid truthfulness with which he treats his subject matter often appears as insensitivity. The subject matter takes complete possession of him; his heart does not lie like some cheap metal right beneath the surface, but rather wants to be sought, like gold, in the depths. Like the divinity behind the structure of the world, he stands behind his work. The *naive poet* is the work and the work is the *naive poet*. You have to be unworthy of the work or not up to it or have already had your fill of it, to ask only about *the poet*.

Thus, for example, Homer among the ancients and Shakespeare among the moderns, despite being two extremely different natures separated by the immeasurable distance between epochs, reveal themselves to be completely the same, as far as this feature is concerned. When, at a very early age, I first became acquainted with Shakespeare, I was infuriated by the coldness and insensitivity that allowed him to joke at a point of the greatest pathos, and to let some buffoon disrupt the heartrending scenes in *Hamlet*, in *King Lear*, in *Macbeth*, and so forth. That same insensitivity restrained him where my feelings carried me away, it tore him cold-bloodedly away from the place where my heart would have so much preferred to have lingered. I was misled by my acquaintance with more modern poets into first looking for the poet in the work, encountering *his* heart and reflecting in common with *him* on his subject matter [*Gegenstand*]. In short, I was misled into looking at the object [*Objekt*] in the subject. As a result I could not bear the fact that the poet in Shakespeare's case nowhere let himself be grasped and nowhere sought to give an account of himself. He commanded all my respect and I studied him for several years before I learned to appreciate him as an individual. I was still not capable of understanding nature firsthand. I could only endure the image of it, as reflected by the intellect and set down correctly according to a rule, and for this the French and also the German sentimental poets, from the years 1750 until about 1780, were precisely the right subjects. Incidentally, I am not ashamed of this childhood judgment, since mature criticism passed a similar judgment and was naive enough to set it down for the world.

I encountered the same phenomenon with Homer, whom I learned to know at a much later period. I remember [434] now the remarkable passage in the sixth book of the *Iliad* where Glaucus and Diomedes thrust at one another in battle and, after recognizing each other as a former guest and friend, exchange gifts. Next to this moving portrait of piety, where the laws of *hospitality* were observed even in war, Ariosto's depiction of the *noble courage of chivalry* can be placed. In that story two knights and rivals, Ferrau and Rinald, the former a Christian, the latter a Saracen, both covered with wounds after a mighty battle, make peace and mount the same horse to retrieve the fleeing Angelica. As diverse as these two examples might otherwise be, they have an almost identical effect on our hearts because both portray the beautiful victory of custom over passion, and both touch us through the naïveté of their sentiments. Yet how completely differently the poets behave in the course of describing this similar action. As the citizen of a world that had fallen away from the simplicity of customs of an earlier age, Ariosto cannot conceal his own amazement and emotion while relating this incident. The sense of the distance between those customs and the customs characteristic of his age overwhelms him. All at once he stops portraying the subject matter and appears in his own person. The beautiful stanza is well-known and has always been especially admired:

> O the noble courage of the ancient rites of knights!
> Rivals they were, divided in their faiths,
> Still suffering from head to toe
> The bitter pain of the wild struggle of enemies;
> Suspicion set aside, they rode together
> Through the darkness of the crooked path;
> The horse, driven on by four spurs, galloped
> Until the way divided in two.*

And now the old Homer! Scarcely does Diomedes learn from Glaucus the story of his enemy's being a guest and friend of his people from the time of his forefathers than he plunges his lance into the ground, speaks with him as a friend, and agrees with him that in the future they will keep out of each other's way in battle. Yet, let us hear Homer himself: [435]

> And so from now on I am your guest in Argos
> As you are mine in Lycia when I visit that land.

*Ludovico Ariosto, *Orlando Furioso,* canto 1, stanza 22.

For this reason let us avoid each other's lances in the heat of
 battle.
Indeed, there are enough of the Trojans and their famous allies
For me to slay, if God permits it, and to cut down;
And there are also enough Achaians for you to kill what you
 can.
But let us both exchange our armor so that even others
See how we take pride in being guests from the times of our
 fathers."
Thus those two warriors spoke with one another, and
 swinging down from their chariots,
They shook hands and extended friendship to one another.

A *modern* poet (at least one who is a modern in the moral sense of this term) would hardly have waited until then to testify to his delight at this action. We would forgive him all the more easily, since we also pause in our hearts while reading and eagerly distance ourselves from the subject matter in order to look at ourselves. But there is not a trace of any of this in Homer. As though he were reporting something commonplace, indeed, as though he himself had no heart in his breast, he continues in his dry, matter-of-fact way:

Still, Zeus so excited Glaucon, that he, unthinkingly,
Traded his gold armor for the bronze armor of Diomedes,
Armor worth a hundred young steers for armor worth nine.*

In an artificial age poets of this naive sort are rather out of place. In such an epoch they are also scarcely possible any more, or at least they are possible only by *running wild* in their age and being protected from its mutilating influence by some benign fortune. They can never emerge from society itself, but outside it such poets still occasionally appear, though more as strange individuals whom people stare at and uncultivated nature boys who offend them. As valuable as their appearances are for the artist who studies them and for the authentic connoisseur who appreciates them, on the whole these poets are not very fortunate in their century. On their foreheads they bear the mark of someone who is in control and in

**Iliad*, Book VI, v. 224–36.

command; [436] but we would rather be rocked in the cradle by the Muses, we want the muses to carry us. The critics, the real border patrol of taste, detest these naive poets for *disrupting the boundaries* and would rather see them suppressed. That even Homer is granted some validity by these judges of taste might be traced simply to the force of more than a thousand years of testimony. It becomes a disagreeable enough matter for them to affirm rules contrary to his example, and to assert his reknown, contrary to their rules.

The poet, I say, either *is* nature or he will *seek* it. The former makes for the naive poet, the latter for the sentimental poet.

The poetic spirit is immortal and humanity cannot lose it. It can disappear only when humanity and the predisposition for poetry disappear. For if the human being by the freedom of his fantasy and intellect puts some distance between himself and the simplicity, truth, and necessity of nature, then not only does the path to it still stand forever open to him, but a mightier and more indestructible instinct, the moral instinct, drives him ceaselessly back to it. The capacity for poetry stands, moreover, in the most intimate relation to this instinct. This capacity, in other words, does not vanish with the natural simplicity, but only works in another direction.

Even now nature is still the only flame that nourishes the poetic spirit. The poetic spirit generates all its power from nature alone, and even in the case of an artificial human being, that is to say, the human being conceived in culture, it speaks to nature alone. Any other manner of working is alien to the poetic spirit. Thus it may be said in passing that the practice of labeling all so-called works of wit "poetic" is completely unjustified, although for a long time, misled by respect for French literature, we have confused such works with poetic works. Even today, in the artificial condition of the culture, it is nature, I say, that gives the poetic spirit its power. Only now it stands in a completely different relation to nature.

As long as the human being is still part of nature that is pure (which, of course, is not to say "unrefined"), he operates as an undivided sensuous unity and as a harmonizing whole. Sense and reason, receptive and spontaneous faculties, have not yet divided the tasks between them; [437] still less do they contradict one another. His feelings are not the formless play of chance; his thoughts are not the empty play of imagination. The former proceed from the law of *necessity*, the latter from the law of *actuality*. Once the human being has entered into the condition characteristic of culture and art has laid its hands on him, that *sensuous* harmony within him is overcome and he can only express himself as a *moral* unity, that is to say, as someone striving for unity. The agreement between his feeling and thinking, something that *actually* took place in the original condition, now exists only *ideally*. It is no longer in him but rather outside him, as a thought that must first be realized, and no longer as a fact of his life. Suppose now that the concept of poesy [*Poesie*], understood as nothing other than the concept of *giving humanity its most complete possible expression*, is applied to both these conditions. In the original condition of natural simplicity, where the human being still acts as a harmonious unity with all his powers at once, and where consequently his entire nature fully expresses itself in actuality, the most complete possible *imitation of the actual* is *what necessarily makes someone a poet*. On the other hand, here in the condition of culture, where that harmonious cooperation of the human being's entire nature is merely an idea, the elevation of actuality to the ideal or, what comes to the same, *the portrayal of the ideal is what necessarily makes the poet*. And, in general, these two are the only possible ways the poetic genius can express itself. They are, as one sees, completely different from one another. Yet there is a higher concept that encompasses them both, and it should not strike anyone as strange that this concept coincides with the idea of humanity.

This is not the place to pursue this thought further; it can only be cast in its full light by a separate elaboration devoted to it alone. However, anyone who is capable of setting up a comparison between ancient and modern poets* in terms of the spirit of their poetry, and not simply the forms their poetry happens to take, will easily [438] be able to convince himself of the truth of this notion. The ancient poets touch us through nature, through sensuous truth, through living presence; the modern poets touch us through ideas.

*It is perhaps not superfluous to recall that, if the modern poets are contrasted here with the ancient poets, it is not so much the difference in the age as the difference in the manner that is to be understood. In modern times, indeed, even in the most recent times we also have naive poetry in all classes even if no longer of a completely pure sort. Among the ancient Latin poets and in fact even among the ancient Greek poets there is no shortage of sentimental poets. Not only in the same poet, even in

This road taken by the modern poets is, moreover, the same road humans in general must travel, both as individuals and as a whole. Nature makes a human being one with himself, art separates and divides him; by means of the ideal he returns to the unity. Yet because the ideal is an infinite one that he never reaches, the cultured human being in *his* way can never become complete as the natural human being can be in his way. If we pay attention solely to the relation in which both stand to their respective ways of proceeding and to what is optimal for each, then the cultured individual would necessarily lag infinitely behind the natural individual in perfection. On the other hand, if one compares their two approaches with one another, then it becomes apparent that the goal for which the human being *strives* through culture is infinitely superior to the goal that he *attains* through nature. Thus the value of the one consists in absolutely reaching a finite greatness, while the value of the other lies in approaching an infinite greatness. Yet because only the latter admits of *degree* and *progress*, the relative value of the human being wrapped up in culture and taken as a whole is never able to be determined. This is true although that same person, considered individually, finds himself necessarily at a disadvantage in relation to someone in whom nature works in all its perfection. Insofar, however, as the final goal of humanity is unattainable other than by that continual progression, and the human being in nature cannot progress other than by cultivating himself and thus passing over into a civilized state, there is no question as to which of them has the advantage in regard to that final goal. [439]

The very same thing said here of the two diverse forms of humanity may be applied to those two corresponding forms of poets as well.

For this reason people either should not have compared ancient and modern—naive and sentimental—poets with one another at all, or should have done so only in terms of some common higher concept (there actually is such a concept). For obviously, if people first extract the generic concept of poesy one-sidedly from the ancient poets, then nothing is easier, but also more trivial, than to put down the modern poets in relation to them. If one calls poesy

---

the same work, one frequently finds both types united as, for example, in *Werther's Suffering*. Such creations will always make for the greater effect.

only what at all times works uniformly on the simple nature of someone, then it is unavoidable that one will have to dispute whether modern poets ought to be called "poets," precisely in regard to their sublimest beauty, the beauty most peculiar to them. For here the modern poets speak only to the child of art, and have nothing to say to the child of simple nature.* For anyone whose mind is not prepared to pass beyond the actual world into the realm of ideas, the richest content will be an empty illusion and the poet's loftiest flight an exaggeration. It cannot occur to any reasonable person to try to put some modern alongside Homer in terms of what is great in Homer, and it sounds ridiculous enough when Milton or Klopstock is honored by being called "a modern Homer." Yet just as little will any ancient poet and least of all Homer be capable of holding his own in a comparison with what distinguishes the modern poet. [440] If I might be allowed to put it this way, the ancient poet's power stems from the art of something limited, the modern from the art of something infinite.

The ancient artist's strength consists in that limitation ("ancient artist" since with some obvious qualifications what has been said here about the poet can be extended to the fine artist in general). This is precisely what explains the great advantage the plastic arts of antiquity have over those of modern times, and generally the disparity in quality [Wert] between modern poetic as well as plastic arts and both species of art in antiquity. A work for the eye finds its perfection only in something bounded; a work for the imagination can attain its perfection only through something unbounded. Thus, the superiority of the moderns in ideas helps them little in works of the plastic arts. Here the modern is required to *determine*

*It might have been permitted Molière as a naive poet to leave to the opinion of his cleaning lady, the decision as what was to remain and what to be left out in his comedies. It would have been valuable if the masters of the French buskin had attempted this experiment a few times with their tragedies [Trauerspiele]. But I would not have advised that a similar experiment be set up in the case of Klopstock's odes and the most beautiful passages in the *Messias, Paradise Lost, Nathan the Wise,* and many other pieces. Yet what am I saying? This experiment is actually being conducted and Molière's cleaning lady rationalizes all over in our critical libraries, in philosophical and literary annals and travel accounts concerning poetry, art, and the like. Only, as usual, on German soil this takes place with a little less tastefulness than it does on French soil, as suits the servants' quarters called "German literature."

in space down to the smallest detail the picture he imagines and, as a result, he is forced to measure himself against the ancient artist in that very respect in which the ancient has the indisputable advantage. It is different in poetic works. Here, too, the ancient poets wins the day insofar as it is a matter of the simplicity of the forms and what is *physical* and capable of being displayed sensuously. But the modern poet in turn has the better of the ancient when it comes to the richness of the material, to what cannot be portrayed and uttered, in short, what in works of art people call *spirit*.

Since the naive poet merely follows simple nature and feeling, limiting himself solely to imitation of reality, he can have only a single relation to his object and, in *this* respect, he has no choice regarding the treatment. The diversity of impression in naive compositions rests solely on the different *degree* of one and the same manner of feeling (provided that one sets aside everything in it belonging to the content and considers that impression exclusively and purely as the work of the poetic treatment). Even the diversity in the external forms can produce no change in the quality of that aesthetic impression. The form may be lyrical or epic, dramatic or descriptive, and we can well be affected in a weaker and [441] stronger, but never in a different way (as soon as we abstract from the content). Our feeling is thoroughly the same, proceeding completely from a single element, so that we can distinguish nothing in it. Even the difference in languages and ages alters nothing here, for it is precisely this pure unity of its origin and effect that is the mark of naive poetry.

In the case of the sentimental poet things work in a completely different way. This sort of poet *reflects* on the impression the objects make upon him and only on the basis of that reflection is the emotion founded, into which he is transported and into which he transports us. The object here is related to an idea, and his poetic power rests solely upon this relation. The sentimental poet thus always has to deal with two conflicting images and feelings, with the actual world as a limit and with his idea as something infinite. The mixed feeling aroused by him will always testify to this twofold source.* Hence, since a plurality of principles is to be found

*Whoever takes note within himself of the impression made upon him by naive poetry and is in a position to separate the portion of it owing to the content, will

here, it depends upon which of the two will *outweigh* the other in the feeling of the poet and in his presentation. Consequently, a difference in the treatment is possible. The question then arises whether he dwells more on the actual or on the ideal—whether he wants to develop the actual world as an object of aversion or the ideal as an object of affection. His presentation will accordingly be either *satirical or elegiacal* (in a broad sense of this word, which will later be explained). [442] Every sentimental poet will cling to one of these two sorts of feeling.

The poet is satirical if he takes as his subject matter the distance from nature and the contradiction between the actual and the ideal (in their effect on the mind both come to the same). He can accomplish this seriously as well as facetiously, with passion as well as levity, depending upon whether he dwells on the domain of the will or the intellect. The former happens by means of the *censuring* or pathetic satire, the latter by means of the *amusing* satire.

Strictly speaking, the purpose of the poet is compatible with neither the tone of censure nor that of amusement. The former is too serious for the play that poetry should always be; the latter too frivolous for the seriousness that should lie at the bottom of all poetic play. Moral contradictions necessarily interest our heart and for that reason rob the mind of its freedom, and yet all real interest, that is, all relation to a need, should be banned from poetic emotions. Intellectual contradictions, on the other hand, leave the heart indifferent, while the poet has to deal with the supreme interest of the heart, with nature and the ideal. It is thus no mean task for him in the pathetic satire not to violate the poetic form that consists in a free play, and in the amusing satire not to lack the poetic content that must always be something infinite. This task can only be resolved in a single way. The censuring satire achieves poetic freedom by becoming something sublime, while the comical satire sustains poetic content by treating its subject matter in a beautiful manner.

---

find this impression always joyful, always pure, always peaceful, even in the case of very pathetic objects. In the case of the sentimental the impression will always be something serious and tense. This is so because, in the case of naive depictions, whatever they seek to treat, we always take pleasure in the truth, in the living presence of the object in our imagination, and do not look for anything beyond this. In the case of sentimental portrayals, on the other hand, we have to unify the image of the imagination with an idea of reason and for that reason we always end up wavering between two diverse conditions.

In the satire, the actual world as something lacking is contrasted with the ideal as the supreme reality. It is, incidentally, in no way necessary for the ideal to be articulated if the poet simply knows how to awaken it in the mind. But it is absolutely necessary that he does this, or he will have no poetic effect at all. Thus, the actual world in this case is necessarily an object of aversion, but what is most important, the aversion must itself spring in turn from the contrasting ideal. [443] The aversion could also have a merely sensuous origin and be grounded solely in a need frustrated by the actual world. Frequently enough we feel a kind of moral indignation at the world when we are simply exasperated by a conflict between it and our inclinations. It is this material interest that the vulgar satirist brings into play and, because he does not fail to make us emotional, he fancies that he has our hearts in his power and that he is a master in pathetic matters. Yet every pathos springing from this source is unworthy of the poetic art, an art that may touch us only through ideas and reach our hearts only through reason. In addition, the vulgar satirist's impure and material sort of pathos always exposes itself by an excess of suffering and an embarrassingly jejune mentality. By contrast, genuinely poetic pathos is recognizable by a preponderance of spontaneity and by a freedom of mind persisting in the midst of passion. If the emotion itself springs from the ideal opposed to the actual world, then every inhibiting feeling disappears into the sublimity of that ideal, and the magnificence of the idea we are filled with elevates us above all experience's limitations. In the presentation, then, of an actuality that we find revolting, everything turns on this, that the basis of the poet's or storyteller's depiction of that actuality be necessary and that the poet know how to predispose our minds to ideas. As long as *we* simply remain honorable in our evaluation, it does not matter at all if the subject matter is at the same time contemptible and beneath us. When the historian Tacitus portrays for us the profound decadence of the Romans of the first century, it is a case of a superior spirit looking down at the inferior, and our frame of mind is truly poetic because it is precisely that lofty plain on which he himself stands, and to which he succeeded in raising us, that rendered the subject matter inferior.

Hence, the pathetic satire must always flow from a mind vividly permeated by the ideal. Only a prevailing urge for harmony can and may engender that deep sense of moral contradiction and that burning revulsion at moral perversion, a sentiment that becomes the inspiration of a Juvenal, Swift, Rousseau, Haller, and others. [444] If circumstances had not given their minds this specific direction early on, the same poets would necessarily have written with equal success in gentle and tender genres. To a degree they have actually done this. All those mentioned here either lived in a degenerate age and had a horrible experience of moral decay right before their very eyes, or their own fates had strewn bitterness in their souls. Also, because it separates the illusory from the essential with unyielding rigor and penetrates into the depths of things, the philosophical spirit inclines the mind to the rigidity and austerity characteristic of the way Rousseau, Haller, and others portray the actual world. Yet these external and contingent influences, which always work in a restrictive way, may at most determine the direction, but never supply the content of the inspiration. In every case this content must be the same and, free of every external need, it must flow from a burning drive toward the ideal, a drive that is, indeed, the only genuine calling of the satirical poet in particular, and the sentimental poet in general.

If the pathetic satire is designed only for souls that are *sublime,* then the mocking satire can only succeed in hearts that are *beautiful.* For the sublime soul is already secure from frivolity by virtue of its serious subject matter. However, that beautiful heart, which is permitted to treat only a morally neutral material, would unavoidably dissolve into that material and lose all poetic value, if the treatment did not ennoble the content and the *subject* [*Subjekt*] of the poet did not represent his object [Objekt]. Only a beautiful heart, however, has been granted the privilege of stamping each of its expressions with a perfect image of itself, completely independent of the subject matter [Gegenstand] of the work. The sublime character can announce itself only in individual victories over the resistance of the senses, only in certain moments of an upsurge and by an instantaneous exertion. In the beautiful soul, on the other hand, the ideal acts like nature, that is to say, uniformly, and for that reason can also reveal itself in a state of calm. The deep sea appears most sublime in its surging movement, the clear brook most beautiful in its gentle flow.

Many times there has been a dispute over which of the two,

[445] the tragedy or the comedy, deserves to be ranked ahead of the other. If what is being asked by this question is simply which of the two treats the more important object [Objekt], then there is no doubt that the tragedy has the advantage. But if one wants to know which of the two demands the more important subject [Subjekt], then the verdict might come out rather on the side of comedy.—In tragedy so much happens already by virtue of the subject matter, while in comedy nothing happens because of the subject matter; everything happens because of the poet. Now, since the material never comes into consideration in cases of judgments of taste, then naturally the aesthetic value of these two genres of art stands in inverted relation to the importance of their material. The object [Objekt] carries the tragic poet along; the comic poet, on the other hand, must prop up and sustain his object in the loftiness of the aesthetic, through his subjectivity [Subjekt]. While the tragic poet is permitted flights of fancy, which do not require so much, the comic poet must remain himself; that is to say, the comic poet must already *be* there and be at home there where the tragic poet can only get to by leaps and bounds. And it is precisely this that distinguishes the beautiful character from the sublime. Every sort of greatness is already contained in the former, it flows unforced and without trouble from his nature; as far as his ability is concerned, there is something infinite about him at every juncture along his path. The sublime character, on the other hand, is able to discipline and elevate himself to any level of greatness; by the force of his will he can tear himself from any state of limitation. Thus, while the sublime character is free only by fits and starts and with a struggle, the beautiful character is free always and with ease.

To produce and nourish this freedom of mind in us is the beautiful task of comedy, just as the aim of tragedy is to help restore freedom of mind by aesthetic means when it has been violently overcome by a passion. Thus, in the tragedy the freedom of mind must be overcome artificially and experimentally, since the tragedy proves its poetic power by restoring that freedom. In the comedy, on the other hand, the poet must be on guard never to reach the point of overturning the freedom of mind. Accordingly, the writer of tragedies always treats his subject matter practically, while the writer of comedies always treats his theoretically, even if the former (such as Lessing in his *Nathan*) indulges a whim of working on some theoretical material and the latter (the writer of comedy) of working on some practical material. [446] A subject matter is rendered tragic or comic, not by the domain from which it is taken, but rather by the forum before which the poet brings it. The writer of tragedy must take care to avoid placid argumentation, he must always interest the heart. The writer of comedy must guard against pathos and always entertain the intellect. Thus the former displays his art by constantly arousing passion, the latter by constantly fending it off. This art is naturally greater, the more abstract the nature of the subject matter is in the case of tragedy and the more it leans toward the pathetic in the case of comedy.* Hence, if tragedy starts from a more important point, then it must be acknowledged on the other hand that comedy moves toward a more important goal and would render all tragedy superfluous and impossible if it achieved that goal. Comedy's goal is the same as the supreme goal of human striving: to be free of passion, to look around and into oneself always with clarity and composure, to find everywhere more chance than fate, and to laugh more about absurdity than rage and whine about maliciousness.

As in real life so also in poetic depictions one often encounters beauty of soul being confused with simple lightheartedness, the talent for being pleasant and agreeable, a cheerful goodnaturedness. Since common tastes generally never rise above things that are agreeable, it is an easy matter for such *likeable* spirits to usurp that fame that is so difficult to deserve. Yet there is an infallible test, [447] by means of which that natural kind of lightness can be distinguished from the ideal lightness, like the virtue due to temperament, can be distinguished from a genuinely moral character. This probe occurs when both put themselves to the test on some difficult and great object. In such a case the easygoing genius

*In *Nathan the Wise* this did not happen. Here the frigid nature of the material casts a chill over the entire artwork. But Lessing himself knew that he wrote no tragedy [Trauerspiel] and in his unique concern—and this is only human—he simply forgot the teaching established in dramaturgy that the poet is not authorized to apply the tragic form to something else as the purpose of the tragedy. Without quite essential changes it would scarcely have been possible to transform this dramatic poem into a good tragedy. However, with merely incidental alterations it might have yielded a good comedy. To the latter end what is pathetic in the drama would had to have been sacrificed, to the former end the rationalizing. There is probably no question on which of the two the beauty of this poem most rests.

unfailingly descends to the level of platitudes, while someone virtuous by temperament turns into someone materialistic. The genuinely beautiful soul, on the other hand, just as certainly becomes something sublime.

As long as Lucian simply lampooned absurdity, as in *The Wishes, The Lapides, Jupiter Tragödus,* among others, he remains a master of parody and delights us with his merry humor. However, a completely different man emerges from many passages of his *Nigrinus,* his *Timon,* and his *Alexander,* where his satire concerns moral decay as well. "Oh, hapless soul," he writes as he begins the dreadful portrait of Rome in his *Nigrinus,* "why do you leave the sunlight, Greece, and that happy life of freedom and come here to this din of pompous servility, of attendance at court and banquets, of sycophants, flatterers, poisoners, gold diggers, and false friends? And so on." On these and similar occasions there can be no mistaking the high level of seriousness of the feeling, a seriousness that must lie at the bottom of every play if it is to be poetic. Even in the malicious parody of Socrates, his mistreatment at the hands of Lucian as well as Aristophanes, there is a glimmer of a serious reason avenging the truth on the sophist and contending for an ideal that it simply does not always articulate. Without doubt Lucian demonstrated this character in his *Diogenes and Daemonax* as well. Among the moderns what a magnificent and beautiful character is expressed by Cervantes at every appropriate occasion in his *Don Quixote!* What a splendid ideal must have lived in the soul of the poet who created a *Tom Jones* and a *Sophia!* How immensely and powerfully the laughing Yorick is able at will to stir our minds! I also recognize this seriousness of feeling in our Wieland. A gracious heart animates and ennobles the mischievous plays of his moods; this graciousness puts its stamp even on the rhythms of his songs and there is never [448] a shortage in him of that surging power of lifting us up, at the right moment, to the highest summit.

No such judgment may be passed on Voltaire's satires. To be sure, even in the case of this writer it is solely by means of the truth and simplicity of nature that he at times moves us in a poetic way, be it the case that he actually achieves this in some naive character, as happens several times in his *L'Ingénu,* or that he seeks it and avenges it as in his *Candide,* among others. Where neither of the two is the case, he can, of course, amuse us as a witty head but certainly not move us as a poet. Yet everywhere there is too little seriousness at the bottom of his ridicule, and this renders his calling as a poet justifiably suspect. We always encounter only his intellect, not his feelings. No ideal reveals itself under that airy wrapping and there is hardly anything absolutely solid displaying itself in that endless movement. His wondrous complexity in regard to external forms, far from establishing something about the inner fullness of his spirit, instead bears considerable witness against it. For in spite of all those forms he did not find a single one in which he would have been able to express his heart. Hence, one almost has to fear that in this rich genius it was merely the poverty of heart that determined his calling to satire. Were it otherwise, then somewhere on his broad journey he would have had to depart from this narrow track. Yet with all the massive turnover of material and the external form, we see this inner form recur in endless, impoverished monotony. Despite his voluminous career he still did not complete the human journey within himself, the very circuit one happily finds completed in the satirists mentioned above.

If a poet sets nature off against art and the ideal off against the actual world, such that the presentation of the ideal dominates and the satisfaction taken in it becomes the prevailing feeling, I call him *elegiac*. This genre, too, like the satire, has two classes under it. Either nature and the ideal are objects of mourning, when the former is presented as something lost, the latter as something unattained, or both are objects of joy, because they are represented as something actual. [449] The first class yields the *elegy* in the narrow sense, the second class the *idyll* in the broadest sense.* [450]

*To readers who have penetrated more deeply into the matter I will hardly have to justify my use of the names "satire," "elegy," and "idyll" in a sense broader than usual. My purpose in doing so is in no way to disrupt the boundaries that previous observance has with good reason set for the satire and the elegy as well as for the idyll. I look merely to the manner of feeling prevailing in these types of poetry and it is indeed sufficiently well known that this manner of feeling does not allow of being enclosed in those narrow boundaries. We are not only touched in an elegiac manner by the elegy that is explicitly so called. Even the dramatic and epic poets can move us in an elegiac fashion. In the *Messiade,* in Thomson's *Seasons,* in *Paradise Lost,* in *Jerusalem Saved,* we find several portrayals that are otherwise peculiar solely to the idyll, the elegy, the satire. It is also more or less the same in every poem of pathos. Yet, that I count the idyll itself with the elegiac genre, appears rather to require a justification. One might remember, however, that here we are

Like the indignation in pathetic satire and the mockery in sarcastic satire, the sadness in the elegy may only flow from an enthusiasm or inspiration [Begeisterung] awakened by the ideal. Only by this means does the elegy sustain any poetic content, and every other source of it is completely beneath the dignity of the poetic art. The elegiac poet seeks nature, but in its beauty, not merely in its agreeableness, in its correspondence with ideas, not merely in its obligingness to need. Sadness over lost joys, over the golden age that vanished from the world, over the departed happiness of youth, of love, and so forth, can only become the material of an elegiac poetry if those conditions of sensuous tranquility allow themselves to be represented at the same time as objects of moral harmony. For this reason I cannot consider the lamentations composed by Ovid from his place of exile at Euxin, as touching as they are and as much poetic quality as individual passages possess, to be a poetic work as a whole. There is much too little energy, much too little spirit and nobility in his pain. Need, not inspiration, gives rise to those laments. In them there breathes, to be sure, no common soul, yet it is the common mood of a nobler spirit whom fate has pushed to the ground. Of course, if we remember that it is Rome, and the Rome of Augustus he mourns for, we forgive the son of pleasure his pain. But even Rome in its splendor and with

---

talking only of the sort of idyll that is a species of sentimental poetry. It is part of the essence of sentimental poetry that nature is set off against art and the ideal against the actual. If this is not explicitly done by the poet and he places before our eyes a portrait of nature unspoiled or the ideal fulfilled purely and independently, that contrast is still in his heart and will betray itself, even without his willing it, in every stroke of the pen. Indeed, were this not the case, then the very language he must use will bring to mind the actual world with its limitations, civilization with its artificiality. For the language bears the spirit of the time in itself and experiences the influence of art. Indeed, our own hearts would set the experience of corruption in contrast to that image of nature in its purity and thus make the manner of feeling in us elegiac, even if the poet had not intended that. This is so unavoidable that even the supreme enjoyment afforded the cultivated human being by the most beautiful works of the naive genre from ancient and modern times does not long remain pure, but instead sooner or later will be accompanied by an elegiac feeling. Lastly, I note that the division attempted here, precisely because it is based simply upon the manner of feeling, should determine nothing at all in the division of poems themselves and the derivation of the poetic types. For since the poet, even in the same work, is in no way bound to the same manner of feeling, that division cannot be taken from the manner of feeling, but rather must be gathered from the form of the presentation.

all its felicities, if not first exalted by the imagination, is merely a finite greatness and thus an unworthy object for the poetic art. For this art, elevated above everything erected by the actual world, only has the right to mourn for what is infinite.

The content of the poetic lamentation can thus never be an external object [Gegenstand]; it can only be an inner, idealistic object. Even if it deplores a loss in the actual world, it must first transform it into a loss in an ideal sense. The poetic treatment consists exclusively in this transformation of what is limited into something infinite. The external material is thus in itself always irrelevant, since the poetic art can never use it as the art finds it. Rather, only what the art makes of it gives it poetic value. The elegiac [451] poet looks to nature, but as an idea and with a completeness in which it never existed, even if he bewails it as something that once had been and now is lost. When Ossian tells of bygone days and vanished heroes, his poetic power has already transformed those images of memory into ideals and those heroes into gods. The experiences of a specific loss have grown into the idea that everything passes away [allgemeine Vergänglichkeit], and the affected bard, haunted by the image of the ever-present ruin, soars to heaven in order to find in the course of the sun a sensuous image of something that does not pass away [Unvergängliche].*

I turn now to the modern poets in the elegiac genre. Rousseau, the poet just as much as the philosopher, tends only either to seek nature or to avenge it on art. Depending upon whether his feeling dwells more on the one or the other, we find him sometimes moved in the manner of an elegy, sometimes mesmerized by Juvenal's satire, other times transported to the plain of the idyll, as in his *Julie*. Without question his compositions have poetic content since they treat an ideal, only he does not know how to use that content in a poetic way. To be sure, his serious character never allows him to sink to frivolity, but it also does not permit him to elevate himself to the play of the poetic. Caught in the straights of passion at one time, of abstraction at another, he seldom or never brings it to the sort of aesthetic freedom that the poet must assert over his material and communicate to his reader. Either his sick sensitivity prevails over him, driving his feelings to a painful level, or the

*One might read, for example, the splendid poem entitled "Carthon."

power of his thought ties up his imagination and by the rigor of the conception destroys the gracefulness of the portrayal. Both properties, the internal reciprocity and union of which really make the poet, are found in this writer to an uncommonly high degree. What is missing is simply the expression of them actually united with one another; what is missing, in other words, is a greater blending of Rousseau's spontaneity with his feeling and his sensitivity with his thinking. Thus, too, [452] in the ideal of humanity that he sets up, too much attention is paid to the limitations of humanity and too little to its capability. Everywhere in this ideal a need for physical *peace* is more visible than a need for moral *harmony*. His passionate sensitivity is responsible for the fact that, simply in order to be rid of the conflict in humanity as soon as possible, he would rather see it led back to the spiritually empty uniformity of its original condition than see the battle ended in the spiritually rich harmony of a thoroughly developed culture. He would rather not let art begin at all than wait for its completion; in short, he wants to set the goal lower and to scale down the ideal simply in order to attain it all the more quickly and certainly.

Among Germany's poets in this genre I would like to mention here only Haller, Kleist, and Klopstock. The character of their poetry is sentimental. They move us by means of ideas, not by means of sensuous truth, not so much because they themselves are natural as because they know how to make us enthralled by nature. Meanwhile, what is true of the character of these poets, like all sentimental poets *as a whole,* naturally does not for that reason in any way rule out their capacity *individually* to touch us with naive beauty. Otherwise none of them would ever be poets. It is only that it is not their distinctive and dominant character, to feel with a calm, uncomplicated, and easy sensibility and to exhibit the feeling in just this way. The imagination involuntarily crowds the intuition, the power of thought anticipates the feeling, and they close eyes and ears in order to sink, meditating, into themselves. This mentality can endure no impression without at the same time looking to the play of its own mind and, by reflection, setting up outside and opposite itself what it has in itself. In this way we never receive the object [Gegenstand], but only what the reflective understanding of the poet makes of the object. Even when the poet himself is this object, when he wants to show us his feelings, we do not experience his situation immediately and firsthand, but rather as that situation is reflected in his mind, in other words, what he, observing himself, has thought about it. Consider Haller mourning the death of his [453] spouse (the beautiful song is well-known), beginning as follows:

Were I to sing of your death
O Marianne, what a song!
When sighs wrestle with the words
And one thought flees the others.

We find this description precise and genuine, but we also feel that the poet does not really communicate his feelings. Instead he communicates his thoughts about them. His affect on us is, moreover, just that much weaker since his feelings must have already become cooled quite a bit for him to be able to be an observer of his emotion.

The largely supersensuous material of Haller's and in part also of Klopstock's compositions already excludes them from the naive genre. Since that material could not assume a corporeal nature and consequently could not become an object of sensuous intuition, it had to be transported to the realm of the infinite and elevated to an object of spiritual intuition, from the moment it was supposed to be worked over in an exclusively poetic way. In general, only in this sense is a didactic poetry thinkable without internal contradiction. For, to repeat once again, poetry possesses only these two arenas. It must dwell either in the world of the senses or in the world of ideas, since it absolutely cannot thrive in the realm of concepts or in the world of the understanding [*Verstand*]. Still, I confess that I am acquainted wth no poem in this [didactic] genre, from either ancient or more modern literature, that has brought the concept it is working over either down to the level of the individual or up to the level of the idea in a pure and complete way. The usual case, if it goes well at all, is that of an alternation between the two of them, while the abstract conception dominates, and the imagination, which ought to have the say on the poetic plain, is merely permitted to serve the intellect. We must still await that didactic poem in which the thought itself would be poetic and also remain so.

What is said here in general of all didactic poems obtains especially in those of Haller. The thought itself is no poetic thought, but occasionally the execution becomes poetic, [454] sometimes through the use of images, sometimes through the impetus toward ideas. Only in the latter respect do these poems belong here. Power and depth and a seriousness full of pathos characterize this poet. His soul is ignited by an ideal; in the serene valleys of the Alps his ardent feeling for truth searches for the innocence that has disappeared from the world. His lament is profoundly touching. While he sketches the errors of the intellect and heart with an energetic, almost bitter satire, he lovingly portrays the beautiful simplicity of nature. Yet the concept dominates everywhere in his portraits, just as within himself the intellect plays the master over his feeling. Thus, he always *teaches* far more than he *discloses,* and when he does disclose, he always does so with features more forced than they are gentle. He is great, bold, fiery, sublime; but he has seldom or never risen to beauty.

As far as content of ideas and profundity of spirit are concerned, Kleist is quite inferior to this poet. He may surpass him in gracefulness if indeed we are not, as sometimes happens, reckoning as a strength on the one hand what is a lack on the other. Kleist's soul, so full of feeling as it is, revels most at the sight of rural scenes and customs. He is happy to flee the empty bustle of society and find in the lap of inanimate nature the harmony and the peace that he misses in the moral world. How stirring is his longing for peacefulness!* How genuine and full of feeling, when he sings:

> Oh, world, you are the tomb of true life.
> A hot urge often pricks me to virtue
> A torrent of melancholy cascades down my cheeks
> Example conquers and you, oh fire of youth
> Quickly you dry up the noble tears.
> A true human being must be far from human beings.

Yet if his poetic impulses drove him from the suffocating circle of relationships into the spiritual solitude of nature, the frightful image of his age and, alas, even its chains also hounded him all the

*See Ewald von Kleist's poem, "Sehnsucht nach Ruhe," v. 115–20.

way there. What he flees is in him; what he seeks is eternally outside him. He can never recover from the evil [455] influence of his century. His heart may be sufficiently aflame and his imagination energetic enough to breathe life into the inert fabrications of the intellect through his presentation of them. But the cold thought just as often kills the living creation of the poetic power and reflection disrupts the secret work of feeling. To be sure, his poetry is colorful and sparkling like the spring he praises in song, his fantasy is animated and energetic. Yet, one might label them fickle rather than bountiful, frivolous rather than creative, ambling restlessly forward instead of being expansive and edifying. Features are exchanged for features rapidly and exuberantly, yet without concentrating on the individual, without becoming alive and completing the figure. As long as he composes solely in a lyrical way and dwells simply on the portraits of landscape, we are permitted—in part by the greater freedom of the lyrical form, in part by the more arbitrary nature of his material—to overlook this deficiency. For in this case we generally demand a display of the poet's feelings more than of the object itself. But the shortcoming becomes only all too obvious when, for example, in his *Cissides* and *Paches* and his *Seneca,* Kleist presumes to depict human beings and human actions. In such cases the imagination sees itself constrained by rigid and necessary boundaries, and the poetic effect can only proceed from the *subject matter.* Here Kleist becomes scant, boring, meager, and reserved to an unbearable degree. This example is a warning to all who, lacking the inner calling, recklessly dare to ascend from the plain of musical poesy to the mimetic realm. The very same recklessness, that is only human, is encountered in the kindred genius of Thomson.

In the sentimental genre and especially in the elegiacal part of it, few modern and even fewer ancient poets can be compared with our Klopstock. In the field of ideality, this musical poet has accomplished whatever there was to be attained beyond the confines of living form and beyond the domain of the individual.* Of course,

*I say "musical" in order to recall here poetry's dual kinship: to the art of sound and to the pictorial art. Depending respectively upon whether poetry either imitates a specific *object,* as the pictorial arts do, or produces a specific *state of mind* without requiring a specific object for that, as the arts of sound do, the poetry can be called pictorial or musical. Thus the latter expression refers not merely to what in the one would do him a great injustice [456] if one tried in general to deny him that individual truthfulness and vitality characteristic of the way the naive poet portrays his object. Many of his odes, several individual features in his dramas and in his *Messias* present the subject matter with striking exactness, situating it beautifully. Not infrequently he has demonstrated a magnificent nature and an alluring naïveté, particularly where the theme is his own heart. Yet *his* strength does not lie here; this characteristic did not allow itself to be conveyed through the whole of his poetic career. As splendid a creation as the *Messias* is from a *musically* poetic point of view, as understood in the elaboration given above, it still leaves much to be desired from the point of view of the *plastic* or *mimetic* side of poetry, where one expects forms that have been specified—and *specified for intuition*. The characters [Figuren] in this poem may be specific enough, but not for the intuition. Abstraction alone has created them, and abstraction alone can differentiate them. They are good examples for concepts, but they are not individuals, they are not living figures [Gestalten]. A poet is still required to turn his attention to the imagination and to control it by the thoroughgoing determinacy of his forms. In Klopstock's case much too much freedom is given to the imagination to visualize these people and angels, these gods and devils, this heaven and this hell. A sketch is provided, within which the intellect necessarily must think of them, but no fixed boundary is set, within which the fantasy would necessarily have to depict them. What I am saying here about the characters holds for everything in the poem that is, or is supposed to be, about life and action. Moreover, such is the case not only in this epic, but also in the poet's dramatic poems. [457] Everything is exactly determined and delimited for the understanding (here I recall merely his Judas, his Pilate, his Philo, his Solomon in the tragedy by this name), but it is much too formless for the imagination. Here, I confess freely, I find this poet completely out of his element.

His element is always the realm of ideas and, whatever he is

poetry actually is music in terms of the material, but rather generally to all those musical effects that the poetry is able to produce without controlling the imagination by means of some specific object. In this sense I call Klopstock especially "a musical poet."

working over, he knows how to transport it into the realm of the infinite. One might say he removes the body from everything he treats in order to make it spirit, just as other poets clothe everything spiritual with a body. Almost every pleasure afforded by his compositions must be wrestled free by exercising the power of thought. All the feelings that he knows how to arouse in us so intimately and so mightily, spring from supersensible sources. Thus the earnestness, the power, the drive, the profundity characteristic of everything coming from him; thus, too, the ever-present tension in which our minds are kept while reading him. No poet (with the exception of Young, who in this respect demands more than Klopstock does, but without compensating as Klopstock does) is less suited to be a favorite and a companion through life than Klopstock, who always leads us only away from life, always summons the spirit alone to arms without invigorating the senses with the peaceful presence of some object. His poetic muse is chaste, supernatural, incorporeal, and holy as his religion; one must confess with amazement that, although he occasionally gets lost in these lofty heights, he has never sunk below them. For this reason, frankly, I admit that I fear the mentality that without affectation can actually consider this poet's work its favorite. By this I mean the sort of book with which we are able to agree in any situation, and to which we are able to return from any situation. I would have thought, too, that one would have seen fruits enough in Germany of his dangerous ascendancy. Only in certain exalted moods can Klopstock be sought out and experienced. For this reason he is also the idol of young people, although he is by far not their most fortunate choice. The young who always strive for something beyond life, who flee all forms and find every boundary too confining, give themselves up with love and pleasure [458] to the endless spaces opened up for them by this poet. If a youth then becomes a man and returns from the realm of ideas to the confines of experience, then much, very much of that enthusiastic love is lost, though none of the respect owed so singular a phenomenon, so extraordinary a genius, so very noble a feeling. Germany in particular owes its respect to such a tremendous contribution.

I called this poet "great" especially in the elegiacal genre, and it will scarcely be necessary to substantiate this judgment in detail. Capable of every energy and master of the entire field of sentimental poetry, at one time he is able to make us shudder through the most extreme pathos, at another time he can rock us to sleep in heavenly sweet sensations. Yet his heart is overwhelmingly inclined to a lofty, spiritual melancholy, and as sublimely as his harp and lyre sound, the languishing tones of his lute reverberate ever more truly, profoundly, and movingly. I appeal to everyone whose feelings are pure and in harmony: would you not foresake all the boldness and strength, every fiction, all the descriptions full of splendor, every epitome of oratorial eloquence in *Messias,* all the gleaming similes (at which our poet is so particularly adept) for the gentle sensations exuding from this genre in the elegy *To Ebert,* in the splendid poem *Bardale, Early Graves, Summer Night, Lake Zurich,* and several others. Thus, as little as it satisfies me as a portrayal of an action and as an epic work, *Messias* is dearer to me as a treasure chest of elegiac feelings and idealistic depictions.

Perhaps, before I leave this area, I should also recall the merits of an Uz, Denis, Geßner (in his *Death of Abel*), Jacobi, von Gerstenberg, of a Hölty, von Göckingk, and several others in this genre. They all touch us by means of ideas and, given the meaning of the term settled upon earlier, they all composed sentimentally. However, my purpose is not to write a history of German poetic art, but rather, by means of some examples from our literature, to make clear what was said earlier. I intended to show the diversity of the [459] path taken by ancient and modern, naive and sentimental poets, and to show that if the former move us through nature, individuality, and a vivid *sensuality,* the latter demonstrate just as great a power over our minds, though not as widespread, by means of ideas and a lofty *spirituality.*

In the examples so far, it has been seen how the sentimental poetic mind treats some natural material. One might, however, also be interested in knowing how the naive poetic mind proceeds with sentimental material. This task appears to be altogether new and to entail a quite unique sort of difficulty. For while such *material* was not to be found in the ancient and naive world, in the modern world the *poet* for this was lacking. Nevertheless, genius also took this task upon itself and resolved it in an amazingly successful manner. The task is resolved by a character who ardently embraces an ideal and flees the actual world in order to contend for a phantom infinite, someone who looks incessantly outside himself for what he just as incessantly destroys within himself, someone for whom his dreams alone are the real thing and his experiences always only handicaps, someone who ultimately sees in his own existence only a barrier and, as is only reasonable, tears it down in order to penetrate to the true reality. This dangerous extreme of the sentimental character has become the material for a poet in whom nature works more faithfully and purely than in anyone else. Among the modern poets this poet is perhaps the least removed from the sensuous truth of things.

It is interesting to see with what fortunate instinct everything that nourishes the sentimental character is concentrated in *Werther.* Raving, ill-fated love, sensitivity to nature, religious feelings, a spirit of philosophical contemplation, finally, to leave nothing out, the world of Ossian, gloomy, formless, melancholy. If one adds to this how little value, indeed, how inimical the actual world is to it and how everything outside joins together to force the tortured soul back into his ideal world, then one sees no possible way such a character would have been able to save himself from such a cycle. In the *Tasso* [460] by the same poet the same conflict recurs, albeit in completely different characters. Even in his latest *novel,* as in that first one, the poetic spirit sets itself off against sober common sense, the ideal against the real, the subjective manner of representation against the objective—but with what a difference! Even in *Faust* we meet the same conflict, though, of course, made cruder and materialized on both sides, as the content requires. It would be worth the effort to attempt a profile of this character's psychological development, spelled out in these four ways so different from one another.

Above it was remarked that simply having a carefree and jovial sort of mind, if it is not based upon an inner fullness of ideas, in no way endows someone with a knack for humorous satire, however generously common judgment takes it for having such. To the same degree, simply having a softhearted and gentle disposition prone to melancholy does not yield some special aptitude for elegiac poetry. In both cases, the genuine talent of poets that is lacking is the energetic principle that must animate the material in order to engender something truly beautiful. Thus, products of this gentle genre can merely soothe us, flattering our sensuous character without stirring the heart and occupying the mind. A continual penchant for this way of feeling must ultimately enervate a person's character, plunging it into a state of passivity from which no reality at all, neither the external life nor the inner life, can emerge. Thus people have acted quite rightly in mocking unrelentingly the evil of *sentimentalism* [*Empfindeley*]* and *whining fashion,* such as began to get the upper hand in Germany some eighteen years ago through misinterpretation and aping of some excellent works. At the same time, although that scorn is appropriate, the way people are inclined to indulge the—scarcely better—parody of that elegiac caricature, the farcical figures, heartless satyrs, and moronic caprice† [461] makes it quite clear that those evils have been castigated for reasons that are not completely innocent. On the scale of genuine taste the one counts as little as the other, since both lack the aesthetic content that is contained solely in the intimate merging of the spirit with the material and in the unified relation of a work to the capacity to feel and have ideas.

People have laughed at *Siegwart* and his story of the monastery, while the *Travels to the South of France* is admired. Yet both works have an equally strong claim to a certain degree of appreciation and an equally slight claim to unconditional praise. The first novel can be appreciated for its genuine, although exaggerated, feelings; the second for its lighthearted humor and astute, refined intelligence. Yet just as the appropriate intellectual soberness is thoroughly wanting in the one novel, so there is a lack of aesthetic dignity in the other. The first novel becomes a little ridiculous in the face of experience, the second novel becomes almost despicable in relation to the ideal. Now, since what is truly beautiful must be in harmony with nature on the one hand, and with the ideal on

*"The addiction," as Mr. Adelung defines it, "to tender, gentle feelings, *without rational intention* and beyond the proper measure"—it is very fortunate for Mr. Adelung that he feels only intentionally and, indeed, on the basis of a rational intention at that.

†Of course, there is no reason to spoil certain readers' cheap thrill for them. In the end, what does it matter to criticism if there are people who are able to edify and amuse themselves with the obscene jokes of Mr. Blumauer? Yet the judge of art should at least refrain from speaking, with a certain respect, of works, the existence of which ought with good reason to remain a secret to good taste. To be sure, in those works talent and wit are unmistakable. But all the more is it to be regretted that both are not more refined. I am not saying anything about our German comedies; the poets portray the age in which they live.

the other, the one novel as little as the other can lay claim to being called "a beautiful work." At the same time it is natural and right (and I know it from my own experience) that Thümmel's novel is read with great pleasure. Since he violates only such requirements as spring from the ideal and since, consequently, those requirements are in no way set up by the majority of his readers (and certainly not by the better ones while reading the novel) and since, finally, he fulfills the remaining requirements of the mind and body to an uncommon degree, his book must and will rightly remain a favorite [462] of our time and all times when people compose aesthetic works merely to please, and when people read merely for pleasure.

Yet is not poetic literature in possession of even classic works that appear to violate the exalted purity of the ideal in a similar way and that seem, because of the material character of their content, to deviate substantially from that spirituality demanded here of every aesthetic work of art? What even the poet, the chaste disciple of the muse, may permit himself to do, should that not be allowed the novelist, who is only his half brother and still touches the earth so much? I may avoid this question all the less in the present context, since there are masterpieces at hand in the elegiac as much as in the satiric genre that appear to look for and recommend a nature completely different from that spoken of in this essay, masterpieces that appear to defend that nature not so much against bad as against good morals. Thus, either these poetic works would have to be rejected, or the concept of elegiac poetry proposed here would have to be assumed to be much too arbitrary.

What the poet may permit himself, it was said, should that not be indulged the person narrating in prose? The answer is already contained in the question: what the poet is allowed to do can prove nothing for someone who is not a poet. In the very concept of a poet, and only in this, lies the basis of that liberty, which is nothing but a perfidious license as soon as it cannot be derived from what is highest and noblest in the constitution of the poet.

The laws of propriety are alien to nature in its innocence. Their only origin is the experience of degenerateness. However, once this experience is undergone and natural innocence has disappeared from morals, they are sacred laws that a moral feeling may not violate. These laws obtain in an artificial world with the same right that the laws of nature prevail in the world of innocence. Yet overturning everything within himself that harks back to an artificial world, and knowing how to restore nature in its original simplicity within himself is precisely what constitutes the poet. If he has done this, then for this very reason he is also exempted from all [463] the laws through which a seduced heart defends itself from itself. He is pure, he is innocent, and what is permitted nature in its innocence is permitted him. If you who read or listen to him are no longer innocent and if you are incapable, even for a moment, of finding your innocence in his purifying presence, then it is *your* misfortune and not his. You may as well take leave of him; he has not sung for you.

In regard, then, to liberties of this sort, the following may be stipulated.

First, only nature can justify them. Hence, they may not be the product of choice and a deliberate imitation. For we can never forgive an encouragement of sensuousness on the part of a will that is always oriented toward moral laws. Therefore, they must always be *naive.* However, in order to be able to convince ourselves that they actually are naive, we must see them supported and accompanied by everything else likewise grounded in nature, since nature is only recognizable in the rigorous consistency, unity, and uniformity of its effects. Only if a heart wholly disdains all artificiality, even where it is useful, are we allowed to exempt it from conventions when they are oppressive and confining. Only if a heart submits to all the bonds of nature do we permit it to make use of nature's liberties. Consequently, all other feelings of such a human being must bear the stamp of naturalness within themselves. He must be genuine, simple, free, open, sensitive, straightforward. All deception, all cunning, all arbitrariness, all petty self-seeking must be banished from his character, and all traces of them must be banished from his work.

Second, only a *beautiful* nature can justify liberties of this kind. They may not be one-sided outbreaks of desire, for everything that springs from neediness alone is contemptible. These sensuous energies must also flow from the whole and fullness of human nature. They must be *humane.* In order to be able to judge that human nature as a whole and not merely some one-sided, common, sensual need requires it, we must see human nature portrayed as a whole, a whole of which those sensuous energies make up only one aspect. [464] In itself, the sensuous way of feeling is something innocent and neutral. It displeases us in a human being only because it is something brutish, testifying to a lack of genuine, complete humaneness within him. It insults us in a poetic work only because such a work lays claim to pleasing us, thereby deeming *us* liable to such a lack as well. Yet, if we see the entire remaining scope of human nature in the individual who has let himself be so surprised and if we find all the realities of human nature expressed in the work in which people took liberties of this sort upon themselves, then that reason for our discontent is removed and we can be enthralled with sheer joy at the naive expression of a genuine and beautiful nature. Thus the same poet who may permit himself to make us share such lowly human feelings must in turn know how to carry us up to all that is magnificent and beautiful and sublimely human.

And so we would have found the standard to which we can safely subject every poet who takes it upon himself to oppose propriety, and pushes his liberty to this limit in the portraying nature. The moment his work is *cold* and *empty*, it is vulgar, inferior, and, without exception, deserves reproach, for that coldness and emptiness demonstrate that its origin is not unintentional, that it springs from a vulgar need and that it is a profane attack on our desires. On the other hand, as soon as it is naive and combines the mind and the heart,* it is beautiful, noble, and worthy of acclaim, regardless of all the objections of a frigid sense of decency.

Someone may say to me that most of the French stories in this genre and their most successful imitations in Germany [465] might very well not survive if the standard given here were adopted, and that in part this might also be the case for many works of our most graceful and ingenious poet, including even his masterpieces. To this I have nothing to reply. The claim itself is nothing new at all, and I am only presenting here the reasons for a judgment that already for some time has been passed on these objects by everyone

*"With *heart,*" because the purely sensuous ardor of the portrayal and the sumptuous fullness of the imagination by far are not what constitutes it. Thus, for all the sensuous energy and all the fire of the coloring, *Ardinghello* always remains merely a sensuous caricature, devoid of genuineness and aesthetic merit. Still, this curious production will always remain remarkable as an example of the almost poetic flight that the *mere desire* was capable of taking.

with a more refined sensibility. These principles may perhaps appear far too strict in regard to those writings. Yet the same principles might be found too liberal in regard to some other works. For I would not deny that the very reasons, on the basis of which I consider inexcusable the seductive portraits by the *Roman* and *German Ovid,* just like those of a Crébillon, Voltaire, Marmontel (who calls himself a moral storyteller), Laclos, and many others, reconcile me with the elegies of the *Roman* and *German Propertius,* indeed, even with many a decried work of Diderot. For while the former works are merely witty, prosaic, and lewd, the latter are poetic, human, and naive.* [466]

IDYLL

It remains for me to say a few words about this third species of sentimental poetry; only a few words since a more thorough development of it, which it especially needs, is reserved for another time.†

*If I mention the immortal author of the *Agathon, Oberon,* and so forth in this company, I must explicitly explain that I in no way wish to have him confused with that group. His portrayals, even the most doubtful from this perspective, have no materialistic tendency (as a more recent, somewhat unreflective critic lately permitted himself to say). Such a tendency is not possible for the author of *Love for Love* and of so many other naive and ingenious works in each of which a beautiful and noble soul is mirrored with unmistakable features. Yet he seems to me to be plagued by the quite distinctive misfortune that those very portrayals were made necessary by the plan of his poetic writings. The cool intellect that drew up the plan demands them and his feelings seem to me to be so far from favoring them that in the execution itself I still always believe that I recognize that cool intellect. And it is just this coldness in the presentation that is harmful to those portrayals when they are evaluated, for only the naive feeling can justify them aestheticaly as well as morally. What I doubt, however, (and concerning this I would be very glad to hear an intelligible judgment) is whether the poet may be permitted to draft the sort of plan that exposes him to such a danger in its execution and, for the moment conceding the foregoing, whether in general a plan can be called "poetic," that cannot be carried out without incensing the chaste feeling of the poet as well as his readers and without making both dwell on objects from which a noble sensibility so readily distances itself.

†Again I must remind my readers that the satire, elegy, and idyll, set up as they are here as the three only possible types of sentimental poesy, have nothing in common with the three particular types of poems known by these names, nothing, that is, except the *manner of feeling* that are proper to the former as well as the latter. However, from the concept of sentimental poetry it may easily be deduced that, beyond the limits of naive poetry, there could only be these three ways of feeling and composing, and that as a result the field of sentimental poetry is completely delineated by this division.

The poetic portrayal of an innocent and happy humanity is the general concept behind this type of poetry. Because this innocence and good fortune seem incompatible with the conventional relationships obtaining in the society as a whole and incompatible as well with a certain degree of education and refinement, poets have moved the scene of the idyll from the bedlam of bourgeois life to the simple pastoral setting and have assigned the idyll a place in humanity's infancy *prior to the beginning of culture*. People readily understand that these characterizations are merely incidental, that they are regarded, not as the purpose of the idyll, but as the most natural means to it. The purpose itself is in each case merely to portray the human being in a state of innocence, that is, in harmony and at peace with himself and his surroundings.

Sentimental poetry is distinguished from the naive by the fact that it relates the actual condition to ideas and applies the ideas to actuality, while the naive remains at the actual condition. Thus, as has already been mentioned above, it always has to do with two competing objects at the same time, namely, with the ideal and with experience. Between them neither more nor less than the following three relations are thinkable. Either the mind is preeminently concerned with the *contradiction* or the *agreement* between the actual condition and the ideal, or the mind is divided between them. In the first case it is delighted by the force of the inner conflict, *by the energetic motion,* in the second case by the harmony of the inner life, by the *energetic rest,* and in the third case conflict *alternates* with harmony, rest with motion. This threefold state of one's feelings gives rise to the three distinct types of poetry, to which the usual names *satire, idyll,* and *elegy* perfectly correspond, as soon as one recalls the mood into which the respectively named types of poem transport the mind, while abstracting from the means by which they bring this mood about.

Thus anyone who here could still ask among which of the three genres I rank the epic, the novel, the tragedy [Trauerspiel], and many more would have completely misunderstood me. For the concept of these latter forms as *individual types of poems* is determined either not at all or not solely by the manner of feeling. Rather one knows that such types of poems can be executed in more than one manner of feeling, hence even in several of the types of poetry I have proposed.

Finally let me add that if one is inclined, as is reasonable, to consider sentimental poesy a genuine type (not merely an aberration) of the true art of poetry that expands that art, some attention must be paid to it in determining the poetic types just as, generally, in the entire poetic legislation that is still always one-sidedly based upon the observance of the ancient and naive poets. The sentimental poet deviates from the naive poet in regard to elements that are too essential for the forms introduced by the sentimental poet everywhere to be able to conform to those of the naive poet in an unforced way. Of course, it is difficult here, always to distinguish correctly the exceptions demanded by the difference in type from the ruses that ineptitude permits itself. Yet experience teaches this much, that no single type of poem in the hands of sentimental poets (even the most outstanding ones) has re-

Yet this condition does not take place only prior to the beginning of culture. Rather it is also what the culture aims for as its final goal, if culture is supposed everywhere to have only one specific tendency. The mere idea of this condition and the belief in its potential reality can reconcile a human being [468] with all sorts of evils to which he has been subjected on the path of culture. Were it merely a chimera, then the complaints of those who decry the society at large and the cultivation of the intellect simply as an evil, and who pass that abandoned state of nature off as the human being's true end, would be completely justified. It is thus infinitely important for the human being caught up in culture to receive a tangible confirmation of the plausibility of realizing that idea in the world presented by the senses, in other words, a confirmation of the potential reality of that condition. Since actual experience, far from nourishing this belief, constantly contradicts it, here as in so many other cases the capacity for poetry comes to the aid of reason in order to bring that idea to an intuition and to realize it in an individual instance.

That innocence of the pastoral setting is also, of course, a poetic image and the imagination must already have proven itself to be creative in that setting. In addition to the fact that the task was incomparably simpler and easier to resolve there, the particulars were already provided by experience itself so that the imagination needed merely to select and weave them into a whole. Beneath a serendipitous sky, in the uncomplicated relationships of that original condition, and with limited knowledge, nature is easily satisfied and a human being does not become a savage until need produces fear in him. All peoples with a history have a paradise, a state of innocence, a golden age. Indeed, each individual human being has his paradise, his golden age that he recalls with more or less enthusiasm, depending upon how poetic his nature is. Thus, experience itself presents enough features for the depiction of the subject matter of the pastoral idyll. For this reason, however, it always remains a beautiful, an uplifting fiction and, in the portrayal of this fiction, the power of poetry has worked for the ideal. For the human being who has at one time deviated from the simplicity of nature and

mained completely what it was for the ancients, and that under the old names very often quite new genres have been executed.

has been perilously handed over to his own reason for guidance, it is infinitely important to see the legislation of nature in a pure exemplar once again, and in this faithful mirror to be able once again to purify himself of the corruptions introduced by art. [469] However, in the course of this there is a circumstance that lessens the aesthetic value of such compositions all the more. Set at a time *prior to the beginning of culture,* they exclude, along with all the advantages of culture, all its disadvantages as well and in essence find themselves in a necessary conflict with culture. Because they lead us forward and ennoble us in a *practical* sense, they lead us backward in a *theoretical* sense. Unfortunately, they place *behind* us the goal *toward* which they are supposed to *lead* us. Thus they can inspire in us only the sad feeling of a loss, not the joyous feeling of hope. Because they carry out their purpose only by overturning all art and simplifying human nature, they have, for all the rich content they supply the *heart,* all too little for the *mind,* and the journey through their one-dimensional region is too quickly completed. Hence we are able to love them and seek them out only if we are in need of rest, not if our energies are looking for movement and activity. They can only *heal* the sick mind, they cannot *nourish* the healthy one. They cannot motivate, they can only soothe. All the arts of poets have not been able to make good this defect grounded in the very essence of the pastoral idyll. Of course, this type of poetry does not lack for enthusiastic devotees, and there are plenty of readers who can prefer an *Amintas* and a *Daphne* to the greatest masterpieces of the epic and dramatic muses. But in the case of such readers it is not so much taste as individual need that passes judgment on the artworks, and consequently their judgment cannot be taken into consideration here. A reader with élan and feeling does not, of course, fail to recognize the value of such compositions, but he feels himself seldom drawn to them and very quickly sated by them. For that reason, their effect is all the more powerful at the right, needy moment. Yet true beauty need never wait for such a moment, but instead produces it.

What I am here chiding the pastoral idyll for holds only for sentimental poetry. Naive poetry never lacks for content, since its content is already contained *in the form itself.* Each kind of poesy must have an infinite content; it is by this means alone that it is poetry. But it can fulfill this requirement in two [470] diverse ways.

It can be something infinite in terms of form if it portrays its subject matter *with all its limitations,* that is to say, if it individualizes that subject matter. It can be infinite in terms of material if it *removes all limitations* from its subject matter, that is to say, if it idealizes that subject matter. Thus, it can be infinite either through an absolute portrayal or through portrayal of an absolute. The naive poet proceeds down the first path, the sentimental poet down the second. As long as the naive poet clings faithfully to nature alone, which is always thoroughly delimited, in other words, infinite in its form, he cannot lack for content (Gehalt). On the other hand, nature's thoroughgoing delimitation stands in the way of the sentimental poet, since he is supposed to endow the subject matter with an absolute significance (Gehalt). The sentimental poet thus does not understand his prerogative very well if he *borrows* his *choices of subject matter* from the naive poet, the kinds of subject matter that in themselves are completely neutral and become poetic only by virtue of the way they are treated. Though it is entirely unnecessary, the sentimental poet, by doing this, sets up the same sort of limitations for himself as exist for the naive poet, yet without being able to execute the delimitation completely and compete with the naive poet in the absolute determinateness of the portrayal. Thus, precisely in regard to the subject matter, he ought rather to distance himself from the naive poet, since only by means of the subject matter can he regain the advantage that the naive poet has over him in terms of the form.

Applied to the pastoral idylls of sentimental poets, the foregoing explains why these compositions, for all the expenditure of genius and art, do not completely satisfy either heart or mind. They have led out an ideal and yet remained within the narrow confines of an impoverished pastoral world, when they should have chosen for the ideal either another world or another way of portraying the pastoral world. They are just ideal enough that the portrayal loses something in genuineness by that fact as far as the individual is concerned, and in turn they are just individual enough that the ideal content suffers for that reason. One of Geßner's shepherds, for example, cannot delight us as something natural by virtue of the truthfulness of the imitation, since he is too idealized an entity for that. Just as little can he satisfy us as an ideal by the infinite character of the thought, since he is far too impoverished a creature for that. [471] *Up to a certain point,* of course, Geßner will please all classes of readers without *exception,* because he strives to combine the naive with the sentimental and, as a result, to a certain degree satisfies the two opposing demands that can be made of a poem. Yet precisely because the poet, in his effort to combine both, does not *do complete justice* to either nature or the ideal in its entirety, he cannot completely pass the test of strict taste that cannot forgive anything halfhearted in aesthetic matters. It is curious that this halfheartedness extends even to the language of the poet named, wavering indecisively as it does between poetry and prose, as though the poet were afraid of departing too much from actual nature in rhythm and verse and of losing the poetic élan in prose. Far more satisfying is Milton's splendid depiction of the first human pair and the state of innocence in paradise, to my knowledge the most beautiful idyll in the sentimental genre. Here nature is noble and spirited, possessing at once a fullness of breadth and depth, as the loftiest content of humanity is adorned with the most graceful of forms.

Hence, here in the idyll as in all other poetic genres one must make a choice once and for all between individuality and ideality. For as long as one does not stand at the pinnacle of perfection, attempting to satisfy both demands at once is the surest way of failing on both counts. If the modern feels within himself a sufficient affinity for the Greek spirit to compete with the Greek on the latter's own playing field, namely, on the field of naive poetry, despite all the intractableness of his material, then let him do it wholeheartedly and do it exclusively, disregarding every demand made by a sentimental age's tastes. To be sure, he can attain the level of his paradigm only with difficulty. There will always remain a noticeable distance between the original and the most successful imitator. Still, by following this path he is certain of producing an authentically poetic work.* If, on the other hand, he is driven by

*In his *Luise* Mr. Voß has recently not merely expanded, but also genuinely enriched our German literature with such a work. This idyll, although not completely free from sentimental influences, belongs entirely to the naive genre and because of its individual genuineness and solid naturalness it wrestles successfully—and it is a rare success—with the best Greek models. Thus, regarding what lends it its high renown, it can be compared with no modern poem of its class, but must be compared with Greek models, with which it shares the so uncommon excellence of affording us a joy that is pure, specific, and always unadulterated.

sentimental poetry's enthusiasm for the ideal, [472] then let him pursue this totally, in complete purity, and not stand still until he has attained the utmost, without looking back to see whether the actual world might follow him. Let him have nothing but disdain for the cheap way out that diminishes the content of the ideal in order to accommodate deficiencies in human nature, and excludes the mind in order to have an easier time with the heart. Let him not lead us back to our childhood in order to procure for us, at the cost of the intellect's most precious achievements, a peace that cannot last longer than the napping of our mental powers. Let him rather lead us forward to our maturity in order to give us a feeling of the nobler harmony that is the warrior's reward and the conqueror's prize. Let him make it his task to create an idyll that also realizes that pastoral innocence in those subjected to culture and to all the conditions of the most active and passionate living, the most comprehensive thinking, the most sophisticated art, and the highest social refinement, in a word, an idyll that leads to *Elyseum* the human being who now can no longer return to *Arcadia.*

The concept of this idyll is the concept of a battle completely resolved in the individual as well as in the society, the concept of a free union of inclinations with the law, the concept of a nature purified to the point of supreme moral dignity. In short, it is nothing other than the ideal of beauty applied to actual life. Hence, its character consists in the fact that *every conflict of the actual world with the ideal,* the conflict that has provided the stuff of satirical and elegiac poetry, is completely overcome, and all discord in feelings also ceases. *Serenity* thus would be the dominant impression produced by this type of poetry, but the serenity of [473] perfection, not inertia, a serenity that flows from composure and not from a temporary truce between warring forces, a serenity that arises from fullness, not emptiness, and that is accompanied by the feeling of an infinite potential. Yet precisely because all resistance disintegrates, it will be incomparably more difficult here than in the two previous types of poetry to produce that *movement* without which poetic effect is unthinkable anywhere. While the highest sort of unity must be present, it may take nothing away from the manifoldness; the mind must be satisfied, but without ceasing to strive for this. It is really the resolution of this question that is the task of the theory of the idyll.

Concerning the relation of the two types of poetry to one another and to the poetic ideal, the following has been established.

Nature has given the naive poet the gift of always acting as an undivided unity, of being at each moment a self-sufficient and complete whole, and of displaying humanity in all its significance (Gehalt) within the actual world. Nature has endowed the sentimental poet with the power, or rather it has imbued him with a vital urge to restore, from out of himself, the unity that abstraction had destroyed within him, in other words, the urge to render humanity perfect in itself, and to pass from a limited condition to an infinite one.* However, to give full expression to human nature is the common task of both kinds of poet, and [474] without that task they could not be called poets at all. But the naive poet always has the advantage over the sentimental poet of dealing with sensuous reality, since the naive poet presents this reality as an actual fact, something that the sentimental poet is striving simply to attain. That is also what everyone experiences for himself when he observes himself enjoying naive compositions. He feels all the powers of his humanity active at such a moment, he needs nothing, he is a totality in himself. Without making any distinctions as to his feelings, he delights in his spiritual activity and in his sensual life at the same time. The sentimental poet transports him, on the other hand, into a completely different sort of mood. Here he feels only a vital *urge* to produce in himself the harmony that he actually felt there, to make a totality out of himself, to give complete expression to the humanity within him. Thus, in the experience of sentimental poetry the mind is in motion, it is tense, it pulsates between conflicting feelings, while in the case of naive poetry it is calm, relaxed, one with itself, and perfectly satisfied.

*For the reader evaluating scientifically allow me to remark that both ways of feeling, construed in their supreme conception, are related to one another as the first and third categories. For the latter always arises by the fact that the first is combined with its exact opposite. The opposite of the naive feeling is, namely, the reflecting intellect and the sentimental mood is the result of striving, *even under the conditions of reflection,* to restore the naive feeling in terms of the content. This would happen by means of the realized ideal, in which art again encounters nature. If one goes through those three concepts in terms of the categories, then one will always find *nature* and the corresponding naive mood in the first category, art as overcoming nature by means of the freely operating intellect always in the second category, finally the *ideal,* in which the perfected art returns to nature, in the third category.

On the one hand, then, in terms of reality the naive poet has the better of the sentimental poet. He brings into actual existence something toward which the sentimental poet can only awaken a vital urge. Yet if this is so, the sentimental poet in turn has the considerable advantage over the naive poet of being in a position to give this urge a *more magnificent object* than the naive poet has or could have produced. The entire actual world, we know, remains far behind the ideal. Everything existing has its limitations, but thought is unbounded. Accordingly, because of this limitation to which everything sensuous is subject, the naive poet also suffers, while the sentimental poet's advantage, on the other hand, is the unconditioned freedom of the capacity for ideas. Thus the naive poet, of course, completes his task, but the task itself is a limited one. The sentimental poet does not complete his task, but his task is an infinite one. Everyone, moreover, can learn this from his own experience. People turn from the naive poet to the living present with ease and pleasure, while the sentimental poet will always makes us feel, at least temporarily, out of tune with actual life. This happens because in the latter case our minds have been as it were stretched beyond their natural scope by the infiniteness of the idea, [475] such that nothing at hand can any longer satisfy them. Instead of striving for sensuous objects present outside ourselves, we prefer to sink meditatively into ourselves where we find, in the world of ideas, nourishment for the awakened urge. Sentimental poetry is the progeny of detachment and stillness, inviting us to them; naive poetry is the child of life and it also leads us back to life.

I have called naive poetry a *gift of nature* in order to remind us that reflection has no part in it. It is a lucky throw, needing no improvement if it succeeds, but also incapable of any if it misses the mark. The entire work of naive genius is consummated in feeling; here lies its strength and its limitation. If the naive genius did not immediately *feel* in a poetic, that is to say, completely human way, this lack could not be compensated by any art. Criticism can only help him gain an insight into his mistake, but it can put no beauty *in* its place. The naive genius must do everything through his nature; through his freedom he can do little. The concept of the naive poet is realized as soon as nature merely acts in him by an inner necessity. Now, of course, everything that happens by nature is necessary and so also is every work, even quite unsuccessful ones, of naive genius; nothing is further removed from this genius than arbitrariness. However, the demands of the moment are one thing, the inner necessity of the whole another. Considered as a whole, nature is self-sufficient and infinite; in each individual product of nature, on the other hand, it is needy and limited. This holds accordingly for the nature of the poet as well. Even the happiest moment in which the poet happens to find himself is dependent upon a foregoing moment and, hence, only a conditioned necessity can be ascribed to it. However, the poet is assigned the task of making an individual condition the same for the whole of humanity, in effect, the task of grounding that condition absolutely and necessarily in itself. Thus, any trace of a need of the moment must remain remote from the moment of inspiration, and the subject matter itself, however limited it be, is not permitted to limit the poet. One readily comprehends that this is only possible insofar as the poet from the outset [476] brings with him to the subject matter an absolute freedom and wealth of skill, and insofar as he is experienced at embracing everything with the whole of his humanity. He can gain this experience only through the world in which he lives and which affects him immediately. The naive genius is thus dependent upon experience in a way unknown to the sentimental genius. The latter, we know, initiates his operation where the former concludes his. His strength consists in rendering complete some defective subject matter, taken from himself, and by his own might transporting himself from a limited condition to a condition of freedom. Thus while the naive poetic genius is in need of some external support, the genius of a sentimental poet consists in nourishing and purifying himself on his own. Since the naive genius has to bring his work to completion in sensuous feelings, he must see himself surrounded by a nature rich in forms, a poetic world, a naive humanity. If this help from outside is missing, if a naive genius sees himself surrounded by material devoid of spirit, only two sorts of things can happen. If the poetic genre predominates in him, he takes leave of his species of poetry and becomes sentimental, at least to remain poetic. Or, if the characteristics of the species have the upper hand, he takes leave of the *genre* altogether and becomes an ordinary part of nature, simply in order to remain natural. The *first* scenario was probably the case for the finest sentimental poets in the ancient Roman world and in modern times. Born in another age and transplanted under another sky, those who now touch us through ideas would have enchanted us by their individual genuineness and naive beauty. On the other hand, a poet would scarcely be capable of completely protecting himself from that *second* scenario if, thrown into a vulgar world, he cannot abandon nature.

That is to say, the *actual* nature [*wirkliche* Natur]; as for the *genuine* nature [*wahre* Natur], the *subject* of naive compositions, it cannot be too carefully distinguished from that actual nature. Actual nature exists everywhere, but a genuine nature is all the more rare, since it requires an inner necessity to exist. Every outbreak of passion, however vulgar, is a matter of actual nature; it may even be a matter of a genuine nature, but not a genuinely *human* nature. For each utterance of the latter requires the participation of that self-sufficiency that always expresses itself in a dignified way. [477] Every moral baseness is part of human nature as it actually is, but hopefully it is not part of a human nature that is genuine, since this can never be anything but noble. It should not be overlooked that this confusion of actual human nature with genuine human nature has misled criticism as well as practice into all sorts of distastefulness. Think of the trivialities that have been indulged, indeed praised, in poetry because they are—unfortunately!—found in nature as it actually is. Consider how delighted people are to see caricatures of what in the actual world distresses them carefully preserved and reproduced in a lifelike way within the poetic world. To be sure, the poet may imitate what is bad in nature and the concept of a satirical poet in fact entails this. But in this case his own beautiful nature must *carry over* to the subject matter and the vulgar material must not drag the imitator down to the ground with it. If only he is himself in possession of a human nature that is genuine, at least at the moment he is doing the depicting, then what he depicts for us says nothing. But we can only accept a faithful portrayal of the actual world from someone like this. Woe to us readers, if the buffoon mirrors himself in the buffoon, if the scourge of satire falls into the hands of someone meant by nature to wield a whip much more severe; woe to us, if people utterly devoid of anything called "poetic spirit" and possessing only the ape's knack at vulgar imitation exercise it at the expense of our taste in some grisly and hideous way!

I said, however, that ordinary nature can be dangerous even for the truly naive poet. For, in the end, that beautiful harmony of feeling and thinking that makes up that poet's character is only an idea that can never be attained in actuality. Even in the case of the most fortunate genius of this class, sensitivity will always outweigh spontaneity. The sensitivity, however, is always more or less dependent upon the external impression, and nothing but continuous exertion of the productive potential—something that can hardly be expected of human nature—would be able to prevent the material from wielding at times a blind power over that sensitivity. [478] Whenever this happens, a poetic feeling becomes a vulgar one.*

No genius of the naive class, from Homer down to Bodmer, has completely avoided this obstacle. But, of course, it is most danger-

*The ancient art of poetry can provide the best examples of the extent to which the naive poet is dependent upon his object and of how much, indeed, how everything is a matter of his feeling. The compositions of the ancients are beautiful to the extent that the nature within him and without him is beautiful. If, on the other hand, nature is vulgar, then the spirit likewise deserts their compositions. For example, in their portrayals of feminine nature, of the relation between both sexes, and of love in particular, every reader with refined feelings must sense a certain emptiness and a weariness that all genuineness and naïveté in the presentation cannot remove. Without giving voice to the fanaticism that nature, far from exalting, indeed, foresakes, one will hopefully be allowed to assume that nature, as far as that relation of the sexes and the emotion of love are concerned, is capable of a nobler character than the ancients gave it. People are also aware of the *contingent* circumstances that stand in the way of ennobling those feelings among them. That it was a limitation, not some inner necessity, that kept the ancients at a lower level in this respect is the lesson taught by the example of the modern poets who have gone so much farther than their predecessors, yet without overstepping nature. I am not talking here about what the sentimental poets consciously made of this subject matter, since these poets pass beyond nature into the ideal realm and hence their example can prove nothing in relation to the ancients. I am talking merely about how the same subject matter is treated by genuinely naive poets, for example, in the *Sakontala* [play of the famous writer Kālidāsa, 4th–5th century], in the *Meistersänger*, in many a novel and epic of chivalry [Ritterromanen und Ritterepopeen], and how it is treated by Shakespeare, by Fielding, and several others, even German poets. Here, then, would have been the place for the ancients to render spiritual a material too crude on the outside and to do so from within, through the subject [Subjekt]; that is to say, here would have been the place to recover, by means of reflection, the poetic significance missing in the feeling from the outside, to complete nature through the idea, in a word, to make something infinite out of a limited object by a sentimental operation. Yet they were naive, not sentimental poetic geniuses; hence their work ended with the feeling conveyed to them from outside.

ous for those who have to guard against a vulgar nature from without, or who through lack of discipline become barbaric from within. The former is responsible for the fact that even the most cultivated writer does not always remain free of triteness, while [479] the latter has already prevented many a splendid talent from taking possession of the place to which nature had called him. For that very reason, the writer of comedy, whose genius feeds most on actual life, is most vulnerable to triteness, as the example of Aristophanes and Plautus and almost all subsequent writers following in their footsteps teaches. Think of how low even the sublime Shakespeare occasionally has us stoop, what an assortment of trivialities Lope de Vega, Molière, Regnard, and Goldoni bore us with, and the mire into which Holberg drags us. Schlegel, one of our country's most gifted poets, with a genius that could not fail to shine among writers of the first rank in this genre, Gellert, a genuinely naive poet, just like Rabener and Lessing himself, if I may be permitted to mention his name here, Lessing, the polished progeny of criticism and such a vigilant judge of himself—all of them, more or less, atone for the insipid character of the nature they select as the material for their satires. I mention none of the *most recent* writers in this genre, since I can except none of them from this judgment.

It is not only that the spirit of the naive poet risks getting all too close to some vulgar reality. By the ease with which he expresses himself and precisely by the ever greater approximation to actual life, he encourages the ordinary imitator to try his hand in the area of poetry. Although itself in danger enough from another side (as I will show subsequently), sentimental poetry at least keeps *these* people at a distance, since it is not everyone's thing to elevate himself to ideas. Naive poetry, however, takes it on faith that the mere feeling, the mere humor, the mere imitation of actual nature constitutes the poet. Yet nothing is more offensive than when some vulgar character gets it into his head to try to be kindhearted and naive, while he ought to be hiding himself behind all the pretenses of art in order to conceal his disgusting nature. This is also the source of the unspeakable trivialities that the Germans love to hear under the name of those naive and comic songs and that they like to entertain themselves with, seemingly without end, while seated together at a full table. [480] Given a certain license, the license of caprice and feeling, people tolerate these trifles. Yet they are trifles of a caprice and a feeling that cannot be suppressed carefully enough. In this respect, the Muses on the *Pleisse* form a particularly lamentable chorus, and they are scarcely answered with better chords by the Muses on the Leine and the Elbe.* As insipid as these jokes are, the kind of emotion heard upon our tragic stages is just as pitiful. Instead of imitating nature in its genuineness, it attains only a dull and low-level expression of nature as it actually is, so that after such tear-jerking fare we feel as if we had just paid a visit to a hospital or read Salzmann's *Human Misery.*† Still, as bad as this is, matters are much worse in the case of satiric poetry, and the case of the comic novel in particular. By their very nature they lie particularly close to ordinary life and thus, like any frontier post, they should rightly be in the very best hands. In fact, someone who is the *creature and the very caricature* of his age least has the calling to portray it. Yet even the sworn enemies of every poetic spirit occasionally feel the itch to bungle into this field and to charm a circle of worthy friends with the beautiful offspring, since it is so easy to hunt up some "funny character" and get the caricature crudely down on paper, even if it were only a *fat man*‡ among one's acquaintances. The feelings of someone purely disposed [481] will, of course, never be in danger of confusing these productions of an ordinary nature with the gifted fruits of a naive genius. But it is precisely this pure disposition of feelings that is missing; in most cases people want merely to have some need satisfied without the mind making any demands. The notion, so completely mis-

*These good friends have taken very badly what a reviewer in the *Allgemeine Literatur-Zeitung* [the reviewer was Schiller himself] criticized in Bürger's poems some years ago. The anger resulting from scraping against these thorns seems to be an acknowledgment that, by taking up the cause of that poet, they believe that they are defending their own cause. But in this respect they err profoundly. That rebuke could only hold for a true poetic genius who had been richly equipped by nature, but had neglected to develop that rare gift by his own cultivation. People may subject such an individual to the highest standard of art and should do so, because he had it in his power to do justice to art, if he had seriously wanted to. But it would be ridiculous and at the same time cruel to proceed in a similar manner with people on which nature has not thought, people who demonstrate an utter *testimonium paupertatis* with every product they bring to market.

†The reference is to Christian Gotthilf Salzmann's (1744–1811) novel *Karl von Karlsberg oder Über das menschliche Elend.*

‡The reference is to Christoph Friedrich Nicolai's (1733–1811) *Geschichte eiues dicken Mannes* (1794).

understood yet so true in itself, namely, that people are rejuvenated by works of beautiful spirit, innocently contributes to this indulgence (if it can still be called indulgence where nothing loftier is intimated and the reader profits in the same way as the writer). If someone with a vulgar nature becomes tense, he can only relax in some sort of state of vacuousness. Even a high level of understanding, if it is not supported by a comparable cultivation of feelings, relaxes from its pursuits only in some mindless pleasure of the senses.

If, on the one hand, a poetic genius must be able to elevate himself freely and spontaneously above all *circumstantial* limitations, limitations inseparable from any *specific* situation, so that he arrives at what human nature, in an absolute sense, is capable of, he is not permitted, on the other hand, to transport himself to some place beyond the *necessary* limitations involved in the concept of human nature. For his task and his domain is what is absolute solely within humanity. We have seen that the naive genius is, of course, not in danger of overstepping this domain. But it is probably in danger of *not completely realizing what lies within this domain,* if it makes room for some external necessity or contingent need of the moment at too great a cost to inner necessity. By contrast, in the effort to set aside all limitations, the sentimental genius is exposed to the danger of transforming human nature completely, that is, the danger of not merely elevating or *idealizing* himself beyond any specific and limited actuality toward the absolute possibility—what it is permitted and supposed to do—but rather of passing beyond the possibility itself or *giving himself up to the reverie of impossible dreams.* This mistake of *exaggeration* is based as much on the specific character of the sentimental poet's procedure as the opposite mistake of *being too matter-of-fact* is on the manner of treating things peculiar to the naive writer. The naive genius, namely, [482] lets *nature* prevail within him without the slightest inhibition and, since nature is always dependent and needy in its individual temporal expressions, that naive feeling will not always remain sufficiently *exalted* to be able to withstand the chance determinations of the moment. The sentimental genius, on the other hand, takes leave of the actual world in order to climb up to the level of ideas and control his material freely and spontaneously. Yet since reason by its own law always strives for what is unconditioned, the sentimental genius will not always be *sufficiently restrained* to limit himself constantly and consistently to the conditions contained in the concept of human nature, conditions to which reason must always confine itself, even in its freest actions. Maintaining this restraint would only be possible through a comparable degree of sensitivity, but spontaneity overrides sensitivity in the sentimental poetic spirit as much as sensitivity outweighs spontaneity in naive poetry. Thus, if people occasionally fail to find the *spirit* [*Geist*] in creations of naive genius, they will often ask in vain for the *theme* [*Gegenstand*] in productions of sentimental genius. For this reason both kinds of genius lapse into *vacuousness*, although in completely different ways. For in the aesthetic judgment both a theme without spirit and a play of spirit without a theme amount to nothing.

All poets who fashion their material too one-sidedly from the world of thoughts and are driven to poetic composition more by an inner fullness of ideas than by the urgency of feeling, are more or less in danger of going astray in this way. In its creations reason pays far too little attention to the boundaries set up by the world of the senses, and thought is always driven beyond the point where experience can follow. It may be driven to such an extent that not only can no specific experience any longer correspond to it (the ideally beautiful can and should in fact proceed to this point), but it also contradicts the conditions of any possible experience at all. In this case, moreover, in order to make the thought actual, one would have to abandon human nature altogether. If the thought is driven to this extreme, then it is no longer a poetic, but rather an exaggerated thought, supposing, that is, [483] that it has been articulated in a presentable and literary way. For if it has not done this, then it is already enough if it simply does not contradict itself. If it contradicts itself, then it is no longer exaggerated, but *nonsense*. For what does not exist at all can also not overstep its proper measure. If it is not even put forward as an object for the imagination, then it is just as little an exaggeration. For mere thinking is unlimited and what has no limits can also not overstep them. In other words, for something to be called "exaggerated," it must not violate any logical truth, but rather the truth conveyed by the senses while still laying claim to that sort of truth. Thus if a poet gets the unfortunate notion into this head of selecting, as the material for his sketches, natures that are utterly *superhuman* and *may* not be represented any other way, then he can guard against exaggeration only by giving up any poetic pretense and not even attempting to develop his theme imaginatively. For, were he to do this, then either this would transpose the limits of the imagination onto the theme and make a limited *human* object out of an absolute object (such as, for example, all Greek divinities are and are also supposed to be), or the theme would remove any constraints on the imagination, that is to say, it would overcome the imagination. Exaggeration consists precisely in this.

The exaggerated feeling must be distinguished from the exaggerated portrayal. Here I am speaking only of the former. The object of feeling can be unnatural, but the feeling itself is natural and hence must also speak its language. Accordingly, while an exaggerated feeling can flow from a warm heart and a truly poetic disposition, an exaggerated portrayal always testifies to a cold heart and very often to a lack of poetic talent. It is therefore not a mistake that the genius of sentimental poetry must guard against, but rather a mistake that threatens only the genius's imitator who lacks the genius's calling and thus fails to spurn the collaboration of what is boorish, mindless, even vulgar. The exaggerated feeling is not at all without some truth and, as an actual feeling, it must [484] also have a real subject matter. Thus, too, because it is natural, it permits a simple expression and, coming from the heart, will not lack for heart. Yet since its subject matter is not fashioned from nature, but instead is produced in a one-sided and artificial way by the intellect, it also has only logical reality and the feeling is for that reason not purely human. It is no illusion what Heloise feels for Abelard, Petrarch for his Laura, S. Preux for his Julie, Werther for his Lotte, nor what Agathon, Phanias, Peregrinus Proteus (I am thinking of Wieland's) feel for their ideals. The feeling is genuine, only the object of the feeling is something contrived, lying beyond human nature. Had the feeling confined itself merely to the sensuous truth of the objects, then it would not have been able to have that energy. On the contrary, a merely arbitrary play of fantasy without any inner meaning would not have been in the position of moving the heart, for the heart is moved only by reason. This exaggeration thus deserves correction, not contempt, and whoever denigrates it may well ask himself whether it is not heartlessness that perhaps makes him so clever, and a lack of reason that makes him so astute. For this reason the exaggerated gentleness in the gallantry and honor characteristic of the romances of chivalry, especially the Spanish ones, as well as the scrupulous delicateness, driven to the point of preciousness, in the French and English sentimental novels (of the best sort) are not only subjectively genuine, but even in an objective respect they are not without meaning. They are authentic feelings that actually have a moral source and are only to be reproached because they overstep the bounds of human genuineness. Without that moral reality—how would it be possible for them to be able to be communicated with such strength and intimacy, as experience teaches? The same holds for moral and religious fanaticism as well as for the overdone love of freedom and fatherland. Since the objects of these feelings are always ideas and since they do not surface in any external experience (since what moves the political zealot, for example, is not what he sees, but what he thinks), the spontaneous [485] imagination possesses a dangerous freedom and cannot, as in other cases, be shown the way back to its boundaries by the sensuous presence of its object. However, neither human beings in general nor the poet in particular are permitted to shun what nature legislates, except to commit themselves to its opposite, the legislation of reason. He may take leave of the actual world only for the ideal, since freedom *must* be tied to one of these two anchors. Yet the path from experience to the ideal is quite immense, and in between lies the unbridled capriciousness of fantasy. Thus, it is unavoidable that people in general or poets in particular are *lawless* and, as a result, succumb to fantastic notions, if they use their intellectual freedom to renounce feelings without being impelled to do so by laws of reason, that is to say, if they take leave of nature on the basis of freedom alone.

Experience teaches that entire peoples as well as individuals who have removed themselves from nature's secure guidance actually find themselves in this situation. Experience also provides enough examples of a similar mistake in poetic art. Because the genuine thrust of sentimental poetry is to pass beyond the confines of things' actual nature in order to elevate itself to the ideal, the impulse that is not genuine oversteps every boundary altogether and persuades itself that the wild play of imagination constitutes poetic inspiration. In the case of the geniune poet-genius who would take leave of the actual world only for the sake of the idea, this wild play can never be encountered or only in moments when he is quite lost himself. For, by his very nature, he can be seduced into an exaggeraged way of feeling. However, he can seduce others to the fantastic by his example since readers with lively imaginations and feeble intellects perceive only the liberties taken by the poetic genius relative to the actual nature of things, without being able to keep pace with the lofty necessity in the mind of the poet. What happens to the sentimental genius here is just what we witnessed in the case of the naive genius. Because everything done by the naive genius is carried out through his nature, the ordinary imitator wants to consider his own nature no worse a guide. Masterpieces [486] of the naive genre will thus usually be followed by the most trivial and sordid reproductions of vulgar nature, while in the aftermath of the major works of the sentimental genre there are countless fantastic productions, a fact that is easily demonstrated in the literature of every people.

In regard to poetry there are two principles in use that are perfectly correct in themselves, but cancel each other out in the sense in which people usually take them. Regarding the first principle, "that the art of poetry is for pleasure and recreation," it has already been said that it is conducive in no small way to vacuousness and platitudes in poetic depictions. By means of the other principle, "that poetry contributes to the human being's moral ennobling," exaggerations are provided a safe haven. It is not out of place here to shed some more light on both principles, principles that are so frequently uttered, often so utterly incorrectly interpreted, and so ineptly applied.

"Recreation" is what we call the transition from a violent condition to one natural to us. Thus everything here depends upon what we posit as our natural condition and what we understand by a violent one. If we posit as the natural condition merely an uninhibited play of our physical powers and a freedom from every coercion, then each activity of reason, by offering some resistance to sensuousness, does violence to us, and peace of mind joined with the sensuous movement is the proper ideal of recreation. On the other hand, if we consider our natural condition to be an unlimited capacity for every human expression and the knack of being able to manage all our powers with equal freedom, then any separation and *isolation* of these powers is a violent condition and the ideal of recreation is the rejuvenation of our nature as a whole in the wake of one-sided tensions. The first ideal is thus dictated solely by the needs of the *sensuous nature,* the second by the self-sufficiency of *human nature.* Which of these two sorts of recreation the art of poetry is permitted and required to afford might well be beyond question theoretically; for no one very much wants to be regarded as liable to be tempted to place the ideal of humanity below the ideal of animality. [487] Nevertheless, the demands people are accustomed to make on poetic works in real life are taken chiefly from the sensuous ideal, and in most cases it is this ideal that decides not, of course, the *respect* but rather the *preference* people show these works; they select their *favorite* on the basis of this ideal. The state of mind of most people is a matter of stressful and exhausting *work,* on the one hand, and the kind of *indulgence* that works like a sedative, on the other. The former state of mind, as we know, makes the sensuous need for peace of mind and for a pause from acting incomparably more urgent than does the moral need for harmony and for an absolute freedom of acting. For above all else, *nature* must first be satisfied before the *mind* can make a *demand.* The indulgent state of mind fetters and cripples the very moral impulses that would have to project that demand. Thus, nothing is more disadvantageous to the sensitivity to true beauty than these two all-too-common states of mind, and it becomes self-explanatory why so very few people, even among the better ones, have good judgment in aesthetic matters. Beauty is the product of the accord between mind and senses; it speaks to all the capacities of the human being at once. For this reason it can be felt and appreciated only on the supposition of a complete and free use of all the human being's powers. One must bring to the work an open sensibility, an expansive heart, a fresh and vigorous mind; one must have one's entire nature together. This is in no way the case for those alienated within themselves by abstract thinking, stifled by petty formulas of business, or weary from strenuous concentration. These individuals, to be sure, long for some sensuous material, yet not in order to continue the play of mental powers, but rather to put an end to it. They wish to be free, but only from a burden that further fatigues their lethargic condition, not from a barrier that restricts their activity.

Is there any reason, then, to wonder at the fact that mediocrity and barrenness prosper in aesthetic matters, that weak minds avenge themselves on what is truly and vitally beautiful? [488] They reckoned on being rejuvenated by such beauty, but on being so rejuvenated on their terms, in other words, in the light of their need and impoverished conception. They are annoyed to discover that an expression of strength is then expected of them for which, even in their best moments, they would lack the capacity. Where there is mediocrity, on the other hand, they are welcome just as they are, since, as little strength as they bring with them, they need even less to exhaust the mind of their writer. Here they are relieved at once of the burden of thinking and, in this relaxed state, such natures may indulge themselves in the blissful pleasure of *nothingness,* on a soft pillow of *platitudes.* In the temple of Thalia and Melpomene, as it is cultivated among us, the beloved goddess is enthroned and receives in her ample bosom the stupid savant and the exhausted businessman. Rekindling their numbed senses with her warmth and swaying the imagination to a sweet motion, she rocks the mind to sleep, gently mesmerizing it.

And why would people not indulge in ordinary wits what they are used to encountering even in the best? After every protracted exertion nature demands a respite that it takes upon itself without first being summoned to do so. (Usually people save up only moments such as these for the enjoyment of beautiful works.) This rest is so little conducive to the aesthetic judgment that among the really busy classes of people only very few will be able to judge in matters of taste with certainty and, on what so much depends here, with consistency. Nothing is more common than for scholars, in contrast to sophisticated people of the world, to embarrass themselves by the ridiculousness of their views in judgments concerning beauty, and in particular for those who judge technical skill, nothing is more common than for them to become the laughingstock of all connoisseurs. In most instances their uncultivated, sometimes exaggerated, sometimes crude sensibility misleads them and, even if they have seized upon something theoretical to defend it, they are, on the basis of that theory, capable of forming merely *technical* judgments (concerning the suitability of a work), but not *aesthetic* judgments that must always encompass the work as a whole and thus must be decided by feeling. If in the end they would oblige by renouncing aesthetic judgments and by being satisfied with technical judgments, then they might still always provide something useful enough, since the poet [489] in his inspiration and the sensitive reader in the moment of enjoyment all too easily neglect detail. Yet the spectacle is all the more ridiculous when these crude natures, who after all kinds of trouble and effort can at best develop a single skill within themselves, set up their meager individual tastes as representative of the general sentiment, and by the sweat of their brow pass judgment on what is beautiful.

As we have seen, much too narrow boundaries are usually set for the concept of the *recreation* that poetry has to deliver. The reason for this is that people are used to relating the concept too one-sidedly to the mere needs of sensuous life. In just the reverse manner, the concept of *ennoblement* that the poet is supposed to aim for is usually given much too broad a scope, because people define that concept too one-sidedly in terms of the idea alone.

As far as the idea is concerned, the ennoblement always passes into an infinite dimension, since reason in its demands does not restrict itself to the necessary limits of the world of the senses and does not stand still until it arrives at something absolutely perfect. Nothing that permits something still higher to be thought can satisfy it; no need of a finite nature is excused in the face of its stern tribunal. It recognizes no other limits than those of thought, and we know that thought soars beyond all the limits of time and space. Such an ideal of ennoblement is prescribed by reason in its pure legislation. Hence, this ideal may be no more posited by the poet as his purpose than that lowly ideal of recreation put forth by the sensuous side of human beings. To be sure, the poet is supposed to liberate humanity from all arbitrary limitations, but without overturning the concept of humanity and upsetting its necessary limits. Whatever the poet permits himself beyond these lines is exaggeration, and he is only all too easily misled into doing precisely this by misunderstanding the concept of ennoblement. But what is unfortunate is that he can hardly elevate himself to the true ideal of human ennoblement without taking some steps beyond it. In order to get to that point he must take leave of the actual world, for he can fashion it, like any ideal, only from inner and moral sources. He does not encounter it [490] in the world around him and in the bustle of active life, but only in his heart, and he finds his heart solely in the stillness of solitary reflection. But this withdrawal from life will not always remove only the contingent limitations of humanity from view. More often it will also remove the necessary and indestructible limitations of humanity and, while it looks for the pure form, it will be in danger of losing all content. Reason will pursue its business far too removed from experience, and what the contemplative mind discovered on the serene path of thought, the person acting will not be able to realize on the beleaguered path of life. Usually this is precisely what brings out the fanatic and what alone is in a position to mold the sage. The superiority of the sage might well consist less in the fact that he did not become a fanatic than in the fact that he did not remain one.

Accordingly, if the concept of recreation is not to prove too physical and unworthy of poetry, it may not be left to the working segment of humanity to define this concept in terms of its needs. Nor, if the concept of ennoblement is not to prove too hyperphysical and extravagant for poetry, may it be left to the contemplative side of humanity to determine this concept in terms of its speculations. Yet, since, as experience teaches, both these concepts govern the general judgment about poetry and poetic works, for their interpretation we have to look around for a class of people who are active without toiling and can idealize without getting carried away, in other words, people who combine in themselves all the realities of life with the fewest possible limitations, and are carried along by the stream of events without becoming its victims. Only such a class of people can preserve the beauty of human nature as a whole, something that any toil destroys momentarily and a life of labor destroys continually. Only the *sentiments* of such a class of people can provide a law for the general judgment in regard to everything that is purely human. Whether such a class actually exists, or rather whether those who actually do exist in external arrangements of this sort might correspond to this conception inwardly as well, is another question, about which I have nothing to say here. [491] If this class of people does not conform to that conception, then it has merely itself to blame, since the opposite, working class has at least the satisfaction of considering itself a victim of its occupation. In such a class of people (which I set up here merely as an idea and in no way wish to have designated as a fact) the naive character would thus be united with the sentimental character such that each would protect the other from its extreme. While the naive would protect the mind from exaggeration, the sentimental would ensure it against listlessness. For ultimately we still have to concede that neither the naive nor the sentimental character, considered by itself, can completely exhaust the ideal of beautiful humanity, an ideal that can only emerge from the intimate union of both.

Of course, as long as both characters are elevated to a *poetic* [*dichterisch*] level, as we have also considered them up till now, many of the limitations adhering to them disappear, and even their opposition becomes ever less noticeable to the degree that they become respectively more poetic. For the poetic mood [Stimmung] is a self-sufficient whole in which all distinctions have vanished and nothing is missing. Yet just because both sorts of feeling can come together only in the concept of the poetic, their difference from and need of one another become all the more obvious precisely to the extent that they set aside their poetic character. This is the case in ordinary life. The more they descend to this level, the more they lose their generic character that brings them nearer to one another, until finally all that is left is a caricature of that specific character that sets them off from one another.

This brings me to a rather remarkable psychological antagonism between people in a century in the process of civilizing itself. Because this antagonism is radical and is based on the internal form of the mind, it establishes a breach among people much worse than the occasional conflict of interests could ever produce. It is an antagonism that robs the artist and poet of any hope of pleasing and touching people generally, which remains, after all, his task; an antagonism that makes it impossible for the philosopher, even if he has done everything he should, to convince people generally, something the concept of a philosophy still entails; [492] an antagonism, finally, that will never allow someone in practical life to see his manner of acting approved universally. In short, it is an antagonism responsible for the fact that no work of the mind and no action of the heart can make one class decidedly happy without drawing, precisely for that reason, a condemnation down upon itself from the other class. This conflict is without doubt as old as the beginning of culture and before culture comes to an end it will hardly be resolved other than in a few, rare individuals, who hopefully there always have been and always will be. One of the effects of this conflict is that each attempt to resolve it is futile, since no side can be brought to acknowledge a lack on its part and a reality on the part of the other. Yet, although this is the case, there always remains enough to be gained by pursuing so important a breach back to its ultimate source, and in this way at least bringing the genuine point of the conflict to a simpler formulation.

The best way to arrive at the true conception of this opposition is, as I just mentioned, to remove from the naive as well as the sentimental character the poetic nature that each possesses. What then remains of the naive character is only the following: on the theoretical side, a knack for sober observation and a firm adherence to the uniform testimony of the senses and, on the practical side, a resignation and submission to natural necessity (not, however, to its blind urgency), in effect, a yielding to what is and must be. In the sphere of theory, nothing remains of the sentimental character but a restless spirit of speculation that presses on toward what is unconditioned in all knowledge and, in the practical sphere, what is left is a moral rigor that insists on something unconditioned in actions of the will. Whoever counts himself a member of the first class can be called a *realist,* and of the second class, an *idealist,* though, of course, one may think of neither the good nor the bad sense people associate with such names in metaphysics.* [493]

Since the realist allows himself to be determined by the necessity of nature and the idealist by the necessity of reason, between the two the same relation must obtain as is found obtaining between the effects of nature and the actions of reason. Nature, we know, although an infinite magnitude as a whole, reveals itself in each

*In order to prevent any misinterpretation, I note that this division is not at all intended to occasion a choice between the two, in effect, a favoring of one to the exclusion of the other. It is precisely this *exclusion,* which is found in experience, that I am combating. The result of the present observations will show that only by means of the perfectly equal *inclusion* of both can justice be done to the rational concept of humanity. Moreover, I take both in the most dignified sense and in the complete *fullness* of the concepts of them, a fullness that can only exist in their purity and in the retention of their specific differences. It will also be shown that a high degree of human truth is compatible with both and that their deviations from one another make for a change in the individual, but not in the whole, and in terms of the form, but not in terms of the content.

individual effect to be dependent and deficient. Only in the totality of its appearances does it express a grand, self-sufficient character. Everything individual in nature exists only because something else does; nothing springs from itself, everything springs only from the preceding moment in order to lead to a subsequent one. Yet precisely this reciprocal relation of appearances to one another insures the existence of each individual appearance through the existence of others, and the constancy and necessity of these appearances are inseparable from the dependency of their effects. Nothing is free in nature, but also nothing is arbitrary in it.

And it is in just this way that the realist reveals himself as much in his *knowing* as in his *doing*. The sphere of his knowing and acting extends to everything that exists conditionally. But he also never brings it beyond conditioned sorts of knowledge, and the rules he forms from individual experiences, taken in the strictest sense, are also valid only once. If he elevates the rule of the moment to a general law, then he will unavoidably fall into error. If, then, the realist wants to arrive at something unconditioned in his knowing, he must attempt to arrive at it on the same path on which nature becomes something [494] infinite, namely, on the path of the whole and in the totality of experience. Since, however, the sum of experience is never completely concluded, the most the realist achieves in his knowing is a comparative universality. He builds his insight on the recurrence of similar instances, and thus he will judge rightly in every case that is orderly. On the other hand, in every case presenting itself for the first time, his wisdom returns to its point of departure.

What is true of the realist's knowing is also true of his (moral) action. His character is moral, but this morality, as far as the pure conception of it is concerned, lies not in any individual deed, but only in the entire sum of his life. In each particular case he will be determined by external causes and by external purposes; only those causes are not contingent and those purposes are not momentary, but rather flow subjectively from nature as a whole and refer to it objectively. In the most rigorous sense of the word, then, the motivations of his will are neither free enough nor morally pure enough, since they have something other than the will alone as their cause and something other than the law alone as the objective. But just as little are they blind and materialistic motivations, since what determines the will is the absolute totality of nature, in effect, something self-sufficient and necessary. Thus, common sense, the superior lot of the realist, reveals itself everywhere in his thinking and behavior. The realist fashions the rule for his judgment from individual cases, and the rule for his action from an inner feeling. Yet with providential instinct he knows how to separate everything momentary and contingent from both. By this method he proceeds splendidly on the whole, and will scarcely have to reproach himself for some significant mistake. Only he would not be able to lay claim, in any particular case, to greatness and dignity. Greatness and dignity can only be purchased by independence and freedom, and of the latter we see too few traces in his individual actions.

Things are completely different in the case of the idealist, who draws upon himself and reason alone for his knowledge and his motives. While nature always appears dependent and limited in its individual workings, reason places the character of self-sufficiency and perfection equally in each individual action. [495] It creates everything out of itself and relates everything to itself. What happens by means of it, happens only for its sake; in each concept it puts forth and in each decision it makes there is an absolute greatness. And in just this way the idealist, insofar as he rightfully bears this name, reveals himself in his knowledge as in his deeds. Not satisfied with the sorts of knowledge that are valid only under specific presuppositions, he seeks to press forward to truths that presuppose nothing more and are the presupposition of every other truth. He is satisfied only by the philosophical insight that leads all conditioned knowing back to some unconditioned knowledge, and that attaches all experience to something necessary in the human mind. The very things to which the realist subjects his thinking, the idealist must subject to himself, to the power of his thought. And in this regard he proceeds with complete authority, for if the laws of the human mind were not at the same time also the laws of the world, if reason itself ultimately were subject to experience, then no experience would even be possible.

However, the idealist can have brought matters to the level of absolute truths and yet not much advanced his acquaintance with things by having done so. For while everything is in the end, of course, subject to necessary and universal laws, each individual thing is governed according to contingent and particular rules—

and in nature everything is individual. Accordingly, with his philosophical knowledge he can be master of the whole and in the process have gained nothing as far as particulars and the execution are concerned. Indeed, because in each case he presses for the *ultimate* reasons why everything is able to come about, he can easily forget the *most proximate* reasons why everything actually comes to be. Because he always directs his attention to the universal that renders the most diverse instances equal to one another, he can easily neglect the particulars that render them distinct from one another. Accordingly, his knowledge will be capable of *encompassing* [*umfassen*] a great deal, and for just that reason have *comprehended* [*fassen*] little. What he gains in his overview [Übersicht] of matters he will often lose in insight [Einsicht]. Thus it happens that while the speculative intellect ridicules common sense for its *narrowness*, common sense lampoons the speculative intellect for its *barrenness*. [496] For what knowledge gains in scope it always loses in specific content.

In the case of the idealist, as far as moral evaluation is concerned, people will always find a purer morality on an individual level, but much less moral uniformity on the whole. He is an idealist only insofar as he takes his cues from pure reason. However, since reason proves itself to be absolute in each of its utterances, his individual actions, from the moment they simply are moral, will bear the *entire* character of moral self-sufficiency and freedom. If in actual life there is a genuinely moral action at all and that would remain such even in the face of a rigorous scrutiny, then it can only be performed by the idealist. Yet the purer the morality of his individual actions, the more contingent it also is, since constancy and necessity are, of course, characteristic of nature, but not of freedom. To be sure, it is not as though idealism could come into conflict with morality, this being self-contradictory. That contingency is due rather to the fact that human nature is not capable of a consistent idealism. While the realist, even in his moral action, submits peacefully and uniformly to a physical necessity, the idealist must take flight from it, he must momentarily exalt his nature, and he is capable of nothing except insofar as he is enthused or inspired [begeistert]. Of course, when this happens he is capable of all the more, and his behavior will reveal a character of majesty and magnificence that one seeks in vain in the actions of the realist.

But actual life is in no way suited to awakening that passion in him, and still less of consistently nourishing it. The contrast between the absolute magnificence [Absolutgroße] that unfailingly is his point of departure and the absolute insignificance [Absolutkleine] of the individual instance to which he has to apply the former is much too powerful. Because his will—in terms of its form—is always directed to the whole, he does not want to direct it—as far as its content is concerned—to fragments and yet it is largely by means of small-scale accomplishments alone that he can prove his moral character. Thus, not infrequently it happens that because of the unlimitedness of the ideal he overlooks the limited instance of its application, and, filled with a sense of the maximum, [497] he neglects the minimum out of which alone everything great in actual life grows.

If, then, one wants to do justice to the realist, one must judge him in terms of the entire context of his life. If one wants to demonstrate the same fairness to the idealist, one must restrict oneself to individual expressions of that idealism, but first one must select these expressions. Common judgment, which is so ready to make decisions on the merits of an individual instance, will be indifferently silent about the realists since the individual acts of their lives provide little material for praise and blame. On the other hand, it will always take a position on the idealists, and will be torn between reproach and amazement, because the idealist's deficiency and his strength lie in the individual instance.

With such a considerable discrepancy in principles, it is unavoidable that the judgments of both parties are often directly opposed to one another and, even if they agree about the objectives and the results, that their reasons should be far apart. The realist will ask, *for what is something good?* and will know how to rate things in terms of what they are worth [werth]. The idealist will ask, *whether it is good?* and rate the things in terms of their dignity [würdig]. The realist neither knows nor much cares to know about something having its dignity and purpose within itself (always with the exception, nevertheless, of the whole). In matters of taste he will speak to pleasure, in matters of morality, to happiness, even if he does not make this the condition of acting morally. Even in his religion he does not readily forget his *advantage,* only there he ennobles and sanctifies it in the ideal of the *highest good.* What he loves, he will seek to *make happy*, while the idealist will seek to *ennoble* what he loves. While the realist in his political tendencies aims at *prosperity*, even if it should be at the expense of the moral self-sufficiency of the people, the idealist will make *freedom* the aim, even if it is a threat to prosperity. For the realist independence *of the condition* [*Zustand*] is the supreme goal, independence *from that condition* for the idealist. This characteristic difference may be pursued through their respective ways of thinking and acting. Thus the realist will [498] always demonstrate his proclivities by the fact that he *gives*, and the idealist by the fact that he *receives*. Through what each in his generosity surrenders, he betrays what he most treasures. The idealist will pay for the deficiencies of his system with his individuality and temporal condition, but he pays no attention to this sacrifice. The realist atones for the deficiencies in his system with his personal dignity, but he experiences nothing of this sacrifice. His system holds good in regard to everything with which he is acquainted and for which he feels a need. Why do they bother him, those goods of which he has not the slightest notion and in which he has no faith? It is enough for him that he possesses things, that the earth is his, that there is light in his intellect, and that satisfaction dwells in his bosom. The idealist does not have so kind a fate by far. It is not enough that he is frequently at odds with his good fortune because he fails to make the moment his friend. He is also at odds with himself; neither his knowing nor his acting can satisfy him. What he demands of himself is something infinite, but everything he accomplishes is limited. Moreover, in his behavior toward others he does not disavow this rigor he demonstrates toward himself. Of course, he is generous since in relation to others he is less mindful of himself as an individual, but he is more often unfair since he just as easily overlooks the individual in others. The realist, on the other hand, is less generous, but he is fairer, since he judges all things more *with a view toward their limitations*. He can forgive ordinariness, even vulgarity, in thinking and acting; what he cannot forgive is only the arbitrary, the eccentric. The idealist, on the other hand, is the sworn enemy of everything petty and trivial; he is prepared to reconcile himself with the extravagant and monstrous, if only it testifies to a great potential. The realist proves himself to be a friend of the human, without having a very high conception of human beings and humanity; the idealist thinks of humanity in so grand a manner that he comes dangerously close to despising human beings.

The realist alone would never have extended the sphere of humanity beyond the limits of the world we experience with our senses, he would never have acquainted the human spirit with its independent greatness and freedom. To him everything absolute in humanity is only a beautiful chimera, and belief in it not much [499] better than fanaticism, for he always views human beings only in terms of a definite and, precisely for that reason, a limited activity, never in terms of their pure potential. But for his part, the idealist would just as little have cultivated the sensuous powers and developed the human being as a natural entity, which is an equally essential part of his vocation and the condition of all moral ennoblement. The idealist's striving passes over the sensuous life and the present far too much. He wants to sow and to plant only for the whole, for eternity, and thereby forgets that the whole is only the complete sphere of the individual, that eternity is only a sum of moments. The world, as the realist would like to shape it and actually does shape it around him, is a well-laid-out garden in which everything is useful, everything deserves its place, and what does not bear fruit is banned. The world in the hands of the idealist is a nature less used, but worked out with a much grander character. It does not occur to the realist that a human being could exist for something other than to live well and be satisfied, that a human being puts down roots only to drive his stalk into the sky. The idealist does not consider the fact that, in order to think consistently well and nobly, he must above all things live well; he does not consider that the stalk does not have a chance if the roots should fail.

If something is left out of a system, something for which there is a pressing and unavoidable need in nature, then nature is to be satisfied only by an inconsistency in the system. Both realist and idealist are responsible for such an inconsistency, and this verifies the one-sidedness of both systems as well as the rich meaning of human nature—if, indeed, at this point there still remains any doubt about this. I need not first demonstrate in particular that the idealist must step out of his system as soon as he aims for a specific effect, since every specific existence stands under temporal conditions and takes place according to empirical laws. In regard to the realist, on the other hand, the proposition that, within his system, he cannot do justice to all the necessary demands of humanity might seem more dubious. [500] If someone asks the realist: "Why do you do what is right and endure what is necessary?" he will answer in the spirit of his system: "Because that's the way nature is, because it must be so." Yet this response by no means answers the question, for we are not speaking of what comes with nature, but rather of what he wants as a human being, since it is quite possible for him *not* to want what must be. The question can thus be put to him once again: "Why, then, do you want what must be? Why do you submit your free will to this natural necessity, since you could just as well go against it (although without success, which is in no way the subject of discussion here), and since millions of your brothers actually do so? You cannot say that it is because all other natural entities submit to nature's necessities, for you alone have a will, indeed, you feel that your submission ought to be a voluntary one. Thus, if this happens voluntarily, then you submit not to the necessity of nature itself, but rather to the *idea* of this necessity. For natural necessity compels you, like it compels the worm, in a strictly blind way. But it can get no hold on your will since you, even crushed by nature's necessities, can will something else. But where do you get that idea of natural necessity? Certainly not from experience that provides you only with particular effects of nature, but not nature (as a whole) and only with particular actualities, but no necessity. Hence you do go beyond nature and determine yourself idealistically every time you want either *to act morally* or simply not *to suffer blindly.*" It is thus apparent that the realist acts more honorably than he concedes in theory, just as the idealist thinks more sublimely than he acts. Without acknowledging it to himself, the realist demonstrates through the entire deportment of his life the self-sufficiency of human nature, while the idealist demonstrates through individual actions the neediness of human nature.

On the basis of the sketch given here (the truth of which can be granted without accepting its implication) it will not be necessary for me first to prove to a reader who is attentive and impartial that the ideal of human nature is divided up between the realist and the idealist, without being fully attained by either of them. Experience and reason both have their own prerogatives, and neither can invade the territory of the other without [501] producing deleterious consequences for either the internal or the external condition of the human being. Only experience can teach us what exists under certain conditions, what follows given specific presuppositions, what must happen for specific purposes. Only reason, on the other hand, can teach us what obtains unconditionally and what must necessarily be the case. If, then, we presume by means of reason alone to make out something about the external existence of things, we are simply playing an idle game and the end result will amount to nothing. For, while reason determines unconditionally, all existence is conditional. However, if we let a chance event decide what is contained in the very concept of our own being, we then make our lives an empty game of chance and our personhood [Persönlichkeit] amounts to nothing. Thus, in the first case, what is done is a matter of what our lives are *worth* (their temporary significance), in the second case their *dignity* (their moral significance).

Of course, in the sketch made up to this point, we have conceded the realist some moral value and the idealist some content drawn from experience, but only insofar as neither proceeds in a completely consistent manner and nature operates in them more powerfully than their respective systems do. Yet although neither corresponds completely to the ideal of perfect humanity, between them there is still the following important difference. The realist always fails to do justice to the rational concept [Vernunftbegriff] of humanity, but also never contradicts the understanding's concept [Verstandesbegriff] of it. The idealist, on the other hand, comes nearer to the highest concept of humanity in particular cases, but even the most vulgar concept of humanity is often not beneath him. Now, in practical life, far more depends upon whether the whole is *consistently* humanly good than upon whether the individual is *occasionally* divine. While the idealist is someone more skillful at arousing in us a grand conception of what humanity is capable of and inspiring respect for its calling, only the realist is capable of steadfastly carrying it out in experience and keeping the human species within its eternal boundaries. The idealist is, to be sure, a more noble figure, but [502] also a much less perfect or complete one, while the realist appears thoroughly less noble, but is, on the other hand, all the more complete. For what is noble is already implicit in the demonstration of a great potential, but what is complete consists in the conduct of the whole and in the actual deed.

In the best sense of both, what is true of each character becomes even more obvious in the respective *caricatures* of them. The effects of true realism are beneficial, and only its origin is less noble; false realism is in its origin despicable and in its effects only somewhat less pernicious. The true realist submits, of course, to nature and its necessity, but to nature as a whole, to its eternal and absolute necessity, not to its blind and momentary *compulsions*. He embraces and obeys its law freely, and he will always subordinate the individual to the universal. Thus, too, it cannot fail that in the end he will agree with the genuine idealist, however diverse the paths each takes. By contrast, the vulgar empiricist submits himself to nature as a power and does so in a blind surrender, without choosing to do so. His judgments and his efforts are limited to the individual; he believes and grasps only what he touches, he values only what betters him sensuously. Also, for this reason, he is nothing more than what the external impressions happen to want to make of him. His selfhood is suppressed, and as a human being he has absolutely no worth and no dignity. But as a thing he is still something, he can still be good for something. The very nature he blindly delivers himself up to does not let him fall completely. Its eternal laws protect him, its inexhaustible means of assistance save him, just as soon as he gives up his freedom unconditionally. Although he knows of no laws in this condition, these laws, while unknown, still prevail over him, and however much his individual efforts conflict with the whole, this whole will unfailingly know how to maintain itself against those ambitions. There are enough human beings, indeed, whole peoples, who live in this deplorable state, people who exist merely by the grace of natural law, without sustaining any selfhood, and who, accordingly, also are only good *for something*. [503] Yet, the fact that they merely live and exist demonstrates that this condition is not completely without significance.

Whereas the effects of true idealism are, by contrast, uncertain and often dangerous, those of false idealism are terrifying. The true idealist takes leave of nature and experience only because he does not discover there what reason obliges him to strive for: what is immutable and unconditionally necessary. Out of sheer arbitrariness the visionary takes leave of nature in order to be able to indulge his self-absorption in desires and the whims of his imagination all the more wantonly. He puts his freedom, not in being independent of physical constraints, but in being released from moral ones. Thus the visionary does not merely deny the human character—he denies all character, he is utterly lawless, hence he is nothing and is also good for nothing. Precisely because this fantasy is a deviation, not from nature, but from freedom, because it thus springs from a disposition in itself worthy of respect and infinitely perfectible, it also leads to an infinite fall into a bottomless depth and can only end in complete annihilation.

Translated by Daniel O. Dahlstrom

Acknowledgments

Every reasonable effort has been made to locate the owners of rights to previously published translations printed here. We gratefully acknowledge permission to reprint the following material:

From *On the Aesthetic Education of Man.* © Oxford University Press 1967. Reprinted from *On the Aesthetic Education of Man* by Friedrich Schiller edited and translated by Elizabeth M. Wilkinson and L. A. Willoughby (1967) by permission of Oxford University Press.

THE GERMAN LIBRARY in 100 Volumes

Wolfram von Eschenbach
Parzival
Edited by André Lefevere

Gottfried von Strassburg
Tristan and Isolde
Edited and Revised by
Francis G. Gentry
Foreword by C. Stephen Jaeger

German Medieval Tales
Edited by Francis G. Gentry
Foreword by Thomas Berger

German Mystical Writings
Edited by Karen J. Campbell
Foreword by Carol Zaleski

German Humanism and Reformation
Edited by Reinhard P. Becker
Foreword by Roland Bainton

German Poetry from the Beginnings to 1750
Edited by Ingrid Walsøe-Engel
Foreword by George C. Schoolfield

Seventeenth Century German Prose
Edited by Lynne Tatlock
Foreword by Günter Grass

German Theater before 1750
Edited by Gerald Gillespie
Foreword by Martin Esslin

Eighteenth Century German Prose
Edited by Ellis Shookman
Foreword by Dennis F. Mahoney

Eighteenth Century German Criticism
Edited by Timothy J. Chamberlain

Sturm und Drang
Edited by Alan C. Leidner

Immanuel Kant
Philosophical Writings
Edited by Ernst Behler
Foreword by René Wellek

Friedrich Schiller
Plays: Intrigue and Love and Don Carlos
Edited by Walter Hinderer
Foreword by Gordon Craig

Friedrich Schiller
Wallenstein and Mary Stuart
Edited by Walter Hinderer

Friedrich Schiller
Essays
Edited by Walter Hinderer and Daniel O. Dahlstrom

Johann Wolfgang von Goethe
The Sufferings of Young Werther and Elective Affinities
Edited by Victor Lange
Forewords by Thomas Mann

Johann Wolfgang von Goethe
Plays: Egmont, Iphigenia in Tauris, Torquato Tasso
Edited by Frank G. Ryder

German Romantic Criticism
Edited by A. Leslie Willson
Foreword by Ernst Behler

Friedrich Hölderlin
Hyperion and Selected Poems
Edited by Eric L. Santner

Philosophy of German Idealism
Edited by Ernst Behler

G. W. F. Hegel
Encyclopedia of the Philosophical Sciences in Outline and Critical Writings
Edited by Ernst Behler

Heinrich von Kleist
Plays
Edited by Walter Hinderer
Foreword by E. L. Doctorow

E. T. A. Hoffman
Tales
Edited by Victor Lange

Georg Büchner
Complete Works and Letters
Edited by Walter Hinderer and Henry J. Schmidt

German Fairy Tales
Edited by Helmut Brackert and Volkmar Sander
Foreword by Bruno Bettelheim

German Literary Fairy Tales
Edited by Frank G. Ryder and Robert M. Browning
Introduction by Gordon Birrell
Foreword by John Gardner

F. Grillparzer, J. H. Nestroy,
F. Hebbel
Nineteenth Century German Plays
Edited by Egon Schwarz in collaboration with
Hannelore M. Spence

Heinrich Heine
Poetry and Prose
Edited by Jost Hermand and Robert C. Holub
Foreword by Alfred Kazin

Heinrich Heine
The Romantic School and other Essays
Edited by Jost Hermand and
Robert C. Holub

Heinrich von Kleist and Jean Paul
German Romantic Novellas
Edited by Frank G. Ryder and Robert M. Browning
Foreword by John Simon

German Romantic Stories
Edited by Frank Ryder
Introduction by Gordon Birrell

German Poetry from 1750 to 1900
Edited by Robert M. Browning
Foreword by Michael Hamburger

Karl Marx, Friedrich Engels, August Bebel, and Others
German Essays on Socialism in the Nineteenth Century
Edited by Frank Mecklenburg and Manfred Stassen

German Lieder
Edited by Philip Lieson Miller
Foreword by Hermann Hesse

Gottfried Keller
Stories
Edited by Frank G. Ryder
Foreword by Max Frisch

Wilhelm Raabe
Novels
Edited by Volkmar Sander
Foreword by Joel Agee

Theodor Fontane
Short Novels and Other Writings
Edited by Peter Demetz
Foreword by Peter Gay

Theodor Fontane
Delusions, Confusions and The Poggenpuhl Family
Edited by Peter Demetz
Foreword by J. P. Stern
Introduction by William L. Zwiebel

Wilhelm Busch and Others
German Satirical Writings
Edited by Dieter P. Lotze and Volkmar Sander
Foreword by John Simon

Writings of German Composers
Edited by Jost Hermand and
James Steakley

German Lieder
Edited by Philip Lieson Miller
Foreword by Hermann Hesse

Arthur Schnitzler
Plays and Stories
Edited by Egon Schwarz
Foreword by Stanley Elkin

Rainer Maria Rilke
Prose and Poetry
Edited by Egon Schwarz
Foreword by Howard Nemerov

Robert Musil
Selected Writings
Edited by Burton Pike
Foreword by Joel Agee

Essays on German Theater
Edited by Margaret Herzfeld-Sander
Foreword by Martin Esslin

German Novellas of Realism I and II
Edited by Jeffrey L. Sammons

Hermann Hesse
Siddhartha, Demian,
and other Writings
Edited by Egan Schwarz
in collaboration with Ingrid Fry

Friedrich Dürrenmatt
Plays and Essays
Edited by Volkmar Sander
Foreword by Martin Esslin

German Radio Plays
Edited by Everett Frost and Margaret Herzfeld-Sander

Max Frisch
Novels, Plays, Essays
Edited by Rolf Kieser
Foreword by Peter Demetz

Gottfried Benn
Prose, Essays, Poems
Edited by Volkmar Sander
Foreword by E. B. Ashton
Introduction by Reinhard
Paul Becker

German Essays on Art History
Edited by Gert Schiff

Hans Magnus Enzensberger
Critical Essays
Edited by Reinhold Grimm and Bruce Armstrong
Foreword by John Simon

All volumes available in hardcover and paperback editions at your bookstore or from the publisher. For more information on The German Library write to: The Continuum Publishing Company, 370 Lexington Avenue, New York, NY 10017.

Breinigsville, PA USA
31 August 2010
244636BV00001B/7/A

9 780826 407139